PRAISE FOR

WE DEMAND

Just in time for the suffrage centennial, Anne Gass takes us on the ultimate female road trip, mapping out a journey led by two forgotten Swedish American suffragists whose personalities shine through. There are no better guides than Maria and Ingeborg to take us through the twists and turns, the potholes and unpaved roads, of the class, racial, and ethnic politics of the American suffrage journey. Brava to Gass for reclaiming and reimagining these voices and bringing these characters to life.

—TIFFANY K. WAYNE, PhD, author of *Women's Suffrage: The Complete Guide to the Nineteenth Amendment* (ABC-CLIO, 2020) and other works in US women's history

A thrilling cross-country road trip by three remarkable women promoting women's right to vote was not only an extremely dangerous adventure, but one that made a significant contribution toward helping women finally become full citizens.

—MARSHA WEINSTEIN, President, National Collaborative for Women's History Sites

In this rousing novel, based on a true story, Anne Gass reimagines an epic journey from the point of view of two resolute women who were considered "secondary" figures and brings them to life. Their engaging adventure sweeps us into another time—when women from all backgrounds left their homes and loved ones and bravely crossed the country campaigning for the right to vote.

—ROBERT P. J. COONEY, JR., author of *Winning the Vote: The Triumph of the American Woman Suffrage Movement*

Anne Gass honors two unknown heroes of the struggle to grant women the right to vote on the hundredth anniversary of the Nineteenth Amendment to the US Constitution. Ingeborg Kindstedt and Maria Kindberg are brought vividly to life in this anthem of bravery and determination that advanced the freedom and self-determination of roughly half the US population. Gass has written a novel of adventure, dedication, and sisterhood that should thrill and inspire readers regardless of gender or political persuasion. The characters became so real to me that when I came to their photo at the end of this book, I was grateful to them and their friendship, a true accomplishment for a fine writer.

—MICHELLE CACHO-NEGRETE, author of
Stealing: Life in America: A Collection of Essays

Anne Gass's book is written with great skill and understanding, such that you feel as if you are a passenger in the incredible cross-country automobile journey in support of the woman suffrage movement.

—RUSSELL DiSIMONE, author of *Remarkable Women of Rhode Island*

Anne Gass's feminist scholarship shines through, providing a glimpse of a little-known chapter in the woman suffrage movement. Gass's historical fiction is an informative, page-turning account of Swedish immigrant Ingeborg Kindstedt's experience as one of the three women who made the trip, driving cross-country in 1915.

—JENNIFER PICKARD, Assistant Professor of
Maine Studies, University of Maine

WE DEMAND

The Suffrage Road Trip

A NOVEL BY

ANNE B. GASS

Illustrations by Emma Leavitt of Solei Arts

Designed and produced by:
Maine Authors Publishing
12 High Street, Thomaston, Maine
www.maineauthorspublishing.com

Printed in the United States of America

This book is dedicated to Ingeborg and Maria, and to all those nameless and unacknowledged people who have used their own journeys through life to make the world a better place.

CHAPTER ONE

LATE SEPTEMBER 1915

The car headlamps tunneled through the darkness, picking out patches of desert scrub washed silver in the harsh light. Asleep in the back, Ingeborg came awake when the driver jolted to a stop and almost slammed her nose into the seat in front of her. Sara climbed stiffly from the front passenger's seat holding a lantern in front of her, appearing to look for something. With a curse-filled moan, the driver sagged briefly over the steering wheel before wrenching his own door open and stumbling after Sara.

Ingeborg blinked sleep from her eyes and, yawning, turned to Maria who sat beside her. "What's going on?" she asked in Swedish.

Maria grunted. "Lost," she said. She sounded thoroughly disgusted. "Our driver, who said he knew the way, took a wrong turn. We're on the Midland Trail. He thinks. They're looking for road signs."

"Typical," Ingeborg shook her head. "This is the last time we hire a man to help us drive."

"I agree. We can get lost ourselves—no need to pay a man to do it."

"I have to pee." Ingeborg pried open the door and rose slowly to her feet, stretching her stiff legs and aching back before feeling her way forward in the dark. She'd been told rattlesnakes dove deep into their burrows after sunset but she still stepped cautiously over the uneven ground, listening intently. The only sound was the scrape of wind and sand, and the tick of the car engine as it cooled. She found a low boulder to squat behind, knees groaning, one hand on the rock for balance, and tilted her head back to gaze at the sky. She had never seen stars like this, splattered in thick, pulsing handfuls against the inky dark.

Ingeborg yawned, then regretted it as her chapped lips split, the blood salty and metallic on her tongue. The desert night was biting cold, and she shivered, curling her chin down to her chest for warmth.

Standing, she shook out her skirt and peered over toward the pool of light cast by the lantern, then picked her way carefully toward it. She found Sara and the driver talking to two cowboys who'd been rolled in their blankets asleep near the crossroads.

Ingeborg stared with cold fury at the driver, whose eyes met hers briefly before flicking away. "We pay you to drive, and now we're lost?" she asked, switching to English. He hung his head and blew air into his cheeks, kicking at a rock with his foot.

"We meant to be on the Lincoln Highway," Sara was saying to the cowboys. "On our way to Ibapah Ranch for the night—we should have been there by now."

The men shook their heads. "You're nowhere near the Lincoln Highway, ma'am—or Ibapah, for that matter," said one.

Sara swore. "How far to the ranch?"

Ingeborg glared again at the driver, who kept his eyes pinned to the ground.

"Maybe thirty miles. You'll have to backtrack." The taller of the two men squatted down and brushed his hand across the sand to create a smooth surface. He drew a cross to indicate where they stood and then dragged his finger to show where they'd pick up the Lincoln Highway and where the ranch was from there, pointing out turns and features they'd see even in the dark. Sara fetched some writing paper from her bag and copied the map, going over it with the cowboys until she had it right.

"You be careful," said the tall one, as they thanked him. "The desert's no place to be lost at night."

"It ain't much fun during the day, neither," said his companion. "Get on, now. They'll fix you up at Ibapah."

The travelers returned to the car, and the driver swung it around and headed back the way they'd come, the cowboys already rolled back up in their blankets.

They arrived at Ibapah before dawn, a low-slung, unpainted wood-frame ranch house surrounded by barns and outbuildings. Three shaggy dogs barked a greeting, and Ingeborg cheered inwardly when lamps bloomed in the windows. The travelers unbent stiffly from their seats, so cold their teeth chattered and they could barely shuffle into the house. The grizzled rancher and his wife bustled about building up the fire, and soon the delicious odor of coffee, fried meat, and toasted bread rose from the stove.

Ingeborg edged a little closer to the fire. She thought if she ever warmed up, her bones would melt like icicles until she sank into a bag of skin on the worn wooden floor. Maria sat nearby with her eyes closed and her feet on a hot stone, her bony hands wrapped around a coffee mug for warmth. Ingeborg's eyes roamed over her partner's familiar face, leaner and grimmer from the hard travel. Deep lines bracketed her wide mouth, her lips were chapped and sagged into a grimace. Her skin was deeply sunburned. She still wore the engineer's cap Ingeborg had bought her in San Francisco, the stiff brim pulled low over her forehead. Her barrel-shaped body was swathed in shawls like a Russian doll. Ingeborg watched a little anxiously until Maria stirred, opened her eyes, and gave Ingeborg the tiniest of smiles.

Slightly cheered, Ingeborg bent forward and asked in a low voice, "Are you warmer? Can I get you anything?" Ingeborg worried Maria might not survive this trip, as tough as she was. She was no longer young, older than Ingeborg by five years, and the travel was far more difficult than they'd thought it would be.

Maria shrugged. "No," she said, and took another swallow of coffee. Maria was a person of few words at the best of times, but she'd reached a new level of brevity here. Was she punishing Ingeborg?

"I asked two questions," Ingeborg teased her gently. "No, you're not warmer, or no, you don't want anything?"

Maria stared through her. "Both," she said, and shut her eyes again.

Ingeborg sighed. Maria was annoyed with her, no question about it, but she wouldn't say so in front of the others. So Ingeborg looked over at Sara and the rancher, who were discussing the route to Salt Lake City. Sara Bard Field was almost young enough to be her daughter. In repose her face was pleasant enough, though Ingeborg thought it no better than ordinary. Her large brown eyes were at once wise and infinitely vulnerable, framed by soft, chestnut-colored hair. But when a smile lit her eyes, she'd turn every head in the room, and not just the men. She'd been chosen for this trip because she was a veteran of several state suffrage campaigns—including Nevada's successful effort just the previous year—though Ingeborg didn't quite see how. She barely came up to Ingeborg's shoulder and often seemed on the verge of collapse. After the night they'd just endured, Ingeborg would have thought she'd be prostrate on the couch, demanding they send for a doctor. Yet here she was, bending over the table looking at a map, owl-eyed with fatigue, but alert and in charge. Ingeborg leaned forward to hear their conversation. Maps weren't her department, but she wanted to know what they were in for.

The rancher was saying the spring rains had washed the road out in several places, and it still wasn't repaired. The detour would add hours to their trip.

Despairing, the driver sank down into his chair and took another swig of coffee, inspecting its contents as if he wished it held something stronger.

"Any towns along the way?" asked Sara, her eyes on the map. She looked worried.

The rancher shook his head. "No. Maybe a mining camp or homestead, but they'd be pretty rough. People don't stay put. It's hard living out here."

Sara sighed and dropped her chin to her chest. Her shoulders slumped, and she swayed with such bone-weary fatigue that Ingeborg was afraid she might collapse on the spot. Evidently the rancher thought so too, as he edged closer to catch her if she fainted. But then Sara looked up and turned to Maria and Ingeborg. "I think we should keep going," she said. "After we eat and rest a little. I know we're all dead tired, but we must get to Salt Lake in time for our meetings tomorrow. If we travel today then we can sleep in the hotel tonight. It's a big city, and the hotel will be comfortable."

Ingeborg nodded reluctantly, but looked over at Maria, who stirred and opened her eyes. "Keep going?" Ingeborg asked.

Maria shrugged. "Better do as much as we can in daylight."

Sara asked the rancher to draw a map that showed the detour and how to get back onto the Lincoln Highway. Then she called Maria over, and they went through the route step by step with the rancher to make sure there would be no mistakes this time. The driver sat slouched in disgrace, no one trusting him with directions.

Ingeborg leaned over and said to him with a hint of menace in her voice, "Rest up. You'll be driving a long time."

After breakfast Ingeborg pulled on the stiff, dust-colored, canvas coat she wore to protect her clothes when motoring. As she did so, she caught sight of herself in a mirror. She looked no better than Maria, a wild and grim thing with close-set, deep blue eyes startling out from her weather-beaten face, nose like a prizefighter, stubborn chin. At least she had all her teeth, though there was a gap between the front ones. Her broad shoulders slumped slightly. Just weariness, or was she showing her age? Her last birthday had been her fiftieth, after all. She'd always been proud of her physical strength, but lately she thought twice about tasks her younger self would have tackled eagerly. It was as if the will to launch herself at hard labor was ebbing away—it was easier to ignore grinding tasks or find someone else to do them. She was used to pains that came and went, but at her age they mostly seemed to come and stay, like uninvited guests who refused to leave. After just a week of traveling by motorcar, she hurt all over. By the time they got to Washington she guessed she'd be one giant bruise.

She pushed these thoughts away and finished buttoning the coat from her chin down to her ankles, pulled on her felt hat, and went out to check the car. The last thing they needed today was some mechanical problem that would delay them further. She looked over the engine and then pumped up the tube in the left rear tire that had a tendency to lose air. She hoped she wouldn't have to patch it again before they made it to Salt Lake City.

One of the ranch hands brought over their refilled cans of water and fuel, lashing them to the side of the car. He lingered and watched as Ingeborg worked. "You ladies sure are something," he said admiringly. "Are you really going clear to Washington, DC, all by yourselves?"

"From now on we will be," said Ingeborg. "It was a mistake to hire that driver to help us cross the desert."

"Why make the trip?"

Ingeborg rummaged through a canvas satchel and handed him a document. "We have a half-million signatures on this petition for a constitutional amendment giving voting rights to women. We're bringing them to Congress to demand they pass it."

He laughed. "Suppose they don't?"

"We'll tell the women voters in the West to vote against the Democrats in 1916. President Wilson is a Democrat, and they have the Congress, too. They could pass it if they wanted to. If they don't—the women voters will find someone who will."

The ranch hand whistled. "You tell them Nevada men gave women the vote last year, and we like it just fine. Give it to the rest of you ladies, I say."

Ingeborg said she would be sure to pass that along, and after he'd scrawled his signature on the petition, she returned to the ranch house to let the others know the car was ready. They paid for breakfast and fuel and thanked the rancher and his wife for their warm reception. Then they were back in the car, a long, thick dust plume rising behind them. Sara again sat next to the driver, map in hand, with Maria and Ingeborg in the back seat. As the sun rose higher in the cloudless sky, it became steadily warmer, erasing the chill of the night before. Before long they were stripping off layers and sipping sparingly from their water flasks—they'd bought an extra one at Ibapah—hoping they had enough.

The heat and dust stopped the words in their throats, so they rode in silence, and Ingeborg let her thoughts roam. This wasn't the trip they'd dreamed of, she thought ruefully. She and Maria had planned to cross America slowly, taking their time. This was their last great adventure, so they'd take it slow and choose the route as they went along, stopping where it suited them.

They'd met in Providence back in 1893 at the Swedish Young Women's Home, a respectable boarding house Maria ran for new immigrants. She smiled now, remembering their first meeting. Ingeborg was fresh off the boat from Sweden, looking for a room. It was a frosty January day and Maria was sitting at the kitchen table drinking coffee, weary from being up all night at a difficult birth— she had a side business as a midwife. All the boarders were at work, so the kitchen was empty apart from the cook, who rattled pots and chopped potatoes for the evening meal. Ingeborg was travel-stained and big-eyed at the newness of Providence, and Maria's calm self-possession had awed her. Maria poured her a cup of coffee and offered a plate of biscuits, sliding over a plate of butter and a pot of jam as well. Ingeborg ate three biscuits without stopping, slathering them with butter.

Amused, Maria had watched her over the rim of her coffee cup. "Do you work as well as you eat?" she asked.

Ingeborg had blushed, feeling like a simple country girl. "I do, yes. I'd nothing to eat today, and I haven't tasted anything so good since I got on the boat in Gothenburg. I can pay, though." She reached inside her waistband for the money she kept pinned there.

Maria had waved her hand in dismissal. "Welcome to America. This is the last free meal you'll have. Enjoy it." They shared a smile.

They were an unlikely pair. Maria was as frugal with words as she was with her money; she said both were things you couldn't take back if you used them unwisely. She liked routine and didn't look for trouble but could hold her own if it found her; once Ingeborg had seen her verbally dismantle a cocky coalman who'd tried to short-change her on a delivery. Mostly, though, she was easygoing and steady. The boarders looked up to her, and the man who owned the home claimed he'd never had a better, more honest manager.

Ingeborg was her opposite in many ways. She rode her life like a half-broken colt, plunging from one thing to another, curious and nippy, fighting efforts to rein her in. This could get her into trouble, like the time she'd gambled on a street hustler's shell game for a shiny brooch she impulsively decided to win Maria for her birthday. She'd watched him play a few times—hands a blur as they shuffled the walnuts with the hidden pea—and was certain she could best him. Her loss had cost her a week's pay, and she'd had to borrow her rent from Maria. As time went on Maria helped steady her, but she was always restless, alert for something new.

Maria's reputation as a skilled midwife grew, and she was sometimes away for days. So Ingeborg was glad to quit the factory job she'd hated and take over managing the home instead. She'd done some maintenance, built a barn for their horse and carriage in the back, and found other ways to make herself useful. Before long she and Maria had bought the building and business from the owner. Maria helped out when she could, but Ingeborg found herself in charge much of the time.

She'd discovered that Swedes were in great demand as workers because they were white, Protestant, and mostly sober. For a fee Ingeborg had done background checks and helped place the girls with families and other employers. She eventually tired of watching over the home and decided to expand her business—to do what she called her "intelligence work" full-time. They quickly found a buyer for the home and bought their own place on Westminster Street, across from the Catholic church.

Though they began as business partners, their relationship had blossomed into a deeper intimacy that had caught Ingeborg by surprise. She'd never met a man she wanted to spend her life with— marriage chiefly benefited the husbands, as far as she could tell, and she'd never particularly liked children. So she was content to be single, and hadn't thought of sharing her bed with a woman for any reason other than the warmth and a way to save money—it was cheaper to double up. Everyone did it. At the Swedish Home, their girls were often two or three to a bed.

Then, one night, she and Maria were alone in the kitchen. The girls were all out at a dance or visiting friends, and they were sharing a bottle of aquavit Ingeborg had bought. As they often did, they were gossiping about the girls and their love lives, their petty quarrels, and all the little irritations living in close quarters could bring. Maria was a fierce mimic, and her imitations made Ingeborg laugh until her sides ached and tears ran down her cheeks. "Stop!" she'd gasped,

"I can't laugh anymore!" Still giggling, she'd grabbed the bottle and refilled their glasses, then reached for her handkerchief and wiped her face. Looking up, she saw Maria was looking at her very intently. Ingeborg caught her breath and gazed back at her, her chest thumping in a peculiar way. Slowly, irresistibly, Maria had leaned in and given her the sweetest kiss on the lips, tasting ever so slightly of aquavit, and suddenly a wave of desire had seized Ingeborg, and she'd grabbed Maria and kissed her back, hard.

Ingeborg smiled, thinking of that night and the many others that followed. Their hidden romance also prompted their move into their own place. It was too hard for Ingeborg, in an unguarded moment, not to gaze at Maria the way any lover might. Perhaps every pair of women who shared rooms was up to something more, yet they knew none who lived openly as lesbians, and it was impossible to do so in conservative Providence. But a Boston marriage raised no eyebrows and had suited them both.

Now they were reaping the rewards of decades of hard work and frugal living. They'd shared a nice little cabin on the ship out West, steaming down around the southern tip of Florida and across the Gulf of Mexico, sliding through the new Panama Canal just days before mudslides blocked it up. They'd planned to spend several weeks in San Francisco visiting the Panama–Pacific International Exposition, then buy a car and take their time driving back to Rhode Island.

The Exposition was a marvel—a smorgasbord of art and industry, science and culture. They'd wandered around for days, reveling in the warmth and the Mediterranean color so foreign to their native Sweden and their home in Rhode Island. They walked until their feet ached and their necks cramped from craning their heads at all the sights. They'd toured the Westinghouse Electric exhibits and watched new Model Ts roll off Ford's assembly line.

Maria loved sampling the exotic foods—they'd eaten chow mein and chop suey, Southern grits and Russian pirozhki, and dozens of others. For a Swede, Maria had an unfathomable tolerance for the kinds of spices that made Ingeborg choke and breathe fire. Ingeborg preferred meat, potatoes, and cakes. But by careful choosing, they'd found food that pleased them both.

They were captivated and bewildered by the art they found throughout the grounds. Strolling through the Palace of Fine Arts one day, they'd browsed through a group of modern paintings and sculptures. One was by the young Italian Futurist Umberto Boccioni, titled *Dynamism of a Soccer Player*, and they'd stood for some time puzzling over it. To Ingeborg, it was a chaotic mishmash of color, as if someone had taken scissors to the original painting, pieced it back together in a jumble, and glued it to the canvas.

"Where's the soccer player?" she asked Maria, her brow furrowed. "Do you see him?"

Maria shook her head. "No." Then she pointed to the center of the painting, at what appeared to be the lower part of a leg, and perhaps an eye above it. "Are those parts of him?"

Ingeborg peered closer. Shades of blue and red and purple gave the work a bruised look. "Maybe he missed a goal, and they beat him," she guessed.

Maria laughed. "Might be. I don't understand this modern art. I liked that Homer painting of the women on the rocks. Paintings should be pretty." They'd moved on.

One day, Ingeborg had coaxed Maria to walk through the Zone, the Fair's amusement park, and to ride the Bowls of Joy roller coaster with her, though Maria had screamed and almost lost her lunch. Ingeborg was secretly frightened but also thrilled by the hurtling descents and the brief, breathtaking views of the city from the highest points. She'd have ridden it again, but Maria was adamant.

"You'll kill me!" she declared, cradling her stomach. She'd had to sit down on a bench until her insides stopped whirling.

The nights were Ingeborg's favorite, when she and Maria could stroll arm in arm through the courts and gardens, the air scented with a multitude of flowers and eucalyptus trees, lights sparkling on the Tower of Jewels and in the many fountains. One evening they'd stayed late to watch the fireworks over San Francisco Bay. Standing among thousands of visitors from all over the world, they'd laughed and clapped like children as the rockets hissed into the air and exploded into fountains and sprays and gardens of color. The throbbing booms echoed deep in their bellies.

That night she'd been filled with pride to be a citizen of a country that could produce the marvels they'd seen at the fair, inventions that would change the course of America, and maybe the world. She'd never felt such a sense of possibility, such an irresistible call to be part of the great wave of progress the Exposition celebrated. She searched for the words to express this as she and Maria found their way back to their room late that evening.

"All these inventions, the progress we've seen at this fair," she said to Maria. "Don't they make you wish you were younger?"

Maria peered at her. "No. Why?"

"They make me so excited! Some will change the world." Ingeborg gripped Maria's arm and turned to face her. "Doesn't that make you think?"

"I suppose so," said Maria, wrinkling her brow. "But the world is always changing. We'll see it or we won't. As long as it doesn't change for the worse for us...." She shrugged and then turned back toward their rooms. "Come on, Ingeborg; it's late, and my feet hurt."

Ingeborg had waited for a moment, lost in thought, and had to run to catch up with her. "It's more than just watching—I want to be part of it. But what can I do? I'm too old to be a scientist," she'd lamented as they walked along, her mind spinning with ideas of how, in this vibrant web of progressive movements, inventions, and art she might find a thread of her own that would lead to its very center.

Back in the car, Ingeborg smiled grimly. No doubt that was how they came to be baking in the desert heat almost plowing through dust, great waves of it billowing out from the front fenders and streaming into their faces. Coughing, she pulled out a handkerchief and tied it, cowboy-style, around the lower half of her face.

A few days after the fireworks, she and Maria had shared a lunch table with a woman named Audrey Kendall, from Los Angeles, who told them how she had voted several times. "Women have power if we'd just use it," Audrey had said, dabbing her napkin to her mouth. "California women won the vote in 1911, and since then we've helped pass any number of reforms."

"Like what?" Ingeborg had asked, poking doubtfully at an enchilada Maria had talked her into ordering. She took a little bite and rolled it around her mouth, judging its spiciness. It was all she could do not to spit it back out, and she'd glared at Maria, who ignored her.

"Well, let's see," said Audrey, ticking them off on her fingers. "We helped elect leaders who broke the Southern Pacific railroad monopoly. That was a big one. We now have a fund that gives money to workers when they get injured on the job, we call it Workers Compensation. We also have the eight-hour workday and minimum wages for women working in factories."

Ingeborg was stunned. "Really?" she said. "You did that in just four years?" In Rhode Island they'd been trying for an eight-hour workday for ages. The politicians found all sorts of ways to avoid voting on it—paid off by the factory owners.

"Well, of course it wasn't just the women, the men helped, but I doubt most of those would have passed without our votes. And believe me," said Audrey, with a decisive nod, "now the politicians pay attention to women the way they never did before."

"I don't understand," Maria had said. She pointed to Ingeborg's plate and, when Ingeborg shook her head, emptied half of it onto her own. "If you moved to Rhode Island you couldn't vote, and if we moved to California we could. But we'd still be the same people. It makes no sense." They'd all agreed it was silly to let states decide if women could vote.

The very next morning she and Maria had toured the Palace of Education. Tucked in among other exhibits of the latest voting machines and the Montessori school, they'd found the Congressional Union for Woman Suffrage, its entrance draped in bright purple and gold cloth, with a large sign overhead that read FREEDOM BOOTH.

The Congressional Union was determined to win voting rights for women by amending the United States Constitution—not winning it state by state, as the other national suffrage group, the National American Woman Suffrage Association, had been doing for decades.

Inside the booth they'd looked over a display of dolls from the twelve Western states that had equal suffrage, dressed in bright colors with happy smiles on their faces. Ingeborg chuckled and pointed to Rhode Island's doll huddled together with those from the other states where women couldn't vote. They were all dressed in drab clothing, gloomy, and half hidden behind a low wall.

"That's us," she told Maria. "That's how women look when only men can vote."

Maria shook her head, scowling. "*Tokig*," she muttered in Swedish. Crazy.

Doris Stevens, who managed the booth, had come over then to welcome them. She stood a head shorter than Ingeborg and was much younger, dressed in a well-tailored suit and modish hat. She was well-spoken and had that air of authority people born to wealth always seemed to have. Ingeborg was suddenly conscious of her own simple, worn skirt and blouse and dusty shoes, her battered fedora pulled down over her ears.

But Miss Stevens had been friendly, speaking to them without condescension. "Would you be willing to sign our petition demanding that Congress pass the federal suffrage amendment?" she asked.

"Of course!" they'd said, glad to help in this small way.

"We're planning to drive the petitions to Washington and present them to Congress and President Wilson," Miss Stevens explained as they took turns signing. "We're not sure just how, though. At first we'd hoped to send one hundred cars filled with suffrage supporters, in a grand convoy that no one could miss." She gave a rueful smile. "Everyone loved the idea, but exactly no one has volunteered to do it, so we have no one to send. And we're supposed to launch the trip in a few weeks." Accepting the fountain pen back from Maria, she dropped it into the inkwell. "I'm beginning to feel a bit nervous about it, to tell the truth," she said, with a grimace. "But I expect we'll come up with something."

Ingeborg felt a little shiver of excitement. She and Maria could drive the petitions! She looked over at Maria, who winced and shook her head as she realized where this conversation was headed. She was opening her mouth to object but Ingeborg jumped in first. She looked back at Miss Stevens, worked her face into a winning, gap-toothed smile, and blurted, "We'll do it!"

"I'm sorry," said Miss Stevens, visibly shocked. "Did you say you'll take the petitions?"

Ingeborg's words tumbled out in her excitement. "We're buying a car here to drive back home. To Providence—we live there. There's room for the petitions, and it's not far from Providence to the capital."

Watching Miss Stevens' face change from doubt to surprise and then real interest was worth the scolding she'd get later from Maria, Ingeborg thought. Miss Stevens had clearly underestimated them. Now visibly pleased, Miss Stevens said she would pass the offer along to Alice Paul, the CU's president. "Miss Paul isn't available now, but won't you come back tomorrow to meet her? She can tell you more about what she has in mind."

Ingeborg groaned inwardly and shifted in the jolting car—what had they—she—been thinking? They should have disappeared into the crowd and never gone back. But they'd returned to the booth the next day to meet Alice Paul. She turned out to be a diminutive young woman with a penetrating gaze and an air of quiet certainty. Ingeborg was surprised—it was hard to see in her the tough suffrage general the newspapers made her out to be. They soon learned otherwise.

"Tell me about yourselves," invited Miss Paul, in a friendly tone.

Ingeborg glanced over at Maria and back at Miss Paul. Where to start? She found herself babbling, eager to make a good impression. "We're from Sweden, you might tell from our accents. We're naturalized citizens now," she added hastily. "We live in Providence. Maria is a midwife, and I investigate Swedish immigrants."

Miss Paul looked puzzled.

"To help them find work," Maria broke in. "When they're new, no one knows them. Ingeborg makes sure they're safe to hire."

"I see," said Miss Paul. "But I understand you have some interest in woman suffrage?"

"I have many causes," explained Ingeborg, "but suffrage I like best. In fact, before we left, we formed the Women's Political Equality League of Rhode Island—for working women. I'm president, and Maria is vice-president." She hoped Miss Paul wouldn't ask how many members the new league had, and added hurriedly, "I also joined the Congressional Union."

"I am indeed pleased to hear that," said Miss Paul, with slightly more warmth. "Miss Stevens mentioned you were planning to buy a car here in San Francisco. Have you much experience with automobiles?"

"Yes," said Maria. "As a midwife, a car is useful. It saves time and is safer at night. I've owned a car for two years."

"And I keep it running!" Ingeborg added quickly. "I can change tires and fix most of what goes wrong." She shrugged her shoulders and smiled slightly. "I like mechanical things."

Maria fished in her bag and handed Miss Paul an advertisement for the car they had in mind, a gleaming black Overland Six with a fold-up roof and windows that would fasten down when it rained. It could carry a driver and a passenger in the front seat, and had a rear seat and boot that could carry the petitions and their luggage.

Miss Paul peered closely at the ad. "It looks most suitable for our purposes, but it's expensive, five hundred fifty dollars. Can you afford this?"

Ingeborg and Maria assured her that they could. "We came here by ship intending to buy such a car," Ingeborg said proudly. "Maria sold the other one before we left."

"It's a very good car for the price," added Maria. "The Willys-Overland company made it special for the Exposition."

Miss Paul considered them for a long moment, during which Ingeborg held her breath, suddenly unsure whether she wanted Miss Paul to choose or reject them. Then the younger woman nodded decisively. "It is decided," she said firmly. "You will take the envoys and the petitions with you to Washington, DC, which is, after all, not far from Rhode Island. Since you were planning to make the trip anyway, you will pay for the car and your own expenses. The CU will pay the food and lodging for the envoys."

Maria and Ingeborg looked at each other, confused and alarmed. "But…but…envoys?" Ingeborg stammered. "Who are they? How many?"

"The envoys must come from the equal suffrage states," Miss Paul had explained. "They must represent the women voters of the West, coming to the aid of their Eastern sisters who do not yet have political freedom. Rhode Island hasn't enfranchised its women, so you can't be envoys. The delegates to the upcoming Women Voters Convention will choose them. Please keep this information to yourselves for now, but they will most likely be Mrs. Sara Bard Field and Miss Frances Joliffe, both of whom live in California, where women can vote."

Ingeborg had suddenly felt off-balance and disoriented, just as she had when they'd tried out the Otis Elevator in the fair's Palace of Machinery display. An attendant had guided them into a small room and slid a metal gate across the doorway. He'd then punched a button and the machine clattered upward before lurching to a stop. They'd exited onto a platform quite different from the one they'd just left, with no effort on their part. What had they just agreed to? She suspected they should be asking more questions, but Miss Paul was saying simply, "We are indeed grateful for your help in this matter. And now, if you will excuse me, I must attend to some other details regarding the convention." She smiled, shook their hands, and left.

Maria and Ingeborg had headed straight to a kiosk where they could have coffee, still reeling from this news. "Maybe it will be OK," said Maria doubtfully. "After all, we will still see the country, and we own the car. We can stop when we choose."

Ingeborg agreed. "Yes, it's our car. And it shouldn't matter how we get to Washington."

She was thinking, too, that their little Political Equality League only had a few members. Most working women were too busy, no surprise since they worked six days a week, and long hours, too. Those who could spare any extra time preferred to work on labor issues.

Ingeborg had joined the movement back in 1913 after listening to a young suffragist deliver a speech from a soapbox in the square near their house. In Rhode Island, politics was for men only—except when they needed women to bake cakes and serve coffee. All the causes she cared about—the eight-hour day, better pay, safer working conditions—would be helped if women could vote.

She'd joined the Rhode Island Woman's Suffrage Association on the spot after listening to the organizer's speech. But she'd never felt welcome at the association's meetings. Those women were happy to hire Swedes to cook or clean for them, but they didn't want working women's rumps sitting on their dainty sofas, mixing with their high-class friends.

Once she'd been standing in the entry hall of someone's grand house, waiting to be ushered into a meeting. She'd looked around at the Oriental rugs and the glossy furniture, seeing not one speck of dust. Suddenly, a woman wearing a soft, woolen wrap over a modish frock had bustled in, and taking her for the maid, thrust her wrap at Ingeborg to hang in a closet. Ingeborg had laughed in her face. "I'm here for the meeting, the same as you," she'd told the woman, who'd looked annoyed. Though she'd forced herself to sit through it, balancing her dainty teacup on her knee while the other women blathered on about their children, and nannies, and how hard it was to find a cook, she'd never gone back.

That's why she'd formed the Women's Political Equality League. It had been slow to get going but once word got out about this trip, she'd have something to talk about, all right! People would line up to come to her lectures and invite her to their suffrage teas.

So they'd agreed to take the envoys.

Posters for the convention soon appeared all over the Exposition— Ingeborg and Maria had surreptitiously slipped one off a wall and into their bag as a souvenir. "The World's First Ever Convention of Women Voters!" the headline blared, showing a woman holding a long trumpet to her lips. Ingeborg couldn't help but smile every time she saw one, and there was a little swagger to her step. What would her family in Sweden say if they knew she was part of such an important trip? Little Ingeborg Kindstedt, a leader of the American suffrage movement!

The conference began on September 14th and would conclude two days later with the ceremony that would launch the envoys. Women arrived from all over the country to take part. Ingeborg and Maria mingled with women voters from states like Wyoming, Oregon, Washington and Nevada, where it seemed that men were more enlightened than they were in the East. The speeches gave Ingeborg a jolt in her middle—like the electricity that woke up the machines in exhibits they'd seen. She loved them all, the high-flying talks of democracy and freedom, and the detailed strategy sessions of how to pressure Congress to pass the federal amendment. She wanted desperately to be one of the women the others strained to hear, to speak with confidence and authority to an audience who applauded her. The little book she carried was soon full of notes to help her remember what to do and say when they got back to Providence. Maria was interested, too, though she insisted they sit in the back row after the luncheons so she could nap when she got sleepy.

The car bounced down a bank and through a dry river wash, startling Ingeborg from her reverie. She hoped the driver was awake—and was glad to see Sara reach out and shake his arm as a warning. The heat danced and shimmered in the road ahead as if daring them to approach. They rode with the top down for the breeze, but that meant the cruel sun pressed down on them with no relief. Sweat trickled down between Ingeborg's breasts and down her back. Behind her bandana she opened her mouth wide, desperately trying to suck in air.

To distract herself she went back to that last night at the convention, so unlike anything she'd ever experienced. The CU had rented the Exposition's Court of Abundance for the event, and it had taken on a magical, mystical feel as the light faded from the sky and star-shaped lanterns lit the night. Orange trees, Italian cypress, magnolia, and beds of flowers breathed their perfume into the soft evening air. Iron serpents mounted around a sunken pool hissed steam from their mouths, and more steam stole from vents on the sides of the towers behind the stage. There was a sense of hushed anticipation from the gathering crowd.

The CU had recruited girls from among the families working at the fair to stand on the stage wearing the brightly colored clothes of their native countries; above them stood women draped with the CU's colors of purple, white, and gold. In the background rippled the American flag, and below the stage hung what the CU called the Great Demand banner: WE DEMAND AN AMENDMENT TO THE US CONSTITUTION ENFRANCHISING WOMEN. They sang rousing suffrage songs set to hymns and popular tunes.

That night thousands of fairgoers had joined the convention delegates, packing into the court so tightly there was scarcely room to breathe. They cheered wildly when Sara Bard Field and Frances Joliffe appeared on the stage—they'd been duly elected as envoys earlier in the day—and the chorus swung into "The Song of the Free Women," new words that Sara, a poet, had set to the tune of "La Marseillaise," the French national anthem.

To Ingeborg, waiting with Maria in the Overland Six behind the stage, the song seemed to rise from the court and concentrate in a mighty lightning bolt overhead, pivoting slowly eastward to aim directly at the US Capitol in Washington, DC. Surely those stuffy men in Congress could feel, as she did, a powerful surge of energy that stood their hair on end and caused their knees to tremble. Her heart swelled with pride, and she added her voice to the song. This must be the answer to the call she'd felt that night at the fireworks to be part of something important, a cause larger than herself.

The convention delegates had agreed they would no longer simply ask for the right to vote, as women had done for so long. The vote was something that should have been theirs from the beginning, with no questions asked. This army of women was demanding to be heard, to be equal at last with the men who controlled their lives. The four million women voters of the West were coming to the aid of their Eastern sisters. The words of the last verse and chorus resounded in the night, pounding off the plastered walls of the court and exploding upward, ten thousand voices singing as one.

No more we bend the knee imploring.
No longer urge our cause with tears.
We have rent asunder blinding fears.
We are women strong for women warring.
We come. We come at last.
Night's portal we have passed.
We come. We come. Trust thou our might.
Thou, too, shall walk in Light.

The song ended to wild cheers and applause from the crowd, and as if in response, a brief spray of fireworks exploded off in the distance, lights dancing across the sky. At length Frances held up her hand for silence and spoke about their upcoming journey. "We are going through the states where women are enslaved in the factories and the mills, where they work long, back-aching hours and cannot register their protests in any way. We are only two women," she said, "but we go armed with the fighting strength of four million to do our best to help set other women free."

Maria and Ingeborg exchanged a glance. Two women? What were the two already in the car, wooden dolls? But that was the cue for Maria to drive around to the front of the stage, and again the audience cheered as Sara and Frances walked down the steps and settled themselves in the back seat. They strained to hear their final cue, uttered by the famous actress, Margaret Anglin. As she said simply, "The hopes and the hearts of thousands of women go with you," the lights in the Court of Abundance dimmed, and women began forming a lantern-lit procession. Maria began to inch the car forward, peering through the suffrage flags and streamers draped over the car, trying not to bump anyone. They crept on toward the heavy wooden gates of the Exposition which swung open at their approach, and then, with the crowd roaring behind them, the car slipped through and disappeared into the night.

Ingeborg sighed. Even now, the memory of that event sent a tingle through her limbs, made her want to stand up and sing. But she wondered whether she and Maria would have decided differently if they'd known how difficult this trip would be. At the moment, exhausted, sweating, and aching all over from the jolting car, she had her doubts. But when the crowds were large and shouted their approval, the politicians were friendly, the roads flat and fast, and the scenery a wonder to behold, on those days she wouldn't trade her seat in the car for anything.

CHAPTER TWO

OCTOBER 3, 1915

After leaving the Ibapah Ranch they'd driven straight through the day and into the night, arriving at the luxurious Hotel Utah in Salt Lake City early the following morning. They'd made it through the worst of the desert. The most dangerous part of their trip was behind them—they hoped.

Sara had sat up front with the driver the whole way, holding the map and talking to him, speaking sharply at times to keep him awake. When they arrived at the hotel, Ingeborg and Maria had insisted that he help carry their luggage into the lobby. Sara counted out his money, fingers fumbling with cold and weariness.

Ingeborg regarded him grumpily. "Next time someone hires you to drive, make sure you know the way," she said.

"It was dark," he whined. "I missed a turn. Anyone could have done the same."

"Anyone could have figured it out a lot faster," Ingeborg hissed at him. "Instead you drove and drove. You could have killed us all!"

The driver looked as though he wished he'd at least killed Ingeborg. His eyes narrowed, and he screwed up his face with the effort to come up with some retort.

"Enough!" Maria cut in, glaring at Ingeborg. "I have to lie down or I'll fall over. Stop your yelling; we're here now."

Sara finished paying the driver, and he left to find cheaper rooms. As they checked in, Ingeborg looked around the opulent lobby with its soft carpets, high ceilings, and gold accents. It was certainly the fanciest place she'd ever stayed. She hoped Maria wouldn't insist they find something cheaper tomorrow. Or later today, she corrected herself.

The room Ingeborg and Maria shared was large and clean, and the bed was soft. They splashed water on their faces and hands and collapsed into bed, sleeping late into the next morning.

When they finally descended to the lobby in search of coffee and breakfast, they found Mabel Vernon sitting at a desk, catching up on letters while she waited for them.

Mabel greeted them warmly. "I'm so glad to see you! And oh, my goodness, look at you both so sunburned! Was it awful? Let's order some food, and you can tell me all about it."

Mabel was their advance agent, traveling ahead of them by train and working with local suffragists to set up mass meetings in the larger cities along the way. She was tall and slender, with tawny hair, a prominent, slightly crooked nose, a sweet smile, and large, intelligent eyes. Ingeborg sometimes wished that they had Mabel in the car with them rather than Sara, who could be moody and petulant. Mabel seem to have infinite patience and was always willing to listen to the Swedes' complaints about how the trip was going. She managed to treat them as equals, even though it was also clear she made the decisions. Whenever Ingeborg and Maria got upset about the fast pace, the lack of rest, and the fact that Sara did all the public speaking, Mabel would soothe their injured feelings and make them feel they were the real heroes.

They filled her in over a hearty breakfast of scrambled eggs, fried meat, and pastries, the first real meal they'd eaten since leaving Ibapah Ranch. Mabel listened intently and was gratifyingly alarmed at how close they'd come to disaster. "Just think, if you hadn't come across those cowboys," she said, wincing. "What would have become of you? We certainly chose the right women to make this journey—I can't think of anyone who would have managed as well."

Ingeborg thought to herself that, since they were the only women who'd volunteered to go, there hadn't been much choosing done, but decided to let it go since Mabel was making such a nice fuss over them.

Mabel told them Sara had been up earlier but had gone back to her room to do some writing. She would see them later. "You have a few hours to yourselves now," said Mabel. "You can sightsee if you wish, but you should make sure to take care of your personal needs and see to the car. We have a big meeting later today."

She explained that at three o'clock they were to drive out of town and decorate the car with the CU flags and the Great Demand banner. Then they'd drive back in, as if they were just arriving, and local suffragists in automobiles would meet them at the corner of Fourteenth South and State Streets to escort them to the hotel. From there a marching band would lead them up the winding road to the Utah state capitol building where the speeches would happen on its front steps.

"Who will be there?" Ingeborg asked.

"Governor William Spry, Mayor Samuel Park, and Congressman Joseph Howell, plus at least fifty local suffragists, maybe more," Mabel told them. "Utah women have had the vote for twenty years, and the Mormon Church is behind us, so there's tremendous support, and they're very interested in your trip. We should have an enthusiastic crowd."

"Any word from Frances Joliffe?" asked Maria.

Mabel frowned and shook her head. "No, nothing. I've written to ask when she can rejoin you, but she hasn't replied."

Frances was from a wealthy and prominent San Francisco family. Ingeborg had heard that her brother-in-law was a big anti-corruption crusader, although Frances herself was more focused on the arts. She was supposed to hobnob with the high and mighty and raise funds for the CU as they made their way across the country. While she'd only recently taken up the suffrage cause, she was an able speaker, and the crowds liked her. Sara and the Swedes came from more humble backgrounds, and Miss Paul seemed to think they needed someone like Frances.

So they'd all been stunned when, right after they'd finished their very first mass meeting in Sacramento, Frances had suddenly announced she was leaving. "I'm ill and can't continue," she'd said, though to Ingeborg's skeptical eyes she looked no different than she had when they'd left San Francisco. They'd gaped at her, all of them standing next to the car and ready to leave for Reno.

"But you can't abandon us now; we've scarcely begun!" said Sara, anger slipping into her voice. Frances simply stood there, her face closed up and eyes averted. "All the speaking will fall to me, now. And I'm not well either. I'm just over malaria, and my heart gives me trouble." She put her hand on her heart as if to emphasize her weakness.

"I'm sorry you're not well," Maria told Frances. "It does make travel very hard." Ever the peacemaker, she tried to probe gently into the nature of her ailment, to see if she might help, but Frances's mind was made up.

"I'm afraid I made a mistake, and I simply can't continue," Frances said, little spots of color appearing in her cheeks, her voice rising. "I'll join you later if I can. Good luck." She turned and walked away quickly, her skirts swinging around her long legs. Ingeborg, Sara, and Maria stood there and watched her go.

"I guess she figured out she's used to a different type of travel," said Ingeborg, bitterly.

Sara was seething. "She told me she'd come back from a long trip to Europe just before the convention started. I bet she traveled in style. She must have decided her pampered ass was too soft for this kind of trip." While she'd picked up some education along the way and styled herself a poet, she grew up in a family that watched their pennies. She wasn't poor, but she wasn't in Frances' class either. And since her divorce she'd had to work to support herself.

"This is a trip for women used to working," said Ingeborg, flatly. She turned and opened up the car door. "So let's go." The others followed suit.

A furious silence had reigned as the three travelers wove their way out of the city. At length, Ingeborg shifted in her seat and, raising her voice to be heard over the chattering engine, she said, "We should bet on how soon Frances comes back. What do you think, Sara?" She turned to look over her shoulder.

Sara sat braced in the corner of the backseat, arms folded across her chest, gazing angrily at the parched landscape. "I still can't believe she quit," she fumed. "Maybe Alice can talk her into coming back sooner, but I bet we don't see her until Denver."

Ingeborg was skeptical. She thought there was no way Frances would rejoin them that soon. "You think Denver? What about you, Maria?"

Maria wrestled with the steering wheel, which was wider than her shoulders and stiff to turn. It took a lot of strength to muscle it around. She shook her head and said, "Denver might be too soon— this is a big country. I bet we don't see her until New York."

"Hah!" Ingeborg had said. "I say she joins us in Washington in time to meet President Wilson, and takes credit for the whole trip. That's the way the rich are." They'd laughed and lapsed into silence.

Back in the hotel, Maria and Ingeborg exchanged glances. "Sara needs help with the speeches," Ingeborg told Mabel. "She isn't strong. The travel is hard for her—some days she can barely get out of bed."

Maria nodded in agreement and added "She says her heart hurts, and not just because she misses Erskine. There's something wrong with it."

Charles Erskine Scott Wood was Sara's lover, a former Indian fighter turned corporate lawyer who represented unions on the side and wrote poetry, too. She was finding it unbearable to be separated from him.

Mabel shifted uncomfortably in her seat. "You know how much we appreciate your help," she said. "I believe this trip is the most important thing the Union has ever done. And the two of you came forward when no one else had. But Miss Paul...." Here she hesitated, looked away, and then turned back to look Ingeborg in the eye. "Sara is a veteran of suffrage campaigns in Oregon and Nevada. She has a lot of experience. We very much appreciate your offer to help with the speaking, but the fact is the two of you don't live in an equal suffrage state. You can't speak for the women voters of the West. I know Sara has been unwell at times, but we'll just have to keep her going as best we can."

Ingeborg tried to keep the bitterness out of her voice. "We don't wear pretty clothes, and we don't talk English like you. But we've made our way with no help from men. We know how women are treated. Maria, she's delivered two thousand babies, some to mothers half-dead from too many children already. We see how employers grow rich off their workers. The rich get the best of everything—but they do nothing. You and Sara and Frances talk about how the vote will help working women, but we've lived it!"

Maria nodded.

"I know you have," said Mabel soothingly, "and believe me, when the time is right, we'll certainly ask you to speak. But we have orders from Miss Paul that Sara—and Frances, when she rejoins us—speak as the envoys, and I'm afraid I can't change them." She gathered up her papers and placed them in her bag. "I'm sorry, I must run now. I'm meeting Mrs. Cherdron at noon to plan the final details of our meeting later today. I'll be waiting for you when you get back with the suffrage escort. Enjoy your day and rest up. We have a busy evening ahead of us."

She smiled and walked quickly out of the hotel restaurant. Ingeborg stared moodily at her plate. "I don't believe for one minute it's because we're not from an equal suffrage state," she grumbled to Maria in Swedish, which they spoke when they were alone. "Back at the Woman Voters Convention did you see anyone who looked like us? Talked like us?"

Maria sighed but fixed Ingeborg with a warning look. "Don't make trouble about this. It isn't worth it. Just be glad you don't have to worry about speeches and fixing the motorcar, too. Imagine trying to write a speech while you're under the car or mending a tire."

"It just makes me so angry—"

"Ingeborg! You promised me you wouldn't get upset. Now let's go take care of our business. That car surely needs work after what it's been through."

Ingeborg made no reply, though she had a mulish set to her jaw as the two women left the breakfast table. Maria went back to their room, but Ingeborg crossed the lobby and found her way out the back door of the hotel to the low wooden sheds where they'd stored the

Overland Six. She went behind the car and, after glancing around to ensure no one was looking, quickly unfastened the row of buttons that went from mid-thigh down to the hem of her skirt, in front and behind. Then she refastened them, joining the buttons and button-holes down the inside of each leg, creating a set of loose pantaloons that preserved her modesty as she worked beneath the car.

In the boot she found the apron she used to protect her clothes, and the canvas ground cloth. Yesterday she'd heard an ominous rattle in the steering column, and she also wanted to check the brakes and the shifting mechanism. After oiling the bearings and check-ing the spark plug timing, she crawled underneath the car with her tools. Presently, two workmen walked past and sat on a bench nearby, taking a break. Soon their pipe smoke drifted past her nose, and she listened with half an ear to their conversation.

"He'll hang all right when Governor Spry is through with him," said one. "He's guilty as hell. What kind of a man shoots someone in cold blood in front of his own son?"

"I don't know, Martin," the other man replied. "Do we know for sure he was the one pulled the trigger?"

"How else did he get shot?" Martin demanded. "The grocer winged the man, his boy said so. Old Joe has had plenty of chances to come up with a different story, and he ain't done it. No, they got the right man."

Ingeborg realized suddenly they were talking about Joe Hill, a fellow Swede famous for the songs he wrote for the Industrial Workers of the World, a radical labor union. Ingeborg was a Wobblie too—as the IWW members called themselves. She'd never met Joe, but she'd sung his songs countless times, and she knew the details of his story. With a start she remembered he was awaiting execution in Utah's Sugar House Prison, right nearby. She'd followed his story in the newspapers, and of course the Wobblies took a great interest in his case and talked about it all the time. She rested her tools on her belly as she thought about what had landed him in jail.

She knew that after moving around the country looking for work, Joe had come to nearby Park City because the Silver King Mine was hiring. He was staying with friends. One night he'd staggered back to his cot with a bullet wound in his chest, and it was his bad luck that the same evening, a Salt Lake City grocer named Morrison had been fatally shot by a robber. Morrison had managed to shoot his assailant, but the man had gotten away. The only real eyewitness, the grocer's son, had said at first that Joe Hill wasn't the man he'd seen, but he later changed his story. They'd arrested Joe Hill for the crime even though they had no murder weapon or motive.

Ingeborg found it maddening—everyone did—that Joe refused to say who had shot him and why, or where he'd actually been that night. He just hinted there was a lady involved. She figured that might be true, but it didn't seem worth dying for. Why wouldn't he just name her? Especially since, when it came to trial, the jury quickly found him guilty, and the judge sentenced him to death.

The IWW leader Big Bill Hayward came to Joe's defense, calling on members across the country to raise money for an appeal and to protest his conviction. They all knew Joe had really been convicted for being a foreigner, a Wobblie, and a radical who wrote songs ridiculing the wealthy and powerful.

In her bones Ingeborg knew he was innocent. He might've been up to something that night with some other man's woman, but he wasn't the sort to murder someone in cold blood. The police couldn't find the actual killer, so they'd just seized the chance to get rid of a man they thought was a nuisance. It was scary how the government went after working people just for demanding their rights.

It came to Ingeborg suddenly that she should visit Joe. She felt a buzz of excitement in her chest as she turned the thought around in her mind. Why not? She'd always wanted to meet him. And he believed in suffrage, too!

She'd read that he'd given up all hope of leaving prison alive and urged his friends to stop defending him. What if a visit from a fellow Swede and a Wobblie would change his mind? She could tell him what his songs had meant to her, to everyone, and thank him for helping working people.

The more she thought about it, the better she liked the idea.

She'd have to keep it quiet, though. Maria would understand, though she wouldn't like it, but the idea would scare Mabel and Sara half to death. The CU was happy to work with labor unions as long as the workers did as they were told. But the IWW didn't want to work with politicians the way the CU did. The CU leaders Ingeborg had met were mostly members of the ruling class already, so they had no interest in overthrowing the capitalist system. They would be deeply unhappy with anyone who pushed too far in that direction.

The two men finished their smoke and moved on as Ingeborg continued working on the car. It had held up surprisingly well, considering how much it had been knocked about on the trip so far. The Lincoln Highway, hah! A grand name for something that was little more than a cart track most of the way. A fancy signpost on the side of the road meant nothing if the roadbed was washed out or deep with ruts. Their detour the day before had taken them eighty miles out of the way.

Thinking of their jolting ride reminded Ingeborg that she was still tired and sore, so she hurried to finish up. She wanted a long bath and a nap before they went out this afternoon. She stowed her tools in the boot and went up to their room.

Maria's newly washed undergarments were hung to dry from the spindle of the one chair and in the wardrobe. She sat by the window mending a torn seam and looked up as Ingeborg came in. "How is it?" she asked.

"It needed some grease. I adjusted some things but it's holding up. It's a good machine." Ingeborg began stripping off her outer garments.

"Good," said Maria. "This trip is costing a lot, and I don't want to pay for repairs, too. I was glad Mabel said the CU would pay for that idiot driver we hired."

"He was a waste of money," agreed Ingeborg. "From now on you're our driver, no matter what the roads." She hesitated a moment, and then said, "I'm going to visit Joe Hill tomorrow."

Maria looked at her sharply. "The desert must have cooked your brains, Ingeborg. Why do this? Mabel won't like it."

"Who cares?" Ingeborg asked, bristling. "Mabel herself said we can do as we like with our free time. I can visit a fellow Swede who's down on his luck if I want to."

"Who happens to be accused of murder," said Maria, stabbing her needle into the seam. "I know you don't think he shot that man. I don't either. But people fear the IWW. If they found out—"

"It won't harm this precious trip!" Ingeborg snapped. She splashed water in the basin to wash her face and hands.

"I meant I'm worried for you. What if they decided to make an example of you, too?"

"For what? For being a suffrage-loving automobile mechanic? Why would they lock me up for that?" Ingeborg wiped her hands on the towel.

Maria shook her head. "This country is changing, Ingeborg. It scares me. The war in Europe is frightening people. They're suspicious of foreigners, of anyone who threatens wealthy people. They send police and soldiers to break up strikes. They charged Joe with murder, and they could invent something to charge you with, too. What you did in Providence before we left—"

"No one knows about that here, Maria. And I was never arrested."

"But you almost were. I'm just asking you to be careful. Think about what you have to lose. We've worked hard. Why risk everything to visit a man you've never met?" She knotted the thread and snipped it off with a pair of tiny embroidery scissors she kept in a muslin pouch with needles and extra thread. Her brow furrowed.

Ingeborg sat down heavily on the bed. "Please, Maria. I always hoped to meet him. Soon they'll kill him, and I won't have another chance."

"You'll have it your way in the end, Ingeborg, you always do," said Maria. "But be careful. Promise me you'll keep your temper. Do nothing to anger the guards. If they ask, we'll tell Mabel and Sara that you're visiting a cousin."

"They won't ask," said Ingeborg, with a shrug. "We're just the help." She grabbed a towel. "I'm going to soak that desert out of my skin," she said, heading off to the tub.

* * *

At three o'clock Ingeborg and Maria went downstairs to bring the car around to meet Sara in front of the hotel. They had resumed their customary positions, Maria behind the wheel and Ingeborg beside her in what they called in the West the "shotgun seat," a phrase Ingeborg secretly rather liked.

Closing her eyes, she imagined herself holding an actual shotgun as they drove along, scanning the road ahead or peering up at rocky bluffs for signs of an ambush, the way they did back in the stagecoach days. They'd hear a great whoop! and the next thing they knew, men on horseback would be galloping up behind them, and she'd yell, "More speed!" to Maria and swivel to pull the shotgun up and fit its stock to her shoulder, preparing to blast away at the bandits. In her daydream they were congressmen who blocked passage of the federal amendment, their blue serge suits coated with dust, homburgs bouncing on their backs, caught round their necks by strips of rawhide. She'd line up the gunsights on Massachusetts Senator Henry Cabot Lodge, the blue-blooded snob, and boom! She'd send him toppling backward into the dust. Next to press the attack would be Representative Edwin Webb, who chaired the House Judiciary Committee and hated suffrage. He'd gallop up with one hand wrapped around the saddle horn, hanging on for dear life—and her shotgun would buck and roar and then he, too, would disappear in the dust cloud boiling up from the wheels of the racing car.

She opened her eyes and slanted them over at Maria, who sat patiently behind the wheel. Ingeborg wouldn't share these fantasies with her. Maria would never imagine shooting congressmen bandits, no matter how mad they made her. She would just sit quietly, as they were waiting now for Sara, who was late again. The minutes ticked by, and just as Ingeborg was about to go up and drag her out by her hair, Sara burst through the front doors and tottered down the steps. She looked tired and pale under her sunburned skin, and her eyes threatened a flood of tears. Tiny to begin with, she had lost weight since the trip began, and her brown wool traveling suit hung from her small frame.

She collapsed into the back seat with a muttered apology. Maria and Ingeborg exchanged a glance, and then Maria started the car and pulled out into the road, maneuvering around the piles of dung a passing cattle herd had left in the streets. After some moments Maria looked back at Sara.

"Sara," she said kindly. "Do you have pain?"

Sara shook her head mutely.

"What is it then? Your children, are they well?"

Sara heaved a sigh. "I—yes, they're fine, I think." She hesitated, then blurted out "It's just that I have my period." She choked back a sob.

Maria clucked sympathetically. "Too bad. With this travel, and the meeting, too." She thought for a moment. "Do you have what you need? Ingeborg has some rags, I think—"

"I have what I need," said Sara miserably. "It's just that—I had so hoped to be carrying Erskine's child." Her voice quivered, and tears trickled down her cheeks.

Maria froze, her eyes pinned to the road ahead. Ingeborg spun in her seat and gaped at Sara. "You wanted to be *pregnant*? On a trip this hard? You want to have morning sickness, too?"

"I didn't think it would be this hard," Sara said in a small voice. "And Frances was supposed to be with us, so she could have managed if I were unwell."

They continued in silence, digesting this news. Ingeborg thought about Erskine, who at sixty-three was thirty years older than Sara—he could be her father! He lived with his wife and family in Portland, Oregon, while Sara lived in San Francisco. Sara hadn't shared much information about him, but it seemed their affair had been going on for several years, and Sara had left her husband and two children for him.

He'd come down to San Francisco after the Woman Voters Convention to say good-bye—despite their grand exit from the Court of Abundance that last night, they'd lingered on for more than a week to rest and make final preparations. Sara had eyes only for Erskine, and he was quite attentive in return, giving her a well-tanned buffalo skin to use in the car, a warm coat, and provisions for the trip which she'd generously shared with Maria and Ingeborg. He was a majestic figure: tall, with flowing white hair and beard, and deep, brooding eyes. A handsome man, and perhaps a great lover, but so what? A baby was a burden to a single woman, quite apart from the scandal. How would Sara have managed? Privately, Ingeborg thought that Sara should give up on Erskine and find someone younger who lived in the same city, at least. Preferably someone unmarried. Ingeborg wasn't a prude, but she thought it best to be practical.

Outside the city limits, Maria found a quiet spot where she could pull the car over and park. She turned around to face Sara. "I'm sorry for your news," she said. "What do we do? Soon you must shake the governor's hand and make your speech. Should we tell Mabel you're ill?"

Sara sniffed and wiped her eyes with the heel of her hand. "No," she said. "I can do this. We've come too far not to. It's just that—I lost his child once before. This may have been my last chance—who knows when I'll see him again?" Her chin wobbled, and she looked ready to cry again.

"When was that?" Maria asked.

"Two years ago," Sara said wearily, shoulders slumped in dejection. "I was very ill with tuberculosis, and Erskine sent me to a sanitarium in California. I didn't find out I was pregnant until after I got there. Because I was so sick, Erskine wanted me to have an abortion, but then I miscarried." She sniffed again.

Ingeborg kept quiet. This was Maria's domain. Back when they ran the Swedish home, Maria was the one all the girls went to with their man problems, though usually they wanted to end the pregnancy rather than keep a baby that could mean getting fired or branded as a loose woman. Ingeborg couldn't imagine Alice Paul would be pleased if Sara turned up in Washington to meet President Wilson pregnant with the child of a man who was married to someone else.

"Oh, Sara, how hard for you," said Maria, her voice warm and comforting. "To be so sick and lose a baby, too."

"You must think me awfully silly. But I love Erskine so very much. Even if he never leaves his wife, our child would be something to remind me of him, something we had made together."

"Of course you want a baby with a man you love," Maria said, sympathetically. She hesitated, then asked, "Does Erskine also want a child?"

Sara searched though the pockets of her brown wool suit for a handkerchief and blew her nose. She frowned, considering. "Not quite as much as I do, I think. He has five already, after all, and he does complain about all the people he has to take care of."

"Would he help you, if you had one?"

"Oh, yes!" said Sara. "We're married, after all, though not in the conventional manner."

Ingeborg glanced at Maria, eyebrows raised. "How do you mean?" she asked. She couldn't believe they were having this conversation. Sara was supposed to be the envoy! She had no business being pregnant. She was so frail that a pregnancy would certainly have done her in, and then where would they be?

"He's still married to her—legally," said Sara dismissively, as though that carried little weight. "But we had our own private ceremony during the Oregon suffrage campaign. We were on a speaking tour east of the mountains and managed to steal some time together." Her voice took on a dreamy quality as she remembered, and she closed her eyes. "One night he led me into the woods to an ancient oak tree with great gnarled branches that arched above us, creating a sort of dome. An exquisite, silvery moonlight poured through the branches and bathed our faces. We were kissed by a tender breeze. There, we joined hands and said our vows. 'From now on,' he said, 'all our nights would be bridal nights.'"

"That's what marriage should be," said Maria, visibly moved by this image of Sara and Erskine under a magical moon. "A joining of souls. There's no need for a minister or a church—they just get in the way."

Ingeborg added, "That's the way for babies, too. How can a baby be illegitimate? That's foolishness. I've worked in an orphanage. We knew the mother, but many times—well, the Holy Ghost must have been the father."

"Exactly," said Sara. "I know Erskine would be proud to call our baby his child. He believes in free love, and so do I!" She lay back in her seat, looked up at the sky, and continued in a low voice, "He does love the ladies, though. I really just want him and no one else, but Erskine—he gets so attached to other women." Her voice grew stronger and she said, defiantly, "I don't care, though. We're married, no matter what anyone says."

Ingeborg sighed. It was all very well to talk about free love, but it seemed that men had all the freedom while women were saddled with love's results. She'd seen young mothers at the orphanage, some hardly more than children themselves, cradling their fatherless infants to their breasts, weeping, near collapsing with sorrow. They were doubly damned; for getting pregnant out of wedlock, and then for turning their backs on their babies, even as the sledgehammers of poverty and public shame drove them into the ground and made no other choice possible. Meanwhile, the fathers were nowhere to be found. The very picture of innocence—their hands in their pockets and whistling a tune—they were looking out for their next conquest.

A truck clattered past, a heifer standing spraddle-legged in the back, her head lowered as she fought for balance. The driver, trim-bearded, idled to a stop, stuck his head out the window and asked if they needed help. They waved him on, but Ingeborg checked her pocket watch and exclaimed at how late it was. "Maria and I will get the car ready," she said. "Sara, you fix your face."

Sara stepped out of their way and did her best to remove the traces of her recent crying, pouring water onto her handkerchief and blotting her face with it. She took some deep breaths and paced around, squared her shoulders, chin up, and summoned up the first few lines of her speech.

Maria and Ingeborg shook out the canvas Great Demand banner and stretched it across the back of the car, securing it with ties. They bound suffrage flags to the corners of the windows and stuck a sign that read ON TO CONGRESS to the top of the windshield. The car was still coated with the dust it was wearing when they'd arrived the night before, just as they still wore their travel-stained driving suits, as a badge of distinction. Congressional Union sashes of purple, white, and gold completed their attire, though on Maria and Ingeborg they strained across their large bosoms.

When the car was ready, Maria walked over to Sara. "You look fine," she said. "Tired. Sunburned. Just like us." Then she launched into Sara's "Song of the Free Women" that had been sung at the convention, marched over to the car, and slid behind the wheel. Sara laughed at her slightly off-key warbling, but she and Ingeborg joined in as they climbed into the car, and they drove back down the road to meet the local suffrage contingent, the flags snapping in the breeze.

We come. We come at last.
Night's portal we have passed.
We come. We come. Trust thou our might.
Thou, too, shall walk in Light.

* * *

As Maria steered the car onto Fourteenth South, they could see up ahead a dozen automobiles gaily decorated with CU banners and VOTES FOR WOMEN signs. A great cheer went up from the assembled women and they surged into the street to surround the Overland Six, giving the travelers a warm welcome. Ingeborg was secretly pleased to overhear one woman exclaim, "Oh, look how dusty and worn the poor things are! They must have had a terrible time."

In short order everyone got back into their motorcars and fell into line behind the Overland Six, heading back to the Hotel Utah. The band was already playing when they pulled up, and curious passersby crowded the streets and sidewalks to peer at the spectacle. Mabel Vernon waited for them on the steps of the hotel, and the assembled women applauded as she walked down and joined Sara in the back seat of the car. At a word from Mabel the band struck up a military tune and began marching slowly up the winding road to the capitol. Maria swung the car in behind them, and their escorts followed.

Ingeborg looked around with interest. The sun was edging toward the western mountains, casting long shadows and bringing some relief from the heat. The sidewalks were full of people walking and visiting the shops that lined the street, and they stopped and clapped as the little parade passed by. Across the way she could see the six spires of the Mormon Tabernacle poking their stone fingers toward heaven. She shook her head in wonder and leaned over to say to Maria, "The Mormons build everything big." Maria nodded. The Tabernacle, the wide, empty streets that could easily fit three of the narrow lanes in Providence, and the new state capitol building sprawling on a high bluff overlooking the city—all built on a grand scale.

She was curious about the Mormons, who had twice voted to enfranchise their women, with polygamy at the center of the issue each time. The first time, in 1870, some reformers had promoted the idea as a way to end polygamy, mistakenly believing women would outlaw it the first chance they had. The Mormon elders knew their women better, though, and when polygamy remained legal, an exasperated and Protestant Congress in Washington, DC, passed a law to end both plural marriage and women suffrage in the new territory.

Eventually, Church elders recognized Utah would never be accepted as a state unless they gave up polygamy, which they voted to do, albeit reluctantly. When it came time to write the new state's constitution in 1895, Mormon women realized they'd better hustle to make sure their voting rights were included, but since their votes were no longer essential to the church, they'd had to campaign hard to get them back. Even the famous Susan B. Anthony traveled out from her home in New York to help. When it suited men's own interests, women had no trouble getting the vote, Ingeborg thought, but otherwise it was a fight every time.

Before long, the cavalcade drew up in front of the capitol, built of white marble with rows of columns framing an open promenade. Its towering gold dome rose over the very center of the building, lit by the setting sun. Ingeborg could see a crowd of people, mostly women, massing on the steps waiting for them.

The band marched over to stand at the bottom of the steps and continued to play. Leaving the cars below, Mabel and Sara led the way up the stairs to meet local suffrage leaders who included Margaret Zane Cherdron, whom they'd met at the Woman Voters Convention in San Francisco. Annie Wells Cannon and her mother, Emmeline B. Wells, were also there to greet them. Emmeline was a tiny, ancient woman shaped like a drooping sunflower, shoulders bowed forward and face pointing earthwards, so she had to crane her head sideways in order to see whomever she was addressing. Ingeborg had to resist the urge to stoop down and look upward at her, to give the poor woman's neck some relief.

Emmeline had worked with Susan B. Anthony to write suffrage into the state's constitution twenty years before, so everyone there treated her like royalty, which Ingeborg supposed she was, in a way, suffrage royalty, at least. She often wondered what you had to do to be suffrage royalty. Being white-skinned was clearly top of the list, and being native-born or having the right foreign accent helped too. Graciousness might be part of it as well; Emmeline spoke simply and sweetly as she welcomed the three travelers, though Ingeborg couldn't help but notice that it was Sara she tugged over to stand beside her once the speeches began.

Margaret Cherdron introduced Sara and the Swedes to Governor William Spry, Congressman Joseph Howell, and Mayor Samuel Park. The governor was about Ingeborg's age, sporting a neatly trimmed goatee and spectacles, his smug paunch assaulting his waistcoat buttons. In fact, all three men looked as if they were taking full advantage of their business dinners. They stood in a little huddle with their backs to the capitol wall, facing out at the crowd. They'd said all the right things about supporting the federal amendment but Ingeborg could detect no passion for it. She thought she glimpsed on their faces the patronizing smirk most men slipped into when women reached for something more than what society allowed them. Like a cat watching a mouse trying to leap to freedom up the smooth sides of a metal bucket, the fun was watching women try, again and again, not really caring whether they made it on the first try or the hundredth, or ever. It made her want to box their ears. What would they actually do to help women, in the end?

Ingeborg's other grudge against the governor was that he'd refused all requests to reconsider or delay Joe Hill's execution, even ignoring a telegram from President Wilson and the pleas of the Swedish Ambassador. He was in the pocket of the rich mine owners who were doing their best to stamp out the IWW and all unions—silencing men like Joe Hill would earn him their undying gratitude. It was rumored he was interested in higher office, perhaps even the presidency, and he needed the mine owners' backing. Despite his friendly words about suffrage, Ingeborg was having a hard time feeling grateful to him. She was glad she had to do no more than shake his hand.

The speeches continued as the sun slipped lower over the Oquirrh Mountains west of the city, bathing the capitol with a warm, honeyed light that pressed the crowd together into a single living organism with a single purpose. Ingeborg heard a woman behind her murmur that it seemed as though God himself were smiling down on them, and though Ingeborg had long since ceased to believe in any god, let alone one who concerned himself with humans' toils and cares, she could allow herself to hope this was true.

She raised her face to the light, moved by the setting, the spirit that united women past and present in pursuit of this one great cause—to win recognition of women's right to a civil life, to be recognized under the law as citizens—as people. Like a journey by stagecoach, progress had taken many drivers, many teams. Each stage had required countless hours stolen from family chores, and precious pennies counted out carefully from thin purses. It humbled her to think of it that way, and she said a silent thanks to the Utah women—and men—who had done their part to win voting rights for the women of this state. If this trip could speed the passage of the federal suffrage amendment, it would be worth the difficulty and hardship.

A soft wind welled up from the city below, carrying with it the smell of coal fires, the sounds of children playing, and the clop of horses pulling wagons through the streets. A large hawk soared into view from around the corner of the capitol, riding the warm breeze rising up from the valley floor. It tilted its wings slightly left and right, head and neck craned down, trying to ignore the flock of sparrows that danced close in, harrying and tormenting it, hurling outsized threats against this enemy that was so immense that a single swipe from one of its great claws, a quick snap from its curved beak could have ended their lives. She saw they were determined to drive the hawk away from their nests; they darted in by turns, diving at the hawk's head and uttering shrill cries. Before long, the hawk grew tired of the abuse and flapped its wings lazily to rise up and away from the pestering flock below. She smiled to think that the suffragists were like those tiny sparrows, hectoring Congress and the president by whatever means until at last they moved in the right direction.

Sara stepped forward to speak, still struggling to keep her emotions in check. Her face was layered in sadness, and her voice wobbled at the outset, but rather than trying to hide it, Sara simply admitted that the beauty of the setting and the warmth of their welcome had moved her to tears. She spoke about the Woman Voters Convention in San Francisco and the great work they had set out to do. She recalled how, in 1906, Susan B. Anthony had addressed a suffrage convention in Washington, DC. "Anthony told the crowd that the congressmen had advised women to wait until the time was right for the vote. So they had waited while Negro men won the right, Filipino men were enfranchised, and immigrant men from almost every country on earth were given the right to vote, while their wives, mothers, sisters, and daughters stood by and waited for their turn. Susan B. Anthony knew then she would die before women won the vote, but still she pressed on."

Sara raised her voice, and Ingeborg felt a little thrill up and down her spine at her next words. "Now, my friends, women who are brainy enough to bear and raise children are brainy enough to make laws. The people gathered tonight in the interests of suffrage are doing a great work which will go down in the world's history. For years women have been beseeching, praying for their rights, but now, with twelve equal suffrage states and four million enfranchised women, we are no longer begging for our rights, but are saying—" She paused, and raised her voice to a shout, "We *demand* an amendment to the Constitution enfranchising women!" The crowd clapped and cheered in response.

Finishing up, Sara recognized Maria and Ingeborg for providing the car and accompanying her on this epic journey to Congress. Frances Joliffe, she explained, had been detained by illness and would rejoin them later in the trip, so a speech she'd been scheduled to give in the fairgrounds that evening was canceled. Ingeborg listened to this excuse with an inward eye roll. When would Frances return?

The ceremony came to an end with all those present signing the petition. In the gathering twilight, six young girls clad in white led them back down the steps to their waiting automobiles while singing "America," a favorite among the suffragists because of its emphasis on freedom. Ingeborg understood the song was supposed to inspire, but it seemed to her a syrupy lie. "Sweet land of liberty…." Whose liberty? When laws prevented women or the colored race from voting, were they free? She decided instead to hum the tune while silently replacing the lyrics with ones from the IWW songbook, which seemed a more apt description of the America she knew.

My country 'tis of thee
My private property
Of thee I sing.
Land where the millions toil
That out of "Standard Oil"
I wealth may wring.

My native villainy
Is what enables me
To make my pile.
I have the rocks and rills
Of oil my barrels fills,
With gold and bonds and bills—
That's why I smile....

She felt a hand on her arm and, startled, looked up to see a tall man in a battered cowboy hat, notebook and pencil in hand, asking to speak to her. She stepped to the side to allow others to walk past. "Thank you, Miss Kindstedt. I'm Hans Blodevelt from the *Deseret News*. I'm curious, do you really work on the car yourself?"

"Of course," said Ingeborg.

"How'd you learn to do that?"

"My father could fix anything, and I used to watch him. My uncle was a blacksmith, and I spent hours in his shop, too. I liked mechanical things, so I just asked questions and learned how."

"That's remarkable," Hans said. "I've never met a lady mechanic."

Ingeborg snorted. "Why, do you suppose? We teach girls only to sew and cook and clean, and take care of babies, while their brothers learn the mechanical things. And often boys are sent to school while their sisters stay home."

"Interesting. So you really believe that if we gave them an equal chance girls could do whatever boys could do?" asked the reporter. He sounded skeptical.

"Of course!" replied Ingeborg, trying to suppress the little flame of irritation rising in her chest. "In any factory today, you'd find women doing quite difficult work. And that's with just a little training. With the same opportunities, women would do as well as men, or better!"

"Goodness," he laughed. "Then what would men do?"

Ingeborg laughed. "Good question. Maybe learn to cook." She turned and walked down the steps to the car.

CHAPTER THREE

OCTOBER 5, 1915

Ingeborg was still determined to visit Joe Hill. They'd decided Maria would drop Ingeborg off and drive away; the car was too well known, and they thought it best not to leave it outside the prison.

That morning they'd found Mabel alone at breakfast. She was full of praise for how the event at the capitol had gone and said again how much the CU appreciated what they and Sara were doing. "Everyone says this is the best thing the Union has ever done," she said, her cheeks flushed with excitement. "It can't help but make a difference." Maria and Ingeborg agreed. The Utah women were now awake to the fact their Eastern sisters couldn't vote, and they were determined to make sure their congressmen backed the federal amendment.

The talk then turned to the upcoming stages of the route. Mabel was taking the noon train to Evanston and would work her way toward Denver, via Laramie and Cheyenne. A side trip to Ogden was canceled as the envoys needed to catch Congressman Frank Mondell, who would be in Evanston the following evening.

"He's a Republican and has been our chief champion in the House for years," Mabel told them. "We'll try to use your visit to generate more publicity—I'll see if I can recruit some local leaders to accompany you. See what he thinks about the amendment's prospects in this session."

Ingeborg nodded, trying to act as if visiting congressmen at their homes was an everyday occurrence for them, though she felt a small clutch of alarm at the thought. It still startled her that this was her life now. How could she be the same person who had boarded the ship in Providence earlier this summer?

"I have something for you," Mabel said next. With a flourish, she produced a Lincoln Highway map that somehow no one had thought to procure in San Francisco. Ingeborg and Maria cheered and began poring over it. Their pleasure in the map quickly changed to dismay when they discovered it would be over eighty miles to Evanston, followed by one hundred miles to each of the next three stops. They eyed each other doubtfully and turned back to Mabel.

"How are the roads?" asked Maria.

"I asked around," Mabel said, vaguely. "I hear they're not bad, and you'll be able to make good time."

Ingeborg felt a hot prickling warmth spread out through her arms and back and rise into her face. Beads of sweat moistened her hairline, gathered between her shoulder blades, and rolled down her chest and belly. She looked around, suddenly edgy and irritable. Was there a window she could open? She couldn't understand why the hotel would overheat the dining room; they must spend a fortune on coal. Then she turned back to Mabel and said, her voice almost hissing, "You push us too hard. We didn't agree to this. We said we'd take the petitions to Washington, and then Miss Paul stuck on the envoys. So we said all right to that. And now you want us to drive miles out of our way to visit some congressman in this city and that! If we went straight to Washington, we wouldn't have to hurry so much."

Mabel spoke soothingly. "I know this has been hard, but it will get easier, I promise you. The roads in the East are much better, and the cities are closer together. We just have to get to Denver—there will be time to rest there." She smiled. "You both have been splendid, and Miss Paul is so pleased. We're indebted to you."

Ingeborg huffed and shook her head. "People and machines, both, they have a breaking point, Mabel. If you drive us too hard, something will go wrong."

"We'll all just have to do the best we can," said Mabel, with a shrug.

"It will be winter soon, too," Ingeborg warned. "We'll freeze in that car, I'll tell you right now. And what if it snows? We should go south— that's what we planned to do."

Mabel glanced at Maria, who was gazing out the window, pretending to be lost in admiration of the Mormon Tabernacle's towers. Ingeborg knew that Maria was also unhappy with the route but didn't like fights, especially those she suspected she wouldn't win. She was staying out of this one.

Lowering her voice, Mabel leaned forward and said in a low voice, "We have to rally our supporters in the Northern states. You know as well as I do the Southern congressmen oppose the federal amendment because of the race question; there's no point in going there. And voters in Michigan, New York, New Jersey, and Pennsylvania will vote on suffrage bills this fall, so we must visit those states."

Ingeborg fanned herself with the map and mopped sweat from her neck and face. "Why? I thought we were just for the federal amendment."

"Every state that passes suffrage strengthens our hand when it comes to pressuring Wilson and Congress, and no Eastern state has done this," said Mabel. "A visit from the suffrage envoys will help with publicity. And if they lose, as we suspect they will, we want women to know they can join the CU to work on the federal amendment instead." She smiled. "We benefit either way."

Maria turned toward them and nodded reluctantly, but Ingeborg scowled, unconvinced.

"Let's take it one stage at a time," coaxed Mabel. "It's going so well; maybe our luck will hold. Sara thinks she can make it to Denver, and we'll talk then."

Mabel could be just as stubborn as Alice Paul, in her own way, so they eventually agreed, though Ingeborg still grumbled.

A short time later Maria drew the car to a stop outside the front entrance of Sugar House Prison. They sat and looked it over. It was a commanding building faced with brick, with an arched portcullis and narrow windows that glared malevolently down on the street. To each side spread high stone walls topped with barbed wire; armed guards peered down at them from the corner turrets. Cool, dank air lingered around the entrance, as from a living tomb. Ingeborg cursed in Swedish and sank down in her seat. She pictured being brought inside in chains and hearing the iron gates clank shut.

"You don't have to do this," said Maria quietly, turning in her seat to look at Ingeborg.

"No," agreed Ingeborg, looking down at her hands, which were chapped and gnarled, with small scrapes from working on the car. She turned and faced Maria. "But I have to try. It's just worse than I thought. No justice can be found in a place like this, I think." She opened the door and stepped out.

"I'll be back for you," said Maria, "Watch yourself."

Ingeborg walked through the gate and found her way to the prison office where a uniformed guard sat behind a counter, his face framed by a thick window with a small opening through which they could speak. She told him she'd come to see Joe Hill. The guard looked her over carefully, taking in her worn traveling coat neatly buttoned over her dress, her weathered face. He wore a crisp, dark blue uniform and his hair was cut close under a peaked cap with a broad bill that half hid his eyes. "What's your connection?" he barked at her.

"Cousin," said Ingeborg, forcing herself to look over the guard's left shoulder and settle her face into the impassive, unreadable mask every immigrant learned to adopt when dealing with authorities.

The guard hmphed skeptically. "He hasn't mentioned any cousin. Not sure I see a resemblance, either. Let's see your papers." Ingeborg handed over her identification and naturalization papers, and he examined them carefully before handing them back to her. He glanced up in surprise. "You came all the way from Rhode Island to see him?"

"Yes, sir," said Ingeborg.

"Well, he's refused other visitors. He may not see you."

Ingeborg nodded gravely. "I had to try," she said. "He's very dear to us." That came close to the truth, at least. "My mother would want me to," she added.

"Wait here," said the guard, and disappeared behind a door he'd unlocked using a set of keys dangling from a chain on his belt. She'd never seriously considered the possibility that Joe might not see her. Surely he'd want to see a friendly face, even a stranger's. She fretted as the minutes ticked by.

The keys jangled in the lock and the guard reappeared with a prison matron who patted Ingeborg's clothes for weapons or contraband. Then she nodded at the guard to unlock a barred door to the right of the office. Another guard escorted her through the door and down a dim corridor built of the same stone that formed the prison walls. The stale air was thick with the scent of unwashed bodies and despair.

The matron brought her to a large room that featured several scarred, heavy oak tables bolted to the floor, with benches on each side similarly secured. The guard pointed to a table and told her to sit and wait. Ingeborg peered around the room. There was one window high up, its vertical bars carving the light into strips that fell across the table in front of her. She blew out a breath and tried to compose her thoughts. Now that she was here, what would she say?

Presently a guard appeared, leading Joe Hill to the table and shackling his hands to the massive iron ring bolted to its top. The guard patted Joe lightly on the shoulder. "You know the rules, Joe," the guard said, almost kindly. "You have thirty minutes to visit with your cousin. She's come a long way to see you."

"Thanks, Stan," said Joe. Then he joked, "We may step out for some coffee, but I'll be here when you get back." The guard left. Joe fixed his eyes on Ingeborg and waited. Ingeborg returned his gaze, taking in his gaunt face, stubbled jaw, and the ill-fitting, black-striped prison uniform that hung off his body. In the photos she'd seen, he was youthful, with a stubborn set to his mouth, deep-set, intelligent eyes, and thick hair swept back from a high forehead. This Joe seemed older and infinitely weary. His face was lined. Red blotches bloomed on his skin, and his light brown hair was cut shorter than in the photos, threaded with silver. He regarded her now with curiosity and a touch of humor.

"Well, Cousin, we meet at last," he drawled. "Which branch of the family are you supposed to be from?"

Ingeborg colored slightly and stammered in Swedish, "Forgive me. I was in Salt Lake and I wanted to see you." Fool! She'd scarcely thought about what she would say. She plunged on. "I'm also from Sweden, you see, and in the IWW. I—I wanted to tell you how proud you have made me, and how I love your songs." It sounded lame to her ears, but it was the best she could do.

Joe raised his eyebrows and nodded. "Thank you," he replied in Swedish.

She babbled on. "I'm from Karlstad, but I live in Providence now. I'm an organizer, and I remember the first time I heard one of your songs. They handed around copies of the little red book at a labor meeting I went to. We sang 'We Will Sing One Song' and then 'Ta-Ra-Ra Boom-De-Ay,' a couple of others. I wish you could have seen it. These workers dragged in the door and just sagged onto the benches, so beaten down they could barely lift their heads. The Italians, the Poles, the Swedes all sat in their little groups, not speaking or looking at each other. But when the singing started, they raised their voices together, and through the songs we became the one big union, all fighting the same fight for the same rights. You gave them hope. It was like a miracle."

Joe just stared at her with no expression on his face.

Ingeborg fumbled on. "I was so proud you were Swedish, too. I love all your songs—especially the ones about women."

Finally he stirred, lifting his manacled hands off the table and setting them back down. The chain rattled dully. "If hope were food, then maybe I'd really have given them something," said Joe, his voice flat. "But I wonder, sometimes, how much good I've done?"

"I don't understand." Ingeborg stared at him, bewildered. Did he really not know how beloved he was by working people all over America, all over the world? His songs were sung everywhere, in many languages.

He shrugged. "If I lifted people's spirits with clever lines, so what? From where I sit, the bosses just get stronger. We won a few fights, sure, but more and more they have the politicians and the courts in their pockets. They can beat and arrest and kill anyone and get away with it. And the union leaders squabble over how to fight back. I hate to think my songs inspire hardworking people to strike and get their heads bashed in for nothing."

Ingeborg reached over and covered his manacled hands with her own. "Stop, Joe Hill," she said, her voice urgent. "Why live at all if we can't hope for a better future?" She leaned toward him; her voice urgent. "Your songs, and the IWW, show the workers someone cares about them, knows what keeps them poor, tries to help. With your songs in their heads, they can keep fighting."

Joe shrugged again. Ingeborg considered him. The uniform's rough fabric had chafed his skin, leaving it red and rough at the base of his neck where his collarbones jutted out. His lips were chapped. and there were gray circles under his eyes.

Ingeborg sat back. "I don't know what's worse," she said angrily, "that you're in prison, or they've made you doubt yourself."

There was a brief silence as they regarded each other. Ingeborg read resignation and defeat in his face. A profound despair clenched her heart until she thought it might burst. She gulped in some air. She saw that his eyes were a flat, deep blue, and she was reminded suddenly of a Swedish lake under dull gray skies. As she watched him, though, he shifted and lights began dancing in their depths.

"Oh, don't worry about me!" said Joe, rousing himself. "I'm all right, I just get a little down sometimes. But hey, they give me three meals a day, a bunk to myself, and time to read and write. It would make the Mormons mad to hear it, but it's a little like paradise for me. I've known harder times."

"Is there anything you need?"

"No, no," said Joe, shaking his head emphatically. "You want to know the truth, I'm tired of waiting. I'm ready for it to be over. And I'm tired of talking about it. Tell me what really brings you to Salt Lake City, Cousin Ingeborg."

Relieved to change the subject, Ingeborg quickly told him about the Congressional Union and the petitions and their drive to Washington. He gave a low whistle. "That's some stunt. Think the car will make it?"

"Well, it should," Ingeborg said, a little proudly. "My friend Maria bought it brand new, and I keep it running."

"Is that a fact?" said Joe, smiling. "I never owned a machine myself, and the ones I rode in convinced me that jumping freights was a better way to travel. You ladies have done very well for yourselves. I'm proud of you. And I have no doubt you'll make it to our nation's capital on the day appointed, with banners flying. I only hope they have the sense to listen to you."

Ingeborg reddened slightly, pleased by his praise. "Do you have a message for the president?" she half-joked, and then cursed herself as the smile faded from his face and he looked somber.

"Tell him to open his eyes," he said. "Millions of good people in this country are going hungry. No parents should have to tell their crying children there's no supper tonight, and maybe no breakfast tomorrow. Tell him to quit calling out the army to bust up strikes. The strikers want to work, the bosses just don't pay them enough to put a roof over their heads, let alone take care of their families. They call me a radical, but what's radical about wanting a fair shake for people who work themselves to death to make the bosses rich? Tell him I said he should give women the vote, that'll help clean things up." He paused, and then added gruffly, "And you can tell him thanks for trying to get me out of here."

They could hear the guard returning, calling, "Time's up!" His key rattled at the door.

"Just a little more time," Ingeborg begged, but Joe was leaning back from the table so the guard could unlock his hands. Her heart thumped. How could it come to this? Was there really nothing to be done? Tears welled up and her throat closed over the words she wanted to scream at the guard. She stared at Joe. How did she say good-bye to a condemned man? He looked up and saw her discomfort; a little smile twisted his lips.

"Don't mourn, now. Go to Washington and give 'em hell!"

He rose to his feet and turned to let the guard lead him away. "Joe," Ingeborg managed to say. He turned to look at her "Thanks," she said hurriedly. "We won't forget you." He nodded and the guard led him away.

Ingeborg dug out a handkerchief to blot her tears. The matron came to escort her back to the main entrance. Outside she found

Maria waiting with the car. She took a deep breath of the warm, pine-scented air. After the dim coolness of the prison, the light was harsh and bright, and she had to squint to see. A horse-drawn wagon rumbled by, and children's voices rang out from a nearby yard. Down the street people bustled in and out of shops. She wanted to call out to them, "Don't you know? Joe Hill is in prison here. They plan to kill him for caring about working people like you. Pay attention! It could happen to you, too."

She climbed heavily into the front seat, suddenly very weary, and sank back against the cushions. Maria looked over at her, eyebrows raised.

"I saw him," said Ingeborg. "Now let's get out of here."

CHAPTER FOUR

OCTOBER 7, 1915

They left Salt Lake City for Wyoming under the blue tent of the sky, following the Lincoln Highway signs. As she drove east into the rising sun, Maria sometimes shaded her eyes against the glare to see the road in front of them. The air was cool, and they huddled under their wraps, knowing that before long they would be cursing the heat and dust.

Ingeborg was feeling snappish, like a cat when its fur is ruffled backward so it strikes out with its claws. She'd woken that morning from a dream so dull even the people in it had yelled at her to wake up and end their misery. What was the point of such a dream? she thought irritably. If it were true that dreams revealed something important about the unconscious then hers must be a thick blanc-mange, devoid of any flavoring whatever.

The dream had followed a restless night interrupted by waves of heat lightning that prickled to life in her lower back and swept up her spine, a spreading warmth erupting into showers of sweat that soaked her nightdress and the bedsheets and left her gasping for breath. They'd been happening more frequently of late, and not just at night. Sometimes during the day she'd feel that warning prickle race up her spine, and she'd just have time to grab her handkerchief before the storm broke and she had to mop the sweat from her face and neck, feeling it trickling down between her breasts. Afterward, her soaked underclothes dragged unpleasantly across her skin. The episodes left her wrapped in a dense, damp fog, edgy and exhausted. She kept waiting for other signs of illness to emerge—a sore throat, a hacking cough—but none ever did.

She hadn't mentioned her heat storms to Maria at first, fretting privately they augured some desperate condition that would eventually carry her off. But the second time she'd complained of a fever that Maria's thermometer failed to register, her partner had peered more closely at her and asked some probing questions. Finally, she'd shrugged and given Ingeborg a rueful smile.

"There's nothing wrong with you, *käresta*," she'd said, using a Swedish endearment. "You're just going through the change."

This possibility hadn't occurred to Ingeborg, and she'd eyed Maria distrustfully. "The change! What are you talking about? I'm sick—"

"No, Ingeborg," Maria interrupted her. "You're a woman. And this happens to women your age. All the symptoms fit. I should have guessed—you've been so cranky lately."

Ingeborg had slumped onto the bed, regarding her partner with an anxious frown. "What can I do about it?"

Maria blew out her cheeks and tilted her head from side to side as she considered this. "Well, rest and cool baths can help—"

"We're in the desert!" Ingeborg snapped at her, tugging her shirtwaist away from her chest. "And we're driving all day. Stop with this nonsense! Isn't there some medicine?"

"There are all sorts of potions—ovarian extracts, for one. The Indians use black cohosh. Some people swear by Lydia Pinkham's tonic, if we can find it out here." Maria gave her a sympathetic smile. "It will go away eventually."

"How long?" Ingeborg demanded.

"At least a year. Maybe two," said Maria. "It varies."

Ingeborg had moaned and fallen backwards on the bed. "I'll go mad," she declared.

She was also annoyed because Sara had once again delayed their departure; she'd been penning a final note to Erskine, to whom she mailed thick envelopes bursting with pages at just about every possible stop, along with frequent telegrams. Ingeborg and Maria seldom wrote anyone, and then only to tell of a change of address, or to reply to important news from family in Sweden. Ingeborg was mystified as to what those letters contained. How many times could you describe the poor food, the hard travel, or yet another suffrage meeting?

In truth, Sara was struggling to keep going. She was also short of sleep, having stayed up late writing most of the letter whose completion delayed their departure this morning. She missed Erskine like a missing limb, the ache of his absence a constant presence. Not knowing when she would see him again left her utterly depressed. At the same time, the prospect of being joined at the hip to the two Swedes for the foreseeable future was almost more than she could bear.

That's what she'd been writing to him this morning. "At first I thought we were kindred spirits," she wrote. "Ingeborg so radical, and Maria so sweet and caring. But now I suspect Maria will smother me to death with attention. And Ingeborg half-wishes my heart truly will give out so she can take over the speaking." She'd hastened to assure Erskine that she didn't feel at risk from them. "It's just I would so much prefer that it were you in the car beside me as we jolt along these impossible roads. At least I'd know the comfort of your arms at night." Recalling those lines, she tugged the buffalo skin around her with a heavy sigh.

Ingeborg forced herself to look about at her surroundings. For the first time since they'd left San Francisco, it felt like fall. The scrub oak, cottonwood, and aspen were tinged in yellow and gold. Smoke from cooking fires rose from chimneys and curled around the roofs, filling the air with its sharp scent. Ingeborg inhaled deeply and shifted in her seat. Fall made her want to put up food, buy coal, and ready their house for the winter. Instead she was sitting idly in this car day after day, and it made her twitchy.

She wondered when they'd hit their first storm. It hadn't rained since they'd left San Francisco, but their luck wouldn't last, especially as they left the desert behind them. Eventually, as she'd warned Mabel, they'd run into bad weather, and she hoped the little car—and its passengers—could handle it. She and Maria were tough enough to survive the cold and snow, but she worried about Sara who was lying back against the cushions, the buffalo skin that Erskine had given her pulled up under the tip of her nose, her eyes shut. Ingeborg turned around sometimes to see if she was still sitting up and breathing. Sara's fragile health added worry to a trip that was already hard enough. What would they do if her heart really failed?

Ingeborg imagined driving up to a suffrage rally in a big city with an automobile escort, a military brass band, a governor and a congressman or two ready to greet them—and a suffrage corpse in the back seat. What a mess that would be. And would the CU let Ingeborg speak then? Probably not, she thought sourly. While Sara sometimes annoyed her, Ingeborg had to concede that she was very good in front of an audience. Even when she looked done in beforehand she would somehow rally on stage and deliver a speech that combined poetry with purpose, humor with pathos, and made clear to her listeners what they should do next. Ingeborg couldn't help but feel a little jealous.

By late morning Ingeborg was roasting like a potato in a hot oven. She shifted in her seat and took gulps of air, wondering if human bodies could explode in the heat the way potatoes did when they weren't first pricked with a fork. Exploding might actually be a relief, she decided, assuming she lost the power of thought along with it. Sweat streamed down her back and between her breasts and thighs, soaking her clothes, even as the hot, dust-laden air choked their throats. When they came upon some rare shade under the curve of a canyon wall, Maria pulled the car off the road, and they sprawled on the ground, removing every layer modesty permitted. Sara complained that her heart was racing, and she did look ill, wilted and pale under her browned skin. They spread her buffalo skin out for her so she could lie down. After resting for a bit, she was able to sit up and nibble on the food they'd brought.

She looked over at Ingeborg. "You mentioned having worked in an orphanage. When was that?"

ANNE B. GASS

"In Sweden," Ingeborg replied. "I joined the Salvation Army for their officer training school, in Stockholm. They had me work in the orphanage."

"The Salvation Army!" Sara gaped at her in surprise. "You? I don't believe it. How on earth did you end up there?"

Ingeborg snorted and shook her head, wiping sweat from her face with her handkerchief. "I was young, living with my parents. Not happy. I wanted more than to marry a farmworker or be someone's maid. In Sweden those were my choices. Right, Maria?" She looked across at her friend, who nodded. "But then the Salvation Army came to Karlstad. One night I meant to join friends at the theatre but I arrived too late—the play had started. It was too cold to wait for them outside, so I slipped into a nearby hall where the Salvation Army band was playing."

She paused, remembering the welcoming warmth of the hall after the bitter cold outside, and the joyful, if not always tuneful way the band thumped its instruments. No Church of Sweden service she attended ever had music like that! But most of all, she'd been riveted by the fact that the whole spectacle was commanded by a woman, Major Hanna Ouchterlony, a picture of crisp efficiency in her military uniform.

Ingeborg had watched in amazement. The Church of Sweden let women clean the church and stitch the altar cloths and raise the next generation of parishioners, but they certainly weren't permitted to preach or to lead a group of men. But that night Major Ouchterlony directed the program and welcomed people up on stage to testify about the Army bringing them to God. She spoke simply but power-fully of the work the Salvation Army was doing in Stockholm among the poor, and Ingeborg had known at once that this was what she'd been looking for. Here was work that spoke to her soul—serving the poor, protecting children, and restoring the dignity of women who had been led astray. She'd felt a tingle run from her neck down her spine and she'd shivered, thinking it the very finger of God reaching out to her.

"Did you join on the spot?" asked Sara.

Ingeborg grimaced and shook her head. "No, I took a few days to decide. My family wasn't faithful—I'd often failed our pastor's annual catechism—but my parents had nothing good to say about the Salvation Army. I knew they'd be angry. When I finally told them I wanted to join and become an officer, my father threw me out of the house."

"Fathers!" Sara exclaimed, disgusted. "Mine would have done the same. What did you do then?"

"Father offered to buy me a ticket to America, but I wasn't ready to leave Sweden. Women could have important roles in the Salvation Army, just like men. I wanted that." Ingeborg was quiet for a moment. "I guess I didn't think about the religion so much. I realized soon enough I'd made a mistake."

"How so?" asked Sara, picking up a biscuit and taking a small bite.

"Well, I was never seized by the spirit. I hated how they made poor suffering people hear hours of preaching for their simple meal and a place to sleep. Why not just help them and let them find their own way to God? And women weren't equal. There were a few women in high positions, like Major Ouchterlony, but soon I saw how the Army promoted men and dismissed what women said."

Sara shook her head. "A familiar story. Is that why you left?"

"Partly. One of my jobs was to talk to people when they brought children to the orphanage—almost always just the mothers. They'd be weeping, shaking, clutching their babies. I'd seen poverty, but never like this. Like a giant weight pressing down, crushing them, crushing them. So women sold themselves for bread, and husbands drank wages instead of feeding their families. And no way to stop new babies from coming, even if already there were too many to feed. Why did we demand people's souls in exchange for our help? Why not challenge the things that kept them poor? They told me to be quiet and obey." Ingeborg shrugged. "I knew I couldn't. So I wrote my father for that ticket to America."

"Ah, that's when you became a radical," said Sara, smiling. "But what brought you to suffrage?"

Ingeborg peered up at the cloudless sky, remembering. "Women need the vote to make life better, I believe that. For their families. And for workers. But also, I just believe in equality. If men vote, women should, too. It should be simple. And when I learned how long women had been fighting for it I got angry. So I joined."

While they spoke Maria had been consulting her timepiece. "Ack!" she said now. "It's late! We must get going."

They were soon back in the car, Maria maneuvering carefully around potholes and the boulders that had tumbled down from the canyon walls above them. Ingeborg risked a peek down to her right and decided she was grateful it was so dry. The ground sloped steeply from the road's edge down to the river far below. With a wet road, and no fence, it would be easy to slip sideways, and once the car began falling only the canyon floor would stop it. Her stomach clenched, and she pinned her eyes forward to the next bend of the road. Maria drove white-knuckled, sitting bolt upright, until the danger was past.

A dusty, faded sign proclaimed the road crossing into Wyoming, and on either side the high plains stretched away in undulating folds, the dry grass dusty and gold-tipped after weeks of little rain. Ingeborg missed trees. She was awed by the Western deserts and plains, but their vastness left her feeling unmoored, insignificant, the way she felt on board a ship. Trees brought shelter and scale. You could stand next to a tree and know right where you were, how far it was to the next tree, and that you had firewood to warm your house, cool shade on hot days, shelter from battering winds. The desert had too much space between things and no place to hide.

Maria slowed to bump the car down a slope into a dry wash, then stepped hard on the gas pedal to make it up through the crumbly dirt on the other side. Over the roar of the engine Ingeborg could hear Maria clucking *nck nck*, as if she were urging on a horse. The last horse they'd had before Maria bought her first car was a flea-bitten gray gelding with a loose lower lip they called Fritz. Fritz was a one-speed horse. No matter how much you slapped the reins on his back or popped the whip, he would never manage more than an ambling shuffle, and Maria had developed the habit of clucking to him just like this. It had as much effect on Fritz as it did on this car, and it was beginning to drive Ingeborg crazy.

She'd tried teasing Maria about it. "Why do you cluck at the car? She can't hear you."

Maria had smiled and shrugged. "I can't help it," she'd said. And that was that.

Ingeborg took a deep breath and looked out at the sere landscape to keep her mind off the clucking. Fenceposts and telegraph poles ticked past, and flocks of white-coated sheep dotted the landscape, black faces buried in the dry grass. From time to time they'd see a lone horse and rider circling the herd, or riding along the fence, checking for breaks. Once, the road wound close to some railroad tracks, and a coal train thundered by, belching smoke and cinders, heading west.

She spotted a ranch house perched on a distant ridge, and wondered what it was like for the women to live out here on these lonely ranches, cooking the food that fueled the men's work, cleaning up after them, washing their clothes, with little to alter the monotony of their days and few other women around. Not a life she'd want to live.

They rumbled down Evanston's dusty main street in the late afternoon looking for the hotel of the same name, which proved to be a blocky, three-story brick structure not far from the Bear River. Ingeborg was pleased to see that its plain front proudly announced it had been constructed in 1912; it was relatively new, at least. Maybe the beds would be comfortable, and there would be fewer bugs.

Maria settled the Overland Six in front of the hotel and they climbed out, sticky and stiff. They'd stopped outside of town to drape it in the Great Demand banner and the CU flags, and they'd attracted a few curious glances but little more. Wyoming had come into the Union as an equal suffrage state, so the issue had been settled here for decades. Indeed, the real surprise for Wyoming people was that other states hadn't done the same. Ingeborg had heard that the early white settlers, almost all men, had hoped to lure more women to the territory with the promise of voting rights. She and Maria agreed they'd have needed much more than the vote to follow a man out here.

Once cleaned up and rested, they drove out to Congressman Frank Mondell's house. Mabel had left word for them that no local women were able to help with the delegation, so they would have a private meeting with him.

Mondell was a bluff man with twinkling eyes and a mustache thick as a street broom, who looked more like the corner grocer than a politician. Ingeborg decided she would have liked him straight away, even if he hadn't been championing their bill through Congress. He welcomed them into his parlor, offering them coffee or, with a grin, "maybe something a little stronger, after your drive today." They'd accepted the coffee, refused the spirits, and settled down for a chat.

Mondell seemed genuinely interested in their trip, and was impressed by their harrowing adventures in the Nevada desert. He chuckled at the story of the man they'd hired getting them lost and praised their spirit and toughness. "I know those roads," he said. "Some would be better done on horseback than in an automobile. Many a man has rued the day he attempted them. This is excellent publicity for the Congressional Union."

Sara then steered the conversation toward the federal amendment and its prospects in the upcoming session. Mondell wasn't optimistic. "You've got a couple of big problems," he explained. "The Democrats are angry because you campaigned against them in the last election."

"But we only did that in the states where women already had the vote," said Sara.

"I understand that," Mondell said. "But the fact is, some of those Democrats were suffrage supporters, and, from their point of view, suddenly the women were coming after them because the Democratic party hadn't moved the bill through Congress. They thought they were being treated unfairly."

"Another time we can talk about who's been treated unfairly," said Sara, dryly. "The Democrats control Congress. They alone have the power to move this through. Can you think of another way we can persuade them to do it?"

"You're right, it's in their hands," said Mondell. "My Republican colleagues are coming around on this issue, aside from some of the more conservative ones in the East, but we don't have the votes. You have to convince the Democrats it's in their interest to vote as you want or you'll find replacements who will."

"That's what we're trying to do," said Ingeborg. "Are you saying it's not working?"

"Not at all," Mondell replied, leaning forward. "We like to say if you grab a rattlesnake, you'd best grab it by the head. Now, these Democrats, they act like you've got them by the tail, and they're going to try like hell to whip around and bite you. But you've got them by the head, see? You hang on tight and they'll snap their jaws and shake their rattles like fury, but in the end you'll be able to put them in the sack where you want them." He sat back. "We're just in the rattling phase right now, that's all."

"How long will that last?" asked Sara.

"No way at all to tell," said Mondell. "I don't think you'll get it through in this Congress but maybe in the next. These things take time. You keep doing what you're doing."

"You said we had two problems, Congressman," Ingeborg reminded him.

Mondell sighed. "Well, that would be the South, of course. Nothin' new there. The Southern states are worried about the Negro vote. In some districts Negroes outnumber the whites, and there's no way those white men will allow a bunch of 'niggers and women' to make the laws, if you'll pardon my bluntness."

"How do you suggest we handle that?" Sara wanted to know. "As you know, this puts the CU in an awkward position. We feel for our Negro sisters and want them to vote like the rest of us, but there's enough prejudice against women as it is. If we take on the race problem, too, we might never get the amendment through Congress. And so we wink at Southern states' brutal ways of ensuring Negro men don't vote. We loathe this, but that's the way we read the politics. Do you have other advice?"

Mondell shifted his gaze out the window, where a bored horse in a wooden-planked corral banged a food bucket, demanding its supper. "Slavery ended with the Civil War, but I fear the race prejudice that justified slavery will always be a part of this country. I can tell you—" He paused, and then said, "I have never witnessed such vitriol and contempt as I have seen in some congressmen's eyes when they speak of the Negro race. They will have to answer to someone about that, if only to God in the hereafter. For now, though, their white constituents seem perfectly happy with what they're doing in Washington."

They considered this quietly for a moment. Ingeborg knew he was right about the hate. Hadn't she seen it herself? Immigrants got their share of hate, though Swedes, fortunately, tended to fare better than the Poles, the Italians, the Irish, or the Jews. She knew her business thrived in part because the people she placed were white. And yet, the IWW had shown her that workers could see past their different races or accents, and hold fast to what they had in common. Was there something the South wanted so much that its people could see Negros as welcome partners? She decided to ask. "Congressman Mondell, can we really do nothing about the race question? I've seen the prejudice you talk about—but I've also seen people change when they work for the same cause." Not knowing where Mondell stood on the IWW, she didn't mention it directly. "Suffragists want all women to vote. Can't we find a way for that to happen?"

Mondell cocked his head at her. "You sure all suffragists want to enfranchise Negro women?" he asked mildly. "That's not what I hear."

Ingeborg frowned as she considered this. "Some might not, I guess, but most would."

"From whom have you heard otherwise?" Sara asked. "Was it NAWSA?"

"I believe you could find in both suffrage associations those opposed to Negroes voting," said Mondell, peering at her over his spectacles, eyebrows raised.

"And you think that this comes not just from political expediency, but something deeper?" asked Sara.

"Yes, I think so, although from the Negro point of view, the effect is the same—they're still left with no vote and no voice. It would be a mistake, though, to think this is merely a congressional—or a Southern—problem. You lack votes from the North for the same reason."

"So what do you think we should do?" asked Ingeborg.

"Get back in your automobile tomorrow morning and drive like hell for the US Capitol. There will be more battles to come over the race problem, but don't concern yourselves with that now. Stay away from that issue. It will sink your cause." He rose to his feet, ushered them to the door, and wished them well on their journey. "I'll be there in Washington to greet you," he said. "I know Miss Paul is planning something special for your arrival."

They drove back to the hotel, the western sky a bruise of red and purple. They were silent, each with her own thoughts. Ingeborg felt suddenly that she couldn't continue the trip; it was too far and too hard, and it wouldn't achieve everything she wanted it to.

It was false at its core.

She felt her insides twist and clench, and her mouth tasted sour, as though she had swallowed something bitter. Not for the first time, she wished she and Maria had thought it through more, had asked more questions before agreeing to this journey. *Pucko*—idiot! This is what came from saying "yes" before hearing all the story—a lesson she would never stop learning, it seemed. If only they had pinned Alice Paul down on the details: who would speak, the distances, the roads. And she'd given no thought to the race question at all. She had been foolish, swept into the cause like some giddy young girl, just like with the Salvation Army. She should have known better.

She imagined herself back in San Francisco before the convention, facing off with Alice Paul, setting the conditions under which she and Maria would take the trip. With no alternatives, Miss Paul would have had to agree to them. Ingeborg considered what would she have demanded—no more than eight hours a day of driving, with at least one day off each week. Equal status as an envoy with Sara and Frances, with speaking rights. Insisting that they include Negro suffragists.

When Miss Paul objected, Ingeborg would draw herself up to her full height, and with a slight smile say, grandly, "I regret Maria and I will be unable to assist you," and then turn on her heel and walk away, leaving Miss Paul with no other option than to come running after her and agree to everything. But even as she thought this, she knew she was being childish. Miss Paul was far too skilled and determined to get set back on her heels in that way, and Ingeborg had been far too eager to leap at the chance to make her mark with the legendary suffrage leader. But she hadn't even tried. And Maria had just been towed along.

Another image came to her of an IWW meeting back in Providence, where she would be talking about the trip, fielding questions from the members about the Negro women's clubs, what the prospects were for securing voting rights in the South. She'd have to stammer, her cheeks flushing redder as her excuses piled high in a stinking mass. They would know her to be a radical in name only. Their faces would fall in disappointment, and they would turn away from her in silence.

"I can't do this," she said suddenly, surprised to utter the words aloud.

"I beg your pardon?" asked Sara.

"I can't be part of this trip," said Ingeborg, hot anger washing over her. "It's a lie."

"What are you talking about? You mustn't quit too," Sara protested. "I can't do this alone. I can't even drive!" She sat forward anxiously in her seat. "What's happened?"

"We say we want this one thing, for all women to vote, and look at us! How many Negro women will we see on this trip? Or Indians—what about them? We pretend they don't exist, and why? We call ourselves radicals, but what radical cares only for those who'll be all right anyway? If we don't care about the ones who have the least, who will? It makes me sick. I want no part of it."

Sara opened her mouth to respond but closed it with a sigh and shook her head, slumping back in her seat. They traveled in silence for a few minutes, and then Maria pulled the car into a grassy spot by a river and turned off the engine. After so long in the desert the sound of water gurgling over the rocks was soothing, and they drew in great lungsful of the moist air. A cool mist hovered over the river, dripping off the bulrushes and sedge grass that lined its banks. On the far side Ingeborg could just make out a towering cottonwood tree, its trunk hidden by the mist, upper branches suspended over the water as if hung from a hook high above. Ingeborg opened her door and crunched through the brittle grass to the water's edge. Crouching down, she cupped her hands in the icy water and dribbled it through her fingers before pressing them to her face, massaging the water into her weathered skin. She stood then, wiping her hands on her skirts.

She heard the car door slam and then Maria was beside her, slipping an arm around her waist and pulling her close. Ingeborg leaned into her, close to tears. "We can't stop now," said Maria, in Swedish. "We have to finish."

"I thought we were doing something good, something pure and important," said Ingeborg, her voice strained. "I was just fooling myself. This isn't what I wanted."

"So what else is new?" asked Maria. "We have dreams, we make plans, sometimes they work out, other times not. Sometimes what we end up with is good enough for now."

Ingeborg shook her head.

Maria turned and wrapped her arms around her friend, pulling her into a tight embrace. "Oh, Ingeborg." They stood like this for some moments, before Maria stepped back and grasped Ingeborg's shoulders, giving them a slight shake. "Listen to me."

Ingeborg raised her head and looked Maria in the eye.

"We're immigrants, right?" Maria went on. "What immigrant leaves her country knowing what the future will bring? She just hopes that by leaving everything behind, risking everything, she can make a better life. When she comes to America, she has nothing. Then she finds work and buys some things she needs. Little by little, her life gets better. But she doesn't know what will happen. Maybe the factory where she works will close. Maybe she gets married and her husband beats her. As hard as she works, some things won't turn out as she hoped. Does that mean she should never have tried?"

"What are you saying?"

"This trip, this suffrage work is like that. We don't know what will happen. We can't decide everything. We just work for a better future, knowing it won't happen all at once." She turned and pointed at the cottonwood across the river. "Behind the mist that tree is solid, rooted in the ground. We can't see it, but it's there. Tomorrow, the sun will warm the air until the mist is gone, and the whole tree will be there for us to see. That's the tomorrow we work for, even if today we just see the branches."

Still miserable, Ingeborg wasn't convinced. "But how do we know it's there?"

Maria stooped over and picked up a few stones from the river bottom. Straightening, she chucked one at the cottonwood's trunk; it sailed past and disappeared into the mist. "Oof," she said. As she threw the next one her foot slipped and the stone arced into the sky, landing with a splash into the rushing water. Then she planted her feet firmly and took aim at the tree trunk. They heard a plunk as it hit the tree and then bounced back to splash in the water. "See? It's there," said Maria. "We just have to keep trying."

Ingeborg turned and stepped a few paces away, her arms cradling her body. She glanced back at the car where Sara waited. "I don't know," she said, her voice low. "What if we're asking for too little when we could get so much more by working together? Like the IWW's one big union? Women and Negroes and immigrants, all the poor can belong because people with nothing can only change things by working together." She turned to face Maria. Taking a deep breath, she said slowly "Maybe we're no better than those Southern racists."

Maria shrugged. "Ingeborg, this country fought a war over slavery. You heard the congressman. The South lost, but they feel no different now. And we know people in Providence who think the same. This race business makes people crazy. Maybe the way to change it is for most women to vote, and the sooner the better."

"Do you believe that?"

"They say that where women can vote, they've made a difference. Why not on race, too?"

In the deepening twilight the crickets and frogs sang in sleepy counterpoint. A thin red glow edged the western horizon, and Ingeborg tipped her head back to look at the stars emerging hard and bright in the darkening sky. She felt the world shrink away until it was just her standing there, alone in the darkness. What did she believe? What did she want? What was possible?

Suddenly she remembered when she'd joined the Salvation Army, all those years ago. She saw herself standing pale and trembling before her red-faced, furious father as he shouted that she was a *pucko*, and a disgrace. He'd threatened all manner of harm before throwing her bodily out of the house, but nothing could shake her conviction. She'd been a wall of smooth stone, tall and strong, impenetrable. She'd vowed to see it through no matter what the cost. Yet soon enough she had written her father to ask for a ticket to America, her zeal extinguished by the Army's smothering piety.

Would she quit this, too? She considered what would happen if she did. The CU would end the trip. She'd no longer be welcome as a suffragist. And what good would that do, in the end?

In frustration and fury she reared her head back suddenly and roared into the vast, uncaring darkness, a howl of despair that erupted from her throat with an intensity that startled her, echoing off the nearby cliffs.

Then she looked down at her feet, and it came to her that she would stay in this trip to the end. She wouldn't quit, not this time. Maybe she was giving up too easily, but she already felt at the limits of her strength. Maria was right. The ocean of racism surrounding the Negro people could swamp them. On this trip she would play by the CU's rules, but when she got back to Providence she would do things differently.

She turned and looked at Maria. "All right," she said.

"Feel better?" Maria asked, with a smile, as she came and slipped her arm into Ingeborg's.

"A little." Ingeborg turned as Sara bolted from the car and raced over.

"What happened?" asked Sara, breathlessly.

"Nothing," said Ingeborg, wearily. "Let's go back to the hotel. Tomorrow will be a long day." She slid her arm around Sara and the three walked back to the car together.

CHAPTER FIVE

OCTOBER 10, 1915

Three days after leaving Evanston, they drove down Laramie's dusty main street looking for the Connor Hotel. All afternoon a gusty wind had driven tumbleweeds across the plains and blasted road dust into their faces, chasing the clouds across the sky to pile up over Laramie and the mountains nearby. Now the clouds hung low over the town, muttering snow.

They had crossed southern Wyoming in hundred-mile gulps, the glorious Lincoln Highway just a two-wheeled cart-track that often forced Maria to throttle down to a walking pace. Each day they'd departed early, their breath sending great plumes into the chill morning air. They ate in the car, stopping only briefly at ranches to buy fresh milk to drink and to stretch their stiff limbs. They'd arrive late at a shabby hotel, faces chapped and sunbaked, weary to the point of collapse, to find musty rooms where bugs and spiders visited them in the night. Once, Maria woke up to find a mouse scampering around the threadbare quilt on their lumpy bed. Suppers were "veiled in mystery," as Sara put it one night, glumly stirring the glop in her bowl.

It was maddening, Ingeborg thought, as she took the wheel to give Maria a break, to be racing at a snail's pace toward that evening's meetings. Her body ached from the constant rocking and slamming over ruts and long-dried mudholes, and the rattle of the engine rang in her ears for hours after they stopped for the day. Desperate for stillness, they had no choice but to press forward to stay on schedule.

The monotonous landscape did little to relieve their weary miles. Muted greens and golds and tans stretched away in mottled sameness so that Ingeborg figured God Himself must have been bored with it. At intervals they'd overtake a rancher in a wagon pulled by mules or oxen, their plodding progress not much slower than the Overland Six. The animals would toss their heads and shy sideways when the car edged past them, threatening to spill the wagon and its contents as the driver swore and popped his whip.

To pass the time Ingeborg and Maria told Sara stories about growing up in Sweden and coming to America. Sara sat wedged in a corner of the back seat in an effort to ease the jostling. Her face was ashen, and the lines carved on her face were deeper than when they'd left San Francisco. She complained that her heart disliked the high plains and said she hoped she'd survive until they returned to sea level. But her eyes were open, and she listened, though she said little.

One afternoon, though, Sara asked them about men. Had they never married? Never wanted children?

Maria, usually the quiet one, was the first to speak. "My mother grew up very poor. When she was old enough her parents sent her to work on a farm. She was homesick, and the work was hard."

"Was she bitter about being sent off to work?" asked Sara. "Was she able to visit her family?"

Maria shrugged. "She had to work to live. It's the same in Providence—poor children still work in the mills when the laws say they shouldn't. But in Sweden, *pigas*—what you'd call a maid, or servant—signed a contract for a year. If you ran away the constables could bring you back. And it was a long way to her home so she only saw her family once a year, when the *pigas* all went home for a week." She paused for a moment. "It was hard that no one looked after her.

One evening, she was only sixteen, she was at the evening milking when her boss pulled her into the haymow and raped her."

"How awful!" said Sara. "Oh, the poor thing! Would no one help her?"

"There was nothing she could do. The farmer owned her for the year. Of course he shouldn't have raped her, but there was no one to stop him. He did it many times. He said he'd hurt her if she complained—say she forced herself on him."

Sara shook her head in disgust. "As if she would. The women always get blamed. How did she get away?"

"When the year ended she went home for her week. By that time she was pregnant. Her parents turned her out—said she'd shamed them. The baby was born a few months later. She had no other way to earn a living so she sold herself. There was always some man around, each worse than the last. I stopped learning their names." Maria paused as she negotiated a deeply rutted section of road. "I have two sisters and a brother. All different fathers. I'm the youngest."

"Did your own father ever acknowledge you?" asked Sara.

"No," said Maria. "I doubt she knew who it was."

They were quiet for a time. Ingeborg knew this story but it still made her grind her teeth in fury. She'd heard similar stories from so many other women.

"How did you avoid the same fate?" asked Sara, finally.

Maria braked to avoid a jackrabbit that shot across the road in front of them. "After I was born, Mamma married a widower who gave me his name. He was poor, too, but kind. So she was lucky in the end." Maria thought briefly and added, "I was lucky." She clucked absent-mindedly to the car as it climbed a small rise, lost in thought.

Then she went on. "I didn't know about the rape until I grew old enough to work as a *piga*. That was the work poor girls like me could do. I could tell my mother was sad when they found me a place. A few days before I left, she told me what had happened to her, as a warning. I was shocked. And so afraid of it happening to me, too."

Sara squirmed in her seat, vainly trying to find a more comfortable position. "And did it?"

"No. I was lucky to find a place with a good family. The couple who owned it treated their *pigas* well, though they worked us hard. I was there for two years."

"But you didn't stay—why?" Sara prompted.

"The other *pigas* said farms in Norway paid more and gave more food. And they got a full day and an evening off each week instead of just Sunday afternoons. At that first farm we worked much harder and got almost no pay—just room and board. So when my contract ended, I found a new place in Norway. And it was better. I became close to a girl named Gilla. She loved dancing and having a good time with the boys. Then she got pregnant."

Sara groaned. "It's always the woman who pays. If men could get pregnant, then every store would sell birth control. Instead, we have Comstock's chastity laws. What happened to her?"

"The baby's father wouldn't marry her. She was desperate. People told her about a local midwife who could help." Maria sighed, and Ingeborg reached over and rested her hand on her friend's shoulder. Maria continued on so quietly Sara had to lean forward to hear her. "Gilla begged me to go with her, so I did. But the midwife—she was dirty and more concerned about counting the money Gilla gave her. Yet what could Gilla do? She would have lost her job, and her parents would throw her out. What sort of life would she have, all alone with a baby? The midwife poked at her insides with a long, sharp needle."

"How far along was she?" Sara asked.

"Enough to be sure there was a baby, but not enough to show." Maria stopped, and then went on, her voice flat. "Something went wrong. There was so much blood. It poured out of her, and the midwife couldn't stop it. Gilla clung to my hand and cried for me to save her but I didn't know how. The midwife put some herbs inside her, and pushed on her belly, but she kept bleeding. It was like butchering a pig. I'd never seen so much blood, it was all over her—and us. She grew very pale, and died as I held her. I wanted to die too."

"Maria, how awful!" Sara exclaimed, leaning forward and clutching the edge of the front seat. "What happened then? Was there an inquiry?"

"They hushed it up. The midwife knew many secrets about the powerful families—whose babies were whose, and babies that were never born. She threatened to tell if they punished her. I decided right then to become a midwife and help women have their babies safely. Or not have them. Whatever they wanted. Sweden was training midwives then—too many mothers were dying in childbirth. I got trained, and apprenticed with a midwife who was very skilled. She was a good teacher. I was with her until I saved the money to come to America."

"Such a sad story," said Sara, shaking her head. "Poor Gilla. You turned that tragedy to good purpose, though. How did you happen to settle in Providence?"

"I had friends there. There weren't enough midwives, and no one who would go anywhere, as I did. It was hard at first, but word soon spread. It's been a good life."

"What about you, Ingeborg?" asked Sara.

"The Swedish church made women pledge obedience to their husbands," said Ingeborg. "I was never good at that," she turned to give Sara a wry smile.

Sara laughed. "But when you came to America, you had more choices, surely?" she asked. "And no parents around to please—you were a grown woman then—you could please yourself."

"There were more men, yes, and plenty liked the money I earned, too. One man, a German, courted me for months. He would come after work and sit in a corner of the kitchen at the boarding home. Do you remember him?" she asked Maria. "Heinrich?"

Maria laughed. "Of course! He came around even after you told him no—he couldn't believe any woman would refuse him. After working all day in the fish market, he'd come looking for you—nothing could get the stink of fish from his skin, his clothes. Poor Heinrich, Ingeborg broke his heart."

"How'd you finally get rid of him?"

"I came back late one evening and there was Heinrich—perched on his stool, waiting for me. Again! I'd made it clear I didn't want him. I chose a knife from the drawer and began sharpening it, looking at him all the while. I made a great show of testing the blade, running my fingers along it, and giving him a crazy smile. He began shifting in his chair, looking uneasy, clutching his cap in his hands. Then I threw it at his head."

"You what? Ingeborg, you might have killed him!" protested Sara, half laughing.

"No, I wasn't trying to. Otherwise, I might have." Ingeborg shrugged. "What did he expect? I told him no enough times. In Sweden my brother taught me how to throw knives. I was good at it, too. I still had the knack. It landed in the wall three inches from his head. Not a bad throw," she said, nodding approvingly.

"What did Heinrich do then?"

"He turned white like snow and bolted out the door," said Maria. "He never came back. And when he saw Ingeborg in the street he'd cross to the other side. He thought she was crazy."

"He might have had reason," said Sara, shaking her head. "Did no one ever tempt you?"

"Not really," said Ingeborg. "I met nice men here and there, but Maria was my partner, and I never wanted anyone else."

There was a short silence. Maria's face got pink, and Ingeborg could feel the warmth rising up her own neck. Surely the tips of her ears were now red, a sure sign of embarrassment, and she was grateful her hat was pulled low to cover them. But Sara had her own unconventional love life, so how could she judge them? Sure enough, there was a low chuckle from the back seat.

"Partners!" Sara looked delighted. "I wondered. I mean I have friends who're like that, but, well, I guess you didn't seem the type."

Ingeborg turned and glanced over her shoulder. "What type do you mean? Because we're Swedish? Or old? We were younger once," she grinned at Maria. "It's hard enough to be an immigrant—we should tell people we're lesbians, too?" She gave a short laugh.

"Isn't it silly we can't just love whom we choose," said Sara. "Why is it anyone's business but our own? That's what Erskine and I think. Though maybe it's changing a bit. Do you know Dr. Marie Equi?"

Ingeborg and Maria shook their heads. "Should we?"

"She's a friend from Portland. She's a doctor, but also a suffragist and union activist. Erskine represents her when she gets arrested for whatever she's speaking out against. And she lives openly as a lesbian. She's a real radical."

"She still has patients even when people know she's a lesbian?" asked Ingeborg. "That could never happen in Providence. Too conservative. Too many Catholics."

"Well, she sees patients the male doctors won't. And she does abortions, too. She's pro-labor and very outspoken about it, so the workers love her."

"I can't imagine," said Ingeborg, shaking her head in wonder. "Maybe someday workers in Providence will see the light, too. But women often live together, so we've never had any trouble. Why would a woman choose another woman over a man?" They laughed.

* * *

Laramie's Connor Hotel proved to be an elegant, four-story, yellow brick building on the corner of 33rd Street and Grand Avenue. Lamps glowed cheerfully behind large, plate glass windows. Sara and Maria climbed stiffly out of the car and limped into the lobby, while a bellboy followed with their bags. Ingeborg stayed back to flip the roof up over the car against the snow that threatened. The wind beat leaves against the car's dusty flanks.

After dinner Sara hurried off to speak to a gathering of University of Wyoming students. Maria and Ingeborg returned to their room to rest and go over the next day's route. They were due in Cheyenne by the afternoon for a rally with the governor. It was only sixty miles, but the road wound through a deep, narrow canyon and then over a high mountain pass.

Maria's face was grim, and exhaustion creased deep lines in her face. "If it rains we have mud, and if it snows?" She shook her head. "I guess we find out if the Overland people told the truth when they said Emilie could handle it."

Emilie was the name they'd given the car. After so many hours in her company, it seemed impersonal to refer to her merely as "the motorcar." She had a cheerful personality and spoke a language the Swedes had come to understand well; she would chatter happily when she felt rested and cared for, but had a surprising vocabulary to describe her aches and pains. She was willing—to a fault—to plunge ahead where others might hold back, but so far had stood up to the rigors of the journey, and they liked her brash confidence. So they named her Emilie Rathou, who was the first woman in Sweden to publicly demand equal suffrage.

"Emilie hasn't failed us yet," said Ingeborg, gathering Maria in a close hug. "And you can drive in snow."

"Not over a mountain!" said Maria. She pulled away from Ingeborg and crossed to their window to peer up at the sky. "Who knows how those roads will be? If the snow's deep, we won't see the potholes before I drive into them."

Ingeborg was more worried about finding the road at all but kept that thought to herself. "I'll find a rope and some grain sacks and sand in case we get stuck."

Maria agreed. "Good. And settle up tonight so we can leave early— try to beat the storm."

Ingeborg went off in search of the hotel manager, a short man with rheumy eyes and thick muttonchop whiskers. He scowled at her and shook his head. "You can't travel tomorrow, ma'am. Those roads are treacherous at the best of times. If it snows, that pass will be no place for ladies, if you don't mind my saying so."

Ingeborg did mind but smiled politely. "We're very experienced," she assured him. "We've already driven this car over a thousand miles. We just need a few things." She explained what she wanted.

"At least let me find a man to drive you," he pleaded.

Ingeborg gave a short laugh. "Last time we hired a man he got us lost—almost killed us. We'll manage."

"You'll never make it," he predicted. "We've lost good men up there in storms."

"Well, they ought to have hired a woman," said Ingeborg, irritably. "You'll have those sacks, the sand ready for us in the morning? Oh, and we'll need a shovel, too. We'll pay tonight so we can be on our way early."

* * *

They left soon after dawn, snow boiling out of the skies in the creeping gray light, the road before them little more than a suggestion.

How much was new snow, and how much was simply being scoured from the ground and tossed back into the air? Ingeborg wondered. She thought maybe two inches had fallen so far. Emilie's headlamps poked uncertainly into the storm.

Ingeborg glanced at Maria, who was crouched over the broad steering wheel, her hat pulled low and her eyes glued to the road, lips pressed in a thin line. There was no better person to be with at a time like this, Ingeborg thought. When Maria set her mind to a task, she simply would not be stopped. How many scrapes had Maria hauled her out of over the years? Ingeborg turned and looked back at Sara, who sat staring out into the storm. She appeared wan but resolute.

The road led east out of town and past the fairgrounds into the open plains, where the wind slammed into them. The car's top blocked the worst of the gusts, but it rattled and shook, and snow trickled in through gaps between the fasteners and drifted in small piles on the floor. They had hot bricks beneath their feet and flasks of coffee, which kept them warm—for now, at least. Ingeborg squinted ahead and wondered how cold and snowy it would be at the pass. She thought briefly of the hotel manager who had seen them off that morning. He'd acted as if he was surely sending them to their deaths and begged them once more to wait a day, or to hire a driver. Now she wondered if they should have listened.

They crawled steadily along and saw only a handful of cars heading toward Laramie—no one seemed to be going their way. After an hour or so they came to a rocky outcropping that sheltered them from the wind, so they stopped to stretch their stiff limbs and drink some coffee. Maria flexed her hands and stamped her feet while Ingeborg looked over the car as best she could, topping up the fuel so they wouldn't have to stop on the way up.

Sara, hunched into her traveling coat with a scarf wrapped around her neck, peered up at Maria. "Do you really think you can manage this?" she asked. "We could turn back now."

Maria shrugged, unsmiling. "We'll see. All right so far."

They'd just resumed their progress when headlamps appeared out of the swirling snow ahead of them. Maria eased Emilie to the side of the road and slowed to a stop; the other vehicle pulled up alongside. The driver popped the fasteners on his window and stuck his head out, heavily hatted, and peered at them in surprise. "What in the name of God are you ladies doing out here in this storm?" he demanded. "Are you lost?"

"Headed to Cheyenne," Maria told him. "How's the road?"

"What road?" he thundered. "You can't hardly see it. Snow's blowing fast and thick. You should turn back. We did." His three passengers grunted their agreement.

"We have to go on," said Maria. "The governor is expecting us."

The man snorted. "Tell him to wait. No one'll cross that pass today. Too dangerous."

"We'll make it," said Maria, and put the car in gear. "Good day." With that, she gently steered around the other vehicle and back out onto the road. The other car quickly vanished in the swirl of snow, and the three women faced the road alone.

"We'll make it," repeated Ingeborg, stoutly.

"We have to," said Sara.

Maria just kept driving. They saw no other cars. They were climbing steadily now, holding their breath whenever Emilie slipped on an icy patch. Ingeborg used a rag to wipe moisture from the inside of the windshield so Maria could see. There was nothing else she could do but peer ahead and listen for signs of engine trouble. She tried not to imagine what it would be like to have to climb under the car in the snow, with her gloves off and hands freezing to the metal as she tried to lever off some bolt to replace a part. If they got stuck, how long would it take for help to arrive? A road crew would come out at some point, but not until after the storm was over. By then they might find three stiff bodies huddled in the car, frozen solid. She pushed the image from her mind.

The women were silent as Emilie ground toward the pass, which remained hidden from view. The snow grew deeper, and it became harder to pick out the red, white, and blue Lincoln Highway signs set at intervals to show the way. Ingeborg thought of offering to spell Maria but decided it was too risky to stop. Her muscles ached with tension and the creeping cold, and she had to remind herself to breathe. The bricks had cooled, draining the warmth from her feet. She wiped the windshield again.

The trees grew thicker and pressed closer to the road, snow sheathing their trunks and gnarled branches. The white on white was dizzying, making it hard to judge distances and get her bearings. Ingeborg tried to summon images of the blazing sun in the desert east of Reno, the heat pooling into ponds on the road in front of them. She'd cursed it then but now longed to be back in that oven. It occurred to her that now would be a good time for one of those heat storms, and closing her eyes, she tried to coax along the heat prickling up her spine and surging into her upper body. No luck. She opened her eyes again.

The air grew thinner as they climbed, and Ingeborg glanced back again to check on Sara. She was wedged into her corner, a scarf pulled up over her face, very still. Ingeborg's heart caught in her throat, and she opened her mouth to call out, but relaxed when she saw Sara shift her position slightly.

The pitch grew steeper. Emilie's engine fought to out-roar the storm and almost did, her tires slipping and catching but somehow managing to churn forward. They were the only thing moving, even the wind-riding ravens were hidden. Where did they go in these storms? Ingeborg wondered. Maria's eyes were pinned to the road, her face set and still. Tension blanketed the car. Breathe, Ingeborg commanded herself. How far to the pass? It couldn't be long, surely, they'd been driving for hours.

With no warning a front tire caromed off a boulder, and they skidded, sliding off the road, canted sideways at a crazy angle. Maria cut the engine and set the handbrake, and they sat for a moment in silence. The wind tugged at the roof. Ingeborg watched snow land on the car's bonnet, melting and trickling off the sides. No one spoke.

Then Ingeborg tugged her hat down over her ears and snugged her scarf around the lower half of her face. "I'll go see." She forced open her door and clambered out, awkward and stiff from sitting so long in the cold, clumsy in her bulky outer garments. She had to force her door open and up, and then reach down to feel for her footing in snow that was halfway to her knees. Clutching the car for support she waded uphill and around the bonnet to peer at the damage, her heart nearly stopping when she saw that Emilie's front and back wheels on the driver's side were planted firmly in a ditch. If the wheels had dropped a little lower the car might have rolled, and she could see nothing to stop it in the slope below. Her stomach clenched, and she took a deep breath of cold air to steady herself. What to do? If they could lift the front of the car so the forward wheel came back onto the road, maybe the sand and burlap sacks she'd brought could provide Emilie enough traction to get the rest of the way.

Ingeborg tapped on Maria's door frame to get her attention, and, pitching her voice above the wind, told her to get out carefully on the other side. "Sara too." She waded back around the nose of the car to meet them and explain her plan, then waddled down to the boot and extracted the shovel. She tried to dig a ramp up to the roadbed for the front tire but the dirt was frozen solid, so she scraped away the snow in front of the car so they could stand without slipping. Then she positioned herself facing the hood, closest to the ditch, putting Sara next to her and Maria on the other side. Sara was gasping for breath in the thin air and looked as though she could barely hold herself up, let alone be of much use lifting. But when Ingeborg and Maria bent their knees and squatted down, finding hand holds under the car's frame, she crouched and did the same. "On three we lift together and pull it toward Maria," said Ingeborg. "One…two…three!" She straightened her legs and felt the strain as she took the weight of the car.

Emilie's nose moved a short distance. "Stop!" Ingeborg gasped, and they relaxed their grip only to have the car slide back down into the ditch. Ingeborg swore fluently in English and switched to Swedish when she ran out of words. She turned to her companions. "We have to move it farther next time. Now we know we can do it. Use all your strength and keep lifting and pulling until I tell you to stop. Come." She squatted back down and found her hold again, taking some deep breaths and making sure her feet were secure. When she saw they were in position she nodded and gave the count again. "One…two…." On three she exploded upward with a guttural cry and yanked the heavy car to the left. Her muscles screamed. Her right foot nearly slipped out from under her, but she snatched it back and planted it again, heaving to the limits of her strength. When she couldn't bear it anymore she cried, "Stop!" and they all slumped down, gasping for breath. She peered around and saw they'd moved the car's nose about six inches. The left front tire was dangerously close to the top of the ditch, but it was on the road surface, at least. She turned and nodded. "It will do."

Moving carefully, Ingeborg checked the rear wheel and found it angling up the side of the ditch, pointing toward the roadbed. Maybe she could wedge a rock behind the rear tires to keep the car from rolling backward—if the car slid backwards down the hill they were finished. Then if they laid down the sacking and sand in front of the tires they might just have enough traction to get under way again. But they had only enough sand for one try. If it didn't work…. She pushed that thought from her mind and called instructions to the other women, who were huddled over, backs to the blowing snow, their coats spattered with white. "Maria, see if you can clear the road of snow ahead of the front wheels. Not the whole road. Just where the wheels will go." She passed Maria the shovel. "Sara, use your hands to clear out the snow in front of the rear wheels. Try to get it down to the dirt. I need to find some rocks." Sara nodded and crept toward the back of the car. Ingeborg walked uphill, feeling with her feet and looking side to side for shapes of rocks under the snow. After several fruitless efforts to move rocks that were frozen in place she was able to kick one free and lug it back down the hill. Sara and Maria were making progress, though the frigid wind kept blowing the snow back onto the road.

When she was satisfied the car wouldn't roll back Ingeborg went to the boot and found the burlap sacking and sand. With trembling hands she spread the sand in front of the wheels and tucked the sacking in as far as she could cram it, her gloves wet and her fingers aching with cold. At length she stood and surveyed her work, nodded, and looked over at Maria. It was a pity Sara couldn't drive. Then she and Maria could stand behind and push, and the lighter Sara could steer the car back onto the road. But she needed Maria behind the wheel. "Ready?" Maria nodded.

"What should I do?" asked Sara.

"Maria will drive," said Ingeborg. "You get in the back."

Sara frowned. "Where will you be?"

"I'll push," said Ingeborg. She turned to Maria. "Once you're moving, don't stop. Drive 'til it's flat enough to get moving again when you stop. I'll catch up." She watched as they got into the car and Maria switched on the engine. Ingeborg moved around to the back of the car and set her feet, bracing her hands across the boot. When she was ready, she knocked twice. The engine began to roar and Ingeborg leaned in and pushed with all her strength. The tires whined, and sand and burlap flew backward as the car slowly gathered speed and then without warning shot across the road. Ingeborg fell to her knees and watched with her heart in her mouth as the car nearly plunged off the other side, Maria spinning the wheel at the last second and fishtailing up the slope. With a shout Ingeborg rose up and ran after it, quickly dropping back to a walk, gasping in the thin air. Emilie disappeared around a bend.

Ingeborg trudged upward, wondering how long her walk would be. She might not have needed to push, she reflected, but she couldn't just sit in the car and hope. At least she was warmer from the walking. She just hoped it wouldn't be too long. She rounded the bend and saw Emilie up ahead sitting calmly in the middle of the road as if wondering what the fuss was all about. Ingeborg grinned and tried to walk faster, her chest heaving with the effort, her breath coming fast.

Soon Ingeborg was able to wrench open the passenger door and clamber into the car. Though coated with snow and damp from her exertions she turned and threw her arms around Maria, giving her a big wet kiss. "Maria! You did it."

Sara leaned forward and clapped them both on the shoulders. "You both did it!" she cried. "I've never been so scared in my life!"

Maria smiled over at Ingeborg. "Hope we don't have to do that again."

She slipped Emilie back in gear, and soon they were climbing again, the road bending and weaving past cliffs and rocky outcroppings. The sky grew lighter, and the snow eased to a flurry, opening the view to broad meadows dotted with clumps of trees. Suddenly Ingeborg leaned forward and wiped the windshield again, peering intently ahead. "There it is!" she cried triumphantly. "The pass sign!"

The three women cheered as they drew abreast of the sign. They decided to risk stopping so they could relieve themselves, and beat some warmth into their chilled limbs. They lumbered around like swaddled bears, laughing and dancing. "I wish those men could see us now," Ingeborg crowed. "Let a woman do the driving, she'll make it."

Maria shook her head at Ingeborg. "Too soon to celebrate," she reminded her. "We still need to get down." She turned and looked at Emilie, whose headlamps peered out undaunted from her thatch of ice and snow. "But she's doing all right," she said, approvingly. "That's a good car."

Soon they were under way again, creeping forward cautiously. Emilie seemed to want to charge down to Cheyenne like a horse returning to the barn, and Maria had to work the brake, especially in the steeper sections. There were frightening moments when Emilie simply slid on her own, heedless of the brake or the steering wheel. The snow and wind once again lashed the car and obscured the terrain on either side of the road, and Ingeborg tried not to think about disappearing over some unseen cliff. Sometimes Emilie yawed sideways like a half-broken horse before coming to rest, and then Maria had to coax her into pointing her nose back downhill. This went on for some time until the road leveled out a little and they could all catch their breath. Maria's eyes were wide and staring, her hands locked on the steering wheel, and Ingeborg thought she could see her friend trembling beneath her heavy coat.

They crept forward, and suddenly Maria brought the car to a stop. "Look ahead," she said hoarsely. "Too steep."

Ingeborg grabbed the cloth and wiped away at the windshield, and they squinted out over Emilie's bonnet. The road simply disappeared into the storm. Ingeborg pried open her door and got out to look. The snow was over her boot tops and the wind whipped her skirts; she just managed to grab her hat before it whirled off her head. She stepped forward carefully to peer over the hill, and her heart stopped. Maria was right. The road dropped steeply for several hundred feet before curving around to the right and disappearing into a tunnel of falling snow. Even if they could make it down the first steep section she had no idea how they'd make the turn once the car started sliding, as it surely would, or what they'd hit at the bottom. The cold pressed in on her, sending icy fingers down the back of her neck, and she knew they couldn't wait until the storm cleared. They had to keep going.

She looked around and off to her right saw a thick pine, its gnarled bark coated with snow. If she tied the rope to the car, then wrapped it around the tree, she and Sara could pay it out to slow the car's descent, at least partway down the hill. She trudged back to the boot and got the rope out, shaking out the loops. She could see right away that it wasn't nearly long enough, maybe thirty feet or so. She put the rope back.

They'd have to ride it down as best they could. She yanked open the passenger door and climbed back into the car, bringing with her a blast of wind and fresh snow. "It's steep," she said, "but we can't stay here. We'll freeze." She turned and looked at Maria, and said with more confidence than she felt, "The snow's deep, and it's drifted into a bank down at the bottom, on your side of the road. Then it curves to the right, and I can't see after that. If we start over on the left here and go down as slow as we can, maybe you can gun it around the turn when we get near the bottom. If not, we'll slide into the bank and have to dig out. Either way, we'll manage. You ready?"

Maria nodded, and backed up several feet so she could maneuver over to the left side of the hill. They could just make out a Lincoln Highway marker poking out of the snow halfway down, suggesting the outlines of the road. She inched the car forward. Gas, brake. Gas, brake, until the car was fully over the crest of the hill and began to slide. Maria's face was pale, and her foot rode the brake so hard she was half rising out of her seat. Emilie began sliding to the left so Marie cranked the steering wheel to the right, the car overcorrecting and sliding almost sideways down the slope. Ingeborg wondered briefly if the wheels would pop off but that thought quickly left her as the car nosed into a snowbank on the righthand side and then spun fully around so they were sliding backward down the hill, gaining speed.

Maria worked the brakes and the steering wheel to no avail, and the sides of the road were sliding past them at a frightening rate. Time seemed to slow down and the storm outside was forgotten. Sara let out a little moan, and Ingeborg looked around frantically to see what they might hit. Just as she noticed that they seemed to be sliding more to one side, the car's left rear wheel became lodged in a snowdrift and they thunked almost to a stop. Maria steered to the right and got her foot back on the gas, spinning the wheels until the weight of the engine pulled the car around and the nose was once again pointing downhill. This was better, but they were still sliding; again they picked up speed and the curve at the bottom of the hill was approaching quickly. "Get ready!" Ingeborg gasped to Maria, and then, a few seconds later, "Now!"

Maria stamped on the gas, and the engine screamed as the tires fought for purchase, spraying snow into the air all around them. The car fishtailed wildly and then leaped forward across the road toward an open meadow. Maria quickly spun the steering wheel to the left. "Brake, brake!" shouted Ingeborg, and Maria spun the wheel back to the right and tapped the brake hard, let up, and then hard again, bringing the car back under control. As the slope lessened she was able to bring Emilie to a halt. She was shaking.

They sat in shocked silence for a moment and then Ingeborg and Sara erupted in whoops, and Ingeborg leaned over to embrace Maria, who sat slumped over the steering wheel with a grin stretched across her broad face. "You did it!"

"That was close," Maria gasped.

"I was sure we were dead," said Sara. "I don't know how you managed."

"My heart is jumping," said Maria. "Let me rest a bit."

Ingeborg insisted that she take over as driver. Maria was done in by the tense hours behind the wheel, and they had to be through the worst of it. The road grew more level, the snow not as deep. The car lurched and slid a few more times, but soon the going was easier, and they made good time. The wind tore ragged patches from the racing clouds, and the sun danced over the snow. They sang as they drove; first a psalm, and then Sara led off with "Hello, Frisco" and Maria followed up with "If That's Your Idea of a Wonderful Time (Take Me Home)." The singing warmed them and lifted their spirits, and before long they began passing homes that signaled they were getting closer to Cheyenne. They stopped and with stiff, half-frozen hands tied the We Demand banner and flags to the car, puttering into the town square less than an hour after they were due. They could see a small crowd of men and women bundled against the cold, standing in front of the stage.

Ingeborg drove right up, tooting the horn. The crowd turned to see and let loose cheers and huzzahs, parting long enough so she could bring Emilie, still caked with ice and snow, right next to the stage. The little brass marching band struck up a jubilant victory march, and as the three women climbed from the car, the crowd pressed in to shake their hands and offer hearty congratulations. Ingeborg could feel the vibration of the steering wheel in her hands and throughout her body; she had never been so thankful to arrive anywhere. As she helped Sara mount the steps to the platform, she wondered whether the younger woman would be able to speak, she seemed so weak. Ingeborg was little better off; her feet were blocks of ice that she had to pick up and place very deliberately on each step to stay upright. If Sara fell she would go down as well, she thought, and her bones would shatter like icicles.

Cheyenne Mayor La Fontaine and a Mr. Sinclair welcomed them, standing in for the governor who—naturally—had been called elsewhere on urgent business. Ingeborg and Maria stood flanking Sara. Mabel had already left for Denver. The mayor raised his arm for quiet, and the applause subsided. The band fell silent.

"Ladies and gentlemen, may I present to you the courageous suffrage envoy Mrs. Sara Bard Field, and her companions Miss Kindberg and Miss Kindstedt!" The crowd clapped and stamped their feet, perhaps as much to warm them as to make more noise. "No one else came from Laramie in this storm. These women alone braved the pass and won the day! Mrs. Field, tell us about your journey and what this trip means for woman suffrage."

Sara stepped forward, swaying a little, and for a moment Ingeborg thought she might faint, but then she took a deep breath and her back stiffened. Her voice was pitched low, and the crowd strained to hear it above the wind that whistled across the square where they stood.

"We are come, my companions and I, from San Francisco to seek the aid of the voters of Wyoming, whose far-seeing men entrusted women with the ballot from the state's very birth. The women voters of the West must come to the aid of our Eastern sisters, who are manacled and silenced by their men's refusal to give them equal status as members of our great democracy." Sara took another deep breath and continued, her voice strengthening. "We have crossed deserts by day and night, navigating eastward, and the only time we were lost was when we hired a man to drive us!" She paused for laughter and jeers to subside, and then said, "Today we ventured through a storm and over a pass that no man dared attempt. We fought our way through, the car plunging through drifts and skating down hills, and only the courage and prowess of my companions saved the day. I tell you, ladies and gentlemen, if you want to get somewhere in a storm—hire a woman to drive you!"

The crowd clapped and cheered. Sara smiled and then motioned them to silence.

"The good men and women of Wyoming know that the future of our country requires the assistance of every citizen. The women of this country are eager to share this responsibility. We have with us today the signatures of more than half a million who visited the Congressional Union booth at the Panama–Pacific International Exposition, demanding an amendment to the United States Constitution enfranchising women. We call on you to sign our petition, and to lend your voice and hands to this great campaign, so that the women of this country can at last be included in the promise of this democracy in which we live."

The crowd shouted their approval as the mayor and Mr. Sinclair affixed their signatures to the petition, and others lined up to do the same. The crowd quickly dispersed, eager to warm chilled hands and toes. Ingeborg turned to see a small woman mounting the stairs. Mr. Sinclair hurried over and introduced her as Mrs. John Kendrick, the governor's wife. Ingeborg liked her immediately; she had brilliant blue eyes, a determined chin, and a ready, dimpled smile. Mrs. Kendrick welcomed them graciously to Cheyenne and complimented them on their achievement. Then, turning to Sara, she said, "Mrs. Field, I insist that you come home with me. You must be worn out and half frozen. My car is just over there." She motioned over to where a uniformed driver stood next to a large, gleaming black car.

Sara murmured her thanks, and obediently followed Mrs. Kendrick off the stage. Ingeborg and Maria trailed after them, only to have Mr. Sinclair cut in smoothly and say "There are rooms reserved for you ladies at the Plains Hotel down the street. The dining is generally thought to be the best in Cheyenne." Ingeborg and Maria stared at him and then glanced at each other. "We're not invited to the governor's house," Ingeborg said flatly, more of a statement than a question.

"Mrs. Kendrick wished for a more intimate dinner with Mrs. Field," said Mr. Sinclair.

Ingeborg thought about this. The three of them weren't always together; just last night she and Maria had rested instead of attending Sara's talk at the university. But that had been their choice. When it came to meetings with political leaders, they were always on the platform or in the room, and at least so far there hadn't been any suggestion they shouldn't be. While she sometimes lost patience with Sara's dawdling, her frailty, Ingeborg realized she'd come to think of the three of them as united in this mission. They took care of each other, and when circumstances demanded, each was capable of taking charge. Sara had dealt with that foolish man when they were lost in the desert. Maria had piloted Emilie over the pass today as few men could, and Ingeborg had rescued them from the snowbank. They were equals. They needed one another, and the Congressional Union needed them, too, to bring the petition to Congress. This was a clear snub. Why hadn't Sara protested?

As quickly as these thoughts flitted through her mind, Ingeborg understood that of course they weren't equals; she and Maria were immigrants, workers, uneducated. They were the help. She flushed, a wash of anger rising from her toes to the top of her head. She realized Mr. Sinclair was speaking and tried to focus on what he was saying. "You will find everything you need at the Plains Hotel, Miss Kindstedt." Ingeborg glared at him. She wanted to tell him, "Everything but respect," but Maria grasped her arm and began steering her toward the stairs. "Come, Ingeborg, my feet are frozen to the ground." Reluctantly, Ingeborg let her friend guide her, and when he'd seen them to the car, Mr. Sinclair turned away with a wave.

Emilie sputtered to life, and Maria drove down the few blocks to the hotel. Not many people were out now that the light had dimmed and the temperature was plummeting. Ingeborg glowered, and Maria glanced at her. "Don't be angry," she said, in Swedish. "We're better off at the hotel. For myself, I want coffee, a hot bath, a good meal, and then bed. Sara will have to sing for her supper over there." She paused, and then added, "I feel sorry for her."

Ingeborg wasn't mollified. "We're not good enough for the governor's wife, I guess. Why didn't Sara stand up to her? We should have been honored too."

Maria sighed. "Probably because she was half dead with the cold and the travel today. You know she's not strong."

"What did she do today except sit in the back seat? You and I did all the work, and she gets all the credit. She can't even drive!"

Maria parked the car. "You're right, of course. But what's new?"

"I'm just saying that for all her fine talk about equality for women, it's clear that in her mind that some people are more equal than others," Ingeborg said bitterly.

Maria shrugged. "Like I said, Ingeborg, what's new? Let's find our room."

CHAPTER SIX

OCTOBER 12, 1915

The following morning the sun blazed in a clear sky as if in apology for the previous day. By noon they were back in the car, bowling quickly along some of the best roads they'd had yet, heading to Denver. Emilie purred happily along, charging up the hills with her engine ticking smoothly, tires thrumming on the smooth surface.

Maria was in good spirits, but Ingeborg still seethed quietly over the snub they'd received and made no effort to join in the conversation. Secretly, she was pleased to hear Sara complain that she'd been up nearly until midnight, with one reporter after another calling on her to get the story. Serves her right, thought Ingeborg, spitefully. If she'd shared that burden, she might have gotten to bed at a reasonable hour. Despite all the demands on her time Sara had still managed to pen another long letter to Erskine; Ingeborg had noted the thickness of the envelope she'd left at the front desk in the lobby for mailing. No wonder she's always so tired, Ingeborg thought, huffing a little. Writing to Erskine adds hours to her day.

Mabel would meet them in Denver and had wired Sara in Cheyenne to expect a busy round of mass meetings, dinners, and deputations. She had also promised them a much-needed extra day's rest. Ingeborg and Maria were nearly out of cash and planned to use their time off to replenish their supply. Sara had assured them they could take care of that in Denver, but Ingeborg lay awake at night with her mind twisting and turning over whether the money would be there, if they had the right papers to prove their identity, and what they would do if the bank refused them. When she and Maria had traveled back to Sweden, and to Europe, they'd just carried the money they needed with them. This business of wiring money from one bank to another seemed suspicious to her. How would the Denver bank know how much money they had in the bank in Providence, and how would it travel over the wires to them in Colorado? What if it took a wrong turn and ended up in Detroit instead? It made her nervous.

A sign soon welcomed them to Colorado, which to Ingeborg looked a lot like Wyoming. Baked earth flecked with sagebrush and dotted with patches of snow stretched to the horizon, and the land humped and folded in on itself. Train tracks ran on a raised bed parallel to the road, cinders littering the slopes below. Cattle grazed in the distance, and deer lifted their heads and gazed at them as they rumbled by. An occasional jackrabbit dashed across the road. This was empty country, but the road and telegraph poles flashing by suggested more settlement was coming. Ingeborg still hadn't warmed to this bleak landscape and couldn't understand the attraction.

They reached the hotel in Denver by late afternoon and found Mabel waiting for them there. Mercifully, they'd been able to slip into town quietly, as the usual automobile escort was scheduled for the following day.

Mabel looked tired, and her clothes hung on her already slender frame. For the first time Ingeborg considered how draining the trip must be for her. She had to arrive in towns, often knowing no one, and find food and lodging. She then had to drum up support among strangers for the envoys who were never far behind. No companionship, and always having to look backward and forward at the same time. Ingeborg admired her and felt her ill humor over Mrs. Kendrick's snub ebb away under Mabel's warm welcome and the shower of praise she heaped on them.

"You three are the talk of the town for having made it over the mountain to Cheyenne while the men turned back," she said. "You must tell me all about it! However did you manage?"

They found their rooms and met in the hotel's dining room for dinner. Mabel marveled at their accounts of the blizzard. "How absolutely terrifying! You might have plunged over a cliff at any moment." She confessed that when Alice Paul had conceived of this idea, they hadn't considered the details of the actual travel. "We guessed the envoys might encounter some difficulties but couldn't imagine the true conditions. Alice just said the envoys would be able to overcome whatever obstacles they faced. That was the point, after all. And she was right! I'm very grateful, though, that we didn't have a hundred cars going over that pass."

"That would have been a disaster," agreed Ingeborg. "A driver not accustomed to snow, or a car breaking down. For sure we'd have lost some of them."

"Better to have just the three of you." Mabel beamed at them. "You've shown such unswerving devotion, such extraordinary grit in arriving just where we need you to be. We're stirring up women—and men—to fight for the amendment as never before."

"Do you think we'll get it through in 1916?" Maria asked.

Mabel blew out her breath and shook her head. "We can only hope. They might have a better sense of that at headquarters, but I've had no word we're that close."

"What's the schedule for tomorrow?" Sara broke in suddenly, her voice peevish. "This trip has worn me to a nub. My heart is wobbly at these altitudes, and we've had no rest since Salt Lake City. I can't speak for Maria and Ingeborg, but I am dead tired. I can't keep this up."

Mabel looked sympathetic, but with a certain set to her eyes that meant she was also bracing to deliver bad news. "Your rest day is coming," she assured Sara. "But first we have a great deal of activity planned here in Denver. The suffragists here are thrilled you're coming and have been very busy."

Sara groaned and slumped backward in her seat. "Mabel! You promised us!"

Mabel plunged on. "There are a number of reporters who wish to speak with you, and I've arranged for them to come here tomorrow morning. A photographer will also want to take some pictures of you and the car. In the afternoon you'll drive out of town to ready the car with the banner and signs, and then meet Mrs. Lucius Cuthbert, a lovely woman who is on our executive council, and a few other members. They'll escort you to the auditorium for a mass meeting. From there a larger automobile escort will accompany you to the east portico of the state capital, where you will meet Governor Carlson. Bertha Fowler, who is the head of our state branch here, will also greet you, along with Mrs. James Belford, who's the president of the Woman's Woodrow Wilson Club. I'll be there as well." Mabel paused.

"Will that be all?" asked Sara, with faint sarcasm.

Ingeborg saw the fatigue of the last few days had pooled under her puffy eyes and seeped into the fine network of new lines on her face. She looked over at Maria who shook her head slightly and lifted her shoulders in a resigned shrug.'

"Not quite," Mabel said. "We'll all continue on to a reception at Mrs. Cuthbert's home so people can meet the three of you, and there will be a dinner afterward. On Friday there are a number of events planned, including some street speaking."

"We have to visit a bank," said Ingeborg. "We're almost out of money. When can we do that?"

"Some of these events Sara can do on her own, though we will, naturally, require your services any time we need the car," said Mabel. "You'll have some time tomorrow morning."

"Sara is right," said Ingeborg. "We all need rest. The last week has been very hard and Emilie needs some work, too. We can't keep going at this pace."

"Emilie?" said Mabel, looking confused.

"The motorcar," said Ingeborg. "We named her for a Swedish suffragist, Emilie Rathou."

"I see," Mabel said. She frowned slightly. "I wonder that you didn't choose the name of an American suffragist. We could have called her Elizabeth, or Susan."

Ingeborg just looked at her steadily, refusing to drop her eyes or look away. At length she said slowly, "It's our car. I guess we can name her whatever we like."

"What about the rest day?" Maria broke in smoothly. "Will that be in Denver? We arranged to have funds wired here, and we must get them or we can't continue. Sara must have business to take care of, too."

Mabel turned to her with a smile. "When we're done here you'll drive down to Colorado Springs and rest there. It's surrounded by mountains and will be a delightful place to spend an extra day." She paused, and then said quickly. "You'll just have a few meetings there before you rest."

Sara yawned. "I don't care where we stop as long as it's soon and the bed is soft and doesn't move. Every muscle in my body shrieks from being slatted about by the car—there's never enough time to rest."

"This trip is hard on all of us," agreed Mabel. "I feel it, too. But we're receiving such splendid attention from it, and—"

"You must build in more rest days, then," said Sara flatly. "Change the route if you must. I'll work for this cause but I won't die for it; I have children to think of. Who will continue this trip if I can't? I begged Frances to take over for me here, and she refused. I'm starting to doubt we'll ever see her face again."

Ingeborg's irritation with Sara subsided, replaced by a grudging admiration as she listened to her challenge Mabel. It still surprised Ingeborg that no one spoke poorly of Frances. In fact, the CU thought she was so valuable they still pretended she was with them. Sometimes the newspapers breathlessly welcomed Frances as one of the envoys and left the Swedes out entirely. If Sara walked away, her poor health would be blamed, not her dedication to the cause. Ingeborg thought that if she and Maria quit, it would be held against them as immigrants; people would point and say, "See there? They can't be trusted; they care only for themselves."

Ingeborg turned her attention once again to Mabel and Sara, in time to hear Sara ask heatedly, "Is that what Alice wants, a martyr? I tell you it won't be me."

"Of course not," said Mabel, soothingly. "We're just trying to reach as many people as we can in advance of the upcoming session of Congress. Wouldn't it be worth making the maximum effort if we can get the amendment through next year? That's all we're trying to do. The fight for suffrage has been going on for decades already. We want to win this as quickly as possible so we can all move on to other things."

"Sara's right, though," said Ingeborg, determined to make Mabel listen. "The harder we push, the more likely something will go wrong— we'll get sick, or the car will break down. How will it help the CU if we fail to turn up at a meeting, with everyone waiting for us? That almost happened in Cheyenne. We need time to rest and recover."

"I'll see what I can do," Mabel said, with a shrug. "But you know it's difficult to make changes once things are set in motion. The suffragists in states we visit need time to prepare for our arrival, and the farther east we go, the more resistance we'll encounter to suffrage in general and to the CU in particular. NAWSA has many followers in the Eastern states, and some of those women have no love for us; they require careful handling. It will be no small feat to persuade them to join us in mass meetings."

"Skip them," suggested Ingeborg, irritably. She pictured driving straight across to Washington, DC, from Denver, or even taking a southern route that would avoid the snow, riding with the top down through a lush green countryside. "We can take our time, have more rest days, and we can hole up somewhere if we have to. Maryland, maybe, or Virginia. You must have a wealthy supporter with a country place and spare rooms."

Mabel's smile looked sewn on. She looked around the table at each of them in turn. "We've been over this. New York, Massachusetts, New Jersey, and Pennsylvania will all vote on woman suffrage in state referendums within the next few weeks." Her hands twisted the napkin in her lap. "While the CU stands only for the federal amendment, any publicity for suffrage will be helpful. We have to include them. And if the state campaigns fail, as at least some are sure to, we want people to know the CU and the federal amendment are a better alternative."

There was a pause as they considered their positions, Sara and Ingeborg looking grim, and Mabel no less resolute. As she so often did, Maria spoke up to bridge their differences. "And so we agree," she said. "We will go as far north as Michigan, and through New York and the other Eastern states on our way to Washington, instead of going straight across the country from here. In return, Mabel will make sure the schedule includes more rest days." She looked at each companion in turn. "Yes? We agree on this?"

"Yes, but—we need to see the new itinerary," said Ingeborg. She looked at Mabel. "Before we leave Denver."

"I'll need to confirm with headquarters," said Mabel. "But I'll try."

"I'm at the absolute limit of my strength," said Sara simply, looking at Mabel. "At some point my heart will give out and it won't matter what I agreed to. The doctors I've consulted all tell me to rest. If it means going to fewer states then so be it. But you have to help us—no one else can stand up to Alice."

"I understand," said Mabel. "Believe me when I say that no one knows as well as I do how hard this has been for you. We're all sacrificing."

"Some more than others," said Sara. "But that's enough for tonight. I want to lie down. What time will the reporters come tomorrow?"

They made the final arrangements for the following day and headed to their rooms. Ingeborg climbed in next to Maria and scooted over to hold her, relaxing into her soft curves and inhaling the faint fragrance of the soap from her bath. Maria gave her a sleepy smile and then subsided into gentle snores. Not even the clang and hiss from the steam radiators could prevent Ingeborg from following suit.

* * *

Ingeborg wiggled her fingers and toes for warmth and tugged her hat down more firmly against the cold wind probing her neck, staring out over the crowd gathered before the steps of the capitol and half listening to the speeches. It had been a long day already, with more to come, but she had to admit that Mabel and the Colorado suffragists had organized things brilliantly. So far everything had gone like clockwork, and thanks to the advance publicity, their little car was recognized everywhere they went. The streets were bustling with automobiles; other drivers tooted their horns as they passed, and people on the sidewalks clapped and cheered. If they pulled over to the curb, passersby quickly gathered to admire Emilie and ask them eager questions about their trip.

Indeed, this morning Ingeborg had emerged from under the car to find several cowboy-hatted men standing around, amazed to see a woman in skirts wielding tools they'd thought were their sole domain. She'd had a very satisfying conversation with them about Emilie's performance and the relative merits of the new starter mechanism in the Overland Six. It was a pleasure to talk about solenoids and generators for a change, and she could tell they were impressed with her knowledge. They'd also given her some good tips as to who had the best prices on fuel and where she could find some parts she needed.

As they parted they told her that the Colorado men were in full support of woman suffrage. "You tell those men in Washington that having women voting has helped clean up the politics in our state. We'll never go back. We need women's help to move our state forward."

She enjoyed talking to them. While Sara faithfully recognized the Swedes during her speeches, somehow the rarity of women owning, driving, and maintaining their car wasn't what the reporters cared about. Instead, they focused mostly on Sara, her speeches, and the suffrage petitions.

Ingeborg turned her attention to Mrs. Bertha Fowler, who had just taken the podium. Mrs. Fowler was an imposing, beak-nosed woman with a wintry smile. She spoke eloquently about why their Eastern sisters were depending on the women of the West to help win their fight for suffrage. "We who have voted can show the country how women can bring sunlight into the darkness and muck of politics. As rotted food and dank air have no place in the home, so do they not belong in the political sphere. Colorado has shown that when women do vote, we have better schools, cleaner streets, and healthier food for our families. We do not pretend to have the same interests as our husbands, fathers, and sons. Women's sphere is protecting the family and the home. But only when every woman across our nation can exercise her right to vote will the great promise of our democracy be realized."

Idly, Ingeborg watched a stooped figure at the edge of the crowd; a hatless man wearing a wool coat that even from a distance Ingeborg could tell had seen better days. His cropped beard was white, and his thinning hair, lifted in the breeze, was a silvery gray. He had a familiar look, but she couldn't make out his features. Perhaps she'd seen him at one of their impromptu street rallies. Was it her imagination, or was he staring at her?

Applause from the crowd signaled that Mrs. Fowler had concluded her remarks, so Ingeborg turned back to the stage. Now Governor George Carlson was signing the petition, and others were lining up to do the same. Soon they'd be on their way to Mrs. Cuthbert's house for the reception, and they could finally return to the hotel. She hoped Mrs. Cuthbert served coffee. She glanced back out at the mystery figure in the crowd, but he had vanished, so she found Maria and headed for the car.

* * *

It was after ten when they finally returned to the hotel, bone-tired and ready to drop into their beds. Ingeborg finished buttoning up the car, and Maria collected the petitions signed that day. Sara went straight in and was nowhere in sight by the time they crossed the elegant lobby, shoes sinking into the deep pile rugs. As they collected their key at the front desk, the clerk directed their attention to a figure sitting in the corner, noting that the gentleman had been waiting for Miss Kindstedt's return. From the clerk's pursed his lips and slight hesitation before pronouncing the word "gentleman," Ingeborg could tell he was unsure if the visitor deserved the term. "He was very insistent that he wait for you, but if he's unwelcome, we'll ask him to leave."

Ingeborg scarcely heard him. She was looking hard at the man she'd seen at the rally earlier, still wrapped in his battered coat and rising from the chair where he'd been waiting. She took a few steps toward him. "Rolf?" she whispered. In Swedish she said, "Is it you?" and with a shout of delight ran to throw her arms around him, nearly bowling him over in the process. She held him at arm's length to gaze at his face and then hugged him again, tears starting in her eyes. "Oh," she said, "I thought you were dead. Where have you been all this time?"

Rolf gave her a lopsided grin and squeezed her shoulders. He looked indescribably weary. She gazed at his features, so familiar and dear to her and yet so ravaged by time. Lines radiated from the corner of his eyes and creased his face. A scar puckered one side of his mouth, and his eyes, once so bright and lively, were a watery blue. "No, not dead, not yet anyway."

"I wrote you, but never heard back," said Ingeborg.

"I moved around a lot and lost your address," replied Rolf. "I didn't know if you were still in Providence."

"I am," said Ingeborg, and, turning to find Maria, noticed the clerk taking in this scene with undisguised curiosity. "Maria," she said. "Come meet my brother Rolf. Rolf, Maria is my partner."

Maria came forward, a warm smile on her broad face, and clasped his hand. "Ingeborg has spoken of you so often," she said. "I'm pleased to meet you at last."

Ingeborg scanned the lobby and saw again the clerk openly eavesdropping on their conversation. "Let's find a quiet place to talk," she said. Looking at Rolf's gaunt frame she asked, "Have you eaten?"

Rolf hesitated until Ingeborg pointedly said that she had money, whereupon he admitted that he wouldn't mind a bite. So they found a quiet corner of the dining room, where Ingeborg and Maria ordered coffee. Rolf, after scanning the menu, opted for coffee and a double portion of meat pie. When the waiter had left, he looked at Ingeborg appraisingly. "You've done well for yourself. Driving a nice car, staying in a fancy hotel. A famous suffragist."

Ingeborg laughed and waved a hand at him. "It's Maria's car, I just keep it running. But Providence has been good to me. I found work right away." She told him briefly about her life in Providence and starting her own business. "The wealthy people paid well to know their children and silver would be safe when they hired a nanny or a maid."

"You were always the smart one," said Rolf. "Father was right when he said you should try your luck in America. Me...." He shrugged. "Are you married? Kids?"

"No," said Ingeborg, opting not to talk about Maria. "And you?"

Rolf shifted in his chair and gave a weary sigh. "I did marry, a woman named Helga I met working at a woolen mill up in Maine, a town called Biddeford. We had a child, a son." He looked at Ingeborg. "We named him Adam, after Father. He was a good boy—full of spirit."

Ingeborg felt her stomach twist at his use of the past tense, and her smile faded. "What happened?"

"One winter the mill laid me off. Helga still had her job, but then her mill cut wages. Every day I walked the streets looking for work but never found much. Too many other guys like me. It was cold. We scrimped on heat and food just to keep a roof over our heads. We tried to make sure Adam had enough to eat, even if we went hungry." Rolf sighed again and seemed to sink into his chair. His voice dropped to a whisper. "Then smallpox hit. Helga got sick first, then Adam. There was nothing I could do. The doctor wouldn't come unless we paid him." He looked at Ingeborg, his face wreathed in despair. "I never got it. I don't know why. Sometimes I wish I'd died, too."

"Rolf, I had no idea," said Ingeborg, aching for him. "If you'd told me I could have sent you money."

"We thought it would get better. The mills would re-hire. I just never thought—" He broke off. "When they died, all I could think of was getting as far from Biddeford as I could. I heard the meat packing plants in Chicago were hiring, so I hopped a freight and rode out there. I found work and survived—after a fashion." He grimaced. "But it was always the same. Just when times were good, the bosses would speed up the line to where it killed you trying to stay with it, or they'd cut wages or lay people off. More immigrants arriving every day, desperate for work—the bosses could name their price. That's when I joined the IWW—must have been around 1908."

"You too!" exclaimed Ingeborg.

"It's the right union for the working man," said Rolf, nodding. "But why'd you join, if you worked for yourself?"

"Organizing," said Ingeborg. "I arrange meetings, do street speaking. They needed someone who spoke Swedish."

"Yeah, that's the thing about the IWW," Rolf said, approvingly. "You can speak any language and be a member, not like some other ones. And there's no one like Big Bill Hayward and Elizabeth Gurley Flynn to fight for us. I've seen them both in action, and they could lead people to hell and back." He folded his arms around his chest and leaned back in his chair. "So I drifted west, worked as a longshoreman on the docks in San Diego, and then north to lumbering jobs in

Washington state. Moved around a lot. There's a whole army of men like me out riding the rails and looking for work. The bosses would rain leaflets on a city saying they had jobs, but when we showed up, they were all taken—and they could cut wages for the ones that were already working, since replacements were standing around ready to take over at any pay. It was a bum deal."

The waiter brought his food, and Maria and Ingeborg sipped their coffee while he attacked his plate with a ferocity that suggested that he hadn't eaten in a while. When he slowed down, Ingeborg asked him, "So what did you do?"

"I was tired of fighting the lumber camp bosses. I'd been in and out of jail some, got beaten up, and I just wanted to work. I'd been black-listed out West but I heard there was work in the Colorado coalfields, so in 1912 me and some buddies hopped a freight and came here."

"And you found work?"

"Yeah, they'd opened up a new coal seam, so they needed men. But digging coal is dirty work. Dangerous, too, and the companies always skimp on safety. Saves money." He frowned, and his voice grew bitter. "The great John D. Rockefeller don't care if his workers die, so long as he has fine houses to live in and fancy clothes and parties. We lost over a hundred men every year to mine accidents. A hundred men!" he repeated, shaking his head in disgust. "Every day we'd drag ourselves from bed not knowing if we'd see it again that night. Most men who died left families behind. Their wives got nothing from the company."

"Wasn't the IWW there?" asked Ingeborg.

"Yes, through the United Mineworkers, but this state's mighty anti-union, and the miners' thugs beat up any organizers they found. The company owned the town—houses too—so if you lost your job you'd have no place to live. We organized in secret."

"It's getting to be the same everywhere," said Ingeborg. "The owners have the police in their pockets."

"And not just the police," said Rolf. "Did you hear about Ludlow?"

Ingeborg stared at him, taking in his battered face. "Some. You were there?" She reached out and touched the scar on his mouth. "Is that where you got this?"

Rolf nodded. His face grew tight, his lips set in a hard line. He picked up his fork to eat some more, but set it down and leaned back in his chair. "I was there. I saw it all," he said hoarsely.

"What happened?"

"We finally struck in the fall of 1913 because we were working so damn hard for so little pay, and so many men were dying—if we were gonna die, we might as well go down fighting. So the IWW led us out on strike. The bosses brought in scabs and Baldwin-Felts thugs by the truckload, with mounted Gatling guns. Gatling guns!" he spat out. "When we just wanted an honest day's pay for honest work, and safer working conditions."

Ingeborg and Maria stared at him, almost unable to bear what they knew was coming next.

"The union helped us set up tent camps. The biggest was at Ludlow. We lived in those damn tents straight through the coldest winter Colorado had seen in years, so cold the piss would freeze in the pot by morning. I was there, and I still don't know how we made it through. Brutal." Rolf shivered, remembering. "We were on private land, leased by the union straight up, and the thugs would come around at night, shine searchlights on the tents, and fire away." He shrugged. "They didn't care who they killed. Women. Children. The tents set close together, and at night you could hear the children crying in fear, the mothers trying to shush them. Made me almost glad Helga and Adam were gone."

Ingeborg closed her eyes. This was heartbreaking to hear but nothing she hadn't seen for herself. In Providence the workers lived in crowded tenements, sometimes ten to a room. They worked six days a week, some of them twelve hours a day, and they still barely made enough to pay for rent and food. Meanwhile, the owners lived in big, glittering houses, waited on hand and foot by servants, well away from the smoke and dirt of the factories. The wealthy treated their prize horses and lapdogs better than the workers. She opened her eyes and looked at Rolf. "Tell us the rest," she said.

"Rockefeller and the other owners refused to negotiate. They didn't have to," Rolf shook his head bitterly. "They just called on their buddy, the governor. Ammons," Rolf said his name like a curse. "The snake.

By April things were tense. We were fighting to keep the coalfields shut down, and there were clashes every day. We were getting slaughtered, but we kept at it, in too deep to give up.

"So the governor called out the National Guard." He paused and looked at Ingeborg. "We thought they were coming to help us." He leaned toward her, his voice low, but shaking with anger. "We actually cheered when we saw them coming. Bastards! They set up machine guns on the ridge above us and fired down on the tents. Shot people trying to escape. For hours we lay there, trapped, but then a train came to our rescue—pulled up and stopped between us and the Guard, so most of us ran for cover in the hills nearby. Not everyone, though." He slumped back in his chair. "Families had dug pits under their tents to hide from gunfire. Some women got together in one tent and took their kids down into the pit. They must've thought it was safer. But when the Guard saw we'd left, they came down into the camp, looting and setting fire to everything. The women and eleven kids—they burned to death. They found them the next day."

"Rolf," breathed Ingeborg, struggling. She looked over at Maria who sat silently, tears welling in her eyes. Maria looked back at her, shaking her head. Despair and grief wrapped Ingeborg in a thick blanket, squeezing the breath from her chest. "How'd you escape?" she asked.

"I'd gone back to the camp to look for ones we knew were missing. I'd helped some get out, see, ones who were crippled and couldn't move fast, women who had more kids than they could carry. I was searching through the tents again when I heard the train start pulling away. I had a granny under one arm and a sack of food under the other, so I lit out for the hills where the rest were hiding. But the granny couldn't move fast, and before we reached cover, the Guard spotted us and opened fire. I took a bullet to my shoulder. Granny got hit in the side and we both went down, but I dragged her behind a rock. The Guard found us there. They beat me senseless and left us. After dark some miners slipped down and carried us to safety. I made it. She didn't."

"The bastards," groaned Ingeborg. "How can those men sleep at night?"

"Simple," said Rolf, and shrugged his shoulders. "They just paint us as anarchists, as outlaws. Dangerous to democracy, they say. When they're the ones take the law into their own hands to keep the bosses rich. We could be cockroaches for all they care. They just stamp us out."

"That was over a year ago," said Ingeborg. "What's happened since?"

"It took me a while to heal, especially after that butcher of a surgeon got through with me. My shoulder still isn't right, never will be, I guess." Rolf reached his right hand over to rub his left shoulder, and Ingeborg noticed then how he kept it hunched up and a little forward. A smile tugged the corner of his mouth, and he said, "I had to spend some time singing hymns with your old pals, the Salvation Army, just for a bowl of soup and a blanket on a hard floor. Funny, since us Wobblies always made fun of them. But an empty belly helped me find my singing voice right quick."

Ingeborg squirmed, and said hastily "They weren't my pals, exactly."

Rolf eyed her. "I never could figure out what you saw in them. What you're doing now seems more the thing. Where're you headed next?"

"We leave for Colorado Springs tomorrow—we're on a tight schedule." Ingeborg glanced at Maria with a rueful smile. "We'd planned a different trip—we wanted to explore America, see the West. But at the Exposition in San Francisco we found out they needed a car, and we offered ours." She reached over and grasped his hand. "I wish we could stay here longer now that I've found you. What will you do?"

Rolf smiled, looking down at her hand and covering it with his own, scarred and leathery. Suddenly her heart twisted with a sharp longing for Sweden. She'd spent half her life in America, but more and more she felt unwelcome, viewed with suspicion. She'd given up her family to make a life here, but sometimes she wondered about her choice. Tears started, and she said in a low voice, "Have you thought of going home?"

"Home? To Sweden?" Rolf eyed the waiter, who was coming to clear the table. The other diners had left, and the kitchen crew had moved on to dishwashing and cleanup, preparing to close for the night. A young woman, clad in black, emerged from a side door with a bucket and began to swab the floor. He turned back to Ingeborg. "No. I don't know where home is, but it's not there. Go back all busted up and without a penny? What would be the point? I'm keeping company with a widow who lost her husband in the coalfields. She's got a couple of kids who'll be old enough to work before too long. We don't have much, but we get by. I'll stick it here, I guess."

"I hate to say good-bye. How do I find you?" Ingeborg hunted for a scrap of paper to write his address down and found the bag with the petitions. "Might as well sign this while you're here," she said, and handed over one of the pages. Rolf scrawled his name, and she flipped it over to jot down his address, and then handed him her card. "Write me," she commanded.

"My," he said, impressed, looking it over. "Look at this. Organizer, eh? Some would say you're just a troublemaker."

She grinned at him. "Runs in the family, I guess." They walked out to the lobby and said their good-byes. She watched him duck through the door out into the cold night and wondered when she'd see him again.

CHAPTER SEVEN

OCTOBER 16, 1915

Maria steered Emilie around a swampy pothole and tooted the horn at a shambling, one-horned steer who regarded them from the center of the road. The steer blinked, shied sideways as Emilie nosed forward, and then broke into a brisk trot with its tail flying high, heading toward a distant herd.

"Ridiculous creature," Sara said, from the back seat.

"Most likely an anti," replied Maria. "Going to warn the others."

"You know, he does remind me of the man who spoke against us at that street meeting in Colorado Springs," Sara said with a chuckle. "The red-faced one with the crooked mustache?"

"Yes, he kept waving his arms, trying to work people up about the dangers of women voting." Ingeborg grinned. "I was glad the crowd shouted him down."

"I'm so impressed by these Colorado women—and most of the men," said Sara, pushing off the heavy buffalo skin and setting it aside. "They seem determined to help us. And I think they'll follow through more than some we've met."

"There is something special about them," agreed Ingeborg. "Maybe it's they've had the vote for so long. More than twenty years, isn't it?"

"Yes," Sara said. "They won it by state referendum—the first to do it that way."

They rode in quiet for a bit, watching the sun chase shadows across the prairie grass. Up ahead a ranch house nestled under some cottonwoods, and cattle ambled toward a water tank served by a spinning windmill. "This is a strange country," Ingeborg continued. "States have some rights, and Congress has others, but no one agrees on who has what. So women vote in the West, but in Rhode Island it's never even been on the ballot. It makes no sense."

"Big waste of time, too," said Maria, scratching her nose. "Think of what women could do if we weren't working all the time for the vote."

"That's just what they're scared of," Ingeborg offered.

Sara tugged her hat down against a passing wind gust. "I'd planned to spend this fall writing a new book of poetry," she said sadly. "Erskine's been urging me to get back to writing. But I needed the money...." She drifted off, thinking about her son, Albert, now a handsome young man of fifteen, and her sweet daughter, Kay. It broke her heart to be away from them, but she couldn't ask Erskine to support them, though he loved them very much. Her ex-husband earned very little as a minister, and in any case was too angry over the divorce to give her any money. "I'm determined to support myself and to help pay for things my children need," she said, stoutly. "So here I am."

Ingeborg rolled her eyes. Sara made it sound like she expected a round of applause for deciding to be independent, even though she still had Erskine to draw on if she really needed something, like that buffalo skin or the new coat he bought her in San Francisco. When had she and Maria done anything but support themselves? She knew Sara wasn't born to money, but she sure hadn't worked the way they had.

As if to punctuate that thought, there was a pop from Emilie's right front flank, followed by a faint hissing sound. Ingeborg groaned and swore. Another tire tube burst. Maria pulled the car off the road under a cottonwood and they pushed open their doors and clambered out. Ingeborg rose slowly to her feet, hanging on to the door frame. A searing pain traveled from her left buttock down the back of her thigh; frowning, she breathed deeply until it eased. Ever since the trip over the pass into Cheyenne it had been bothering her, she must have pulled something then. Riding in the car made it worse but the pain seemed to ease when she was able to move around. Tonight she'd ask Maria to rub some liniment on it.

She shuffled around to the back of the car and rummaged in the boot for the tools to jack the car up and remove the tire. Sara, meanwhile, sailed over to the tree to spread out her buffalo hide, and sat down with her back against the trunk. "I hope it won't take you long this time, Ingeborg," she said. "I want to get in early—I need to write Erskine tonight."

Ingeborg found herself slapping the jack handle lightly against her hand and glaring at Sara as she finished getting herself comfortable. Maria thought Ingeborg was too hard on Sara, but really, it was beyond belief how Sara just sat there in the car, day after day, and did nothing but put on airs while Maria and Ingeborg did all the work. "It *is* nice to be out of the car, though," Sara prattled on. "That back seat is so hard—if they said there were springs in it, they were lying to you."

Maria caught Ingeborg's eye and shook her head, gesturing that she should get to work. Ingeborg attacked the nuts holding the wheel with added ferocity, her jaw clenched. Presently she had the tube out and found the hole, a slice about the length of her thumbnail. She spit on her handkerchief and wiped down the tube, making sure to remove all the dust from around the hole, and waved it around in the air to dry. She'd been hoping for a simple puncture. These longer slices were harder to patch, but she'd try it anyway. They had three days to travel the next five hundred miles, through Lamar and across the state line into Kansas, hitting Dodge City, Hutchinson, and finally Emporia, where Sara had an interview with some newspaper editor that people thought highly of. They only had two other tubes, and who knew what the roads ahead were like?

As she worked, Ingeborg let her mind play over her recent grudges against Sara. They'd stopped for two days in Colorado Springs, a welcome respite from the travel and from each other. Mrs. Cuthbert had whisked Sara off to her house while Maria and Ingeborg had stayed in a hotel in town. When she rejoined them Sara looked better than she had since they'd left Reno, rested and fed and for once not complaining of her heart. She bubbled with enthusiasm for the Cuthberts, their beautiful house and attentive servants and their literary knowledge. "They even knew of Erskine!" she warbled, which clearly vaulted the Cuthberts into a select circle. Ingeborg had grumbled only a little when Sara went off with them; she was too grateful for the rest and to be shed of Sara and her ailments for a time. But Sara's account of her stay with her wealthy friends had Ingeborg snarling once again to Maria in a private moment.

Maria had little patience with her. "Why make a fuss, Ingeborg? Sara doesn't mean anything by it. She loves books, and she loves Erskine, and if she can find someone who loves those things too, we should be glad for her." She sat down in the room's only chair and removed her shoes, rolling her wool stockings down her calves.

Ingeborg's jaw had jutted out. She poured water into the bowl and soaped up her face and hands. "I just hate the way we get treated as the hired help as soon as someone higher class comes along."

"Honestly, Ingeborg!" cried Maria, "You'd think they made us sleep in the stable with the horses. We stayed at a very nice hotel in Colorado Springs. Very good food. I wish I knew what they put in that casserole we had last night." And she was off talking about the meals they'd eaten, something Ingeborg couldn't care less about. She'd allowed herself to be diverted, seeing that Maria wasn't interested, but it rubbed at her like a saddle sore.

The patch seemed inclined to hold, so they were soon on the road again. Ingeborg settled back in her seat and let her mind drift to Rolf's account of the coalfields strike and the Ludlow massacre. When she closed her eyes, she could picture the families cowering in their tents, the flimsy canvas no match for the murderous bullets that rained down on them.

It seemed that government of the people and for the people was only for the rich, after all, just like the Wobblies said. The Civil War hadn't ended slavery; it had just taken a new form. Employees lived in company-owned houses, sent their children to company schools, prayed in company churches, and bought food and supplies in company stores with company script. Company store prices were double what regular stores charged, but there was no place else that would accept the script they were paid in. When workers protested, they were fired and driven out of town. All the way along, workers were cheated and abused and couldn't call on their own government for protection.

Ingeborg frowned unseeingly at the dry landscape. When she'd first come from Sweden, immigrants were welcome because the factories needed workers, the wealthy needed servants, and there were plenty of jobs for everyone. But that trickle of humanity had turned into a flood, and immigrants came now from all over Europe, expecting to find their future and maybe a fortune. Some did, she supposed. But for too many, especially now, the welcome had been replaced by a rude hand shoved in their faces. Or a gun.

They'd seen Mabel off at the train station in Pueblo, and Ingeborg was startled to see signs warning immigrants that their waiting room was behind the baggage depot. One sign had read "*All Irish, German, Italian, French, Greek, Polish, Spanish, Mexican, and Jewish Passengers Must Use the Immigrant Waiting Room!*" The emphasis on the words *Immigrant Waiting Room* made the message extra threatening. She hadn't gone looking for it because Swedes weren't on the list, perhaps because their skins were as white as anyone's, but wasn't that true of the Irish and Germans, too? Who came up with these rules? What happened to people who disobeyed the sign? The same thing as the poor miners, she guessed.

She wondered if they might also encounter such hostility, especially once they left the protection of the states that had already enfranchised women. Three women, traveling alone, could be ambushed easily on a lonely stretch of road. Perhaps she should buy a gun. Maybe when they got to Kansas City. She could slip into a store and tell the proprietor that it was a present for her brother. She had the feeling Sara and Mabel wouldn't approve, but while Ingeborg was willing to suffer the hardship of this trip for suffrage, she damn sure wasn't willing to die for it.

That evening, as they were preparing for bed in their rough hotel room in Lamar, she broached the subject.

"Did you see the signs in the rail station in Pueblo this morning?" she asked Maria. "There's a lot of anti-immigrant feeling around here."

Maria, carefully hanging her skirt and blouse in the armoire, had seen the signs and agreed that it was troubling.

"Do you ever wonder if we're in danger driving on these roads, far away from any help?"

Maria looked over at her, a slight suspicion forming in her eyes. "The roads are dangerous sometimes. But I'm more worried about the weather. The worst we've had so far is people telling us to go back home, take care of our families."

"I was thinking about what happened to Rolf and those coal miners. Couldn't that happen to us? Suppose someone gets mad at what we say and decides to take matters into their own hands. Would the police help us?"

"Ingeborg, that was very different. The miners had guns; they were shooting—"

Ingeborg raised her voice; she could feel her face get hot. "They murdered innocent women and children. And the Guard helped them do it. I'm just saying it could happen to us, especially once we leave the equal suffrage states." She paused, and then said, "I think we should buy a gun."

"Oh, I see now," said Maria, flipping the blankets back and examining the sheets for bugs. She looked over at Ingeborg. "Here we go again, Ingeborg. No. No guns. Remember what happened in Providence last summer? You want that should happen again?"

"Maria, please," pleaded Ingeborg, "I just want to keep us safe."

"We'll be safer without a gun," said Maria, sitting down on the bed. "If Miss Paul wanted us to have a gun she'd have given us one. What would people say if they knew the suffrage envoys were armed?"

"That's the point, Maria," said Ingeborg, walking quickly around to Maria's side of the bed and crouching down to look her in the face. "What if someone held us up and wanted to take the petitions from us? How would it look if the envoys showed up at the Capitol with no petitions?"

"Ingeborg, you promised if we did this trip, you wouldn't get excited. Maybe we need to send you to stay with Frances Joliffe, get some rest." She lay back and pulled the bedclothes up to her chin. "Now come to bed and stop being foolish," she said crossly. "We're not going to buy a gun."

Ingeborg gave an exasperated sigh and slowly climbed into bed beside Maria. "I just think—"

"No, you're not thinking, that's the problem. The last thing we need is you waving a gun around. Please, no more, Ingeborg! Go to sleep; tomorrow will be a longer drive than today." Maria rolled onto her right side, her back to Ingeborg. Presently her breathing grew deeper and her body twitched as she fell into a deep sleep.

Ingeborg stared into the dark and fumed, fashioning arguments she could use to convince Maria. Coyotes howled out on the prairie, and a train whistle sounded outside the window. At length her body relaxed into the soft warmth of the bed, and she slept.

* * *

Two days later they were crawling through mud on their way to Hutchinson. They'd left the good weather behind them in Colorado; it had been raining since they'd arrived in Dodge City the night before, and the roads were getting steadily worse. Maria tried to steer around the potholes, but with so many it was hard to guess which one looked least likely to swallow the car. They'd pulled Emilie's top up and fastened down the windows, but inside they were still damp and cold.

Earlier, Ingeborg and Maria had teased Sara about a piece they'd seen in the Pueblo paper, titled "Motherhood Strike is Suffrage Threat." Sara had been quoted as saying that many women in non-suffrage states "will deny themselves the privilege of motherhood until they receive the vote."

"What does that mean?" said Maria. "Is the CU against marriage?"

"Maybe they'll simply refuse to share their husband's bed," guessed Ingeborg.

Sara snorted. "That reporter! So smug. He was needling me about what would happen if Congress refused to take action on the amendment. Suddenly I remembered an ancient Greek play, *Lysistrata*, written by Aristophanes. Do you know it?" she asked.

They didn't, so she went on to tell the story of an Athenian woman, Lysistrata, who vowed to end war by persuading the women of her city to refuse sex with their men.

"A boycott!" said Ingeborg, "Or a man-cott.…"

"Did she win them over?" asked Maria.

"Yes, in the end she did," said Sara, "but not before the men paraded their discomfort all over the stage."

"So this is the CU's new policy?" asked Maria.

"It will be hard to enforce," said Ingeborg. "Especially those young, pretty suffragists." She turned around to peer at Sara. "What about Erskine? Would he be an exception?"

Sara laughed. "No, it isn't the CU's new policy, and I'll thank you not to plant the idea in Alice Paul's mind. If ever I see Erskine again, which I sometimes doubt, I fully intend to share his bed."

"You'd need the National, too," said Maria, referring to their rival suffrage organization. "They're much larger than us."

"I wish you could have seen the look on that reporter's face," said Sara, laughing. "For a moment there I had him. You could see him thinking, if Alice Paul could have us driving across the country on this mission, and campaigning against the Democrats, she just might be capable of organizing a national sex boycott. I could tell he was calculating whether his wife would go along with it, and how much he'd suffer."

That had led to a lengthy and mirthful discussion of just how such a campaign could be organized. They all agreed that Alice Paul, who appeared to have no interest in sex at all and was instead married to the suffrage movement, would be the natural leader. The Democrats would complain bitterly to Carrie Chapman Catt, the National's president, who would issue denouncements of the sex boycott to the press and encourage her members to satisfy their men at every opportunity.

This in turn would lead to some reduction of the National's effectiveness, as their members were occupied in the bedroom and by the inevitable babies that would result. They disagreed whether this would be beneficial or not to the CU and the federal amendment. Sara thought perhaps it would be, since the uproar would focus more attention on women's demand for political rights. Ingeborg agreed that it would be good to distract the National's organizers, since then there would be fewer state campaigns and they could get women to work on the federal amendment. Maria thought it would make men so angry it would backfire altogether and they'd force women back into the home. "They'd call out the National Guard," said Ingeborg.

But that was hours ago, and they were long past ready for this day to be over. They'd taken a chance and opted for the shortcut through Nickerson and were now regretting that decision. It was pitch dark, and the cold, relentless rain thrummed down on the car's roof, the air thick and swampy. Emilie's headlamps peered no more than five paces ahead of them, which forced Maria to drive at a walking pace. The mud was the real worry, though. In some sections it came halfway up Emilie's tires and she had to plunge through one hole after another. Maria clung to the steering wheel, grim-faced, as Emilie churned along, slipping and sliding. They rode silently, listening to the sound of the engine laboring, all of them fluent now in the language of pistons and sparks and alert to any sign of distress. No one else was traveling this late at night, and aside from the occasional farmhouse they were utterly alone.

Without warning Emilie's nose dropped and there was a sickening slide into deep muck. Her engine wailed as Maria tried first to jam forward through the mudhole, then to reverse backward over the lip they'd just come down. No luck. After a death rattle Emilie quit for good. Water began seeping through the floorboards as Maria ground on the starter, but the engine wouldn't catch.

The women groaned and swore as one, then Ingeborg pushed open her door and stuck a foot out.

"Where are you going?" asked Sara.

Ingeborg turned and gave her a cool stare. Wasn't it obvious? "To see if we can push her out of this mudhole. Unless you have a better idea?" Sara didn't, so Ingeborg continued on, feeling for the bottom as icy water came over her boot tops and the mud tugged at her skirts. When she stood up she was halfway up her thighs in muddy water. Moving haltingly, clinging to the car, she walked around the front to gauge the size of the mudhole, and then worked her way around to the back. Rain pelted down, cold water trickling off her hat and down her neck. The muck was thick and gooey and threatened to suck off her boots. She doubted they'd be able to budge the heavy car on their own but she called to the others to come out and help. "Maria, you push from the driver's door so you can steer. Sara, you come back here with me and we'll push from behind." When they were all in position, she counted to three and they threw their strength into pushing the car forward. Absolutely no response. They tried again and again, their feet slipping and water sloshing, but they were well and truly stuck.

They climbed back into the car for the meager shelter it provided from the rain though they were already soaked to the skin.

"Now what?" asked Maria.

"Let's try calling for help," said Sara. "Maybe there's a house nearby that we can't see." So they unfastened the windows and stuck their heads out. "Help! Help us!" they shouted, over and over again into the pitiless dark, and then waited for a light to come on, or the sound of someone coming to their aid. There was nothing but the rain on the roof top.

"Great shortcut this turned out to be," Ingeborg grumbled, brushing mud and grass off her skirt. "We'll be stuck here all night."

"No, we can't be," snapped Sara. "We have to be in Emporia tomorrow, there's a big meeting there and I'm to be interviewed by William White."

"Why don't you just phone him up and tell him to come get us," Ingeborg shot back.

"You're the mechanic, why don't you do something?" Sara returned.

"I'm a mechanic, not a magician," said Ingeborg. "The only way to get the car out of this mudhole is with horsepower—the old-fashioned kind."

"Enough," said Maria. "Bickering won't solve this. We can stay until daylight and hope someone sees us, or go for help."

Sara grabbed the top of her head with her hands and groaned. "Goddammit! What's the time?"

"I checked my watch when we went past that last farmhouse," said Ingeborg. "I think it must be about ten o'clock now."

Sara groaned. "We *cannot* remain in this bog all night. We have to do something." She stuck her head out the window again and shouted for help until she was hoarse.

Ingeborg and Maria looked at each other, and then turned to face front again. Neither said a word. The way Ingeborg saw it, Sara had created this problem by insisting on taking the shortcut. Ingeborg and Maria had been dubious; the main road was clearly marked on the map and side roads could be rough. Although muddy from the rain, the road they'd been on had a gravel base and would likely have gotten them into Hutchinson just fine. But Sara had scoffed at their fears and after some hesitation they'd agreed. There was no way Ingeborg was going to fight through the dark and mud now to get help. Her leg was still weak and pained her when she walked far. Maria was in no shape to go either. Sara would have to fix this.

The silence stretched on. No help arrived. Then Sara let out an exasperated sigh and began rummaging around the back of the car. Ingeborg turned around to see what she was up to.

"All right, dammit, I'll go, but before I do—where's that flask Erskine gave me?" Sara found it tucked into a door pocket and, pulling it out, took a big swallow before passing it forward. She tugged her hat down on her head. "How far back do you think that farmhouse is?"

"Maybe a mile," said Maria. "Maybe two."

"Well, if I'm not back by morning, come find me. I'll probably be face down in some wretched slough. If I die, don't bury me here. I hate Kansas!" With that, she opened her door, swearing as the icy water found her skin. "Oh, that's cold," they heard her say. She took a step, slipped, grabbed the door to keep from going down, and steadied herself. Then she took another step, slammed the door, and disappeared into the darkness.

Ingeborg and Maria each took a swig from the flask; Maria then tossed it the back seat, settling down to wait. Neither had much to say, but from time to time Ingeborg stuck her head out her door to look and listen for any sign of Sara's return. Almost three hours passed before she heard a harness jingling and could glimpse the light swinging from the wagon. "She did it!" she told Maria, elated. "Someone's coming, anyway."

When the team drew close, Ingeborg and Maria eased out of the car and waded through the mud hole to greet them. The farmer stopped his team, the mules snorting and shaking rain from their long ears. Their backs came nearly to Ingeborg's shoulders and they looked sleek and well-muscled, she noted with satisfaction, which meant that they would probably be up to the job. Steam rose gently from their backs.

Sara climbed down carefully from the wagon, plastered with mud from head to foot, soaked to the skin, and so exhausted she could barely stand upright. She looked like a drowned cat. Ingeborg thought perhaps she'd never seen anyone quite so miserable and felt a grudging respect for her. "Well done, Sara," she said.

Maria waded over and threw her arms around Sara. "You saved us!" she crowed. "I was so worried!"

Sara turned and motioned to the farmer. "This is Mr. Bishop," she said. "He and his mules were good enough to come to our aid." Ingeborg and Maria thanked him.

"Let's see what we've got, here," was all Mr. Bishop said. He jumped down from the wagon and walked around the edge of the bog, looking for firmer footing. At length he climbed back aboard and, clucking to his mules, drove them around to the right of the mudhole, maneuvering them into position in front of the motorcar. Ingeborg followed and stood by the mules' heads while Mr. Bishop hitched a thick rope to the back of the wagon and, jumping down into the mudhole, attached it to the underside of Emilie's nose.

"Should we push?" Ingeborg asked.

"Wouldn't hurt," said Mr. Bishop, so the three women waded into the mudhole and positioned themselves behind Emilie. On three, the farmer shouted "Hyup!" and cracked his whip across the mules' rumps. They jumped forward into their collars and the women leaned on the car, muscles straining, the mud pulling at their boots and cold water sloshing up their legs. With a grotesque slurping sound the mud released Emilie's wheels and the mules pulled her up onto solid ground. The women cheered and staggered through the mud to where the farmer was unhooking the rope, Maria half supporting Sara so she wouldn't lose her footing.

"Stay out of mudholes," Mr. Bishop advised, as he unhooked the rope. "You don't know how deep they get. Steer round 'em if you can." He gave them some pointers on the road ahead and then clucked to his mules and swung them around. Headed back to the farm and their feed bins, the mules pricked their ears forward and had to be restrained from breaking into a trot.

After considerable tinkering Ingeborg got the motor running, and they were back on the road, moving more cautiously this time. It was still dark when they pulled into Nickerson, which had a small cluster of houses and no hotel. They roused the occupants of the largest house, who grumpily allowed them to sit in their kitchen until daylight, but offered nothing warm to eat or drink. The fire in the kitchen stove was banked and cold. They cleaned themselves up as best they could but had to remain in their soaked garments because, knowing the rain was coming, they'd express-shipped their luggage and the petitions through to Kansas City. They sat shivering, soaked, filthy and miserable until daylight arrived and they could venture forth to Hutchinson, about eleven miles away. The rain had stopped, blessedly, and it looked like the weather was set to clear.

They pulled up in front of the Bisonte Hotel in Hutchinson where they'd meant to stay the night before, climbed stiffly out of the car, and entered the front door into the cozy lobby. Logs crackled brightly in the fireplace at one end. The proprietor was chatting with another guest but they both fell silent and gaped as the muddy women walked up to the desk. "Good morning," said Sara, with authority. "We were due to arrive last night but got stuck in the mud near Nickerson. We'd like our rooms now, but just long enough to clean up and have a short rest. We'll also have coffee and breakfast—delivered to our rooms, please."

Ingeborg admired Sara's command of the situation. That was the thing about Sara, she reflected. Sometimes she played the invalid and seemed weak and whiney, but then she'd walk more than a mile through hip-deep mud to summon help. And now she was coolly ordering the staff around as though she arrived at a hotel mud-spattered and disheveled every day.

The proprietor inquired about their luggage. "No luggage," said Sara crisply.

"I see," he said, looking very doubtful, but he handed them their room keys and sent staff to bring them hot water for washing.

By noon they were back in the car heading for Emporia, over a hundred miles away. A brisk breeze chased the clouds around and dried out the roads, so they made good time, running with the top down despite the day's chill.

As they'd prepared to leave the hotel, Ingeborg had gone out ahead of the others to get the car ready, and found three men gathered round Emilie, inspecting her mud-covered flanks.

"Got into some mud, did ya?" said one.

"Sure did," said Ingeborg, briefly describing their trials with the mudhole as she folded back Emilie's bonnet and began adjusting the spark plugs. But instead of the sounds of sympathy she was expecting, or even, yes, admiration for Sara wading through mud and darkness to rouse the farmer, she heard laughter. Surprised, she looked up to see them openly smirking at her. What was wrong with them? Any traveler could tell a story like that. There was no shame attached to having slid into a mudhole on a dark, rainy night on an unfamiliar road. That could happen to anyone, surely? She studied each of them in turn, all younger than she was and clad in patched, mud-splattered overalls, with barely a mouthful of teeth among them. One, a tall, skinny fellow, said insolently, "Oh, we heard you calling for help, all right. We guessed who it was, too. We knew you was coming."

Ingeborg felt her face flush. After the night they'd just been through, she felt brittle and ready to snap. She itched to slap that insolent grin but asked through gritted teeth "Why didn't you help us?"

One of the others, a swarthy fellow in a conductor's cap, spoke up. "We figured if you ladies want the vote so much you should learn to get your own selves out of a pickle. Why should we do everything for you?"

Ingeborg couldn't believe her ears. "You didn't help because we're *suffragists*?"

The men chuckled and nodded. "Yep, that's right."

She stared at each of them in turn, wondering if they bred them simple in this part of Kansas. They were like schoolboys, pleased with their prank and heedless of the misery they'd caused.

"Decent men would've helped us," she said slowly. "Think of women who care for their men when they're sick in bed. Night or day. They don't say, 'Oh, you must learn to care for yourself and not depend on me.'"

Their brows wrinkled as they thought about this. Then the skinny man said, "That's where women belong, in the home. That's what you're made for." His companions laughed and nodded in approval.

"Kansas women won the vote three years ago," she said tartly. "And it's a good thing they did, too, judging from the likes of you. You're three good reasons why women need to vote for themselves." She grabbed the fuel can and began to fill Emilie's tank. As she did so, Sara and Maria emerged from the hotel and walked over to the car.

Ingeborg gestured with her chin toward the men. "These three princes heard us calling for help last night and did nothing. They said if we want the vote we should take care of ourselves." The men eased backward a step and looked a little nervous, especially when Sara rounded on them, eyes blazing, a figure of fury in her mud-stained traveling suit. "I walked three miles through mud up to my waist to find help when you could have come to our aid?" she spat out.

Ingeborg was amused that Sara had doubled the mileage and added water depth, but perhaps it had felt that way to her at the time. And who was Ingeborg to say anything? There might very well have been waist-deep puddles.

The men nodded, shifting uncomfortably, their swagger less noticeable now that they were confronted by three angry women. Sara turned to Ingeborg and Maria. "I guess I was lucky that the farmer who pulled us out was a gentleman, not one of these louts. Let's get out of here." They got in and Maria reversed the car, forcing the men to jump out of the way, and sped off down the road.

The following morning they were back in the car heading to Kansas City, Missouri. Ingeborg shifted uncomfortably in her seat, already stiff and sore. It seemed weeks since they'd left Colorado Springs—had it really just been one? Each long day in the car felt like a beating.

They'd arrived at Emporia's Broadview Hotel around teatime yesterday to find William White, the publisher of the *Emporia Gazette*, sitting in a corner of the lobby smoking a cigar and waiting to interview Sara. He was a portly man with a round face and soft white skin that made Ingeborg think of a milk bottle, but he had a kind smile and a twinkle in his blue eyes. He roared when he saw their muddy clothes and exclaimed over their maltreatment by the men in Nickerson.

White looked at Sara with a broad smile. "I can tell I'm going to enjoy this interview more than any I've had in some time. Could I prevail upon you to speak with me now? I understand you have commitments later this evening, as do I."

Sara tipped her head back and smiled up at him, an impish gleam in her eye. What was she up to, wondered Ingeborg?

"I'd be happy to, Mr. White, but we have a bit of a quandary. I must have my clothes cleaned before tonight's meeting. Would you object to doing the interview in my room? I can cover myself with blankets in the bed, and you can sit in the chair."

Now, that's a little fast, thought Ingeborg, suppressing a smile, and she flicked a glance over to Maria, whose eyes had gone big and round, her eyebrows disappearing under her hat brim. Maria looked meaningfully at Sara, who paid her no attention.

White chuckled. "I'll take it however you'll give it to me."

"Sara," Maria began, "Is this proper—"

Sara cut her off. "I have no time to be proper. I have to be practical. Mr. White needs his interview. We need clean clothes before the meeting. Our spare clothes are waiting for us in Kansas City. You can join me in the room, if you like, to make sure we don't get up to something."

"This is, I concede, a trifle unconventional," said White to Maria. "But I am a gentleman. She's safe in my hands—no, perhaps I should just say that she's safe with me, I assure you."

Maria gave an embarrassed smile and looked at Ingeborg, who shrugged. Sara turned back to White. "Give me fifteen minutes to get myself sorted out. I'm in Room Three-B." White bowed slightly and wished Ingeborg and Maria a pleasant evening.

In the end it had gone as Sara had planned. White got the story and whatever else happened was up to them. Sara had prevailed upon the hotel manager to find someone to work overtime to clean their clothes, and they were ready in time for the evening meeting.

Ingeborg and Maria had talked it over in their room later that night.

"She isn't your daughter, after all," said Ingeborg, pulling the covers down and climbing into bed. "And she and Erskine are free lovers, at least Erskine is, and she says the same. Why should we care what she does?"

Maria was still fretting. "What would Miss Paul say? And she does need looking after. She's not well—look at how much weight she's lost. Like a scarecrow, now. I worry for her."

Ingeborg snorted. "Sara can take care of herself. That's a woman who knows what she wants and how to get it. Look at her. She's divorced, and her children live with their father while she has an affair with a married man and is gone for months on a crazy automobile trip. There are women would pay to change places with her." She thought for a minute. "Well, maybe not for this trip."

"Don't you think she's changed since we left San Francisco?" asked Maria, settling into bed beside Ingeborg.

"In what way?"

"She's more willing to attract attention. Did you notice how she flirted with the men when we stopped for gas today? One of them looked as if he was ready to step behind the building with her, and she might have gone with him."

Ingeborg rolled over on her side to look at Maria, and laughed. "You sound like an old grandmother," she teased. "This is America. Not like when we were growing up in Sweden, thank God. Sara looks after herself just fine. She said herself she just wants Erskine, but she's pretty and the men like her. So what if she flirts a little? And what's wrong with having some fun? We've had little enough lately." She hitched closer to Maria, slid her hand around her and pulled her close, her lips finding Maria's earlobe. "And if it gets the men to help us...." Maria laughed and snuggled into her embrace.

The road to Kansas City wound through farmland wrested from the prairie, the landscape dotted with newer frame houses crouched beside towering windmills. A handful of sod homes remained, some still occupied, judging from the smoke curling from their chimneys, and others slowly subsiding back into the earth from which they came.

The harvest was nearing the end, the coffee-colored fields stubbled with stalks of wheat and corn. Deer scavenged for the leavings and bounded away as the car drew near.

Ingeborg thought back on her conversation with Maria about Sara. It's true that Sara had changed, but Ingeborg felt different, too. In Providence she made sure her clothes were clean and modest, even if her coat was years old and her dress not in the latest fashion. But now she wore her dust-covered clothes and her sun-stained face as a badge of honor. Who cared what others saw when they looked at her? The three of them had faced dangerous roads that turned men back. She'd mended tires in the burning desert, had kept the car running. There weren't many who could have done what they had, certainly not Frances Joliffe, wherever she was now, no doubt hiding under a parasol to protect her dainty white skin.

This was what worried men, Ingeborg thought, and the anti-suffrage women, too. Who knew what mischief women could get up to when they no longer cared what people said about them, or what rules they broke? That's the change she'd seen in Sara. Less care about pleasing others, and more care for doing what she liked. Ingeborg quite preferred the new Sara to the one who mewled over Erskine and looked like a wrung-out dishrag.

Maria was more old-fashioned. Speaking in front of a crowd made her bashful and tongue-tied, but Maria read women like newspapers. One glance at their faces told her the headlines of their day, and with little time at all she could tease out the stories they'd buried in the back pages. Ingeborg connected with women over their fighting spirit, while Maria enveloped them with warmth and soothed the cuts and bruises of their souls.

Sara's suffering over Erskine, her divorce, her absence from her children, and her physical frailty had drawn Maria like a bee to a picnic. She often fussed over Sara. Was she warm enough? Too tired? Rested enough to speak? Mostly Sara seemed to enjoy the attention, and if it helped them both survive the trip, then Ingeborg was all for it. But she drew the line at becoming Sara's chaperone.

Ingeborg clung to the door frame as Maria swerved around a rock poking up through the road surface. They were coming into the outskirts of Kansas City now, houses closer together, the air heavy with smoke and with the reek of the famous stockyards, barely visible off to the west. Ingeborg gazed about with interest. The roads were bustling with motorcars of every shape and size, some electric, some belching steam or smoke. Their drivers honked impatiently and wove in and out of the rumbling wagons pulled by horses, mules, and oxen, their drivers trading insults. Solitary cowboys slouched in their saddles, looking bemused by the mechanical river through which their horses pranced and snorted in alarm.

As they weren't officially due until the following day, they entered the city without fanfare, winding through the streets toward the main business district and the Baltimore Hotel. It was brand-new, an imposing red-brick building so tall Ingeborg had to crane her head back to see the top. Maria parked Emilie by the hotel's front entrance. Uniformed bellboys trotted out to carry their baggage, which they had collected at the train station on their way by.

As they checked in, Ingeborg let her eyes travel around the ornate lobby, a two-storied affair with a balcony around the second floor, marbled columns, and a fountain plinking at its center. A gleaming grand piano stood in a corner, an elegantly attired Negro man at its keys playing lighthearted tunes. Couples strolled through the lobby arm in arm, the women in bright frocks and elaborate hats, and the men in suits and ties. The three travel-worn and sunburned travelers looked out of place amidst this splendor.

The clerk had just handed them their keys when the lobby doors opened, and Mabel came hurrying in, her forehead knotted and her jaw set in anger. When she noticed them, though, she broke into a broad smile and came over to say hello. "I'm so glad to see you!" she said, embracing them each in turn. "How were the roads today, not too bad, am I right?" She turned and scanned the lobby. "We have so much to catch up on, we can sit in that corner," she added, and began ushering them over.

Ingeborg frowned, irritated. She badly needed to pee and had been looking forward to a bath and a nap. She glanced at her companions and saw that they were equally taken aback. She was just about to protest when Sara jumped in.

"Mabel, we've come through purgatory and I, for one, am ready to drop. I simply must get some rest if I'm to make it through whatever torture you have planned for us. My heart has been racing and fluttering by turns all day."

Mabel peered at her, concerned. "I'm sorry you're not well, Sara. Should I send for a doctor?"

Sara did indeed look unwell, Ingeborg realized suddenly. She was ashen under her browned skin, with great dark bags under her eyes. Her body sagged with exhaustion. Maria edged over closer as if to catch her if she swooned. Looking at Mabel, Maria said firmly "Now is not the time for talk." Slipping her hand under her arm, she steered Sara gently toward the elevators. After a few steps she stopped and turned back to Mabel. "And send for the doctor."

Ingeborg started to follow but Mabel whispered urgently "Ingeborg! When did she become ill?"

Ingeborg turned and stared at her blankly. Sara hadn't been healthy since they'd left San Francisco. Surely Mabel understood that? "Two nights ago she walked miles in the rain and mud to get us pulled out of a mudhole," she said instead.

Mabel winced sympathetically. "Poor Sara, that's awful. I suppose my news can wait for dinner—shall we say seven thirty? There's a cafeteria next door—the food is quite good, and cheaper than the hotel. Besides," she said, grimacing, "the Baltimore prefers not to have unaccompanied women in its dining hall."

Ingeborg looked around at the opulent lobby and shook her head. "We pay their prices—we should be able to eat here. If I weren't so tired I'd tell you to reserve a table. It's 1915, for heaven's sake. Even Providence lets women dine alone. But the cafeteria will do—Maria will be happy to pay less." She agreed to carry the message to the others.

Sara didn't come down to dinner. The bewhiskered doctor, after applying his stethoscope and much peering and prodding, ordered her to stay in bed and rest. So it was just the three of them at their table in the cafeteria, a cheerful and efficient space where the staff all wore uniforms of a peculiar apple green.

As they settled down to their meals Mabel brought them up to date on the plans for the next few days, and the local situation that was causing some trouble.

Missouri was the first state they'd been in where women still couldn't vote. A statewide suffrage referendum the year before had failed by a two-to-one margin, and Kansas City suffragists were almost as conservative as the men who had voted it down. "They're all members of the National," complained Mabel, "and desperately afraid that helping the CU will unleash the hounds of social hell upon them so they won't be invited to the next ball. Two separate halls canceled my reservation for our mass meeting when someone told them we were radicals. One of them was the Athenaeum where the Women's Club meets, if you please!" Ingeborg was amused to see that Mabel, whose cool, calm facade rarely cracked, was shredding her bread roll onto her plate, viciously tearing bits off and throwing them down as if dismembering her opponents.

"No mass meeting, then?" asked Maria.

"Oh, we'll hold one all right," Mabel said grimly. "I got Frank Walsh to help me."

"Frank Walsh the labor lawyer?" asked Ingeborg, with surprise.

"He lives here," said Mabel. "And he knows Erskine, everyone seems to, so of course he was happy to help when he heard Sara was coming to town." She paused for a moment and then said drily, "He's quite the ladies' man."

"How so?" asked Maria.

"He's the sort who looks you right in the eye and smiles as if you were the one person on earth he'd hoped to see," said Mabel. "And then he presses your hand a bit too long, sidles up right next to you, and drops his voice as if you were already lovers." She shook her head and wrinkled her nose.

Ingeborg rolled her eyes, and Maria clucked her tongue disapprovingly. "What did you do?" Maria asked.

"I looked around for the door," said Mabel, "And edged in that direction. His secretary is a fine old girl and I hoped she'd come to my aid if he attacked me. He told me how impressed he was with me, and how it must be lonely traveling as I did. He knew this cozy little restaurant that set a fine table, where I could tell him all about it." She choked a bit. "This while he'd picked up my hand and was stroking it. He would help me, and then I could help him. He had an arrangement with the owner, he said, about a room in the back."

"He didn't!" gasped Maria.

Ingeborg wrinkled her nose and said something unflattering in Swedish.

"Oh, yes he did!" Mabel retorted. "I didn't know what he'd try next, so I snatched my hand away and flew out to his secretary. I was getting desperate over the hall, I can tell you, or I'd have set him on his heels."

"Did she help?"

Mabel nodded. "She looked him right in the eye and said, 'May I place a call for you, Mr. Walsh?' He grinned like a schoolboy caught in mischief and told her to phone his friend who owns the Glendale Building, and within a matter of minutes we were back in business."

"What did you do then?" asked Ingeborg.

Mabel laughed. "As soon as the deal was struck I thanked him, said I had an engagement with Mrs. Ess, the leader of the National here, and took off."

Though it happened all the time, Ingeborg was disappointed to hear this. All the union people loved Frank Walsh. His boyish appearance hid a sharp legal mind and the soul of a prizefighter, and he was famous for defending workers' safety, fair wages, and equal rights for women. Working people cheered when President Wilson had made him the head of a new Commission on Industrial Relations to look into the increasing violence in the mills and mines. Newspapers gleefully published details about his tough questioning of captains of industry. After the massacre in Ludlow that Rolf had narrowly escaped, Walsh had summoned John D. Rockefeller himself to take the stand. As part owner of the Colorado coalfields, everyone guessed he was behind the massacre, and they loved it when Walsh went after him.

It was too bad that Walsh, who stood up for the weak and defenseless, would also use his power to win favors from Mabel when she needed his help. Who else could women turn to if not men like Walsh? All the more reason for women to vote, Ingeborg thought.

"Isn't he having an affair with Doris Stevens—the one who works for Miss Paul?" Maria asked suddenly. Ingeborg and Mabel stared at her in surprise.

"How on earth do you know that?" asked Ingeborg.

Maria wore a sheepish smile. "At the Exposition, before we left, I was talking to some of the other organizers. You were doing something with the car, Ingeborg, so you didn't hear this. One of them…Vivian?" She looked at Mabel for confirmation.

"Vivian Pierce?" asked Mabel.

"That's right, Vivian Pierce, she told me he was coming to the Exposition, and she planned to sneak off with him and have 'one mild little riot,' I think was how she put it. But she also told me that he and Doris were lovers."

Ingeborg grinned at her. "You know all the juicy gossip," she said.

Maria smiled back. "I just listen," she said. "And I don't judge." She turned back to Mabel. "Isn't he married?"

Mabel laughed shortly. "Does it matter? Of course he is. He had a photograph of his wife and flock of children right there on his desk." She shrugged. "No wonder he assumed I'd sleep with him; it seems half the CU organizers already have. But it worked out. We have our hall and he's agreed to speak at our meeting. We have another problem, though." She looked around to make sure they weren't being overheard and leaned in closer. "It's about the petitions," she said quietly.

Ingeborg looked at Mabel, eyebrows raised. They'd been faithfully collecting signatures and bringing them into their hotel every night. When they'd express shipped their luggage ahead they'd sent the petitions, too, and had found them waiting when they'd arrived in Kansas City.

"What about them?" asked Maria.

"Just how many do you have in your possession, do you think?" asked Mabel.

Maria and Ingeborg looked at each other, confused. "We don't have them all," said Ingeborg, slowly. "We started with a pile about this high," opening her thumb and forefinger about three inches. "And added maybe a thousand since we left." She stopped and thought about it. "They're in a canvas satchel and not that heavy. Sara can still sling it over her shoulder easily. But we never had them all."

Mabel gnawed on a finger. "That's what I was afraid of," she said.

Baffled, Maria said, "Surely someone has the others, the half-million signatures from the Exposition? What did they do with those?"

"I don't know," said Mabel, uncomfortably, "I wasn't in charge of the booth. Doris Stevens was."

Ingeborg stared at her. "Are you saying," she said slowly, "that we've been claiming there are a half-million signatures, but we only have what we're carrying with us? They must still be at the Exposition. Or maybe they shipped them to headquarters?"

Mabel shrugged helplessly. "You'd think."

"We're in trouble," said Ingeborg. "Some reporter is bound to ask to see them."

"I'm afraid one already has," said Mabel quietly, picking up a fork and pushing food around her plate. Maria and Ingeborg fell silent, looking at her.

"The half-million signatures," Maria asked. "Who counted them?"

"I don't know," said Mabel. "I wasn't out there any longer than you were." She raised her eyes to look at them. "It seems to be Alice who first used that figure."

They stared at her, and then Ingeborg leaned in close to Mabel. "Miss Paul *made that up?*" she hissed. Her mind reeled.

"We don't know if she did!" Mabel said hastily. "I've written to headquarters and to our office at the Exposition to see if they have the missing sheets. We must be careful no one else hears of this."

"What did you tell the reporter?" asked Maria.

"I said that to preserve them from the weather we shipped most of them on ahead." Mabel pushed her plate away and leaned her elbows on the table, a lock of hair escaping from the pins under her hat and falling over her cheek. Wearily, she lowered her head and massaged her temples with her fingers.

Ingeborg's thoughts spun. She raised her hand and covered her mouth, thinking back to the CU booth at the Exposition. There had been visitors stopping by that booth all day, every day. Surely many of them had signed. But perhaps not. Or perhaps the CU hadn't been careful about keeping all the pages together. "She made up a number that would sound impressive," she said, slowly. She was torn between anger at Miss Paul and a grudging respect for her brazen gamble to inflate how many signatures the CU had. It made sense—as long as they didn't get caught. A state like New York or California could easily produce forty or fifty thousand signatures all on its own, so bringing that number from the woman voters of the West wouldn't excite any attention. But half a million. That was something to sit up and take notice of.

"And what happens when we get to Washington, and they aren't there?" Ingeborg wanted to know.

"We'll let headquarters figure that out," said Mabel, absently. "Maybe they'll find them." Despite her calm tone, she looked more worried and harried than Ingeborg had ever seen her. They sat in silence for a long stretch, each with her own thoughts.

Finally, Maria stirred and sighed. "We can't fix that now," she said. "Tell us about the next few days."

Mabel roused herself and rummaged in her satchel, pulling out a sheet of paper. "Tomorrow we motor over to Kansas City, to the library. The high school band will play, and we'll be greeted by Mayor Green, Senator William Thompson, and Representative Joseph Taggart." She looked up at them. "As it's Kansas, they're eager to show their support for suffrage and outdo their larger neighbor across the river, so I've been assured that the local suffragists will turn out in force." She returned to her schedule. "There will be a dinner and speeches, of course, and we'll stay at the Grand Hotel. The following day, a parade of motorcars will assemble in Kansas City and escort us back to the Kansas City Hall on the Missouri side." She stopped and looked up, noting the confusion in her companions' faces. "Is something wrong?"

Maria looked pained. "Why are they both named Kansas City?" she asked. "It makes no sense, like naming both your sons Henry."

Mabel laughed. "Some wisdom known only to the men who founded them, no doubt. It is confusing, but they seem to manage. But you understand the suffragists from the Missouri side will come over to escort us back, and we must arrive at City Hall by one o'clock to be greeted by Mayor Jost. After some remarks there, we've organized a deputation to Senator James Reed, another Democrat but a fierce opponent of votes for women and of nearly every other progressive movement you can name. We're not likely to change his mind, but we must try.

"From there we go to the Glendale Club for the mass meeting at four o'clock, where Frank Walsh and Representative William Borland will also speak. Borland is a Democrat. They'll sign the petition. A dinner for suffrage workers at six o'clock will be followed by a flying squadron and street speaking."

"When's our rest day?" Ingeborg wanted to know.

Mabel kept her gaze on the sheet of paper in her hand. "You'll have one."

Ingeborg waited, but when Mabel volunteered no more information she asked "When?"

Mabel sighed and fidgeted. "We go to Topeka, the capital, the next day. Then you'll rest."

Ingeborg and Maria traded looks. "I hope you have a plan for when Sara gives out," said Ingeborg. "I'm not sure she can manage this."

Maria spoke up. "Perhaps in the future you could give us a rest day first, when we arrive in the city, so we can recover. Sara is really not strong. What would people say if she took ill and died on this trip?"

"I'm sure it won't come to that," Mabel said quickly. "Sara's a veteran of many campaigns. She can handle this one, too."

"But you're the one making up the schedule. What if she dies because you worked her to death?" Ingeborg asked, insisting on an answer. "What will you do then?"

"Well, she'll be a martyr, I suppose," said Mabel, somewhat flippantly. She rolled her eyes as she said it, as if making light of the possibility.

Ingeborg shook her head, startled. She looked over at Maria, who had gone completely still, and then back at Mabel. "A martyr?" she repeated.

"Ingeborg, this is like war. When we send our men to war, they know they could die fighting for freedom. We hope it won't happen, but it could. Why should winning suffrage be any different?"

Ingeborg shot another look over at Maria, who was staring at Mabel as if she'd taken leave of her senses. "We're women," Ingeborg replied. "We don't kill people, Mabel."

"No one's asking you to kill anyone," said Mabel, heatedly. She sat upright in her chair, her slender body radiating tension. She spoke harshly. "But Alice says if more women were willing to commit themselves to suffrage, work at it night and day, pushing themselves to exhaustion as she has done, as we're all doing, that we'd have won our rights long ago. Instead, women treat suffrage as just another club they belong to, and so we poke along at a snail's pace. She has a point."

Ingeborg considered this. It was true not many women devoted themselves to suffrage alone. She was sure one reason the bosses resisted calls for shorter weeks was to give their workers less time to organize. But if working women could squeeze any time from their jobs and families, they often chose labor unions. For them, suffrage was like the mirages they'd seen in the Nevada desert. Looking ahead, you'd see what looked like cool water and soft grass, but it always just turn out to be sand and scrub. The same with suffrage—once they'd won, they'd still have to campaign for new laws, sympathetic candidates, and for the party they thought might deliver on its promises. All of which were led by men, anyway, who couldn't always be trusted to vote as they promised or who, like Frank Walsh, wanted something in return. Over time, having the vote might improve women's lot, but it was less certain compared to winning a wage increase, shortening the work week, or trying to keep their men from dying in the coal mines.

Maria spoke then. "It's true what you say, but many women have other things they must do." She smiled at Mabel. "And perhaps we shouldn't kill off the ones who are willing to work hard."

Mabel smiled back. "Very true, Maria. We don't want to lose Sara, or you two either. We should retire for the evening; tomorrow will be a long day."

"Another long day," Ingeborg murmured.

CHAPTER EIGHT

OCTOBER 21, 1915

ngeborg gazed across the table at Frank Walsh, pleased to be dining with the famous lawyer. He'd insisted on hosting them for dinner at Kansas City's finest restaurant on their return from Topeka. That whole thing had been a disaster and she was eager to forget it. Womanizer or no, he was a generous host, and an amusing one. Sara sat on his right, Mabel on his left, and Maria and Ingeborg across the table from them.

Frank, as he'd insisted they call him, was a gifted storyteller and seemed to have an inexhaustible supply of tales. He'd kept them laughing through the caviar, the delicate consommé, and roast lamb with mashed potatoes and a heavenly gravy. Now he poured the last of the wine in their glasses as they waited for dessert and coffee to arrive.

Maria was unused to wine, though she had drunk less than the rest of them, and Ingeborg could see her listing in her chair like an old boat, images of fluffy white beds circling in her eyes. Ingeborg ignored her; she herself felt energized, stimulated by the conversation and the wine and being in Frank's presence.

Frank sat back in his chair and beamed around the table at them, dropping his hand down on his lap and inching over to place it on

Sara's thigh. Sara brushed it off without comment. "How did it go in Topeka?" he asked.

Ingeborg stiffened, feeling the warmth of the meal slip away. "We didn't make it," she said. Maria's eyes opened wide and she sat upright, looking nervously around the table.

"Not at all?" Frank asked, astonished. "What the hell happened?"

"It was the first time we haven't arrived for a meeting," said Sara. Her eyes flicked to Frank's face and then dropped down to her hands, which were twisted in her large cloth napkin. Suddenly aware of everyone's gaze, she made a show of shaking the napkin out and smoothing it over her lap. Her voice had an edge to it. "We took some wrong turns, and then we had a flat tire. It took ages to fix it."

Ingeborg narrowed her eyes and shot Sara a dirty look. It was true that repairing the flat had taken a long time. She wasn't sure why, maybe the cold air, but several times when she pumped up the tube the patch just blew. It hadn't helped to have Sara fidgeting around and asking every two minutes if she was done yet and why it was taking so long.

They were already late due to having been lost for some time before realizing they were on the wrong road. They'd stopped for directions, at a small shack squatting in a ratty cornfield with children spilling out into the yard, but the mother had gone to help a neighbor, so the children had to fetch their father from the back field where he was mending a fence, and they could see him walking over the furrows toward them, a mere dot moving so slowly that Sara commenced muttering and dancing about with impatience. At length she snapped, "Oh, for God's sake, let's just drive to him, it will be at least another half hour before he reaches us." So they'd jumped into the car, and Maria maneuvered it around the chickens, children, puppies, and flotsam littering the yard, probably picking up the offending nail in the process, and bumped over the field to meet him.

The farmer was deliberate of thought, and painstakingly recited every turn and fork in the road, every major and minor landmark, until he got to the turn the travelers already half-suspected they'd gotten wrong. As soon as he came out with that information they thanked him and climbed back into the car, bumped back over the furrows, and resumed their journey. It was only a few miles later that

Ingeborg heard the slap of the flaccid tire on the hard roadbed and, despite Sara's pleas to just continue driving on the rim, had told Maria to pull over.

Ingeborg wasn't superstitious, but she was inclined to think the very devil was in the tube that day. The patch just wouldn't hold. By the time she'd bolted the tire on and Maria had pointed Emilie's nose toward Topeka, careening along the road at a furious speed, they were all stiff with worry and fear that they were too late. Maria had crouched over the wheel with her eyes locked on the road, moving only when she was forced to shift.

Worse, Ingeborg could feel the telltale prickle of a heat storm climbing up her back. Soon she was mopping sweat from her brow and neck, jaw clenched and almost exploding with irritation. Once the heat subsided, her damp underclothes clung clammily to her skin.

So when Sara began wailing from the back seat about how late they were, and they never should have taken that road by the cornfield, as if every road around here didn't run by a cornfield, and Maria shouldn't have driven over a nail, and Ingeborg should have fixed the tire faster, and how this trip was going to be the death of her, Ingeborg's fragile self-control snapped, and she whipped around to snarl at Sara, "I'm going to kill you myself before this trip is over! Shut the hell up!"

Sara had whimpered and pressed herself back into the seat cushions, and they'd continued on in grim silence, Ingeborg's words hanging over all of them like an evil, foul-smelling vapor. When they finally pulled up in front of the capitol in Topeka only Mabel remained, pacing back and forth across the steps, waiting for them and frantic with worry. Everyone else had gone home. She'd spoken for two hours, summoning up every suffrage lecture she'd ever delivered or heard, weaving them together on the spot to keep her increasingly chilly and dispirited audience entertained. After an hour, Governor Capper, who had waited patiently for them to arrive, declared he had business to attend to and went off with his staff. The rest of the audience had slowly drifted away.

There was nothing to do but turn around and drive back to Kansas City in cold silence, each with her own thoughts. Without speaking it was assumed they would go their own ways to dinner and an early bed, but a message from Frank had been waiting for them, insisting on hosting them for dinner.

Mabel spoke up, eager to soothe away the day's indignities. "These things happen when you travel," she said. "It was unfortunate, since we had the governor there, but everyone knows motorcars are unreliable. He was quite gracious about it."

Sara sensibly remained silent. Ingeborg had been itching to ask about the Industrial Relations hearings that Frank was leading, and now seemed a good time to change the subject. She asked Frank if he thought they would change anything, in the end. Frank fell quiet, his boyish face grave as he considered his answer.

"I often ask myself that," he said slowly. "The hearings have exposed how workers are abused, the power the rich industrialists wield over their lives, how they work in filth and are paid starvation wages. But the facts don't matter when there's money involved. As long as politicians are in the pay of the Rockefellers of the world, I'm afraid we'll continue to see workers shot, and the National Guard called out to end strikes." He picked up his wine glass and drained it, lowered it deliberately to the tablecloth, and blotted his lips with his napkin.

The waiter approached, balancing a large tray with their coffee; right behind him was another bearing plates of apple tart, a hotel specialty, according to Frank. He waited for them to distribute the dishes, and then spoke again.

"We need more agitators, more than we need lawmakers and law governors. More people, at every level, calling for economic justice. The power of massed capital continues to grow, and we must stop it if we hope our country will survive." He smiled. "I like to say of my commission work that for the past two years I have been merely a lawyer, with a struggling democracy for a client."

"But the money is everywhere," said Sara, her voice low and tired. "Sometimes I despair...."

"We must do this a step at a time, patiently," said Frank. "Trying to go a mile rather than one foot at a time will lead to disaster. And we must look to our leading lights, past and present. Abe Lincoln once observed that, while many labor, others enjoy the fruits of labor without having done anything to deserve it. He said 'This is wrong and should not continue. To secure each laborer the whole product of his labor, or as nearly as possible, is a worthy subject of any good government.' When I feel dispirited, I remember Mr. Lincoln's words and find the heart to go on."

"We need women's votes," said Ingeborg. "Men can't do this alone."

"No, we surely can't," agreed Frank. "Women and labor and agitators of every stripe. Together we must find our allies and elect them. Men like Bill Borland, who spoke yesterday at your mass meeting."

"I agree," said Mabel. "A good, thoughtful man, very supportive of suffrage."

Ingeborg sipped her coffee and recalled the contrast between Representative Borland's remarks and their encounter with Missouri Senator James Reed. The two men couldn't have been more different. Borland had a pleasant face, with the broad forehead and open gaze of a man of much intelligence and education. He spoke movingly of the great work the country had before it and how essential it was to engage women—and their votes—in this work. Reed, on the other hand, peered out with sharp eyes under the low bench of his forehead. He was ill-informed, seemed perpetually angry, and had been dismissive of their demands to the point of rudeness. "Not like Reed," she said.

Frank laughed. "No, Reed is another man entirely. He's a creature of the party machine—wouldn't be where he is now without its help. He'll vote as he's told by the bosses. We're old foes, he and I."

"Women's votes won't be enough," said Maria. They all turned to her, surprised. She had been so quiet they'd almost forgotten she was there. She pushed on. "For true change, women must be in every office and position."

"Maria's right, of course, but how do we go about that work?" asked Mabel. "I get overwhelmed, at times, as if we're emptying the ocean with a spoon." She looked over at Frank. "Why do you think men are so opposed to women's equality?"

Frank shrugged. "Ask ten men and they'll give you ten different reasons." He pushed his dessert plate away and sat back in his chair. "At bottom, I think there are two different types of people in this world.

Those who embrace change and those who fear and oppose it—chiefly because they suspect that the benefits they enjoy today may be lost if things change too radically. That's why they're called *conservatives*." He smiled at Mabel, and then looked around the table. "I might ask you the same question. Why do so many women oppose suffrage, or at least refuse to work for it?"

"I ask myself that daily," said Mabel. "We'd have won suffrage decades ago if every woman had demanded it. I think we're reared to be submissive, and to do as men tell us. To see ourselves through their eyes. Once we're trained that way, it's hard to think differently, and it starts in the cradle." She shrugged. "And the laws don't favor women's independence."

"Too many babies," said Maria. "Women spend their lives tending children they have, already pregnant with the next."

"Ignorance," said Sara slowly. "We see the results of sending girls to school—and to college, too. When we're educated we demand more." She sounded weary beyond measure. Ingeborg looked over at her, realizing she'd barely made eye contact with Sara since their fight earlier in the day. Now she could see that Sara was drooping in her chair, her chin lowered almost to her chest. She'd eaten no more than two bites of the apple tart. She looked as though the merest nudge would send her toppling sideways.

Ingeborg knew it was late and they should get to bed, but she was reluctant to end the evening. "Too busy," she chimed in. "Women work all day in the factory, and then go home to cook, clean, and sew. Nurse their families when they're ill. How do they find the time to agitate?"

"Many reasons," said Frank. "When you find the key to convincing all women to support suffrage I'd be obliged if you'd share it with me— perhaps I can use the same arguments with the men. But you see why I say change won't come overnight. We have to approach it from many different directions. And slowly. We're not calling for a revolution, whether in labor or in suffrage. Conservatives can unleash a multitude of fear and ignorance on those who push too far, too fast."

Suddenly, Sara uttered a breathy sigh and slumped sideways, slowly toppling to the floor in a dead faint. Her companions sprang up in alarm and rushed to her, as did several other diners and most of the waiters. Soon a throng of people stood around her, all offering differing opinions as to what should happen next.

"Keep her still," said one.

"Move her to her room," said another.

"Straighten her legs and lie her on her back!"

"Roll her on her side, so she doesn't choke!"

Maria knelt by Sara's head, feeling her brow and calling her name. Sara groaned and began to come around. A rumpled, weary-looking man who said he was a doctor pushed through the crowd. He'd just finished dining and was on his way out of the restaurant when he heard the commotion and turned to see the crowd forming around Sara. Gruffly, he looked up at the spectators and told them to go back to their seats. "The show's over, folks. Give us room." Reluctantly, they turned away and went back to their tables, craning their necks to see what was happening.

The doctor, who said his name was Gibbons, quickly checked Sara's pulse, peered into her eyes and throat, and listened to her breath. Sara began moving her limbs and attempted to sit up. He urged her to lie still and, looking up at Frank, he asked "What happened?"

"We'd just finished dinner and she fainted. No warning."

"She hasn't been well, and she's overtired," explained Mabel. "She's one of the suffrage envoys you may have read about. Poor thing, she's pushed herself to her limit." Ingeborg shot a look at Mabel. Hadn't she and Maria been warning her of this very thing? Who was it set up meeting after meeting and gave them no time to rest?

"Her heart is weak," said Maria, looking stricken herself. " I don't know what's wrong, but it gives her a lot of trouble. She complains of it often."

Dr. Gibbons looked around for the head waiter, who was hovering nearby, and asked him to bring a rolling chair so they could get Sara to her room. By this time Sara was fully alert, looking up at all the faces looking down at her. "Did I faint?" she asked, her voice tired and thin so they had to strain to hear.

"Yes," said Mabel. "But the doctor is here, and we're going to move you to your room in a rolling chair."

"I can walk, let me walk," said Sara, and she struggled to rise.

"You lie still, ma'am," said Dr. Gibbons. "We don't need you toppling over again."

Sara's eyes found Frank. "Don't tell Erskine," she said. "I don't want him worrying."

Frank frowned at her. "Now Sara, I think he should know—"

Sara fought to sit up and the doctor held her down. "Frank, please! I'll write him, I promise. Just don't wire him now."

Dr. Gibbons looked up at Frank and shook his head no, warning him to drop it. A bellhop arrived with the rolling chair, and he and the doctor lifted Sara carefully to her feet and deposited her in it. Sara's face was pale. She drooped back against the chair cushions, her face tilted down and her eyes closed, hands lying limp in her lap. Trailed by Mabel and the doctor, the bellhop headed for the elevators.

Ingeborg looked over at Frank and then at Maria, unsure what to say or do. They were standing in an awkward threesome, still eyed by the diners at nearby tables. Maria was peering anxiously after the wheelchair, watching as the elevator doors opened and swallowed Sara and her attendants. Frank regarded Ingeborg gravely.

"Please sit down," he said. "I won't keep you much longer but I need to understand what's going on." They took their seats and he looked at them. "Has this happened before?"

"She's never fainted like this," said Ingeborg, "at least since we left San Francisco."

"She isn't strong, and we're worried about her," said Maria. "We've had little rest. You wouldn't think riding in the car would be so tiring, but the roads are often bad and though the car is very good, still it bounces."

"And she gives all the speeches, goes to receptions and dinners," Ingeborg added.

"Has she seen a doctor?" Frank asked.

"Of course," said Ingeborg. "They always tell her she must rest." She shrugged. "And then we get back in the car and drive to the next city."

"She's going to need some time," said Frank. "Can the two of you finish the trip alone? Or at least go on without her until she's stronger?"

"Of course," said Ingeborg. She felt a guilty stirring of excitement; maybe this would be her chance. If Sara couldn't go on then someone would have to make speeches.

Frank's brow furrowed, and he asked "Wasn't there another gal traveling with you? I could swear I'd read two envoys left San Francisco."

Maria shook her head. "She quit in Sacramento. She wasn't well either."

Ingeborg blurted out, with more than a touch of irritation. "She's supposed to rejoin us, though who knows if she will? But she's young and pretty, a socialite. The CU hopes she'll attract wealthy donors, so they pretend she's still with us, or has just gone for a few days."

Frank laughed. "So here you are, old enough to be their mothers, and you're the ones still standing. Why is that?"

Ingeborg grinned. "Swedes are tough," she said simply. "Our lives have never been easy. We know how to survive."

Frank laughed again. "I can see that." He grew grave. "I'm sorry Sara's ill, and I hope she makes it. I know Erskine's crazy about her. But it looks to me as if you're going to have to take it from here."

"They don't like us to make the speeches," said Ingeborg, flatly. "They'll cancel the trip before they'd let that happen. We aren't young. We don't look pretty, and we don't talk pretty." She gave a short laugh.

Maria jumped in. "It isn't just that," she reminded Ingeborg. "We live in Rhode Island; we can't speak for a voting state like Sara does."

Frank shook his head sympathetically. "Sorry to hear that," he said. "I think you have a story to tell, all the same." He sighed, sat back in his chair, and signaled to the waiter for the bill. "But this fight you're in, as with labor, it's bigger than you, bigger than all of us. The very heart and soul of our democracy is at stake, and our foes are as powerful and dangerous as those our forefathers faced in the Revolution. They'll stop at nothing to defeat us. And so we must be strong, and stick together. If we let them pit us against each other, they'll win."

Ingeborg considered this. Frank was right, of course, and if she didn't believe it deep down, then she and Maria would have put Sara on a train in some cowpoke town and gone on with the trip alone. But there were so many twists and turns that navigating them seemed as hard as crossing the Nevada desert at night. Which roads would bring them most directly to victory? Which were just side trails that would lose them in the wilderness, or turn them back the way they'd come? Whose rights, whose feelings, would be run over along the way?

Did it matter how they won as long as they did, in the end, win suffrage for women and justice for working people? Given the great work they'd taken on did she have a claim to be treated as more than just the hired help? What difference did it make, really? She couldn't douse this constant flame of resentment, stop herself from comparing constantly how she and Maria were treated. But it wasn't just about her, she reminded herself. It was about all prejudice. Like the sign at the train station in Pueblo that told certain groups to wait in a small, cramped waiting room out of sight of the whites in charge. Was she supposed to ignore that?

She closed her eyes. Her head ached with the wine, and with exhaustion, and with spinning through these arguments she'd had with herself countless times since she'd begun this trip. Suddenly she wished someone would load her into a chair and wheel her back to her room, put her to bed with tender hands and gently wipe her face with a soft cloth dipped in warm, scented water. She was tired of getting bumped and bruised and turned around.

She opened her eyes and looked at Frank, who was signing the bill the waiter had brought over. "I know you're right," she said. "But it's hard to drive past one injustice on your way to fight another."

"I'm not saying you should ignore them, or pretend they don't exist," he said. "Point them out. But don't expect everyone to agree with you, even those you thought were on your side." He smiled. "I've had plenty of experience with that. You should have seen what people wrote about me when I roughed up young Rockefeller at the commission hearings."

Ingeborg laughed. "I'm surprised you weren't tarred and feathered."

"I didn't care a fig then, and I don't know," said Frank. "Some rules are meant to be broken, especially when they only serve the rich. The trick is to break 'em in service to your cause, not just for the sake of breaking them."

"I'll remember," said Ingeborg. She rose to her feet. "Thank you for dinner," she said. Maria pushed back her chair and stood beside her.

Frank rose and came around the table to shake their hands. "Best of luck to you both. Stay the course. The CU needs courageous women like you. If you see Mabel, tell her to stop by and see me before she leaves town. I'll help anyway I can."

When they got to their room Maria sank wearily onto the bed. "I'm too tired to get into my nightgown," she yawned. "Maybe I'll just sleep like this." She let herself fall backwards and closed her eyes.

"Not in my bed you won't," said Ingeborg. "Come, sleepyhead, I'll help you." She stood by Maria's feet and unlaced her boots, pulling them off and tossing them in the corner of the room. "Don't you dare go to sleep yet!" she said in a mock threatening tone.

Maria issued a pretend snore, and then opened her eyes. "Do you think Sara's all right? Will she be able to travel tomorrow?"

Ingeborg held out her hands and Maria grabbed them, letting herself be hauled to her feet. Ingeborg shrugged as she unbuttoned Maria's dress and helped her out of it. Who knew? She really didn't wish Sara ill but in some ways it would be nice not to have the daily aggravation of her company. But she didn't want to think about that tonight. "I've had enough of Sara for one day," was all she said. "We'll sort it out in the morning. Whatever happens." She rummaged in Maria's bag and found her nightgown, helped her into it and gave her a long hug and a quick kiss, and then turned her around and gave her a gentle push toward the bed.

"Go," said Ingeborg. "I'll be right there." But by the time she slid in under the covers Maria was already asleep. Ingeborg quickly followed.

CHAPTER NINE

OCTOBER 26, 1915

Ingeborg woke the next morning with pain radiating through her skull from a tight knot behind her eyeballs. The skin of her throat felt glued together and she could only breathe, painfully, through her nose. She groaned. Was she ill? Maybe she was sick like Sara. She inched her head sideways on the pillow to see if Maria was awake. Maria was snoring lightly, but her wrinkled brow and wincing expression suggested she was similarly afflicted. Ingeborg let her head roll back on the pillow. All three of them had come down with the grippe! What would happen now? Mabel would have to manage on her own. She drifted into a snoozy dream of Dr. Gibbons leaning over her and gravely saying she must spend at least three days in bed, eat nourishing soups, and under no circumstances get back in the car. He would give her some powders for her pounding headache. As she was snuggling back into blankets, trying in vain for a comfortable position on the pillow for her throbbing head, Maria woke with a snort and sat up in bed, putting her hands to her temples.

"Ugh," she said in Swedish. "My head hurts."

"We're sick," said Ingeborg. "Like Sara. Stay in bed."

Maria turned and looked at Ingeborg and huffed with irritation. "We're not sick. It was the wine," she said. "Damn that Frank Walsh."

Ingeborg groaned again and pressed her hands to her forehead. "You're right." She sat up slowly and swung her feet over the side of the bed. Her stomach churned briefly and threatened to heave, but then settled down. Groping her way to the nightstand she poured glasses of water from the pitcher, handed one to Maria, and sat down on the bed to drink hers. She took several swallows, feeling the cool liquid run down her throat, imagining it pushing out into her parched body. Better. Bending over slightly, she leaned her elbows on her knees and inspected her toes, peeking out from under her nightgown. There was a time when waking up to pounding headaches was her daily routine, until Maria had told her to stop or move out. She'd been a bitter drunk, finding fault with everything and everyone. The alcohol loosened her tongue and she said things she regretted afterward—when she remembered them at all. She seldom drank now, but sometimes, when the mood took her and someone offered....

She turned to look at Maria, who was getting dressed, fingers fumbling with her buttons. "We have to see if Sara can travel. Come on, get dressed, Ingeborg."

Ingeborg wanted to ask if she'd misbehaved at last night's dinner but could detect no sign in Maria's face or tone that she had, so she drew on her clothes and packed her bags. Today they would drive to Marysville, in the northeast corner of Kansas, their last stop before crossing the border into Nebraska. She and Maria had gone over the route and it was a long drive, close to 150 miles. They'd need to get started soon.

They found Mabel waiting for them in the lobby. She'd peeked in on Sara earlier and found her sleeping peacefully. After he'd examined her last night the doctor decided she was just overtired. He'd given her a sleeping powder and thought that if she rested today she would be able to travel the next.

"I'm afraid the two of you will have to go on by yourselves," Mabel told them. "There's a congressman in Marysville, and we've been advised he'll only be there one more night before returning to Washington. We need his signature."

"What about Sara?" asked Maria.

"She'll catch the train to Marysville tomorrow morning and will arrive by midafternoon. You can meet her there. Then it's only about fifty miles to Lincoln." Mabel looked at each of them, her face radiating gratitude. "You two are so strong and capable. We're so fortunate that we can rely on you. You'll have most of tomorrow in Marysville to rest. But we must get this signature and tonight is the only time."

Mabel was leaving for Lincoln within the hour and would be traveling ahead of them for several days. They'd next see her in Chicago in a little over a week. They said good-bye, and Ingeborg and Maria ate a hurried breakfast in the cafeteria next door before loading their bags in Emilie and heading out.

Once they left the city behind the road snaked through a monotonous landscape, corn and wheat fields quilting the land where tall prairie grass had once stood. The sky was equally flat, clouds low and leaden and still, pressing down from the sky. It was chilly, with a hint of rain.

Ingeborg's headache was abating, and she was happy to have some time alone with Maria, to let things cool down between her and Sara. This trip was unlike anything else she'd ever done. The hours in the car ought to have given her plenty of time for thinking, but she was constantly distracted—by things they saw, keeping an ear tuned to Emilie, and the chorus of complaints from her own body. Whether they spoke or remained silent, rode in harmony or in chilly irritation, Maria and Sara were also a constant presence.

Her thoughts came now in fractured bursts, events and emotions and images sliding together like a kaleidoscope. Sometimes, now, she had trouble pairing events with the proper city. On a few occasions she'd woken to a dark room and had trouble remembering where she was, the name of their hotel, or even where the door to the hallway lay. She was keyed up and exhausted all at once, forced to keep moving but longing to sit in one place and let the river of events swirl around and past her.

In Missouri they'd had a taste of the reactions they could expect now that they'd left the equal suffrage states behind. As they motored in their flying squadron up and down Kansas City's broad main avenues, pulling over to the curb to let suffrage speakers stand and address any small crowd of people, boys heckled them, telling them to go home and cook supper, do the dishes. Once a well-dressed woman, her children gathered about her, shouted at them, "Who's going to care for my children when I'm voting?" Such narrow-minded fusspots. Who cared for that woman's children now when she went to the market, or to visit her sick mother? As if women's equality should hinge on something so small and solvable. It was no different in Providence, she had to admit, but she'd grown used to traveling through equal suffrage states where people thought women voting was a good thing.

Providence. She shot a side glance at Maria, who was steering Emilie one-handed over the flat roads, left elbow resting casually on the doorframe. She could be out for a Sunday drive, thought Ingeborg. Her face was relaxed, and she hummed a little tune under her breath.

Ingeborg scratched her nose and tucked a bit of loose hair back under her hat. She didn't want to worry Maria but she was feeling nervous about what their reception would be in Providence. By rights they should return as heroines, enjoy a big fuss from local suffragists. But it might be prudent for her to stay out of the newspapers—let Sara have the spotlight, and Frances, if she was back by then. With some luck no one would recall what she'd done in last summer's riots.

* * *

Back in June Providence mill workers had gone out on strike when, almost overnight, local store owners had doubled the price of flour and sugar.

"What can I do?" one shopkeeper had told her. She noticed his pudgy hands couldn't even reach each other around his big belly. He had no trouble putting food on his own table, that was clear. "The war in Europe—it's driving the prices up."

"America isn't even in the war," Ingeborg told him.

"But it might be soon," he'd whined.

Everyone knew they were just taking advantage of the helpless workers trying to feed their families. Factory owners refused to raise wages and—incredibly—took advantage of workers' desperation by demanding even higher production. The strike was peaceful enough at first, but within a few days it turned ugly. Each day had brought a new demonstration and fiery speeches, as well as attacks from both hired thugs and the police.

The press dubbed the protests the "Macaroni Wars" because most of the workers were Italian and used flour in their bread and pasta. But the workers were dead serious about it. They endured so much—families squeezed into tiny flats, neighborhood streets thick with mud and refuse, cruel hours at the mills, and still they were barely surviving. They were at their breaking point. If they couldn't afford to feed their families, then they couldn't—they wouldn't—work.

Ingeborg had been amazed at how much organizing it took to keep workers idle. They needed soup kitchens to feed the hungry. They had to plan the next day's rallies and speakers, and try to get permits for their marches. Find care for those injured by police truncheons, or by the flying rocks hurled by young boys into the melees that marches sometimes turned into. Everyone wanted to help, but that meant there had to be a plan and someone to organize them, and they either had too much help or not enough.

Several times Ingeborg herself had mounted a rickety stage to speak to the workers. Looking out over the crowd she felt such love for them all, white, black or brown, Italian or Swedish. Wherever they hailed from, she told them, they were all Americans now. They had rights, and if they stayed strong and united, they could break the backs of the mill owners. She always ended with a few IWW songs from the little red book, and hearing the songs rise up brought tears to her eyes. The chorus from a Joe Hill song, "There Is Power in the Union" captured exactly how she felt.

> There is pow'r, there is pow'r in a band of working folk,
> When they stand hand in hand;
> That's a pow'r, that's a pow'r that must rule in every land;
> One Industrial Union Grand.

For days, hardly sleeping, she'd supported the strike. The marches and meetings grew angrier, and then workers' fury boiled over. Clashes with the police grew more frequent and violent.

Ingeborg had begun suspecting informers everywhere. She'd insisted on sleeping in a storeroom the police might overlook if they searched for her, and she made sure she came and went at odd hours when their neighbors would be less likely to see her.

"Don't go today," Maria had begged her. "Stay home and rest. They can spare you for one day."

"I have to go!" Ingeborg had insisted, struggling into her dress. "You don't understand, Maria. I'm the only one who can keep the strikers safe from the police."

Ingeborg squirmed in her seat now, blushing at the memory. She could see now that she might have seemed a bit unhinged, although at the time there had been many convincing signs that her presence was somehow crucial. She still thought Maria had overreacted, but perhaps Ingeborg had given her some cause. Once, she'd caught sight of her own face in a mirror and was surprised to see a wild-eyed woman staring back at her, hatless with her hair snaking out, her dress stained and torn.

The end had come one stifling morning in mid-July. They'd gathered at the park, planning to march to City Hall at noon. But the factory owners had hired more thugs and persuaded the Providence police chief to deputize them. Before the march even started dozens of armed men closed in on the strikers, arresting the leaders they could catch. Then they began savagely clubbing the rank and file, who roared with anger and fought back. Shots rang out and she saw workers fall, their blood soaking into the dusty streets. Thugs chased after fleeing strikers and beat them savagely when they caught them.

Despairing, Ingeborg had watched the bitter struggle in front of her. The screams and cries of the strikers, and the shouts of their pursuers pierced her heart and she could scarcely breathe. She had never seen such cruelty and chaos. All around her younger boys hurled chunks of cobblestones they'd pried out of the roadbed. Ingeborg stood rooted to her spot, helpless to stop the violence but unable to flee.

Then she saw two policemen seize an older boy and begin beating him with their nightsticks. His mother screamed and rushed across the road to defend him, grabbing the men's arms and pushing them away. One released the boy and turned his nightstick on her—she fell to the ground, blood gushing from a head wound. The policeman raised his stick and let it fall on the helpless woman again and again. Suddenly Ingeborg found a knotted length of wood in her own hand and she walked up behind the man and gave him a tremendous crack on the head. His knees buckled and he toppled over, lying still. She turned and faced the other policeman, eyes blazing, placing herself between him and his victims. "Go," hissed Ingeborg. She locked eyes with the man she faced and they glared at each other for a long moment.

The policeman she'd felled moaned and stirred, and her opponent glanced down at him briefly, and then looked back at her. "I know you," he said. "Don't think this is the end of it," and to her infinite surprise and relief, he'd dragged his buddy to his feet, gotten his arm around his shoulder, and half-carried him down the road. Ingeborg helped the boy get his mother back to their squalid flat, gave them some money, and then found her way home. She'd stumbled in the door and collapsed in a chair, words coming in a tumbling rush as she tried to describe to Maria what she'd witnessed, and how she'd failed. It took some time to get around to the blow she'd dealt the policeman, but once Maria had pieced the story together it was her turn to get agitated.

"I knew it! Ingeborg, I knew you were getting too excited by this." She banged the kettle down on the stove and poked angrily at the fire. "You must be crazy, beating a policeman! How long before they come for you? I told you to stay away!"

Ingeborg had ranted and wailed, a jangly knot of nerves. Short bursts of the violence she'd witnessed played like newsreels in her mind, again and again. Maria made her some coffee and sponged the sweat and grime off her face and arms, speaking to her in a soothing voice, and then sat holding her until she calmed a little.

Finally, Maria stirred. "Ingeborg," she said. "You're not well. And it's not safe for you here. They'll come for you and lock you up—who knows for how long?"

Ingeborg scarcely heard her, the images sliding past each other in her mind, the woman lying still on the ground, the anguish of her son, the feel of the blow she'd dealt the policeman traveling up the stick into her arm.

"Ingeborg, look at me," commanded Maria, and Ingeborg looked into her partner's sweet face, her eyes anxious and scared. "You're ill, you need to go to the hospital."

"I'm not ill," Ingeborg had protested. "I wasn't hurt."

"That's not the sort of hospital I mean. I've been thinking. Hazel Bowditch is the matron at the Dexter Asylum. I helped her daughter through a bad birth last year. She told me if there's anything she could do I should ask."

"The Dexter Asylum?" repeated Ingeborg, fuzzily trying to follow Maria's line of thought. The Dexter Asylum was where Providence housed people who were poor—and crazy. Why would Maria send her there?

"That's right," said Maria, her voice calm and soothing. "A rest will do you good and the police won't look for you there."

"You think I'm crazy?" shouted Ingeborg. "I'll tell you what's crazy, police beating mothers and children and no one stopping them."

"Calm down, Ingeborg. It's just for a little while. It's that or wait for the police to arrest you. I've delivered babies there, it's much nicer than jail. Cleaner beds. Food. In jail you'd get a lumpy mattress with an old, dirty blanket."

"But I'm not crazy!" insisted Ingeborg.

Maria had looked at her steadily. Ingeborg flinched when she saw that steely look in her partner's eyes. When Maria made up her mind there was no talking her out of it. "You're too excited. You need rest. And we need time for this to blow over. I promise you it won't be long. Just until we decide what to do."

Reluctantly, Ingeborg had agreed. Maria left to fetch the car, and Ingeborg had slipped out the back door to meet her several blocks away, crouching down in the backseat and covering herself with a blanket.

Ingeborg still recalled the terror she felt as they drove through the immense granite walls that surrounded the asylum. It had felt like a prison. The flat stone walls of the main building towered above them, the black window trim flaking paint. The grounds surrounding it were overgrown with tired weeds that slumped in the summer heat. A handful of residents wandered listlessly on the dirt paths.

A thick, tarry despair washed over her. What if Maria meant to leave her there for good? One way to rid herself of her troublesome partner. She deserved no less.

Hazel Bowditch was a rail-thin, fox-faced woman, who was so tall she had to tip her head sideways to pass through the door of her office. Once she'd closed the door Maria had sketched out the details of why Ingeborg needed to hide at the Asylum for a little while. Hazel had eyed Ingeborg, who sat slumped in her chair, depressed and mute.

"People come and go from this place, and seldom of their own choosing," Hazel said to Ingeborg. "I don't think the police will look for you here. We'll try to keep you out of sight, though." She'd asked Ingeborg what farm work she could manage, and they settled on an assignment in the dairy, making butter and cheese. "All the inmates work here," explained Hazel. "It would look odd if you didn't."

Hazel coached her on a few things she could do to convince the other staff and inmates that she was ill. As an extra precaution they agreed on a new name for her while she was at Dexter—she would be Hilda.

Ingeborg was overwhelmed with sadness as Maria drove down the gravel drive without her. She wailed and sank to her knees, then keeled over and lay curled up in a ball, sobbing. She had never felt so helpless and alone, even when she'd first come to America. It was as if all of the pent-up fears and tensions and heartache of not just the last few weeks but of her whole life poured out of her, her tears dampening the scruffy lawn of the Dexter Asylum like those of thousands of lost souls before her. She wanted to die.

Hazel let her lie there for a time and then came out, a young woman in a stained Dexter uniform by her side.

"Get up, Hilda," Hazel said, not unkindly.

Ingeborg peered up at her and said nothing. She felt as if all of her bones had been removed, and if she tried to stand, she'd spread out in a gelatinous glob of skin and tissue.

"Come on, now," said Hazel, less kindly. She gestured to the woman with her, who Ingeborg now saw had a large, strawberry-colored birthmark across her right cheek. Her left eye roamed about independently. "This is Tina. She'll show you around the dairy."

Ingeborg sighed and struggled to a sitting position, and from there slowly climbed to her feet, a movement that seemed to take at least a day and all her strength. She still couldn't speak, so she just looked at Tina and waited.

Tina's smile suggested she'd likely be toothless before long—her teeth were brown and several were already missing. But it had a sweet quality nonetheless, and Ingeborg found herself smiling tentatively in return. "Come with me, Hilda," she said, and held out her hand. "I'll show you around."

Ingeborg grabbed her hand and let herself be led inside where they left her bag on the narrow cot where she would sleep that night. She grimaced as she counted the beds—nine other women would share the small room with her. There was a washstand in the corner and one small window to let in the light. The room was on the second floor, hot and stuffy, and ripe with the odor of sweat and unwashed bodies. For a moment she closed her eyes and pictured the cozy room she shared with Maria, the large bedstand she had made with her own hands, covered with a comfortable featherbed and a homemade quilt. She shook her head and rubbed her face. What had she come to? What if Maria never returned? She choked back a sob, weaving on her feet.

Tina glanced at her sympathetically and then led her to the dairy and showed her around, describing the routine. "The milkers are up early—well, we all are—but they'll bring the full pails into the parlor here. The skimmed cream goes here." She showed Ingeborg the churn, the butter molds, and other equipment she would need to use. Ingeborg felt a little tug of interest in the mechanics of the operation and despite herself looked forward to starting work.

Within a day or so she had settled into the routine and thought she might survive this—as long as Maria came back for her. That anxiety never left her, and every time she heard car wheels crunching on the graveled drive, she poked her head out to see if it was Maria, only to be disappointed.

The days were tolerable if she kept busy. She mostly stayed away from her fellow inmates as much as she could, but there was almost no privacy to be found—even the outhouses were two-holers. She studied the others covertly. Many held passionate conversations with people no one else could see; others crept furtively around, smiling oddly.

Some seemed angry and ready to pick a fight with anyone and everyone. Once, when she was crossing from the main building to the dairy after the midday meal, a swarthy fellow with eyebrows like lobster antennae approached her and poked her in the chest with a stiff forefinger, yelling angrily. Nothing he said made sense. She was frightened, and looked about quickly for something to defend herself with, but saw nothing. Finally, she'd locked eyes with him and said quietly, "I mean you no harm. I'm going to work now." Somehow that had taken the bluster out of him, and he smiled and motioned her off as if that were what he'd been telling her to do all along. She breathed a sigh of relief and walked away.

Nights were the worst. The room was stifling. Some nights it seemed more mosquitoes than air sailed in the open window, and bedbugs feasted on her until her body was a mass of itchy welts. It was then she despaired that she would ever see Maria again. As she twisted and turned to get comfortable, slapping at the biting bugs, she wondered, Where was Maria? Would she ever come back? She was tortured by images of Maria happily carrying on with her life, pleased she no longer had to put up with her crazy partner. Staring into the dark as the biting flies droned in clouds around her head, she wondered if she'd spend the rest of her life at Dexter. She wept into her pillow. All her roommates did the same.

It was a full week before Maria had returned, bearing a broad smile and an envelope holding tickets for the ship that in two weeks would take them west to San Francisco and the Panama–Pacific Exposition. Ingeborg could scarcely believe it. Her fingers trembled as she held the tickets and read the information over and over, tears sliding down her face. Maria held her, laughing and crying at the same time. "We'd talked of going," she said. "Why not now?"

* * *

Speeding along now in Emilie, Ingeborg glanced over at Maria and wondered whether she regretted the decision. Maybe she wished she'd left Ingeborg at the Dexter Asylum. Maria was her North Star, steadfast, unwavering, constant. Whereas Ingeborg was like a jerky child's toy, unseen hands making her jump about. It was easy to see why Maria might get tired of her.

Ingeborg cleared her throat and looked over at her friend. "I was just thinking about Providence," she said. "Do you think they've forgotten?"

Maria looked over at her, eyebrows raised. "Providence? Why worry about that? We won't be there for weeks."

"I was just thinking about last summer, everything that happened. How you saved me." Ingeborg added gruffly, "You're so good to me, and I cause you nothing but trouble."

Maria laughed. "True. I wonder why I put up with you. But my life would be very dull otherwise." She reached over and rested her hand on Ingeborg's thigh. "Besides," she said with a little grin, "I need someone to change the tires and look after the car."

Ingeborg smiled back at her, scooted over on the seat so her body was pressed into Maria's, and gave her a quick kiss on the cheek. Maria settled her right arm around Ingeborg's shoulder and they rode for a while in comfortable silence. Presently, Maria stirred and said, "We'll tell Mabel to not send photos of us to the newspapers in Providence. She can use Sara's photo instead. Tell her not to mention us."

"What will she think?" asked Ingeborg.

"We can explain what happened. She'll be proud of you, an activist for workers and suffrage, too."

"I hope so. I just don't want her to think I'm crazy."

"Don't be silly," said Maria. "Who would think that? You went to Dexter so you wouldn't go to jail."

"Still. I'd rather no one knew about it," said Ingeborg.

Maria glanced at her and looked back at the road. "Ingeborg," she said, "you're not crazy. Sometimes I wish you'd think more before you act. But like Frank Walsh said, we need people like you to stick up for the ones who have nothing. I can help—but I'm not like you. In life we have to decide for ourselves. You're an organizer. As long as I've known you, it's been the same. You can't be anything else."

Ingeborg felt tears prick her eyes, hearing this. "Thank you for seeing that," she said finally, her voice gruff from choking back tears. "And for helping me."

Maria looked over at her again and smiled. "It's all right," she said, leaving Ingeborg unsure whether she was speaking about the trip or their relationship. She decided not to ask.

The next day they were at the Marysville station when Sara's train pulled in, belching smoke and cinders. Sara tottered off the train, still pale but for her nose, which was red from blowing into the handkerchief she applied at intervals. Her eyes were runny, and her voice was hoarse from coughing.

Ingeborg and Maria greeted her with affection and sympathy, moved by evidence of an illness they could actually see and understand, in contrast to her complaints about her heart. Maria placed an arm around Sara's shoulders and guided her to the car, while Ingeborg grabbed her bag.

"You should be in bed," scolded Maria gently.

Sara settled into the cushions in the backseat and closed her eyes against the glare of the sun, which chose that moment to emerge from the low clouds that had hung over the town all morning. "Bed would be heavenly," she said. "But I must keep going." She was quiet as Maria started the motor and guided Emilie out of the snarl of wagons and trucks that had pulled in to meet the afternoon train. Away from the station Marysville's absurdly wide streets were almost empty, little puffs of wind chasing dust along the rutted surface. The air was chilly despite the brightening sun.

"I thought about being like Frances," said Sara, her voice so weak Ingeborg and Maria had to strain to hear her over the chattering engine. Ingeborg turned around to face her; Sara was still lying limply with her eyes closed. She continued, "If ever I were going to quit this trip, it would be now. But I couldn't do it. It's too important. I'm just stubborn, I guess." She was seized by a fit of coughing then, leaning forward and pressing the cloth to her lips before falling back against the cushions.

Ingeborg faced forward, remembering their conversation with Mabel about martyrs, and shivered. Was that just a few days ago? Sara had been exhausted then, but this cold on top of her weak heart made things much more serious. She really ought to be in bed. What good was she at this point, anyway? She couldn't possibly make a speech in her condition.

She felt a grudging admiration that Sara was carrying on despite the many reasons she had for turning back. She wasn't a quitter, not like Frances. But surely there was a limit to what her body could take.

Ingeborg turned back around to face Sara. "What if you died?" she asked bluntly. "Would it be worth it?"

Sara opened her eyes and stared briefly at Ingeborg before shutting them again. A long cough wracked her slender body, and when it ended she said hoarsely "It's funny, last summer I wanted to die. I missed Erskine so much. I had malaria. I was so sick, and I fainted then, too. I was at the beauty parlor having my hair done, and the next thing I knew I was on the ground looking up at all these faces. I didn't see much point in going on." She lay quiet for a moment. "This trip has almost killed me, but in a strange way I feel stronger, surer of myself and my purpose than I have in years. I want to live. I *will* live. I just have to get through this."

Ingeborg faced forward again, glancing at Maria, who still looked worried. They rode in silence for a time, and Ingeborg thought Sara had fallen asleep, when she asked suddenly "How did it go with the congressman?"

"Guy Helvering. A Democrat," said Ingeborg. "He signed." She thought back to their meeting with him the night before, she and Maria dusty and windblown after hours on the road.

Helvering was in his late thirties, she'd guessed, with a shifty, insolent look about him. Ingeborg liked to think her intelligence business had taught her the knack of sizing up her customers' characters within a few minutes of meeting them. Sometimes when she met new people, she entertained herself by speculating what jobs she might recommend them for. Boot black, factory worker.... She thought Helvering would sneak his fingers into the silverware drawer, so she wouldn't possibly recommend him as a domestic servant.

He'd greeted them with the practiced smoothness of a politician but was plainly irritated by the suffrage question and was reluctant to sign the petition. "Ladies, it seems to me you're making a long drive for nothing," he said. "Kansas passed suffrage the way I think it should be done—by the state. Congress should stay out of this."

"If Congress could pass amendments giving Negro men the right to vote, surely they can do the same for women," Ingeborg told him.

"That was different," Helvering had replied "We fought a war over that." He flipped through the pages of the petition to see who else had signed. "I see you got Senator Taggart," he said.

"We're fighting a different sort of war," said Ingeborg. "The votes of the four million women in equal suffrage states are our weapons."

"Yes, I recall you were active in the elections last year," Helvering said. "I had to swear my everlasting allegiance to the Susan B. Anthony amendment or the women would have campaigned against me," he said, and smirked. "Not that it would have made any difference to the outcome."

"Maybe not," replied Ingeborg, working hard not to let this sneering man get her riled. She longed to slap that smirk off his face. "But we'll have more money and workers in 1916—and be better organized."

"Is that a threat?" asked Helvering.

"No, it's the new politics."

"The other national suffrage group, what do they call themselves-?"

"NAWSA," said Ingeborg, using the acronym.

"NAWSA," he repeated, "They don't pull these sorts of stunts, do they? They treat us with more respect."

Ingeborg said, bluntly, "We don't have time for their foolishness. We're playing politics. Just like you." She flicked her eyes over to Maria, who looked slightly alarmed by this exchange. She gave Ingeborg a quick shake of the head.

Helvering had laughed then, and looked at Ingeborg. "I see! You're a bunch of hornets and mean to sting us into submission."

Ingeborg smiled at him. She liked the image of a swarm of women surrounding Helvering, grabbing him by their multiple arms, and burying their stingers into his skin as he screamed and begged for mercy. "That's right."

He'd ended by saying that if Senator Taggart had signed, he guessed he would. "I'm a friend of suffrage, you know," he said as he scribbled his signature on the bottom of the petition.

Now Maria drove due north out of town toward Lincoln, winding through corn fields and pasture and coming into the open plain. Sara sneezed and coughed in the back, but otherwise they rode in silence, arriving after dark. Ingeborg was thankful to pull up to the brightly lit Lincoln Hotel that towered over a grand, cobblestoned boulevard. They checked in quickly and headed to their rooms.

In the morning they met for breakfast in the hotel dining room. Sara still looked ill but had slept well, and thought she could get through the day. They'd been surprised when they'd checked in the night before to find that Mabel was in town—they'd thought she'd be several days ahead of them. She'd stayed in Lincoln to do what she could to raise interest in their arrival. She'd been out when they arrived but joined them at breakfast.

"NAWSA is very strong here," she said. "At first I could get almost no one to turn out for you, except for Mrs. Hardy and Mrs. Hall. The plan is to gather at Lincoln and P Streets at one o'clock and parade to the statehouse, with flags flying. We'll see who shows up." She grimaced. "At the statehouse Governor Morehead will receive us, but I don't know if he'll sign. Mrs. Hardy told me that since Nebraska voters defeated their suffrage referendum last year, he's said his hands are tied. Suffrage is dead, as far as he's concerned."

Sara sighed and looked like she wanted to crawl back into bed. Ingeborg looked at Mabel, concerned. "Is this what we can expect from now on?" she asked.

"There will be some tension," admitted Mabel, who looked as if she could use a few more hours of sleep herself. "But it's worse in these states where there simply aren't that many women to begin with, and few that are active in suffrage. Iowa will be difficult, since of course Mrs. Catt is from Cedar Rapids." Ingeborg knew that Carrie Chapman Catt was a past president of NAWSA and now ran New York's chapter. She was widely regarded as one of NAWSA's most effective state leaders—people spoke of her reverently, like a queen.

"There's a lot of loyalty to her there," Mabel added, sipping her coffee. "But we have more supporters in the East, so even if NAWSA comes out strong against us, we'll have more help."

They went their separate ways after breakfast, Ingeborg to look over Emilie, who had begun making a furious knocking sound about ten miles out of town. It took Ingeborg a few hours to locate the source of the noise, decide what had to be done, and find the part she needed at a local garage. When she finally crawled out from beneath the car, she was amused to see two boys watching her, looking puzzled. She guessed they were no more than ten or twelve years old, with the same round faces and unruly brown hair under their worn caps.

"I told you it was a lady!" said one, elbowing his brother.

"Anyone could see that from her skirts," his brother replied.

"But you said ladies can't fix cars," said the first one.

"This one can," said Ingeborg drily, hoisting herself stiffly to her feet, and wiping the oil off her hands with a rag.

"Why don't you get a man to do it?" asked the first boy, hands deep in his pockets.

"Yeah, he'd probably do it better," sniggered his brother.

Ingeborg looked them over. "Women can do for ourselves. We don't need men to help us. We've come all the way from San Francisco, and I've taken care of this car the whole way. Patched tires, fixed the motor, changed the oil. All of it. And my friend who drives the car is a lady, too. When we hired a man to drive us through the desert, he got us lost." The boys chuckled. "We never did that again."

"Maybe Papa would buy a car, if Ma could fix it," said the first boy to his brother.

"Nah, he never would," said the brother.

"Let's ask him!" And off they ran down the street, Ingeborg watching them with a smile.

As she crossed through the lobby on her way to the elevator, she picked up the morning paper, the *Lincoln Daily News*. Back in the room, Maria sat at a cramped desk writing a letter to their bank while Ingeborg leafed through the paper and found an article about their visit. She read through it quickly, and her wrathful growl pulled Maria's attention from her letter.

"What?" she asked.

"Listen to this," snarled Ingeborg, reading aloud. "Suffragist Sara Bard Field is in Lincoln today to meet with Governor Morehead and Mayor Bryan. She comes as an envoy from the women voters of the West, and brings with her a monster petition demanding that Congress enfranchise women through national action. She is accompanied by her fellow envoy, socialite Frances Joliffe of San Francisco." Ingeborg uttered a rude sound and tossed the paper aside. "No mention of us at all."

Maria shrugged and went back to her letter. "I'm sure the CU gave that reporter our names, too, Ingeborg. Newspapers just get things wrong sometimes."

"It makes me so mad they talk about Frances but not us! We've barely heard from her since Sacramento."

"It's not right," Maria agreed, "but there's no use getting upset about it. It suits the CU to pretend she's still with us, and if the reporters are foolish enough to accept it, why make a fuss?"

"Are we ghosts? Who do they think is driving the car? Isn't that news? We deserve to be in the paper." Ingeborg was agitated, walking with jerky steps around the small room. "At least as much as Frances!" she spat out.

Maria turned to face Ingeborg, a warning in her eyes. "Calm down. Of course you're right, but so what? You want to tell the reporters where they can find Frances? How would that help? Maybe you should write the notices yourself."

"I'm not going to tell—" Ingeborg stopped, and looked at Maria, a smile spreading across her face. "That's a wonderful idea, Maria."

Maria looked nervous. "What?"

"I'm going to write the notices myself. In Swedish. And send them to Swedish newspapers."

"Ingeborg," Maria groaned, shaking her head. "Why do you always have to make trouble?"

"What trouble?" asked Ingeborg, excited, as she hunted for writing paper. "It was your idea. The Swedes at least should know the truth about this trip. Why should we be invisible?"

"What will you write?"

"In my notices you will be featured as the owner and driver of the automobile, and I as the mechanician. I'll say that we are bringing the petitions to Washington on behalf of the CU. Frances won't be mentioned. All true." Ingeborg eyed Maria's fountain pen. "Are you done with your letter? I want to get started."

"Not quite," said Maria, looking earnestly at Ingeborg. "Promise me you won't write anything to hurt us or the CU."

"Maria, who gets to decide the news?" Ingeborg replied, tartly. "That's the point. Swedes might like to know we're making an important trip like this one. But how will they know if they just read the English language newspapers? Or if they can't read English? They should know about us. And I'll bet not many CU members read Swedish newspapers."

Maria gave up and finished her letter, handing the pen over to Ingeborg. Ingeborg bent over the desk, scratching away until it was time to prepare Emilie for the afternoon's meetings. As they left the hotel Ingeborg handed the envelope to the clerk to mail.

They drove over to Lincoln and P streets and found half a dozen automobiles bedecked with suffrage pennants and American flags. Some of the women looked nervous, their eyes darting over the streets and sidewalks to spot acquaintances who might shake scolding fingers at them. Mrs. Hardy, however, was relaxed and smiling and welcomed them warmly. She was a tall woman with blond hair piled under her hat, a firm chin, and merry eyes. I could definitely recommend her as a housekeeper, Ingeborg thought.

"I'm sorry we couldn't have a larger turnout for you," she said, "but the women here are very loyal to NAWSA and worried the CU will ruin their reputations. After our state referendum failed here last year, though, it's clear to me we need to throw all of our effort behind the federal amendment."

"You've done very well," Mabel told her warmly. "It seemed at first we might just have your car in addition to the envoys, so this is wonderful. Shall we begin?"

Mabel signaled to the bugler, whom she'd hired because no band would agree to play for them. He stood up in the rear of Mrs.

Hardy's auto, clad in a bright blue coat with brass buttons, and blasted out the first notes of a military tune on a long silver trumpet. The women hastened to their respective autos and fell into line behind Mrs. Hardy, the envoys in second position. In this way they made their way over to the state capitol where Governor Morehead would receive them. Ingeborg looked around curiously. The city was bustling, automobiles and wagons piled with goods trundling along the wide streets. Hurrying back from their midday dinners, men and women stopped to look at the procession and some stuck their heads out the windows. A few people waved but most stood frowning, or turned a cold shoulder.

When they arrived at the capitol, an aide met them on the steps and ushered them into Governor Morehead's office. The bugler preceded them while blowing madly, cheeks bulging.

Governor Morehead was a pudgy, pale-skinned fellow whose thin hair was receding rapidly from his prominent brow. Ingeborg privately rechristened him Governor Forehead. He welcomed the women courteously enough, but his light gray eyes were cold, and he seemed eager for them to be on their way.

Mrs. Hardy introduced them all, and Sara, wheezing slightly, her voice thickened from her cold, did her usual routine of being the envoy from the Western states. "In every state we've passed through so far, the governor has not only signed our petition, but many have given me letters endorsing the federal suffrage amendment." She smiled sweetly at him and held out the petition. "Will you not add your name? We want you to come with us before the tide has passed by."

The Governor, unsmiling, said bluntly, "I suppose you're aware that this state has recently passed upon this issue? It would be unbecoming of me as general executive of the state to sign a petition favoring an amendment which the state has passed on adversely. I would be advocating against the wishes of a majority of the people."

Sara tried a sweet smile. "The Governor of Oregon signed although his state voted against equal suffrage five times."

"I am here to enforce the law," the governor replied, "and not to ask Congress for anything contrary to what the majority of the people want."

"But, Governor," said Mrs. Hardy, "how can you say that the majority of people oppose suffrage when only the men voted?"

"In most instances we can assume that men vote as their women wish them to," said the governor. Then he added, "The women can trust their men to know what's best for them."

Ingeborg gasped at this ridiculous statement and looked over at Maria, who raised her eyebrows and shook her head slightly. How could men possibly believe they alone could speak for women? How many men would be content for women to vote for them? Not many, she guessed.

"If the women had voted upon our measure last year I think you would have seen that a majority of the *people* desired equal suffrage, Governor," said Mrs. Hardy, warmly. "A majority of *men* voting a certain way can't possibly represent the will of the majority."

"In this state, Mrs. Hardy, the law permits only the men to vote, so on this question they are the only people I concern myself with," said the governor.

"I am sorry to find your mind so made up on this issue," said Mrs. Hardy, looking him straight in the eye. "Women will vote someday, and we will not forget who helped us—and who did not."

"I'll worry about it when that day comes," the governor replied, unconcerned. "I suppose you must have other visits to make." He wished the three travelers a safe and pleasant journey, and an aide ushered them out of the office and back to the statehouse steps.

Mrs. Hardy was fuming. "That smug little prig."

"Yes, it's infuriating," said Mabel. "You answered him well, I thought." The other women nodded in agreement. Ingeborg was pleased to note that the ones who'd seemed ill at ease earlier were now brimming with indignation. There was nothing quite like getting brushed off by a politician to turn a woman into an activist, she decided.

"When we get this through, I'll make sure every woman in Nebraska knows he did nothing for suffrage," said Mrs. Hardy, bitterly.

A chill wind gusted up the steps and swirled fallen leaves around their feet. Sara shivered, and Maria edged over to pull her scarf up around her neck. "When are we due at Mayor Bryan's office?" asked Ingeborg. She wasn't sure how long Sara would last.

"We should leave now," said Mrs. Hardy. "He's expecting us. Might as well get it over with."

They got back into their cars, the bugler tooting notes at intervals. Sara coughed in the back seat and said absently, "I hope Mayor Bryan didn't hear about my meeting with his brother," she said.

Ingeborg turned to look at her. "What do you mean?"

"His brother is William Jennings Bryan."

"Of course!" said Ingeborg. "He's from Nebraska. Why did you meet with him?" She felt a pang of jealousy. How was it possible that Sara met all these famous people? It wasn't fair. Bryan had run for president three times as a Democrat, though he'd never been nominated. He'd been President Wilson's Secretary of State until June, when he'd resigned after the Germans sank the *Lusitania*. Ingeborg appreciated his opposition to war but thought him too preachy and was glad he'd never been president.

"He visited the Exposition last July, and I led a deputation to speak to him," said Sara. "The reporters made a big fuss over it at the time." Ingeborg ground her teeth lightly. The usual thing. Sara once again in the right place at the right time.

Sara was seized by a deep, wracking cough that left her weak and breathless. She found the water and took a sip.

Despite herself, Ingeborg was curious. "What did you say to him?"

Sara grimaced and held the canteen to her lips again. "He'd just finished a speech in which he'd declared, among other things, that world suffrage would bring about world peace. We were waiting for him afterward, and I asked him if he wouldn't speak for the CU's effort to win a federal amendment, considering he's for world peace and thinks enfranchising women could help achieve it."

"What did he say to that?" asked Ingeborg, curious.

"Oh, he got on his high horse and told me he'd never speak for any organization that opposed the Democratic Party. I pointed out that he'd quit as secretary of state over a difference with Wilson. 'Do you believe in standing by your party, whether it's right or wrong?' I asked him. I said we were just trying to win women's freedom in the most direct way possible, using the same methods as men."

Ingeborg smiled. She could picture Sara staring up at Bryan, hands on hips, her eyes blazing. "What did he say then?" she asked.

"Oh, he gave me that smile—the way men do when they think women have missed the point entirely. And then he said, 'The Lord does not ask you to do the impossible' or some such tripe. You know he fancies himself a biblical scholar. But I was raised in the church and married to a minister, for heaven's sake. I know my Bible as well as anyone. I said to him sweetly, 'Oh yes, he does, Mr. Bryan. What of his calling on Abraham to sacrifice Isaac, or David to fight Goliath? There are many such examples.'" She snorted. "Then he switched tactics and asked how much the Republicans had paid us to campaign against the Democrats."

"They always say that," Maria chimed in, as she nosed the car into the curb by City Hall.

"He thought the Democrats should be praised for having handled tariffs and currency reform in this last session, that those were the 'paramount issues'" said Sara, bitterly. "I told him he was wrong, that war was the supreme issue, and low tariffs had no value if the world is fast becoming a well-filled graveyard because the mothers of this country had no say about the destiny of their sons." She blew her nose vigorously and took a last sip from the canteen, preparing to climb out of the car. "He told us to be patient. I told him we had lost patience, and the Democratic Party had better act. He walked away after that, but the reporters had listened to the whole exchange and made a big fuss in the newspapers. My mother even wrote from Detroit to scold me for saucing him."

They joined the rest of the party assembling on the sidewalk and walked up the steps of City Hall. Mayor Bryan waited for them at the top. He proved to be taller than his brother and sported a brushy mustache, perhaps to make up for being nearly bald. He greeted them with a smile and the usual pleasantries. Then he turned to Sara. "I hear you met my brother, Mrs. Field," he said. His voice was grave but a smile twinkled in his brown eyes.

Sara smiled and dipped her head in agreement. "Yes, I had that pleasure in San Francisco last summer," she replied.

"I fear you might have found him not entirely supportive of your cause," he said.

"Supportive, perhaps. But not ready to act on that support in a meaningful way. He seemed to think the tariff more urgent than women's political freedom," she replied, and added drily, "We don't agree."

"William and I agree on many things, but on this we differ," said the mayor. "I would be pleased to sign your petition." The assembled women clapped as Sara handed over the petition, which he signed with a flourish. Several members of his staff did as well. He wished them a safe journey and much success with Congress, and they drifted back down to the waiting cars.

Sara settled into Emilie's backseat, spent from the day's exertions. She coughed again, that deep, wracking cough that left her breathless and weak, and she lay back against the cushions and closed her eyes. Mabel huddled with Ingeborg, Maria, and Mrs. Hardy on the sidewalk to consider what to do.

"She needs rest," said Mrs. Hardy, looking worriedly at Sara. "I think she's feverish."

"We have to get to Omaha tonight," said Mabel. "We have stops planned in Des Moines, Marshalltown, Clinton, and then Chicago."

Mrs. Hardy stared at Mabel. "What good can she do you in her condition? The poor thing's half-dead already! If you push her too hard who knows what will happen?" The question hung in the air. Ingeborg and Maria looked at each other, wondering if Mabel would talk about martyrs.

Mabel straightened her hat. "I'd like to get her to Omaha tonight," she insisted. "Mayor Dahlman there will sign and he's very popular. He'll bring out a big crowd. We can't miss that."

Mrs. Hardy sighed, looked over at Sara, and back at Mabel. "All right," she said. "But what shall we do about the tea we have planned for you? We're supposed to gather at Mrs. Branwell's house at four o'clock."

"Do you think anyone will come?" asked Mabel. "I mean, besides the women who turned out today?" Ingeborg could see them sitting in their cars watching, waiting for instructions. A gust of cold wind washed over them, swirling leaves around their feet.

"I doubt it," said Mrs. Hardy. "They're all so frightened of going against the National."

"Let's skip the tea, then," said Mabel, deciding. "We'll push on to Omaha. I'll ride with the envoys. Please convey our apologies to Mrs. Branwell and say it was due to Sara's illness. And thank you for your fine work here today. We had a splendid deputation and, even if the governor refused to sign, we've put everyone on notice that he did not. And Mayor Bryan did."

"Unlike his brother," observed Ingeborg. They laughed and went their separate ways.

Maria and Ingeborg raised Emilie's top to help keep out the wind. Mabel climbed into the back with Sara and fussed over her while Maria drove to the hotel to pick up their luggage. Before long they were angling northeast toward Omaha; the roads were good and Emilie skipped along, her top rattling in the breeze. They might make Omaha in a couple of hours, thought Ingeborg. She looked behind her. Sara appeared to be sleeping, cocooned under her buffalo skin, but Mabel was alert and looking out the side window, lost in thought.

"Any news about the petitions?" Ingeborg called back to her.

Mabel sighed. "Nothing yet," she said. "We have to discuss it by letter—telegrams are too risky. I may hear in Des Moines—if not, surely there will be word in Chicago."

Ingeborg nodded, and they rode in silence for a bit before Mabel leaned forward and spoke again. "We have another problem, though. How are you and Maria fixed for money?"

Ingeborg raised her eyebrows at Maria, who kept their cash pinned in a pouch under her generous bosom. Maria turned her head slightly to speak to Mabel, her eyes fixed on the road in front of her. "Enough to get to Chicago. We'll get more there."

Mabel nodded. "I'm nearly out. I've wired and written to Alice about it but she hasn't responded. I hate asking her for more funds, as she has the weight of the entire effort on her shoulders, poor thing. Perhaps headquarters has no money either. I know she thought we could appeal for funds as we traveled, but honestly, when are we supposed to do it? Between the travel and organizing the meetings, there just isn't time. Alice probably thinks I'm useless," she concluded, miserably.

Maria laughed. "Hah! You work miracles every day."

"I'll simply have to do better," murmured Mabel quietly, almost to herself. Then, more firmly, she said, "Don't worry. I'll draw on my own bank for now, and the CU will pay me back when they can." She sat back in her seat.

Ingeborg looked out the front window, where the sinking sun picked out the tops of cottonwoods lining an irrigation ditch across a field, briefly turning them salmon pink. She loved this time of day, the aching beauty of the fading light, the trees' bony brown fingers etched against the fading sky. A flock of starlings wheeled and swooped over the trees, hovering as if to land and then shooting off again in a twisting, spinning mass. She felt pulled toward home, and suddenly she thought of the snug place she and Maria shared in Providence. She'd been so glad to leave after the troubles last summer, and more than once she'd thought she might never go back. But now she conjured up an image of their kitchen with the cookstove Maria kept scrubbed and polished, their chairs set off to the side, the framed photograph of her parents on the wall, a faded rag rug on the floor at their feet.

The travel was hard, doubly so when they got little support from the local suffragists. Add to that Sara's bad cold, the missing petitions, and the constant concern about money. This adventure might be over before they ever arrived in Washington, and she and Maria would slink back to Providence in a disgrace they would carry like a stain for the rest of their lives. She slipped into a deep gloom, and silence blanketed the car.

They drew into the outskirts of Omaha around five o'clock, stopped briefly to put Emilie's top down and decorate her, and drove directly to the courthouse. To Ingeborg's surprise over a hundred women and men were waiting for them, and a resounding cheer went up as Maria swung the little car around the corner and came to a stop beside some other machines parked by the roadside. The crowd swarmed Emilie so tightly, at once exclaiming and welcoming and congratulating them, that they could scarcely open their doors. At length they fell back enough for the four women to emerge from the car and walk up the marble steps to where Mayor James Dahlman stood waiting for them, a broad smile on his face. "Omaha welcomes the suffrage envoys!" he boomed, his voice carrying out over the crowd, which again erupted into cheers.

Ingeborg grinned as she shook his hand. Perhaps an inch or two shorter than she, he strutted like a scrawny bantam rooster, holding himself very erect. She was drawn to his eyes, which were set deep in his head and snapped with quick intelligence and an impish gleam. It was obvious he loved being mayor and meant to be the center of whatever stage he paraded across.

Mabel briefly explaining their purpose in Omaha and introduced Sara, who was ghostly pale and fighting to stay on her feet. Nevertheless, she began bravely, "Mayor Dahlman, I come to you from the women voters of the West—" Then she began coughing into her handkerchief, bending over slightly from the waist.

The Mayor eyed her sympathetically. "Save your breath, Mrs. Field," he said. "We need speeches less than you need a sickbed." He raised his voice, again addressing the crowd, which Ingeborg now realized was mostly men, some of whom seemed to be weaving on their feet as badly as Sara, though for different reasons. She saw one man withdraw a flask from his coat pocket and, saluting Mayor Dahlman with it, take a long swig.

"I know the reasons for your visit," Dahlman proclaimed, raising his voice so the crowd could hear. "You seek to advance the right of women to vote by amending the US Constitution!" Muted cheers and calls from the crowd, which to Ingeborg sounded faintly hostile. She looked at the mayor, wondering if he would sign the petition, and if it would help if Sara collapsed at his feet.

Dahlman smiled. "I don't support your cause," he said. "Omaha is a wet city, and we aim to keep it that way!" Great cheers and applause burst from the crowd at this. Dahlman held out his hand to quiet them. "However," he said. "I lose no opportunity to poke a finger in the eye of William Jennings Bryan and the Governor of Nebraska, so I will sign your petition!" The crowd roared with laughter, and there were cries of "I'll sign it!" and "You first, Mayor!" While Maria edged Sara to the side, Ingeborg grabbed the petition and held it out first to the mayor, who signed his name with a flourish, and then to the line of men forming behind him. Within fifteen minutes they'd added another fifty signatures. Mayor Dahlman said his farewells, wished them good fortune on their journey, and the crowd dispersed.

Later that evening Maria sat in the spindly chair in their cramped room, stripped to her underclothes, her shoulders bared. Ingeborg stood behind her, working the knots out of her neck and shoulders with a pungent salve. Wrestling with the broad steering wheel for hours each day cramped her muscles until it was an effort to stand upright. Though she seldom complained, she tossed and turned in bed each night, trying to find a comfortable position. There was a tap on the door, suddenly, and Mabel's voice called to them. Maria flipped a shawl over her bare shoulders as Ingeborg let their visitor in.

"I have news!" Mabel said, her slender face flushed with triumph. "I wanted to share it with you right away." Ingeborg perched on the edge of the bed and Mabel stood next to the closed door.

"What's happened?" Ingeborg asked.

"The president has agreed to receive the envoys when you arrive in Washington!" Mabel said. "I had a wire from headquarters. Tumulty sent a note to Miss Paul this afternoon. It will be in all the papers tomorrow."

"Wonderful!" said Maria, beaming.

"Hurrah!" Ingeborg jumped up and hugged Maria, and then threw her arms around Mabel as well. Joseph Tumulty was President Wilson's personal secretary and was known to favor suffrage, though he hadn't yet convinced his boss of the wisdom of the federal amendment. Wilson preferred to kick it to the states, mostly so he could avoid the race question. He was a Southerner, after all.

"This will help with our publicity as we go East," said Mabel, excitedly. "I was so worried that we'd travel all the way from San Francisco and be refused."

"Will we go straight to the White House, then?" asked Ingeborg.

"I don't think so," Mabel replied. "I don't know all the details, but I believe headquarters is planning a large demonstration. The CU will time its annual meeting for our arrival, and NAWSA's will just be ending, so we should have many supporters on hand. It will be Congress's opening day. They've pulled permits for a parade to the

Capitol, and we'll hold an event there. The meeting with President Wilson will happen afterward. It's all very exciting!"

They chatted about this for a few minutes, and then Mabel recalled her other piece of news. "My mail had gone astray, but some of it caught up with me here. Alice wrote that she's put money into my account so it won't be overdrawn. So we don't have to worry about money, at least for now."

"Is there money to pay a doctor for Sara?" asked Maria. "I'm worried about her."

Mabel nodded. "Yes, he's just been and given her some syrup for her cough. He says it's just a cold and will pass." Ingeborg noticed that she didn't quite meet Maria's gaze, however, and wondered what else the doctor had said.

"We should stop for a day or two and let her rest," said Ingeborg. "She won't recover if we keep up this pace." She gestured to Maria. "The driving is hard for us, too. Maria's muscles are all in knots."

Mabel shook her head. "Sara's tougher than she looks. We need to press on to Des Moines for meetings tomorrow. There's a congressman in Marshalltown we'd like you to visit, and from there you make your way across Iowa to Chicago. Clinton is one of the stops. I'll leave you an updated itinerary. They don't expect you in Chicago until November fifth, I think, so you'll have plenty of time." She smiled sympathetically at Maria. "I'm sorry about this. But you're lucky Ingeborg can look after you. I wish there was someone to rub the knots out of my neck." She sounded exhausted, her frail body propped up against the doorframe.

Ingeborg looked at her curiously. She realized she'd never thought of Mabel's private life. Did she even have one, or did she just work all the time? She was a young, attractive woman, despite her too large and slightly crooked nose, and more than once Ingeborg had seen men eye her appreciatively. Mabel never seemed to notice. But Miss Paul sent her all over the country on CU business, so if there was someone waiting for her, he was very patient. She opened her mouth to ask but Maria beat her to it. "Do you have someone special?" she asked. "At home?"

Mabel's smile had a touch of sadness, and she shook her head. "No, this work is too important right now. There will be time after we pass the amendment. I don't think I could travel as I do if there were someone waiting for me. And mostly I don't think of it, but I do get lonely sometimes." She looked at them pointedly. "I like the way you two are with each other," she said quietly. And left it at that.

Ingeborg reddened and glanced quickly over at Maria. It was one thing to open up to Sara about their relationship—she was divorced and made no secret of her older lover. She had her own scandals. But the habit of secrecy was too ingrained. People were peculiar about women loving each other, and Mabel was their boss, essentially. It was better to be safe and not bring it up at all.

But Maria was beaming at Mabel. "It's very nice to travel with a woman as your partner," she said. "I recommend it."

"I'll keep that in mind," said Mabel, smiling back, and then she said good night and slipped out of the room.

Ingeborg turned to Maria. "What are you doing?" she demanded, in Swedish. "You want to get us in trouble?"

"What trouble?" Maria replied. "She's like us, anyone could tell. Now get back to rubbing my shoulders, they're killing me." She pulled the shawl off her shoulders. Ingeborg grabbed the jar of salve and worked her muscles with long, smooth strokes as Maria hung her head and uttered little grunts of pleasure.

Ingeborg mused about their recent exchange. She and Maria never told anyone in Providence the true nature of their relationship. There were far too many Catholics around and they had strict rules about sex, mostly that it was for men to have as much as they wanted and women to put up with the results, as far as Ingeborg could tell. And that included the priests. For the sake of appearances, Ingeborg rented a room from Maria and had her own bed and belongings there, although they slept in Maria's larger bed. They'd never been questioned.

But in just the last month they'd revealed their most guarded secret to two near-strangers. She felt a giddy terror, and wondered how many more people would know before the trip was over.

"How did you know about Mabel?" she asked Maria.

"She never flirts with men," said Maria. "Haven't you noticed that? Even when they like her. But she was nervous and tongue-tied around that pretty girl in Denver who came to all the events."

"Which one? There were a lot of them." Ingeborg gave Maria's shoulders a playful squeeze.

Maria rolled her eyes. "Stop, you." She thought for a bit. "What was her name? Miss Penderton? She had that curly auburn hair, and white skin. Wore a green gown to the big dinner. I caught Mabel gazing at her a few times, looking so hungry and wistful. I felt sad for her."

"I remember her now. But I didn't see that Mabel liked her." That was Maria, Ingeborg thought. She liked hanging back, watching and listening to what people said with their words and their movements, or how their faces changed when they thought someone wasn't watching them. She spoke fluently a language Ingeborg had never learned. It was like a telegraph—you couldn't see what passed through the wire but somehow a message got through to the other end. For Ingeborg, and for lots of people she knew, the message was often incomplete, or had words the sender hadn't meant to send at all. Maria got it right nearly every time.

CHAPTER TEN

OCTOBER 30, 1915

T wo days later Sara collapsed again and refused to go on without a rest. They were in Marshalltown, with the meetings in Des Moines behind them. To their surprise and delight, hundreds of suffragists had turned out for them in Des Moines—Ida Cummins, wife of Iowa's Senator Albert Cummins, even rode in the lead car of the parade escorting the envoys to call on her husband. The good senator's eyes twinkled as he declared his willingness to use his utmost influence in the Senate to pass the amendment. He praised the envoys' courage and grit, and thought the stunt couldn't fail to put his colleagues in Congress on notice that the women's train was a-coming and they had better get on board. Perhaps it wouldn't pass in this Congress, he told them, but it certainly would in the next.

So they were all in high spirits at the banquet that followed, and if Sara said little and ate less, no one noticed—there were plenty of other women eager to stand and speak. Mabel had gone on to Chicago, so even Ingeborg stood to speak about their more challenging moments: the desert, the pass to Cheyenne, and the Kansas mudhole misery.

They arrived in Marshalltown the next day, Sara as thin and brittle as the dry leaves blowing down the main street under Emilie's wheels.

A deep cough wracked her chest, and she struggled to breathe. They helped her to her room and summoned a doctor, who prescribed rest and syrups and more rest. After consulting the itinerary Ingeborg and Maria decided there was no point going on to Clinton; rather they should stay put and see if Sara could recover her strength before what would surely be a grueling few days in Chicago. They wired Mabel of their plans, and she replied promptly, agreeing with them.

So it was that they found themselves with time on their hands in Marshalltown, a small Midwestern burg with smug, tidy streets set at precise right angles to each other. After lunch Ingeborg proposed to Maria that they stretch their legs, which felt almost wobbly after being cooped up in the Overland Six for so long, as though they had been on board ship and needed to find their land legs again. So they donned their hats and coats and ventured out onto the street as the sun rode lower in the sky, slipping down from its midday height. A brisk wind tugged at their hats and made them sink their necks into their buttoned-up coats, and they stepped around puddles left by a hard rain that had passed through in the night. The streets were quiet, the sidewalks almost deserted, and the few people they passed walked briskly by, barely acknowledging their presence, as shuttered as the shops that lined the street. Ingeborg wondered if they were always this unfriendly, or if somehow word had gotten round that the suffragists were in town and were to be avoided at all costs.

Despite the chill it was pleasant to be walking again, and they were reluctant to return to their tidy but overstuffed hotel room.

"Do you suppose this town has a movie theatre?" Maria wondered.

"They must—it's big enough. Let's see if someone will tell us where to find it," said Ingeborg. They turned and strolled back up the main street, and presently came upon a man sitting on the steps of a house, puffing on a hand-rolled cigarette. He wore a patched wool jacket over a mended sweater, his hat pulled low on his forehead. He was a few days overdue for a shave.

They halted in front of him and wished him good day. "Is there a movie theater in this town?" Ingeborg asked, politely.

The man laughed. "Not open today. It's Sunday! All the pious people are at home, counting their money and communing with the Lord."

Ingeborg smiled and glanced at Maria, whose lips were twitching as well. She turned back to the man. "Are there other ways to pass the time, then?" she asked. "Dances, music?"

"Ma'am, you're clearly not from these parts. These people are as narrow as a one-lane bridge. There's no two-way about it, you go their way or you plain go nowhere."

Ingeborg wrinkled her brow. This could be Karlstad, her hometown, from thirty years ago. Nothing to do on Sundays but go to church, have a cold Sunday dinner, and spend the rest of the day contemplating the Lord. But even Providence had some entertainment to offer on Sundays, and she hadn't realized American towns could be so provincial. She nodded at the man, and said gravely, "So, no fun at all to be had in Marshalltown on a Sunday afternoon?"

He snorted. "These people wouldn't know fun if it bit them on their well-padded fannies," he said. "But Sundays are the worst. The only sport is watching them try to outdo each other in piety." He pulled at his cigarette, squinting at them, and blew out the smoke in a long, smooth exhale, flicking the ash onto the sidewalk. "What's your business here?"

Ingeborg explained and he gave an appreciative chuckle. "I read about that. So you're those ladies, eh? Good for you." They grinned back at him, and he went on. "Don't think you'll get much support here, though. People hereabouts worry if the women vote they'll run crazy, raise taxes. Look like men."

"Some people think if women do vote they'll clean things up, shut down the saloons. If people around here are as conservative as you say, maybe they'd want that," said Ingeborg. She looked up and down the street, with its neat and orderly progression of storefronts, signs advertising a butcher shop, a bakery, a mercantile. Not a saloon in sight.

"The men like to drink, but they do it in their private clubs, where they can make sure the women and riff-raff like me can't join 'em," said the man, tossing the stub of his cigarette into the street. "They don't want Prohibition. And they want to keep women under their boot heels."

"Old story," said Maria. She looked at him curiously. "What keeps you here?"

"Helping my mother," he said, jerking his thumb toward the door behind him. "I grew up here but never stay long if I can help it. I'll move on soon, looking for work."

He stuck out his hand. "Name's Mike. Nice talking with you." He wished them luck on their journey, and they moved off down the street toward the hotel.

Two days later Sara still didn't feel up to a long car ride in the damp cold that had settled over Iowa, so Ingeborg and Maria agreed to drive to Clinton separately. Sara would take the train to Clinton and they'd pick her up, continuing on to Chicago from there. Maria fussed over Sara while Ingeborg readied the car, and before long they were driving briskly along solid roads toward Cedar Rapids, where they'd spend the night.

It was November now, and the leaden sky pressed down over the rolling hills of central Iowa, cornfields alternating with prairie grass. Frost etched the stalks spiking up from the ground. The cold air swept over and around the windshield and into the car. Ingeborg tugged her shawl up around her neck and gazed at a farm as they drove by, a woman walking out to feed the chickens, a barking dog giving them a halfhearted chase, and cows strolling away from the milkshed to lip the frozen grass between the piles of dung scattered across the barnyard. Two geese engaged in a shouting match, and three more stretched their necks out, hissing at the farm wife's skirts. She turned back to Maria. "This reminds me of where I grew up," she said in Swedish. "Would you ever go back?"

"To live?" asked Maria. She considered briefly, and then said, "No. No real family left. And no reason to love it. My life is here."

"You don't miss living on a farm?"

Maria laughed. "What would I miss? Milking cows and churning butter 'til my arms ached? The animals got better care then we did. On the ship coming over I sang hallelujah each time I puked because I was off the farm for good." She peered at Ingeborg. "Why?"

"I don't know. These farms make me miss Sweden. Providence is so noisy and dirty. Sometimes I think it would be nice to live where I could have some chickens, maybe a little garden."

Maria snorted. "You grew up in Karlstad—going to your grandparents' farm was your holiday. It's different when you can never leave. Try milking when your hands are chapped and raw with the cold. The cows kick you and tip the milk pail over." She shuddered. "You think it's cold now. I was colder working on Swedish farms. You'll never get me back to a farm, or to Sweden to stay. I'll buy my meat at the market, thank you, all cut up nicely, and eat it next to the stove in my warm kitchen."

Ingeborg laughed and said no more about it, but turned over the idea of returning to Sweden someday. They could buy a little red cottage with some chickens in the back, maybe a goat for the milk and the company. She still had family there: her mother, her sisters, and one brother. There were the many nieces and nephews—nearly grown, now. What were their days like? It was comforting, somehow, to think about living with people to whom she belonged. Then she shrugged and put it out of her mind. That decision was a long way off. She was happy living with Maria, and there was still work for her to do here.

They rattled on in comfortable silence. The road grew narrow, and sidetracks split off at angles, disappearing into the prairie grass. They stopped and consulted their road guide, which consisted of a simple map and a list of instructions. "At point four miles turn left at the oak tree," Ingeborg read. "I don't recall seeing any oak tree, at least not at a turn. I think we're on the wrong road." She looked around and spotted a small farm set well off the road and protected by a gate set in a fence of sagging barbed wire. "Let's ask there."

Maria turned Emilie around and bumped in over the lane, stopping just before the gate. Ingeborg stepped out of the car and slipped through the gate, latching it behind her. She didn't see any livestock but she knew to leave gates as you found them, open or shut. As she turned toward the house an angry dog raced around the side of the coal shed, barking and snarling, and dodged in to snap at her skirt. He was reddish brown, the size of a small pony, with long springy legs—if he stood up he could put his front paws on her shoulders.

Ingeborg was scared but stood her ground, knowing that if she fled he'd be on her in an instant. She tried not to imagine the feeling of his teeth sinking into her forearm, and spoke to him soothingly. "Shhh, now, good dog, we mean you no harm. Shh...." He continued to dance around her, barking furiously. The racket stung her ears, and he alternately rushed her and jumped back as if they were boxing. Ingeborg looked about fruitlessly for a stick to fend him off with while she tried to dodge back though the gate. She didn't want to hurt him, but she'd crack him across the head if she had to. Maria had emerged from the car and stood behind the gate saying anxiously, "Get out of there quick now, he'll bite you!"

At that moment the door to the house opened, and a woman stepped out onto the little porch, calling to the snarling dog. "Rusty, come here. Now!" The dog ignored her and redoubled his frantic attacks as she strode down the steps and through the yard to them. "Rusty!" she grabbed him by the scruff of the neck and wrestled him backward, commanding him to sit. To Ingeborg's relief he finally quieted, lowering himself onto his haunches and whining, but keeping his eyes pinned on Ingeborg.

Ingeborg thanked her, taking in her plain, homespun skirt covered with an apron, a heavy shawl thrown hastily around her shoulders. A threadbare scarf covered her hair. Ingeborg guessed she was in her late twenties. She glanced at the house and saw a few small heads peeking through the doorway.

"We're sorry to bother you," said Ingeborg, "but we've lost our way. Can you tell us the road to Cedar Rapids?"

The woman looked back at Ingeborg with small, hard eyes. Her face wore suspicion like a second skin. "You're well off the road to Cedar Rapids," she said, her voice flat and almost as unfriendly as her dog's. "What brings you out here?"

Ingeborg glanced quickly at Maria, then turned back to the woman and smiled reassuringly. "We're suffragists, ma'am. Traveling to Washington to meet with Congress and President Wilson. We want them to amend the Constitution so women can vote."

"The vote? What for?" the woman turned her head and spat. "Politics are for men, I say. I got enough to do here. I got no time for voting. Why, it'd take me half a day to get into town to mark my ballot. That's time I won't get back, you ask me."

Ingeborg suppressed a sigh. Her lucky day—a vicious dog *and* an anti. Thank goodness they needed nothing more than directions—she hated to think if they'd been forced to shelter for the night with these people. "A lot of women think the vote will make life better for their families," she said, calmly. "Better schools. Safer food. Things like that."

"My kids get all the schooling they need here on the farm," she said. "And we raise our own food. Whatever else we need, the Lord or my husband provides."

Ingeborg felt the tips of her ears begin to burn, but she tried to keep her voice mild. "Not every women has a husband, ma'am, and sometimes the ones they have aren't much good. We think women should be able to vote and not depend on men."

"The Bible says, 'Thy desire shall be to thy husband, and he shall rule over thee,'" said the woman, suddenly furious, and the dog began growling again, its hackles raised. "Get away from here with your votes. Don't need 'em!"

She glared at them, standing her ground with her hand on the dog's neck but looking as if she was itching to let him loose. Ingeborg turned and slipped through the gate, muttering to Maria in Swedish. "Let's go." Maria backed the car until she found a place to turn around, and then she swung Emilie back onto the road. Ingeborg groaned. "What's the matter with people? We offer her a banquet table with fine food and wine, and she's insisting on dry bread and water. I don't understand."

Maria shook her head and was silent for a bit. Presently, she stirred and said, "Women like that, people like that, they find comfort in rules. We wrap newborns snugly because they don't know what to do with their limbs. The womb holds them, they're scared when they throw their arms out and don't feel its walls pressing back. They cry. It calms them to wrap them. I think the more fearful people are the more they need walls—rules, beliefs—that make them feel safe."

"They're not curious about what's beyond those walls?" asked Ingeborg. "I would be." She crossed her arms and stared out into the passing fields.

Maria laughed. "You're different, Ingeborg, you're not like that. You probably cartwheeled down the birth canal. Your poor mother."

She shrugged and said, "People often hold onto rules they're taught as little ones. Those are hardest to change, sometimes. For some people, those rules work out for them and they think, why shouldn't everyone else follow them, too?"

"What makes women agree when men say, 'You're not smart enough to vote'?" complained Ingeborg. "They don't have to vote if they don't want to, but why deny it for the rest of us?"

"I don't see it either, Ingeborg, but right now we need the road to Cedar Rapids." She pointed to a farmer, perched on a wagon behind two massive draft horses. "Maybe he can help." She drew close and pulled Emilie over to the side of the road so as not to alarm the horses, and Ingeborg got out and picked her way over. She passed their map up to the farmer, who studied it briefly, nodded, and then traced his finger over it, talking all the while. Ingeborg gave him a big smile and a wave and returned to the car.

"We just have to go up another mile or so. There's a turnoff we missed earlier. He says the signpost is hidden by a branch."

They waited for his team to plod past, and then Maria eased back onto the road. Before long they found the turn and were heading toward Cedar Rapids, reaching it in the midafternoon.

The town looked like many they'd already seen, a broad main street of packed dirt lined with shops. Tidy homes with fenced-in yards bracketed either end of Main Street, while silos poked into the sky on the outskirts. Ingeborg marveled over the methodical grid structure of Midwestern streets. In Providence, as in Sweden, streets wound through towns almost whimsically, some so narrow an automobile could scarcely pass through, joining at odd intervals and crazy angles. The houses had come first and then the streets. Here, the streets had come first and then the houses. She wondered if the way streets were laid out changed people. Did living on identical square blocks with orderly streets make people all the same way, too?

When they checked into the Allison Hotel the clerk handed over a sealed envelope with an invitation to tea from a Mrs. Lila Carey, who lived on Grand Avenue. At the appointed hour Ingeborg and Maria turned up at Mrs. Carey's house, a large affair set back from the road behind the spreading branches of a burr oak tree. The grass around the flower beds was neatly trimmed and not a single leaf marred the expanse of lawn. A uniformed servant answered the door. She took their travel-stained outer garments without a word, though Ingeborg detected more than a hint of disapproval in the way she held their coats by her fingertips and at arm's length. Ingeborg glanced over at Maria, who grimaced, and they followed the maid into the drawing room.

Five immaculately dressed women were arranged around the tea table. Under her breath Ingeborg muttered a curse in Swedish—this was just like those tea parties in Providence that had made her start her own suffrage association. Mrs. Carey was at their center, a slender, blonde woman with mirthless blue eyes atop a perfect little nose. She rose to greet them and ushered them to their seats, asking immediately, "Are there just two of you, then? I was led to believe there were four." She wore a determined smile, but looked as though she suspected the invitation to tea had somehow gotten into the wrong hands.

Ingeborg gave her a big, gap-toothed grin and shook her head. "Mrs. Field is ill and Miss Joliffe returned to San Francisco for a while. It's just us two for now."

"I'm sorry to hear that. When do you expect them to return?" asked Mrs. Carey, as she motioned them into their seats. She completed the introductions and began to pour the tea, passing around plates of savory petits fours. Hungry, Ingeborg helped herself to five of the small, frosted cakes and popped one into her mouth, passing the plate on to Maria. Mrs. Carey's eyebrows rose toward her hairline.

Ingeborg chewed and swallowed as she explained that Sara would meet up with them in Clinton, and they hoped Frances would rejoin them soon. She shifted to talking about their trip, the petitions, and the plans for their arrival in Washington. "There will be a great event at the Capitol," said Ingeborg proudly, "and we'll meet with President Wilson later that day."

"It's the opening day of Congress," Maria added.

Although the women smiled politely, Ingeborg couldn't help but notice that they showed a marked lack of enthusiasm. Finally, Mrs. Carey set down her teacup and saucer and fixed them with a determined smile. Ingeborg thought she now understood what a field mouse might feel like just as it glimpsed the hawk's talons reaching for its back.

"And will you campaign against the Democrats in 1916—as you did in the 1914 elections?" she asked.

Ingeborg looked straight back at her. "If they force us to—yes," she said.

"We're all members of the Iowa Woman Suffrage Association," explained Mrs. Carey. "Mrs. Catt is from Cedar Rapids and we much prefer her methods. Some of those Democrats support suffrage, after all."

"Then they'd better get busy," said Ingeborg, drily. "They have nothing to fear from us if they at least try to move it along."

"Do they have anything to fear from you, really?" drawled Mrs. Carey. "You had very little effect in 1914, as I recall."

"That was the CU's first try," said Ingeborg, trying for a light tone and almost succeeding. She felt her chest tighten with anger and fought to keep her temper in check. "We'll be much better organized in 1916. All the women voters we have now—why, they could stop Wilson from being reelected!"

Mrs. Carey laughed, and her companions smiled thinly. "We're all Republicans, so we'd welcome any help in removing Mr. Wilson from office." Then she frowned. "But this stunt of yours is causing trouble for the majority of suffragists. Mrs. Catt doesn't like it, and neither do we, do we ladies?" The other women shook their heads, regarding Ingeborg and Maria with open dislike.

The woman to Ingeborg's right said firmly, "It's unbecoming of women to behave that way."

Ingeborg turned and considered the speaker. She wore a hobble skirt in a deep green fabric, and a black velvet hat with a tall, pointed feather sticking straight up behind her right ear. "It's unbecoming to insist women be recognized as citizens?" she asked quietly.

The woman sniffed and pointed her nose in the air. "We have no issue with asking for the vote," she said. "Hasn't NAWSA been doing that for decades? Let me remind you that, but for our work, there would be no women voters. The CU is new to this. You'll just have to accept these things take time, dear. Running about demanding the vote makes us look ridiculous—and makes the men very angry. An angry man makes a poor ally."

Ingeborg stared at her. There was no point in antagonizing these women, but she couldn't back down. "Politicians trade votes for support every day," she said, slowly. "The Democrats are angry because we're applying pressure—but it's working! In Swedish we'd say, 'Only dead fish follow the stream.'"

"I beg your pardon?" gasped Mrs. Carey, affronted. She exchanged glances with her companions, who looked equally outraged.

Maria tried to cut in. "What Ingeborg means is—"

But Ingeborg had her blood up and forged on. "We need to try new things. The men like it when you smile and beg and go home crying when they pay no attention. But the CU makes them see we have the power to change things." She shrugged. "If you can't change the vote, change the politician."

Maria jumped in. "Can't we work together? We'd get the vote faster."

"We won't support your methods," said Mrs. Carey, tartly. "It makes no real difference to women if it takes another twenty or thirty years to get the vote. What does it matter, compared to preserving those qualities that make us women? Meanwhile, our men take good care of us, don't they?" She looked around at her companions, who murmured in agreement. "We can afford to wait a little longer."

Ingeborg took a deep breath and looked around the circle of women, their faces closed and watchful. It made her angry to explain this over and over. "Some of us have no men to take care of us," she said slowly. She looked over at Maria.

"Mrs. Carey, why do you want the vote?" asked Maria, simply.

Mrs. Carey's mouth snapped into a thin, straight line, and her fierce eyes bored into Maria's. "We want the vote to protect women's sphere—the home, our children. We're all in agreement on that, surely?"

Maria had gone to the heart of the matter. They weren't just at odds over strategies, they differed over the end goal as well. These women found comfort and security in the confines of their lives. The vote would allow them to decorate it more to their liking, as if they were choosing new wallpaper for their dining rooms.

"No," said Ingeborg, slowly, "we're not." She raised her chin. "We think women should be equal to men in every sphere. We need the vote, but it won't be enough. There will be other fights. But we must finish this one before we get to the others."

"So—you're radicals, then," said Mrs. Hobble Skirt. She spit the word out as if it were spoiled fruit. "You want a feminist revolution."

Ingeborg glanced at Maria, who was sitting upright in her chair, gripping her empty teacup. Her face betrayed no emotion, but her eyes implored Ingeborg to stay calm. Ingeborg attempted a smile, though bitter words boiled at the very tip of her tongue. "We think women should control our own lives, and have more say in this government—we help pay for it, after all. Is that radical? You should thank us—we'll finish this faster."

"Well, I'll tell you something," said a silver-haired woman perched on the edge of an overstuffed armchair in the corner of the room. She'd been following the debate with interest, her sharp eyes darting from one speaker to the other. She thumped her cane on the floor for emphasis and said in a creaky voice, "Mrs. Catt is a particular friend of mine—I knew her parents well. She is a lady through and through. And tough, too. She's done more for suffrage than all of us in this room put together. She knows, in the end, rational arguments will prevail—men will simply see the sense in raising women up and give us the vote. There's no need to play politics. Women should never stoop to that."

Ingeborg gazed at her, groping for a civil response in the riot of words whirling about her brain. To her mind, this notion of ladylike behavior caused women endless trouble. You were a lady or you weren't, and if you had to ask what it meant then you couldn't be counted as one. It was the fear of being cast in with the great unwashed hordes that kept these pinch-nosed women in line. Ingeborg forced herself to remain calm. "When you say *lady*," she asked slowly, "what does that mean? Who decides?" She looked at each of them, their faces identical masks of polite disdain. "It's like a prison you lock yourselves into. Maybe it's time it should mean something different." She looked for a nod, a smile, some agreement, but there was none. The silence lengthened.

Maria stirred. "It's a long drive to Clinton tomorrow, Ingeborg," she said quietly. "We should go." She looked over at Mrs. Carey and smiled. "Thank you for the tea," she said quietly. "And best wishes for your success with suffrage in Iowa." She rose to her feet, and Ingeborg followed suit. "We'll show ourselves out."

The women issued polite but chilly good-byes, which is what any *lady* would do, thought Ingeborg, with an inward sigh. Summoned by Mrs. Carey's bell, the servant met them at the front door and handed over their hats and coats. It had grown dark, and the wind pushed against them as they walked to Emilie and wordlessly climbed inside.

Maria swung the car around and drove back toward the hotel. Ingeborg slumped against the seat cushions, still seething. "What a bunch of pampered hens!" she spat out. "They probably never worked a day in their lives!"

"We don't know that, Ingeborg," said Maria. "Maybe their lives have been much harder than we think, and they're just trying to protect what they worked so hard for." Then she laughed. "I was worried you'd lose your temper in there."

"I might have if Mrs. Hobble Skirt had kept talking. Women like her make me sick. Don't tell me being their sort of lady is the best way to win. If we stick to their methods, you and I won't live long enough to vote."

* * *

They arrived in Clinton the next day in time to meet Sara's train. She descended the steps to the platform looking weary, her traveling clothes speckled with coal ash. As she looked around she mopped her nose with a large handkerchief, and Ingeborg and Maria exchanged worried glances. Was Sara no better?

When Maria called out, Sara looked around, broke into a wide smile, and moved quickly toward them. "There you are! I'm feeling better, even if I look like a coal miner. I have new sympathy for Mabel—all the time she spends on trains. They're only a bit better than motorcars."

Ingeborg studied Sara. When she was ill, or exhausted, or both, as was so often the case on this trip, Sara could be whiny and petulant, and it was hard to remember then that she could be this charming, confident woman. She'd take her over Mrs. Carey and Mrs. Hobble Skirt any day.

They found their way to the hotel and checked in, agreeing to meet for dinner. Then they went their separate ways, Sara to write some letters, Maria to nap, and Ingeborg to make sure Emilie was in top form. The engine had begun backfiring, and the smoke from her tailpipe had gotten thicker and blacker, her way of saying she was overdue for attention.

Ingeborg refastened her skirt buttons to form the loose trousers, tied her apron over her traveling coat, and raised the hood. She checked for worn or loose parts and then adjusted the spark plugs to the precise gap required. She added water to the radiator and topped up the magneto oil cups. Next she wiped down the gears with kerosene and lubricated them with a mixture of graphite and oil, sliding under the car to get at the connections underneath. She worked quickly, her hands now practiced and familiar with the feel of the tools and the way Emilie was put together. It felt good to work with her hands after hours of sitting in the car. Again, her mind strayed back to the tea with the ladies yesterday afternoon, and she smiled when she thought of how appalled they'd be at seeing her crawling around with oil-stained hands underneath the car. To hell with them.

Finishing up, Ingeborg stowed the tools and her apron in Emilie's boot. As she walked through the hotel lobby, she picked up the *Clinton Evening News*, glancing over the headlines as she rode the elevator to the third floor. A photograph of a Negro woman caught her attention, along with the grisly headline "Lynchers Build Bonfire, Roast Two Men." In the South, mobs regularly murdered Black men almost for sport, sometimes doing it in front of crowds. That wasn't new, but it was terrible to see a newspaper cruelly make light of it.

Back in her room she studied the article more carefully. The woman in the photo was Ida B. Wells Barnett, an anti-lynching activist who campaigned for suffrage, too. "Listen to this, Maria," said Ingeborg, and read a little from the piece. "She lives in Chicago. We should visit her!"

Maria groaned. "Ingeborg."

"Why are you groaning? She believes in the same things we do. If she were white, we wouldn't think twice. In fact, we wouldn't have to find her, she'd be on the stage with us."

"You know why, Ingeborg. Remember what that congressman told us. The CU can't provoke Southern states by siding with the Negroes. It's simple."

"But it's not right," fumed Ingeborg.

"Right, wrong, it depends on what you want. People crazy and mean enough to laugh as they burn Negroes for no reason won't pass suffrage if they think the women will vote against them. Standing with the Negroes on this is like teasing a rattlesnake. You might only be bitten once, but it doesn't matter if that bite kills you." Maria glared at Ingeborg. She wore a grumpy frown, her hair still tousled from her nap.

"What are you talking about, rattlesnakes? You sound like a crazy old woman," Ingeborg shot back. "It won't be in the papers. We'll just slip away one day and see her. No one needs to know. Like in Salt Lake City when I saw Joe. There was no trouble then."

Maria hunched a shoulder and looked away.

"Maria, I swear, if we just meet women like Mrs. Carey, you'll need to put me back in the Dexter Asylum when we finish this trip. All these people doing important work, and we drive through their cities like they don't exist."

"You know we've met plenty of people who aren't like Mrs. Carey. You're just stirring up trouble the way you always do," grumbled Maria. "You try my patience sometimes, Ingeborg."

"Aren't you the least bit curious about her?" Ingeborg glanced at the article again. "It says she's one of the foremost voices raised against lynching. She writes articles and books about it. She helped start the NAACP."

"The what?"

"You know, the society to uplift the Negroes." Ingeborg dropped the newspaper on the bed and went to the washstand, pouring water into the bowl. "We read about it—they formed it a few years ago." She stripped off her garments and began soaping up her hands and arms, scrubbing at the oil stains. "You don't have to, but I'm going to see her if I can."

* * *

They left early the next morning and wove through the streets of Clinton, rattling across the bridge over the great Mississippi River and heading east along the Lincoln Highway, the sun still low on the horizon and peeking through stacks of pancaked clouds. The streets near the hotel were busy with motorcars, but farther out they passed horse-drawn wagons rattling into the city, the farmers slouching on the box and reining in their teams to quiet them as Emilie hurried past. Before long they were out in open country, once again passing solitary farmhouses crouched in stubbled fields silvered with frost. Ingeborg breathed out long white plumes; it was cold, though the clear skies promised that the sun might warm them later on. For now she had hot stones at her feet, and she was wrapped in a blanket. She looked over at Maria, crouched as usual behind the wheel, intent on driving. Maria needed her feet free and thus had no bricks, but she didn't complain. She needed a warmer hat, though. Perhaps they'd find one in Chicago.

Chicago. It was hard to picture as they passed through farmland that they'd be there by evening, their largest city yet. She'd never been, though she might have visited Rolf had she known he was there. Chicago was said to be a city built by immigrants—drawn by work in the trainyards and slaughterhouses, in construction, and in factories making clothes and other goods. Its workers were famously unruly—in Providence the unions looked to Chicago for examples of what they should be doing themselves.

Mabel had been in Chicago for several days and was sure to have arranged a full schedule of lunches, teas, and speeches. Still, Ingeborg was hopeful that she'd be able to find time to visit Ida Barnett. Ingeborg had sent her a telegram the previous evening, ducking quickly into the Western Union office next to the hotel before meeting Sara for dinner. She'd named the days she'd be in Chicago and inquired if Mrs. Barnett would be available. With luck there'd be an answer when they checked into the LaSalle Hotel this evening.

Suddenly Sara stirred and asked, "Would you like to meet Clarence Darrow?"

Ingeborg blinked at her, her brow furrowing as she struggled to wrench her thoughts back to the present. Had Sara said something about Clarence Darrow? She and Maria traded glances. Maria grinned. Sara was full of surprises. Darrow was another lawyer, even more famous than Frank Walsh, but for similar reasons. Workers worshipped him, and the moneyed class trembled when they knew they had to face him in court.

"Clarence Darrow?" Ingeborg, trying to ignore the little hiccup of jealousy in her chest. "How do you know him?"

"He and my sister Mary were lovers for years," said Sara casually, brushing some dust off the buffalo hide. "He's also a friend of Erskine's." She smiled at Ingeborg, who had twisted around in her seat to gape at her. "In fact, it was he who introduced us."

"Your sister is Clarence Darrow's mistress?" Maria gasped.

"Not anymore," said Sara. She shrugged. "His wife threatened to leave him, so he broke it off. But Mary got him through some hard times, including when he was tried for bribing the jury in the McNamara case."

"I remember that," said Ingeborg, quickly. "Those two brothers bombed the Los Angeles Times building. Or were accused of it. Do you think they did?"

"They were guilty, all right," Sara said, sitting forward and leaning her arms on the front seat. "I covered that trial for the *Oregon Daily Journal*, and because Mary and I shared rooms, I saw a lot of Clarence. He knew they were guilty—that's why he arranged that plea deal. He hated to do it, but it was the only way he could save their lives."

Ingeborg nodded slowly. "He hates the death penalty." She looked over at Sara. "What's he like?"

Sara wrinkled her nose. "I don't care for him much, and I've often wondered why Mary does. He's brilliant, of course, but I've seen him use that brilliance to torment the people he professes to love, including Mary."

"He's abusive?" asked Maria.

"He hurts with his words, not his fists," Sara replied. "He likes playing with people, probing them, to see how he can pull them to pieces. It's worse when he's drunk, of course, which he often is." She sighed and sat back in her seat. "But he can also be charming and, of course, he's fascinating—people flock to him at any party. I'm glad, though, that he ended the affair with Mary. She's married, now, and has a baby girl. Clarence is too old for her."

Maria and Ingeborg exchanged glances; Sara saw this and laughed. "I know! I should talk. My first husband, Albert, was twenty years older than I am, and Erskine and I are thirty years apart." She shook her head ruefully. "But age doesn't always matter." She lapsed into silence.

Ingeborg watched the road spooling out in front of them with unseeing eyes, her travel weariness forgotten as she imagined meeting Clarence Darrow and Ida Barnett. This trip was taxing in every possible way—she had never been so exhausted and sore, bored and frightened and frantic by turns. But how else would she meet these people she'd read about in newspapers?

Wouldn't she have something to talk about when they were back in Providence! She entertained herself the rest of the way to Chicago with images of herself speaking to labor groups, to the suffrage snobs, and to progressives of every stripe.

CHAPTER ELEVEN

NOVEMBER 8, 1915

Ingeborg grinned as she looked around the crowd gathered at the steps of the Art Institute of Chicago. Behind her, at the top of the steps, a chorus of one hundred women stood grouped on either side of the band, with the Great Demand banner fluttering over their heads. The echoes of Sara's "Song of the Free Women" were closing out to thunderous applause from the huge crowd that had gathered, much bigger than any they'd seen since that last night at the Exposition. Many women were draped with the CU's purple, white, and gold sashes, and against their bright colors the envoys' worn traveling clothes looked drab by comparison. Ingeborg was proud of them, though; each one of the stains on her overcoat, the scuffs on her leather boots had a story behind it that few in this crowd could equal.

Mabel had done her work well. Fully fifty motorcars packed with suffragists and bedecked with suffrage flags and signs had met them at the LaSalle Hotel that morning to escort them to the Art Institute. Their procession was so long that mounted policemen had to escort them as they made their way slowly through the crowded streets. The Chicagoans they passed clapped and wished them luck and thanked them for their work. Ingeborg held her head high, smiling and nodding to the crowd, pretending that she and Maria alone were the focus of the occasion.

Now she turned her attention to Mayor William Thompson, who was formally welcoming them to Chicago. "We have watched the growth of the suffrage movement with great interest," he said. "As you know, we have partial suffrage in Illinois, and a more confusing and nonsensical system man has yet to devise." The crowd laughed. Consulting his notes, he continued, "In Illinois, women can vote for presidential electors but not in party primaries or for delegates to national conventions." Boos from the crowd. "They may vote for university trustees but not for county school superintendents. Likewise, they may vote for county surveyors but not for judges or sheriffs." He looked at the crowd and raised his open palms in question, his face a study in incredulity; they laughed and clapped in return. "In cities they may vote for mayor or aldermen, but not for police magistrates. And no woman in Illinois can vote for candidates to the state legislature or Congress, or for an amendment to the State Constitution." He shoved the paper into his pocket. "Now I ask you," he thundered, "Where is the sense or justice in that?"

The crowd roared in response, "No justice! No sense!"

Motioning for quiet, Mayor Thompson turned to Sara and said, "On behalf of the City of Chicago, I wish you Godspeed and much success on your mission. It is with great pleasure that I agree to sign your petition, with the proviso that my wife be the first to have that honor." The crowd clapped and cheered.

Sara thanked him and stepped up to speak. "I can't help but contrast the kind words of Mayor Thompson with those of the Kansas City mayor a few days ago. He made mention of woman as muse, as the poetry of man's existence." She stopped, and then deadpanned. "Then I think there was something about the sun, the moon, and the stars...." The crowd laughed. Sara took a deep breath and raised her voice higher. "But nowhere in his lofty words was there any recognition of women as citizens, or of the justice of our claims for equality!" She turned and smiled at Mayor Thompson. "I like your approach much better."

Afterward they drove back to the LaSalle Hotel, minus most of the escort but along with the leaders of every one of Illinois' many suffrage organizations, to meet with Congressman Fred Britten. The congressman assured them that he was well-disposed toward suffrage and would support its passage through the House of Representatives. Ingeborg waited impatiently for the ceremonies to end, so she and Maria could sneak away.

A note from Ida Wells Barnett had been waiting for Ingeborg when they'd checked into the hotel the previous afternoon, inviting them to tea and providing directions to her home in the city's south side. Ingeborg fidgeted as the meeting droned on and groaned inwardly every time someone else stepped up to pose a question to the congressman.

At length they made their escape and hurried to the car. Ingeborg had told Mabel she needed to get the car serviced that afternoon. The next day being Sunday, the mechanics would be off; it couldn't wait if they were to leave as planned Monday morning.

"Very well," said Mabel, looking at her curiously. "If you're certain it's something you can't manage yourself?"

Ingeborg busied herself buttoning up her coat and straightening her hat, not daring to look too long at Mabel. "No, we need a special part, and I want them to install it."

Mabel reminded her of the evening's schedule, and Ingeborg and Maria were free to go.

Ida Wells Barnett lived with her husband in a tidy stone rowhouse just south of E 35th Street, not far from Lake Michigan. A tree spread its bare branches over the front yard. Maria found a place by the curb to park Emilie and then looked over at Ingeborg. "I hope this is worth your fuss," she said quietly. "I don't know what you hope to gain from it."

Ingeborg shrugged and shook her head. "Me neither. But I can't stop thinking that we're stronger working together—the way rope is, all those strands. The CU wants women to work together to win suffrage but their rope's all white—they've washed Negro women out like a stain. I hate that."

Ingeborg walked up the steps, Maria trailing behind her, and thumped the ornate brass door knocker to announce their arrival. After a few moments Ida herself opened the door.

"Welcome," she said, with a polite smile. "Come in, come in." She helped them remove their coats and hung them on a stand in the narrow front hall, and then ushered them into the parlor. After the cold drive Ingeborg was grateful for a small coal fire that warmed the room. She glanced around, noting the writing desk in the corner, piled with papers and books. Books also crammed shelves along the parlor wall. "Please forgive my untidy desk," said Ida with a smile, noting where Ingeborg's gaze had landed. "I'm a journalist, you know, and this is my office much of the time. I'm working on a paper I'm to deliver at the NAACP next month."

They exchanged pleasantries as Ida poured tea and passed around a plate of sandwiches. She was older than her photo in the newspapers, about the same age as Ingeborg herself, with fine lines etching her face and her graying hair swept back in a simple bun. Her wool dress lay comfortably over her ample chest and hips, giving her the look of a kindly grandmother. But her gaze was penetrating and steady, and Ingeborg guessed it could bore through any pretenses. She shifted a little, suddenly uneasy at being there. Too late, she wondered once again why she had not listened to Maria.

After a bit, Ida set her cup and saucer down and gave them a questioning look. "I understand you're on a journey to Washington on behalf of woman suffrage, for the Congressional Union," she said.

"Yes," Ingeborg spoke quickly, the words tumbling out. "Maria and I admire your work and since we were in Chicago we wanted to meet you. We were so pleased to find you were available. As immigrants—"

But Ida cut her off. "My pleasure," she said. "Aren't you traveling with some other women—the envoys, I think they're called? Why did they not accompany you?"

Maria choked on the bite of sandwich she had just put in her mouth, and Ingeborg made a show of handing her a napkin and patting her on the back while she decided what to say.

"I'm afraid Miss Joliffe had to return to California—an illness in the family," said Ingeborg, vaguely. "Mrs. Field is otherwise engaged."

"I see," said Ida. She took another sip of tea, eyeing them over the rim. "Is it possible you have a message for me from Miss Paul?"

"No," said Ingeborg, flatly.

Ida sat back in her chair and blew out an exasperated sigh. "In fact, this is not an official visit from the Congressional Union?"

Ingeborg shook her head mutely. Maria kept her eyes on her teacup.

"That's a shame. I had hoped your visit meant the CU had decided to strengthen their numbers by inviting Negro suffrage clubs to join them after all." Ida spoke quietly, but with a controlled fury that betrayed her anger at being snubbed. "If they don't know you're here, just what are you doing in my parlor?"

Ingeborg put her hands on the top of her head, closed her eyes, and took a deep breath. Then she gave Ida a level look and said, "Because I wanted to meet you. Since we left San Francisco we've never once met with Negro suffragists or invited them to be part of our meetings."

"And you never will," said Ida, irritated. "Tell me something I don't know."

"I believe women need to stick together, that makes us stronger, like the IWW that I belong to also." She paused. "It's wrong, what we're doing."

Ida nodded slightly. "Thank you for that, I suppose. How is it you're involved with this CU adventure?"

"Almost by accident." Ingeborg quickly told how they'd stumbled into driving the envoys to Washington, DC. Ida listened closely, offering the occasional nod or "Is that so?" and soon Ingeborg found herself complaining of the CU's treatment of her and Maria, describing the slights they suffered even as the CU depended on them so heavily.

"It doesn't surprise me one bit," said Ida, sighing. "I have my own issues with Miss Paul. Were you at the parade she organized in Washington, the day before Wilson's inauguration?"

"I was," said Ingeborg, remembering. Almost eight thousand women had arrived in Washington to march in the greatest suffrage parade ever held. The procession had drawn such crowds that Wilson, arriving the same day to prepare for his inauguration ceremony, was surprised to find almost no one there to greet him.

The march had started off well, but the police had refused to protect them from the hostile men who'd flooded Pennsylvania Avenue, stopping the women in their tracks. Ingeborg had stood with the Rhode Island delegation as an angry, jeering mob pressed against them from all sides, pushing and shoving, reducing them almost to single file. Beside her Anna Wheaten had fallen to her hands and knees, tripped by a man wearing a sailor's uniform. Ingeborg reached down and hauled her to her feet before she was trampled by the marchers crowding in behind them. Putting Anna behind her, Ingeborg had confronted the sailor, locking eyes with him and trying desperately to project fearlessness even as her insides quaked. She knew instinctively that showing any sign of weakness would invite another attack. The sailor had smirked, and Ingeborg braced herself, but then quite suddenly he turned and disappeared into the crowd.

For ages they couldn't move in any direction, and it seemed entirely possible they would be massacred in broad daylight on the streets of the nation's capital, merely for wanting to vote. After what seemed an eternity the army arrived to restore order and allow the parade to finish. She had been so relieved to see the uniformed soldiers advancing toward them, pushing the mob back to the sidewalks. When the procession moved forward once again, she realized how narrow their escape had been. Scores of women had been injured. "I'll never forget that day."

"Nor will I," said Ida, her voice icy and her eyes snapping with anger. "You may recall that at the last minute, Miss Paul considered having Negro suffragists march together at the rear of the parade, instead of with their states. Apparently there were some who didn't want us to be seen marching with our white sisters."

Ingeborg sank back in her chair, her limbs leaden, forcing herself to meet Ida's glare. She had some hazy recollection of hearing about this after the march, but had forgotten.

"We felt so angry, so betrayed," Ida went on. "To think that women who were demanding political freedom would signal their willingness to deny it to their Negro sisters—with the eyes of the world watching. It was a disgrace."

Ingeborg nodded and slanted her eyes over at Maria, who was gazing at Ida with such sadness it nearly broke Ingeborg's heart. "That was wrong," she said hoarsely, wrenching her eyes back to Ida. She'd heard about this after the parade was over.

"I'm glad you agree!" said Ida, coldly. "Though ultimately she made the right decision, I had already decided to wait in the crowd until the Illinois contingent came by, then I stepped into their ranks and stayed with them to the end. We had words with Miss Paul afterward, I can tell you." She sighed and shook her head, reaching for cup of tea.

"You were that woman! I remember it now." Ingeborg took a deep breath and looked up at the ceiling, then exhaled in a gust and gazed at Ida. "How do we change this?" she asked, miserably. She glanced at Maria. "We're told the Southern states will block the federal amendment if they think it means Negroes will outvote them." Maria nodded, mutely, fingering her teacup.

"They certainly will," said Ida. She leaned forward and fastened her eyes on Ingeborg's. "But I ask you how white women can demand political freedom for themselves and watch it be denied their Negro sisters and brothers? What if people with white skin simply did the right thing and recognized those with black skin as equals in every way?" She got to her feet and crossed to the window, looking out at the street, then turned back to them. "I was born a slave," she said quietly. "How can any of your injustices compare to being owned by another person? Don't leave us behind, I beg you. We need you to fight for us, too, and not just in the South."

"It's no better here?" Maria asked.

Ida shrugged. "It's better. We can move about more freely, but we're always the last hired and the first fired—for the jobs they let us have. We're paid less for the same work. And we can only live in some places, which are already too crowded. Every day more of our brothers and sisters arrive here—fleeing the South where slavery never really ended. It just changed form." She crossed back over and sat in her chair, regarding Ingeborg and Maria with eyes that burned through them.

Ingeborg hung her head. "I'm sorry," she said miserably. She looked down at her hands, strong, calloused, some dirt under her thumbnail, the skin marked with scars from old cuts and a few new ones she'd picked up working on Emilie. With these hands she had worked her way to a comfortable life. She'd worked hard, yes. But her white skin had opened doors that were shut in the faces of people like Ida, whose hands were no different from hers, who worked just as hard for the same chance to build a life. Despair pressed down on her.

"I don't know what we two can do," she whispered, lifting her eyes to Ida. "How we can help."

"Use your voices," said Ida. She sat forward in her chair; her voice urgent. "Speak up! It matters what you say."

Ingeborg thought for a bit. "The federal amendment would mean voting rights can't be denied on the basis of sex. That would include Negro women, surely?"

Ida clapped her hands on her knees, frustrated. "Yes, but the Southern states already prevent our men from voting—poll taxes, literacy tests. Lynching. That's when they try to register. Most are too afraid to even try. How will it be different when this amendment passes?"

"I don't know," said Ingeborg. "But over time…." Her voice trailed off. "Maybe they'll get used to the idea," she finished weakly.

"How long do you expect us to wait for our freedom?" Ida demanded, her voice bitter. "It's already been half a century since the Civil War ended. We need to wake people up to the injustice Negroes face every day." She leaned forward. "There's room in your car for another person, one who looks like me. That's what I'm saying."

Ingeborg took a deep breath. "You're right. We'll do what we can."

Maria looked over at her. "We should go."

Ingeborg heaved herself to her feet and walked over to Ida, who rose to meet her. They clasped hands and then Ingeborg reached out and drew her into a hug. "Thank you," she said softly. "For seeing us, and for your work." She stood aside as Maria approached and hugged Ida also.

Ida leaned against the doorjamb as they put on their outer clothing. Her face was edged in a kind of bitter sadness, but her voice, when she spoke, was soft. "Stay warm," she said. "I'll be watching for news of you."

Ingeborg looked at her. "Stay safe," she said soberly.

The air was chilly, and Emilie coughed to life reluctantly. Maria waited for her to warm up before pointing her nose north toward the hotel. The streets were quieter now, the streetlamps were on, and people hurried down the sidewalks, their collars turned up against the cold. Maria asked, "Did you get what you wanted?"

Ingeborg sighed heavily, a frosty plume that blew back in her face as they motored along. "I don't know. I know she's right. If all women stood strong together, we could shout down the racists."

"But," said Maria, expertly maneuvering Emilie around an icy patch and accelerating down an open street. "Women don't even agree on suffrage. Not the suffragists, even! It could take decades more to pass the amendment if we add the race question."

"It would be worth it if women like Ida could be with us in the car, on the platforms," argued Ingeborg. "You saw her. She's smarter than both of us together. She's like Miss Paul."

"You're right. It isn't fair. But Miss Paul's got her teeth locked on this like a dog on a bone, and she won't give it up for anything."

Ingeborg stared unseeing out the windshield, her face troubled. "Who else will help if we don't?"

Maria shook her head. "Power only goes so far." She thought for a moment and said, "It can be stretched too thin, like when you roll out pie dough. There are only so many pies it can cover before it tears and makes holes."

"Pie dough!" Ingeborg said, exasperated. "What does pie dough have to do with this? Besides, you can just make more."

"What if there isn't any more flour? What happens then?"

Ingeborg had no reply. The arguments circled around her like hornets, she'd slap some away only to have others dive in below her guard and burrow their stingers into their skin. But one thing she knew for certain—it was wrong to ignore injustice. She felt unsettled and angry, and they finished the ride back to the hotel in silence.

CHAPTER TWELVE

NOVEMBER 9, 1915

Giddy with exhaustion and triumph, Sara, Maria, and Ingeborg gathered around a table in a corner of the hotel bar. Mabel had already left for Indianapolis. The Chicago meetings had been brilliant; thousands of supporters had come out, and the press had followed their movements closely and sung their praises. People recognized them everywhere, clapping and cheering as Emilie sailed past flying the suffrage flags. They were more than halfway to Washington with the most difficult driving behind them. Support for the amendment was growing everywhere. Nothing could stop them now.

Ingeborg stared hard across the table at Clarence Darrow, who had joined them for a drink and was bantering with Sara about her sister, Mary. Was this the same man she'd read so much about, the eloquent defender of the poor and weak? She was having trouble believing it. He was older than she'd expected, with deep lines carved on either side of his nose and mouth and across his bulging forehead. His greasy, thinning hair was parted on the side and combed over the top, struggling to hide his bald spot. A sour odor clung to him, and his fingernails were dirty. Lumpy skin and watchful eyes, set wide and predatory beneath his heavy brow, put Ingeborg in mind of a crocodile. If she squinted she could almost see incisors poking out over his lips. How on earth had Mary—or any woman—found him attractive?

Darrow turned his attention to Maria and Ingeborg and said with his toothy smile, "I see Alice Paul has got her claws into you, too. Why don't you just go home and forget about the whole damn thing? To hell with the Congressional Union." He drained his glass and signaled the waiter for another, his second. Now she could see the veins prominent in his nose and cheeks.

Ingeborg eyed him as she took a gulp of her own wine. Surely Darrow favored suffrage? Had she missed something? She darted a question at Sara who looked just as confused. Maria shifted nervously in her seat. The air felt charged.

"The whiskey must have gone to your head, Darrow," said Sara. "I can't believe you mean any such thing. You've always favored suffrage. I remember talking about it with you and Mary many times."

"I'm not drunk, if that's what you're saying," Darrow retorted. "Not yet anyway. But I stand by my statement. Woman suffrage will ruin this country."

Sara laughed at him. "Come now, Clarence Darrow, champion of labor and king of the antis! They must be thrilled."

"I was a suffragist once, but no longer." He looked over at Sara, who was glaring at him. "Don't frown now, honey, you're prettier when you smile," he said, leering at her.

Sara ignored him and looked at Ingeborg and Maria. "I had no idea he'd switched sides. He used to wax poetic on the topic of equal rights for women." She looked back over at Darrow. "Does Mary know about this? She'd skewer you if she heard you're an anti."

"I don't care," said Darrow, "It's none of her business, anyway."

"Wait 'til I tell her," said Sara.

Ingeborg stared at Darrow, disappointed. What was going on? He was so different from what she'd expected. Where would labor unions be without men like him. Or Frank Walsh? They were heroes. Like shiny shells plucked out of the water and held to the sun, everyone admired the layered depths of their beauty. But they were different when you met them face-to-face. The gloss was gone, and a faint stink clung to them, just as seashells did when you brought them home and set them on a shelf. Their ordinariness was revealed. They were no different from any other man—the local fishmonger, or the man who came around to sharpen knives. "What changed your mind?" she asked.

Darrow leaned toward Ingeborg with a pleasant smile that didn't touch his eyes. She suppressed a shiver and wondered if facing him on a witness stand felt like this. "Women are too conservative. We already have too damn many laws, and when women vote they just pass more."

"Perhaps women wouldn't have to pass more laws if men had done a better job in the first place," Ingeborg shot back, nettled.

"Look at San Francisco!" Darrow said, rattling the ice in his glass. "Four years after California gave them suffrage, they've passed every kind of law imaginable—mark my words, temperance is next."

"Oh stop, Darrow!" snapped Sara, exasperated. "Women always get the blame for temperance, but you know it wouldn't have a chance unless men supported it, too."

Darrow shrugged. "But women will clinch it," he said. "And the men know it. That's why they vote against suffrage. Look at New York, Pennsylvania, Massachusetts, and New Jersey—they all denied it just in the last few weeks."

"But that's precisely why we need a federal amendment," Sara pointed out. "It's so much more work to push it through the states, and when we lose, we go backwards because everyone just talks about how suffrage lost, not how many people voted for it."

"That's the fortunes of war—and politics," grinned Darrow. The waiter set his new glass down in front of him. Darrow picked it up and took a deep swallow.

"Anything more for you ladies?" asked the waiter. Sara and Maria quickly refused, but Ingeborg asked for another glass. Her blood was up. Darrow would insist on covering the bill, anyway, so Maria couldn't complain of the cost. Maria put a warning hand on Ingeborg's thigh, but Ingeborg ignored her.

Darrow drew his hand across his mouth and continued. "States should decide who votes," he declared. "Congress has no business interfering."

His words hung like a thunderclap in the air. Sara was the first to recover. "What about the Fifteenth Amendment?" she demanded. "Though it gave only Negro men the vote and left women out," she added. "But it set the precedent."

Darrow eyed her. "They were wrong," he said simply. "It isn't up to Congress who should vote."

"If Congress hadn't acted, there would be states where Negroes would never vote," said Ingeborg. "Neither would women."

"The Negroes don't vote in those states now," Darrow pointed out. "Jim Crow laws see to that. And no one's proposing to fight a war over Jim Crow. That I know of, anyway," Darrow raised the glass to the women. "To the good fight," he said gallantly, taking a sip.

"You're just being impossible," said Sara. "You don't believe half of what you're saying."

"Oh, I surely do," said Darrow, lowering his gaze to set his drink down precisely on the wet ring left by the previous one.

"But it's not fair when only half the people are free," protested Ingeborg.

"When has it ever been otherwise?" asked Darrow, throwing up his hands. "It's more equal now than it was at the start—at first only property-owning men could vote."

Sara snorted. "But it wasn't long before men without property could vote, and they hardly had to ask for it. Women have been begging for the vote for decades. And times have changed. Did you see that poll of newspaper editors in the *Literary Digest* a few weeks ago?"

"No," said Darrow.

"Well, they asked a thousand editors about their policy on suffrage and whether their communities supported it. A good two-thirds of the editors favored it, and almost half of their communities did—a lot of them hadn't made up their minds yet. So suffrage is coming, whether you like it or not."

Darrow shrugged. "The Founding Fathers were worried about putting too much power into the hands of the common man. And they were right if you ask me. Democracy is overrated."

"But it's not fair!" repeated Ingeborg.

"Oh, that I'll grant you," said Darrow. "It's never been fair. But voting is a states'—"

"To hell with states' rights," Ingeborg snapped. "Men just hide behind that to avoid talking about women's rights." Darrow's unexpected betrayal had sent a surge of anger coursing through her, and the wine she'd drunk made her reckless. She opened her mouth to go on but Maria administered a sharp kick under the table.

Darrow gave a raspy chuckle. "You're not entirely wrong there," he conceded. "But we're 'the United *States* of America,'" he reminded her, "Not just *America*. If there are some states that want to molder in the darkness, under our Constitution that's their prerogative."

"Well, let them molder over something besides voting rights for women," said Sara. "We're going for the federal amendment, and we're going to win. We've been at this too long."

* * *

They left Chicago the following morning in a cold drizzle that strengthened to a steady downpour as they reached the outskirts of the city. Rain cascaded down the windshield, and with the top up, their breath fogged the inside of it, requiring Ingeborg to wipe it frequently so Maria could see to drive. Still, Maria had to peer out her side window to steer Emilie around the larger puddles, so it was almost as damp inside the car as out. The rain pounded on the car's top, which rattled and shook in the wind. Conversation was impossible.

Ingeborg was cocooned in gloom. In Chicago she'd become convinced—they all had—that this trip would drum up such support for the amendment that Congress would pass it in the next session. The loss of Darrow's support had brought her back down to earth with a thud. And over the state's rights issue, too, she thought with disgust, a fig leaf men pulled out whenever they wanted cover for refusing women's demands for equality. Hiding behind the US Constitution was so easy. "What can we do?" men would say, feigning regret. "So sorry! Our hands are tied." For years Congress sent them to the states for voting rights, and the states lobbed them straight back to Congress, and women ran back and forth like tennis balls. To hell with all of them. Congress had set the precedent with the Fifteenth Amendment, and women were going to ride that straight into the voting booth.

She gave a deep sigh and huddled under her traveling robe, shifting her feet. It could be years before they won. How did they keep on with it, Stanton, Anthony—thousands who'd worked almost all their lives on suffrage and died knowing it was far from won? She'd only been at this for a few years, and she was already sick to death of it. Weary of the priggish men—and women—who were determined to keep women in a box, as if women were all just one kind of thing, and not free spirits able to do anything they liked. Let the women who wanted to live in a box do it, and leave everyone else to make their own decisions.

* * *

"Get your *Suffragists* here! Twenty-five cents each. Read how the Congressional Union works to win the vote for women!" Ingeborg roamed through the crowd, waving a bundle of *The Suffragist* newspapers like a carnival barker and making change from a pouch tied around her waist. Bored with standing on platforms where she had to smile and keep her mouth shut, she'd volunteered to sell copies of CU's paper to help raise money. It was warmer moving around, and she could talk to people. The skies had cleared but it was quite chilly. Plumes of steam rose from the assembled onlookers, and they stamped their feet to stay warm, driving their hands deep into their pockets or hand muffs.

Sara and Maria and the local dignitaries were standing on the statehouse steps in downtown Indianapolis, facing Morton's monument. Members of Indiana's Equal Franchise League crowded up front, but a number of men stood at the outskirts of the crowd, eyeing the proceedings with skepticism.

"Step right up, don't be shy!" cried Ingeborg. "We women don't bite, we just want the vote!" She turned and spotted an older gentleman wearing a fine wool coat that fell to his knees, and a derby tugged down around his ears. His beard was neatly trimmed and flecked with gray. He waved her over and she made her way to him. "Good morning, sir, surely you can spare at least twenty-five cents for a good cause. More if you can spare it!" He dug in his pockets and handed her a dollar. Ingeborg was delighted. "Thank you! That will help us get to Dayton." She dropped it in her pouch and grinned as she handed him a paper.

"You've drawn a good crowd today," he said. "I wondered how many people would come out."

Ingeborg looked around—she guessed there were about seventy-five people, most of them women. "We never know how many will come," she agreed. "Between the weather and whatever else is going on." Then she leaned in close and said in a stage whisper, "We always claim at least a hundred in the larger cities."

The man laughed. "Good plan! The antis inflate their numbers, why shouldn't you?"

"Are the antis strong here?" Ingeborg asked him, curious.

"Not too many, but a few that make a lot of noise." Then he said, in mock outrage, "The head of it made the papers just last week—she said suffragists want the vote so they can promote polygamy."

"Hah!" Ingeborg retorted, flapping her handful of newspapers at him. "If that were true, the men would have let us vote long ago!" They laughed, and she moved on.

The crowd began applauding, and she looked up at the stage where the ceremony was getting started.

Eugenie Nicholson, a member of the CU's national Advisory Council, welcomed everyone and introduced Jacob Dunn, who was representing Mayor Joseph Bell.

The mayor, Eugenie had explained ruefully when she arrived at the hotel that morning to lead the caravan to the statehouse, was mysteriously unavailable, and the only man they could find to speak at the event was the city comptroller.

"The mayor's a Democrat," Eugenie said. "Chosen by the party machine, and they're angry because the CU campaigned against Democrats in the last elections. We expect that's why he's not available, though they haven't said so directly."

To his credit, though he was a last-minute stand-in, Mr. Dunn welcomed the travelers graciously and congratulated them on their accomplishment. Sara gave a spirited account of the Woman Voters Convention and their plans to bring the petition to Washington; she was close to her own self again after her terrible cold. Ingeborg could see the men who'd been standing on the outskirts of the crowd press in closer so they could hear better. She was pleased to hear murmurs of surprise and encouragement from those around her, and to have them line up to sign the petitions that Ingeborg and some other local suffragists offered around.

A small luncheon followed the ceremony. Only a dozen or so local suffragists were there, and they left promptly when the meal and the speeches were over. Eugenie Nicholson lingered with the travelers over coffee.

Ingeborg watched Eugenie with fascination. She was lovely to look at, with creamy skin and a tumble of glossy curls, but she was also smart and well-spoken. She told some amusing stories about her interactions with Alice Paul, which made her an instant ally. Her husband was some sort of famous writer—Sara was excited and clearly wanted to push the suffrage talk to the side so they could discuss books and, inevitably, Erskine.

Sara hadn't been talking as much about Erskine lately, it occurred to Ingeborg, except about his long story-poem, "The Poet in the Desert." Sara had lent them a copy, sections of which Ingeborg and Maria had read aloud to each other one night in their room, sending them into gales of laughter. More than anything else, the desert seemed to remind Erskine how much he loved women! Mother figure, temptress, goddess—all of them. Sara thought it high literature and was scheming to find a publisher for it in New York.

Ingeborg returned her attention to the conversation. Eugenie was apologizing for the poor turnout at the day's events. "The National Association is strong here," she said. "You know Ida Harper is from Indiana, and they're all proud of that. And they're all *ladies*, you know...."

"Yes, everyone knows the CU is full of ultra-feminist harpies, hell-bent on converting every woman to androgyny," Sara said, her voice laden with sarcasm. She rolled her eyes.

Eugenie laughed and shook her head. "There is that," she admitted. "But they also seem to think all they need to do is to be sweet and charming—then of course the men will oblige them." She inserted a cigarette into a pearl-handled holder, lit it, and after a deep pull sent a long stream of smoke into the air.

Sara nodded thoughtfully. "I've often suspected that this is some sort of cat-and-mouse game. As long as we play by their rules and don't cause trouble they can keep us busy on suffrage without making much progress. Oh, they'll let us have a state referendum now and then, and occasionally we'll even win one."

"Exactly," said Eugenie, looking around for an ash tray. Finding none, she tapped her ashes into her coffee cup. She raised her eyebrows and, looking at each of them in turn, said in a hushed voice. "But some worry that demanding the vote will raise the brute force in men."

"What breed of men do you rear in Indiana?" Sara glanced at her in amusement, and then picked at a stray thread on her sleeve. "Are they such brutes?"

"No more so than anywhere else, I imagine," said Eugenie. "I can see them getting thundering mad, but I don't expect it will come to blows. Though if they feel that threatened, who knows?"

"Are women here worried they'd be lynched?" asked Ingeborg. "Like the Negroes?"

"We're white and we're women, so I hardly think they'd dare be so public about it," Eugenie replied. "Don't most men prefer to beat their wives in private?"

"Men who already beat their wives would do so over suffrage, I think," said Sara, "Because they worry we might pass laws to make it illegal. I feel terribly for those women but we can't let that stop us." She drained the coffee from her cup and set it down. "We go to Ohio next. What can you tell us about the women there?"

Eugenie pondered this. "Where are you stopping?"

"Three cities," said Maria. "Dayton and Columbus, and then we go up to Detroit, then back to Cleveland."

Sara groaned.

"Three cities!" said Eugenie, her brow furrowed. "Why so many?" She ground her cigarette out. "You had just one stop in Indiana."

Sara shrugged. "We have a lot of CU members in Ohio," she said. "But my guess is Harriet."

Ingeborg glanced at Maria, who shook her head. "Harriet?" asked Ingeborg.

"Harriet Taylor Upton," Eugenie told them. "She's the queen of suffrage in Ohio. Served as NAWSA's treasurer for many years." She turned back to Sara. "But will she help the CU?"

"Mabel seems to think so," said Sara. "Ohio was beaten badly in its last two state suffrage campaigns, in 1912 and 1914. From what I hear she'll do almost anything to win."

"Watch yourselves," warned Eugenie. "She's a hellcat when she's crossed and can make things hard for you."

* * *

They arrived in Dayton just after noon the following day, Maria swinging Emilie down Dayton's wide main street and steering around people running to catch the interurban train. Thin clouds lingered over a watery sun, and sharp gusts of wind sent leaves scudding down the sidewalks.

As Maria pulled up in front of their hotel, Ingeborg caught sight of something a couple of blocks down the street. "Look at that!" she said, peering intently.

"What?" said Sara, looking around.

"That suffrage booth. The sign says Dayton Woman Suffrage Association," said Ingeborg.

Sara pulled herself out of the car and began unstrapping her bag from where it was cinched against the side. "Maybe they have some new campaign going on," she said, tugging her bag free. "I swear if I don't get to a washroom this instant I'm going to explode on the sidewalk." She disappeared through the hotel's revolving doors.

"Ingeborg," said Maria, who was rummaging around in the boot for her belongings. "Give me a hand with these bags."

"Wait," said Ingeborg. "Come look at this."

Maria walked around to stand beside her and looked down the street to the booth. After a moment, she said in some surprise, "The ladies running the booth are colored!"

Ingeborg looked over at her and grinned. "I'll be right back—I want to talk with them."

The two women standing behind the booth wore thick hats pulled low over their ears, and fur-trimmed coats. They stood chatting with each other behind a broad shelf on which suffrage literature was arranged in neat piles held down with paperweights, but they lapsed into silence as Ingeborg hurried up.

"We're here to assist with any and all suffrage emergencies." said the woman on the left, who stood a full six inches over Ingeborg and had a lanky form. Her face was arranged in a suitably grave expression, but her eyes twinkled. "How may we help you?"

"Oh!" cried Ingeborg, startled. "There's no emergency. It's just—oh, you're teasing," and she grinned at the women. "I'm glad to see colored women in charge of a suffrage booth in the center of town."

They grinned back at her. "Thank you. We do things differently here in Dayton, I believe," the tall one said.

"Yes, you do," said Ingeborg, with feeling.

"I'm Miss Hallie Brown," said the taller woman. She placed a hand on the arm of her companion, who was shorter and more amply endowed. "And this is Mrs. Jewelia Higgins. We have charge of the booth one day a week."

"The Dayton Suffrage Association lets Negroes be members?" asked Ingeborg, shocked.

"Of course," Miss Hallie replied, with a smile. "It's our only suffrage association."

"And who might you be?" asked Mrs. Higgins. "Are you new to Dayton?"

"No—that is, yes, I've just arrived but won't be here long." Ingeborg quickly introduced herself. "We're driving to Washington with petitions for Congress and the president."

"You're one of the envoys!" Mrs. Higgins cried.

Ingeborg grinned and stood up a little straighter, pleased to be recognized. "That's right."

"Your reputations precede you," said Miss Hallie. "We will certainly attend your mass meeting later this afternoon."

"As well as the dinner afterward," Mrs. Higgins chimed in. "We're all eager to hear about your trip. What adventures you must have had!"

Ingeborg gaped at them in amazement. "But—how? To be frank, we've found that colored women aren't usually welcome."

The women looked at each other and smiled. "The association here knows every vote counts when it comes to suffrage," Miss Hallie told Ingeborg. "They don't care where it comes from. Labor. Negroes. Not many colored people live in Dayton, so maybe that helps, too. The whites don't feel so threatened."

Ingeborg shook her head, puzzled. "Why can't the rest of America be like Dayton?" Then she excused herself, saying, "I'll look for you later today."

* * *

The next few days felt to Ingeborg as if they were stuck in a movie reel playing at high speed. They dashed in Emilie from one meeting to the next, with little time to rest.

Despite Harriet Taylor Upton and her NAWSA association's efforts to snub the envoys, a gratifying number of Ohio Woman Suffrage Association members had turned out to see them in Dayton and Columbus. And the news coverage had been good, though as Ingeborg scanned the newspapers in the lobby each morning there was practically no mention of the Swedes, only of Sara and Mabel. Even Frances, who hadn't been seen or heard from for weeks, merited more than one mention. Ingeborg shook her head in disgust and grumbled to Maria about it one night as they'd prepared for bed. "I hope some of the Swedish newspapers are printing what I send them," she said grimly. "Swedes should hear the whole story, even if no one else does."

Maria snorted. "How is it the whole story if you only mention us?" she wanted to know. "You're no better than they are if you leave them out."

"Serves them right," Ingeborg insisted, stubbornly. Maria refused to hear any more about it.

The head of the CU branch in Ohio, Dorothy Mead, had welcomed the envoys to Dayton. She was a slender woman with a ready smile who carried herself with an air of confidence and assurance. Ingeborg was even more taken with Jesse Leach Davisson, who lived in Dayton and had recently been appointed to the CU's advisory council. It was Jesse who had insisted that colored women be allowed to join the Dayton Woman Suffrage Association, and made sure they were included in all suffrage activities. Her light blue eyes were set wide apart in her broad, pleasant face, and she had an unflappable air about her. She greeted Maria and Ingeborg warmly when they were introduced. "And you are the ones, I hear, who supplied and pilot the automobile!" she said with a smile. "I think it's absolutely marvelous. We need more women like you." She turned and looked at Dorothy Mead. "Now when men talk about women drivers, we can speak of Miss Kindstedt and Miss Kindberg."

Dorothy agreed. "The papers are full of stories of men who crash their motorcars," she said. "But men say women are dangerous drivers."

Ingeborg glowed. Dayton was the most enlightened city they'd seen yet. When they'd gathered at the courthouse for their open air meeting, she was thrilled to see a sprinkling of colored women—and men—in the crowd, including Miss Hallie and Mrs. Higgins, who smiled and waved. She wove through clumps of people, hawking *The Suffragist,* and detected no tensions between the races. Here was a model for the CU—for the whole country.

She'd stopped to speak with an older Negro man who stood quietly on the edge of the crowd. His team of mules was tied to a post nearby, long ears swiveling lazily back and forth, heads drooping and hips cocked as they caught a quick nap.

Ingeborg approached him. "Want to buy *The Suffragist*?" she asked.

"Well now, let's take a look," he said, with a pleasant smile, and held out his hand to take a copy. He looked it over and then tilted his head at her. "How much?"

Ingeborg eyed the man's worn clothes and told him she'd take whatever he could offer.

"I got five cents—that's all I can spare," he told her.

Ingeborg beamed at him. "Sold!" They laughed and shook hands.

"Name's Henry Tallen," he said. Ingeborg introduced herself.

"My wife will be glad to know I met you," he said. "She wanted to come, but she's working. What you women are doing is a fine thing. I never did understand why Congress gave just the colored men the vote after the war. Makes no sense."

Ingeborg lifted her shoulders in a shrug. "You're right—it would've saved us all a lot of trouble if they'd enfranchised everyone."

Henry looked over at his mules and then turned back to Ingeborg. "Them mules got more sense than people do," he said. "They don't care if they're alongside horses or sheep or cattle or goats. Long as they got enough to eat, they don't care. Wish people could be as smart as mules."

"More mules, fewer fools!" said Ingeborg. "That's what we'll say from now on." They laughed, and then Ingeborg moved on through the crowd, waving the paper. Soon she became aware of a different speech some distance away, an acrid counterpoint to the suffrage ceremony. Irritated, she craned her neck around to locate the source and spotted a man standing on a soapbox across the square. A woman stood beside him, nodding approvingly.

Ingeborg drifted closer and saw the woman was holding a neat, hand-lettered sign that read, THE OHIO ASSOCIATION OPPOSED TO WOMAN SUFFRAGE. A handful of men and women stood around, listening intently.

The speaker, a thickset, heavily jowled man with a beard dribbling off his chins, pointed a finger at his audience and thundered on. "Feminists teach sex freedom and birth control. They want trial marriages and easy divorce. They want the state to rear their children for them so they can run about with their licentious behavior! Is this what wholesome people want?" The onlookers shouted, "No!" in indignation.

"Of course not," the speaker continued, and then he lowered his voice conspiratorially. "Directly across this square are those who would have us abandon morality." He pointed dramatically at the suffrage rally. "Suffragists!" he pronounced, his voice dripping venom.

Ingeborg turned with the rest of the group and was relieved to see the crowd she'd just left was largely oblivious to the anti on his soapbox. The blood rose in her face, and her chest tightened as the man roared on. She took a few steps forward and saw that he was wearing a clerical collar. It was only a matter of time before he brought the church into it, she figured.

Right on cue he proceeded to do so. "The church must set its face—and speak—against those who desire to destroy morality as we know it. We have a duty to a higher power than individual rights. I ask you, what about the divine creed of duty to God, to posterity, and to the state?"

The small group whooped and cheered and stamped their feet. "That's right!" they yelled back at him. "God provides, we need only ask Him."

"Many women believe this, too," the man continued. "I am a minister, yes, but some may think that as a man I have my own interests in women remaining in the home. Ladies and gentlemen, I give you Mrs. Harry Talbott, president of the Ohio Association Opposed to Woman Suffrage!" He stepped down heavily from the soapbox, took the sign from the woman holding it, and helped her onto the box in his place.

"Thank you, Reverend Brandenburg," she said, as the small group of onlookers clapped in welcome. Her voice was mesmerizing, low and rich. A voice of education and privilege, Ingeborg thought. "We are indeed grateful to the clergy for helping stem the evil tide of feminism—and equal rights for women!"

Ingeborg grumbled to herself. Why did some women want to be unequal? Like insisting on going through life on your knees—it made no sense. She turned to eye the suffrage stage where Sara was stepping up to speak and decided to stay put for now. This was the first time the antis had mounted a counter-rally and she wanted to keep an eye on them. Mrs. Talbott rolled on.

"We are opposed to woman suffrage because woman's God-given function of motherhood is of central importance to the future of our nation. In fulfilling this role, we reach the pinnacle of our utility. Our government entrusts to women the task of laying the foundation for good citizenship while our children are in their most impressionable years. Think!" she implored. "The entire human race passes through our hands. Are we to turn away and let the seeds grow as they may? Or shall we nurture them, tend them carefully, and help them grow straight and strong?"

So they can die in your wars and waste their lives in your factories, thought Ingeborg, irritably. She lowered her head a little, looking up at Mrs. Talbott through her eyelashes.

"We deny the right of a few women to force upon us responsibility for government which we neither asked for nor desire," proclaimed Mrs. Talbott. "Remember," she said, as she drew in a deep breath and held herself erect, "the noblest women in history have been those who stood behind and served the greatest men of all time."

"Hogwash!" Ingeborg burst out, surprising herself and everyone else.

"I beg your pardon?" asked Mrs. Talbott, peering down at her from the box.

Ingeborg stamped up and planted herself in front of Mrs. Talbott. Reverend Brandenburg drew closer as if to shield her from Ingeborg's wrath. The onlookers pulled in closer to watch the ruckus close up. "I'm sick of women like you. Go home! If that's where women belong, why are you here?"

"I came to speak the *truth*!" said Mrs. Talbott, haughtily, looking down her nose at Ingeborg. "I could not stand by and let the ultra-feminist lies of the other side go unchallenged. Women do not belong in government, and we do not want the vote."

"Then don't vote!" Ingeborg shot back. She shook her head angrily. "You anti women are like the organ grinders' monkeys. You think it's fine because the organ has some gold paint, and maybe your master gives you a new suit or a sparkling toy. But the *truth* is," she spat out the word, "you're just monkeys tied up with string. And you dance to the same tired tunes, over and over again. That's no life."

"Look here," said Reverend Brandenburg sternly to Ingeborg. "You have a lot of nerve coming here and making a scene. We're just trying to speak to the people."

Ingeborg rounded on him. "As we are!" She flung her arm toward the suffrage meeting, then narrowed her eyes and jutted out her chin. "But we have a lot more people," she pointed out.

Some of the onlookers chuckled. "She has a point there," one man said. Mrs. Talbott glared at the speaker and then back at Ingeborg. "I demand that you leave us at once! We want nothing to do with ultra-feminists like you!"

Ingeborg gave a short laugh. "Lady," she said, looking up at Mrs. Talbott, "we're going for an amendment to the US Constitution enfranchising women. And you can't stop us." With that, she turned on her heel and stalked back across the square to where people were lining up to sign the petitions.

* * *

Late that evening they huddled with Dorothy Mead and Jesse Davisson to talk about the day's events and strategize over the meetings in Columbus and Cleveland. Dorothy yawned and stretched. "I'll take the early train to Columbus in the morning to meet with the state association and make one last try for their support. I don't expect it, though. Upton is dead set against the CU." She shrugged, and then said with a smile, "I begin to see what it must be like to be an envoy. I'm so tired! I don't know how you keep up this pace." She looked around the room at them.

Sara had pulled a second chair in front of her, taken her shoes off, and placed her feet on its seat. Strands of hair had pulled out of her bun and dangled over her cheek. She looked completely used up. Maria was slouched in her chair, almost asleep. Ingeborg herself was fighting the urge to lean forward and cradle her head on her folded arms. She was afraid to go to bed while the others were still plotting in case they came up with some scheme that would make the next few days still harder.

Mabel, though, was shuffling through a pile of papers in front of her, looking as if she had another few of hours of work left in her. Ingeborg eyed her sourly. The woman wasn't human. How did she do it?

Mabel looked up at Dorothy. "I spoke with Mrs. Upton as well. She was adamant that NAWSA and the state associations will only be harmed by the CU's tactics and she wants nothing to do with us."

"She won't admit it but she doesn't have the control she used to in Ohio," observed Jesse.

"That's right," agreed Dorothy. "We should have a good turnout in Columbus—in part because Governor Willis and his wife are for us. They'll sign the petition tomorrow."

"The governor's support is important," Mabel observed. "Particularly since you still have some congressmen who need convincing."

Jesse snorted in disgust. "Yes. We visited Brumbaugh a few weeks ago. He follows Wilson's lead—favoring suffrage through state action. He thinks the federal amendment will be too difficult to enforce."

"Wilson's come some little distance since he was elected," Mabel said, thoughtfully. "He began his first term saying he hadn't thought of suffrage at all. Now he favors it but thinks states should decide. He made quite a show of voting in New Jersey's referendum in October."

"Do you think he'll ever come around to the federal amendment?" asked Dorothy.

Mabel set her mouth. "We have to make him see it's in his interest. He's a Southerner, and needs Southern support to win reelection. So it won't be easy."

"We told Brumbaugh that the party that puts suffrage through will have a halo around it," said Jesse, fishing a gold filigreed compact from her bag. She squinted at the mirror and powdered her nose. "He was unmoved."

"We have to make them believe we can prevent Wilson's reelection if the Western women vote against him," said Mabel firmly.

Maria snored softly and Ingeborg noticed her friend's chin had dropped down onto her chest. Ingeborg rose to her feet. "Time for bed," she said, putting her hand on Maria's shoulder and giving it a gentle squeeze. "What about Cleveland?"

"Harriet and her group won't dare make a fuss in Columbus," Dorothy said. "Not with the governor there. Watch for something in Cleveland, though."

"I still have friends in Cleveland," said Sara, smothering a yawn and slowly struggling to her feet. "My ex and I lived there for eight years. I think they'll come out for us."

"Splendid," said Jesse. "We're doing our best to drum up support as well. And now, off to bed. We'll see you in Columbus tomorrow."

* * *

The envoys were early to their rendezvous point with the Columbus suffragists, so Maria pulled the car over, and they sat in silence for a few minutes, listening to the plink of Emilie's engine cooling. The air was freezing and quite still. Ingeborg was thinking about the next few days. It seemed wrong, somehow, that they'd leave Columbus for Detroit and then reenter Ohio for the Cleveland meetings. It felt like going backward. It was better to leave each state behind, not looking back, thinking only of the next one and the next until they arrived at the capital. Not too many more states to go, she thought hopefully, counting them on her fingers. Ohio, Michigan, New York, Massachusetts, Rhode Island, New Jersey, Pennsylvania, Delaware, and Maryland. Nine. And then Washington. She sighed. Still too many.

"What's Cleveland like?" she asked abruptly, turning around in her seat to look at Sara.

Sara was half reclining against the seat cushions, gazing unseeing out the window. There were deep bluish-gray circles under her eyes. With a visible effort she turned her head to look at Ingeborg and frowned a little as she thought about her answer. "It's all right, I guess," she said vaguely.

"You said you'd lived there?" asked Ingeborg.

Sara shifted. "Oh, my husband was called to a church in Cleveland. I never felt as though I fit in. They fired him after a time, and we moved to Oregon."

"They fired him?"

"It was my fault, I suppose," said Sara. "I was quite taken with Tom Johnson, the mayor at the time. He introduced me to the writings of Henry George—do you know him? He wrote *Progress and Poverty*. I thought it was the most important book I'd ever read and threw myself into helping the poor in our parish." She paused, remembering. "I persuaded Albert to preach against the rich and powerful who kept people poor, and the church didn't like it."

Maria made a rude sound with her lips. "They want to save poor people from hell in the next life—not this one," she said.

"Something like that," Sara admitted. "I told you I felt I didn't belong. It was ugly at the end. Everybody was angry—with us, with each other." She shrugged. "On top of everything else, I was beginning to realize I didn't love my husband. So it was a difficult time. But an important one for me, nonetheless. I feel I grew up in Cleveland."

"But you grew up in Detroit?" asked Ingeborg.

"I did, but I married so young—just eighteen. And Albert was so much older, for a long time I sort of trailed after him. Cleveland's where I learned I wanted something different."

"A different old man," said Ingeborg, playfully. Maria frowned at her.

But Sara smiled. "Yes, Erskine's older, but he couldn't be more different from Albert." She checked her watch. "The parade will be here any time now. We'd better get ready."

They piled out of Emilie and had just finished decorating her when a long, low-slung touring car came around the corner and pulled up, followed by a dozen others. Dorothy Mead emerged from the passenger seat of the lead car and walked over with its driver, a rather nervous looking woman wearing a large, flowered hat tied severely under her chin, whom she introduced as Mrs. Walter Popkin.

"Oh," Mrs. Popkin tittered, when they thanked her for coming. "I wouldn't have missed it. Mrs. Mead was determined I should come, after all."

Mrs. Mead smiled blandly. "That's right. I wouldn't take no for an answer." She looked over at the three travelers. "No luck with the state association, I'm afraid," she said lightly. "We'll simply have to go on without them."

"At least you brought some friends," said Ingeborg. She looked over the entourage. "Is that a milk truck?" She looked closer. "And a Black Maria?" She glanced back at Dorothy, whose face was grave, though her eyes were twinkling. "Are we in trouble already?"

"Beggars can't be choosers," said Dorothy, tossing her head. "With the state association opposed to us I had to scramble to find an escort. I called in some favors. One was to the police chief."

"Good for you!" said Ingeborg, laughing. "Let's go meet the governor."

As they drew up to the statehouse, a military band with a dozen members was playing bracing airs to the assembled crowd. The chief of police waited to escort them into the building, and together they marched up the steps through the west entrance and into the reception hall where Governor Frank Willis, his wife, Allie, Mabel Vernon, and local CU leader Mrs. James Rector were waiting for them, along with about three hundred other people. Ingeborg was startled by the size of the crowd, no less so than Dorothy, judging by the look on her face. Governor Willis must have called in favors of his own.

He and Mrs. Willis made a handsome couple. Their open, generous faces were wreathed in smiles as they met the envoys, and Mrs. Willis expressed warm and genuine thanks for them undertaking such a difficult journey.

In his remarks, the governor made it clear that he supported both woman suffrage and the federal amendment. "Some questions are purely local in nature," he said. "But the question of who is to vote concerns everyone across the country. You are right to present this issue to Congress, and Mrs. Willis joins me in sincerely hoping you meet with much success when you arrive at their doorstep in early December." They signed the petition and the governor returned to his office, while Mrs. Willis remained behind for a light luncheon and more speeches.

The hall was crowded with tables. Some two dozen attractive young women draped with purple, white, and gold sashes threaded their way through the crowd bringing trays of refreshments to the guests. Mabel and Sara stood in the reception line next to Mrs. Willis while Ingeborg and Maria sat down at a table facing the front, their backs to the rest of the room. With so many people crowded into the room the noise quickly grew deafening, making conversation across the table impossible. Ingeborg and Maria lapsed into silence and looked around.

The room was a long rectangle with a low dais at one end, the front edge of the platform draped with red, white, and blue bunting; a large American flag stretched across the back. Ingeborg was idly watching the crowd when a door in the side of the hall opened and a man and a woman entered, scanning the room. Ingeborg cocked her head. Where had she seen them before? The man was large and carried his head like a buffalo—set low on thick, rounded shoulders— and he had a wispy beard. The woman with him was neatly done up and she held herself very erect. Her nose wrinkled slightly as though she were in the presence of a bad smell. Ingeborg sat bolt upright and clutched Maria's arm. "The antis!" she hissed in her ear. "The ones I told you about. They're here!"

"What? Where?" asked Maria, excitedly, and Ingeborg pointed them out. "Are you sure?"

"Of course I'm sure," said Ingeborg. "How could I forget? It was just yesterday." She paused, and then gasped "They're coming this way!" She turned quickly and faced the front of the room.

The antis had spotted the empty seats next to Ingeborg and the woman led the way through the crowd to her table.

"Are these chairs taken?" the woman asked. Ingeborg turned her face up to the woman and gave her a big, gap-toothed smile. "No," she said. Mrs. Talbott's eyes widened as she recognized Ingeborg, and her face grew very red.

"You!" hissed Mrs. Talbott. "What are you doing here?"

"I'm one of the guests of honor," Ingeborg pointed out. "Why're *you* here?" She looked over at the reverend, whose gobbling face almost matched the puce wallpaper.

He opened his mouth and closed it again, and with a sly glance at Mrs. Talbott he said. "We're here to listen. And to observe."

Mrs. Talbott nodded and she sat down next to Ingeborg, with the reverend to her left. An uneasy silence blanketed the table. Ingeborg sat bolt upright and watched them from the corner of her eye, convinced they were up to something. The other suffragists were puzzled by the obvious tension among them, but soon Mrs. Rector called the gathering to order, urging everyone to take their seats. The crowd fell silent.

Ingeborg sat quietly and watched as Mrs. Rector introduced Sara as the envoy. She made no mention of Maria and herself, though Ingeborg noticed that Sara, as usual, made sure to point them out as her driver and mechanician. Still just the hired help, Ingeborg thought. But she and Maria smiled and nodded to the crowd, which clapped politely.

Beside her, Mrs. Talbott fidgeted with the gloves she held in her lap, twisting them one way and the other. From time to time she'd slip her left hand surreptitiously into her coat pocket, finger something, then pull it out and resume twisting her gloves. Reverend Brandenburg sat quietly enough but glanced several times at Mrs. Talbott, brow slightly furrowed.

What did Mrs. Talbott have in her pocket? Ingeborg wondered. She didn't want to make a fuss as Sara was speaking, but she was certain the pair was up to something and she was determined to stop them. Quietly, she worked her left foot over and hooked it behind the front leg of Mrs. Talbott's chair. Sara was talking about the petition, all the signatures they'd added in every state they'd passed through since they'd left San Francisco, and praising Governor Willis and other Ohio suffragists for their vision in supporting suffrage through national action.

Suddenly, Ingeborg saw Mrs. Talbott plunge her left hand into her pocket while at the same time giving the reverend a brief nod. She began to pull her hand out while rising to her feet, thrusting her chair back. The reverend rose with her and she opened her mouth to call out, but Ingeborg yanked her left leg forward and toppled Mrs. Talbott over backward. The reverend tried to catch her but got tangled up in his own chair and instead fell heavily in an awkward sprawl across her left arm. Mrs. Talbott shrieked in pain.

Bedlam ensued as people from surrounding tables stood to gawk. The police chief pushed his way through the crowd to where Ingeborg was crouching over the antis, pressing her hand on Mrs. Talbott's right shoulder to prevent her from getting up. She caught his eye and said firmly, "Mrs. Talbott felt faint. She needs air. We have to move her." The chief nodded and summoned some men who helped Mrs. Talbott and the reverend to their feet and led them out a side door. Ingeborg followed them, hearing Mrs. Rector encouraging people to please quiet down and return to their seats.

They found a small meeting room and settled Mrs. Talbott into a chair. One of the men, a doctor, started gently helping her to remove her coat. She gasped in pain and hugged her left arm across her body, giving a vigorous push to the doctor with her right arm. "It hurts!" she wailed.

"Wait!" said Ingeborg, suspecting that there might be another reason for Mrs. Talbott's discomfort. "She has something in her left coat pocket. See what it is."

"Look here," Reverend Brandenburg said, trying to insert his bulk between Mrs. Talbott and the doctor. "The lady has experienced serious injury, all due to that dreadful woman." He pointed at Ingeborg. "Arrest her!"

Ingeborg turned and locked eyes with the police chief. "Check her pocket!" she snapped. "They're antis, I saw them in Dayton yesterday. They're up to something."

The chief looked startled, but after a long look at Ingeborg he moved over in front of Mrs. Talbott and directed the doctor and another man to hold her in the chair. She writhed in their grasp and sought to struggle to her feet. "Stand back!" he barked at Reverend Brandenburg, putting a hand in the middle of his chest. "We must get to the bottom of this." The reverend moved aside reluctantly, and the chief turned to stand in front of Mrs. Talbott.

"Ma'am," he said to her. "What's in your pocket?"

"Nothing!" she snarled. "You have no right to hold me like this!"

"I'm going to ask you once more," said the chief. "What do you have in your pocket?"

Mrs. Talbott gritted her teeth and refused to speak, so the chief leaned forward and patted the outside of the pocket carefully, before gently sliding his fingers in and coming out with a gleaming black pistol. Shocked exclamations came from around the room. Reverend Brandenburg took a step backward, appalled by the sight. "What have you done?" he gasped. Mrs. Talbott kept her eyes on the floor and said nothing.

The chief glanced briefly at Ingeborg. "How did you know about this?" he asked.

Ingeborg shook her head. She was feeling a bit trembly from everything—the sight of the pistol left her cold. "I didn't trust her, I knew she was an anti. I was watching her and she kept putting her hand in her pocket. I never saw the gun until now." She looked over at Mrs. Talbott, who was beginning to cry silently, fat tears rolling down her cheeks. The two men kept her pinned to the chair. Ingeborg leaned over and pushed her face into Mrs. Talbott's. Narrowing her eyes, she demanded, "Who were you going to shoot?"

"No one!" Reverend Brandenburg said, "That is—"

"I'll handle the questioning," the chief broke in, "at the station." Telling Ingeborg to step back, he directed the men holding Mrs. Talbott to guard her. He left the room to make arrangements, carrying the pistol wrapped in his handkerchief.

Silence descended on the room. Ingeborg stood against the wall near the door and watched the guilty pair. Mrs. Talbott sat head down and motionless apart from the occasional shuddering sigh. Tears slid down her cheeks. The reverend appeared to be praying over his clasped hands, lips moving soundlessly.

Ingeborg's anger still simmered. Who would have been in Mrs. Talbott's sights had she pulled the trigger? Sara? Mrs. Rector? Ingeborg herself? What could she possibly have thought to gain from waving a pistol in front of a room full of witnesses?

"You should have taken your own advice," blurted Ingeborg, suddenly.

Mrs. Talbott raised her head and stared at her, eyes unfocused and watery. "What do you mean?" she asked.

"Yesterday, in Dayton. You climbed on that soapbox and made a speech saying women should stay home, stand behind their men." Mrs. Talbott shrugged and dropped her head. "It's always the same with you antis," Ingeborg pressed on. "You say women should stay home—then you run about making speeches." She stopped, considering. "Though you're the first anti I've seen with a gun."

"You and your screeching, sobbing sisters," said Mrs. Talbott, bitterly. "You want to ruin everything. All women need are children at home and husbands to protect them. That's what I was trying to defend."

"By shooting someone? You're crazy!" Ingeborg yelled at her. "You think all women are like you?" She crossed over and stood in front of Mrs. Talbott, who shrank back in her chair. "Look at me, are we the same?" Mrs. Talbott raised her head. "I never had a husband—I left my family in Sweden and I came here and worked. Every damn day. No man gave me anything. The vote is the protection I need!" She raised her hands and clapped them back down to her sides in frustration. "Stay home on election day if you want. But don't stop the rest of us because you're too lazy or scared to vote."

Mrs. Talbott sniffed and looked down at her hands.

"I hope they lock you up for a good long while," said Ingeborg, and went back to the hall.

CHAPTER THIRTEEN

NOVEMBER 13-19, 1915

They pulled into Detroit in the early afternoon two days later, too tired to shiver any more from the cold that wrapped their limbs in ice. Maria pulled Emilie to the curb in front of their hotel, and they sat unmoving, grateful for the stillness.

Their departure had been delayed by the investigation into Mrs. Talbott and her plot to harm the suffragists. The police had interviewed Ingeborg several times, reviewing the details of her story. She was glad the police seemed to be taking the threat seriously, but her patience was almost at an end.

An inspector faced her across the table, his face inscrutable. "Tell us again what you saw as you sat at the table with Mrs. Talbott. Where were her hands?"

"As I've told you six times already," Ingeborg replied, fighting the urge to scream at him, "she kept her right hand in her lap. But I could see her touching her left coat pocket, and sometimes she'd slide her hand in and then jerk it back out. That seemed odd and so I kept watching her from the corner of my eye."

"How many times did she touch her left coat pocket?" the inspector asked.

"I couldn't say for sure," Ingeborg frowned, thinking back. "A lot, though. Maybe fifteen times?"

And on and on.

They were all frantic that the police investigation would cause them to miss their next meeting. At length Mabel appealed to Governor Willis, who directed the police to let Ingeborg go, and off they went.

Due to the delay they'd had to race to Detroit, Maria crouched over the steering wheel looking grim and determined, Ingeborg and Sara hanging on for dear life as she swerved around potholes, banged over scalloped surfaces that set Ingeborg's teeth clacking like castanets, and shot across narrow bridges. They hadn't stopped for lunch, so they were famished as well.

Sara sighed and reached for the door handle. Maria and Ingeborg stirred and followed suit, dragging their stiff and weary bodies out of the car and into the hotel. Mabel was pacing around the lobby, waiting for them, and she pounced as they limped in the door. She looked as gaunt and worn as they did themselves, though her skin was less ravaged by the sun and wind. A faint air of coal dust clung to her suit.

"You're here!" she said, her voice a mixture of relief and annoyance. "I've been so worried, I expected you hours ago!"

"Not now, Mabel," muttered Sara as she made straight for the hotel desk. "We're tired and hungry and cold as corpses." Ingeborg and Maria tottered in her wake, ignoring Mabel, who was fairly hopping up and down with nervous anxiety.

Mabel hopped over to Sara and hissed in her ear. "Something's come up! We must talk this instant."

Sara stopped and eyed Mabel warily. "What?" she brusquely.

"The Episcopal Bishop of Detroit. He—he has concerns. About you." Ingeborg and Maria pulled in closer to listen to the conversation.

"About me?" asked Sara, exasperated. "I don't even know him. Why, I haven't lived here in years."

Mabel glanced over at the desk clerk, who was watching them curiously. She turned her shoulder to him. "He's heard about you and Erskine," she whispered.

Sara gazed up at the ceiling, drew a deep, impatient sigh and looked back at Mabel. "So?" she asked, with an edge to her voice.

"It matters because we've asked him to take a big role in the events here. He's for suffrage, and well liked. But someone must have told him about you and Erskine, and now he's threatened to pull out."

Sara was torn between tears and exasperation. "This is too much!" she managed to spit out between clenched teeth. "I'm to be held to account for loving a man I don't live with and have barely seen for the past two years." She stopped and looked at Mabel, brow furrowed. "How does the bishop even know about this?"

Mabel shrugged. "It seems to be an open secret. Your mother still lives here. Maybe she's been talking?"

"Just wait 'til I get my hands on her," muttered Sara, angrily. "What do we do now?"

"The bishop wants to meet with you as soon as possible," said Mabel. "We should leave as soon as you've checked in—let the bellboy take your bags to your room." To Ingeborg's relief, Mabel looked over at Maria and said, "It's just a few blocks from here—we won't need the car."

Ingeborg eyed Sara sympathetically and thought that if she had to meet with a bishop right now, she couldn't be trusted to keep her temper. Erskine, she thought, shaking her head. That man had caused Sara such trouble—she hoped he was worth it.

Maria edged closer to Sara and touched her arm. "I'll go with you."

Sara stood there, head down, swaying a bit, caught between duty and profound exhaustion. She drew in a deep shuddering breath and let it out slowly. Duty won. She gave Maria a weak smile and shook her head. "Thank you, but I can do this. You rest." Then she squared her shoulders and looked over at Mabel with a look of deep dislike. "Let's get this over with," she said flatly. She grabbed her bags and walked over to the desk, signing the register with a quick scribble. The desk clerk signaled the bellboy to take her bags. Then the two women marched out through the hotel's revolving door. They clutched their hats to their heads as a damp wind rose from the Detroit River and chased them down the sidewalk.

Maria looked worried as they walked to the elevator. "They push her too hard."

"She'll be all right," said Ingeborg, slipping her arm through Maria's. "At least she's not pregnant. What would the bishop say about that?"

* * *

That evening they were back in the car, along with Mabel Vernon, leading a procession of cars bedecked with yellow lanterns. Crawling along at walking pace toward the courthouse several blocks away, there was time for a quick exchange of news. Sara shrugged off her meeting with the bishop. "He'd heard rumors and worried we might be spreading the gospel of free love as we drove across the country. I was in no mood to dissemble, as you can imagine, so I simply told him the story of how Erskine and I fell in love. By the end, he accepted that we share a very enduring love that's gone through many years of waiting and hardship. He'll speak tonight." She paused, looking out unseeing at the people who eyed them curiously as they rolled slowly past. "He's a good man," she said. "Instead of condemning me outright, he sought the facts from me directly and made up his own mind. I was glad to speak with him—somehow it brought Erskine closer."

"What a relief!" said Mabel, adjusting her scarf to keep the cold air off her neck. "I panicked when I heard. The suffragists here have done fine work, and we want his blessing." She laughed. "Do you know the Whittemores?"

"Yes," said Sara, "I met Margaret in San Francisco—she set up the booth at the Exposition, I think?"

"That's right," Mabel replied. "They're from Michigan and some of our most able organizers. They've been working for weeks to prepare for your arrival."

"That was a good dinner tonight," said Ingeborg. They'd been hosted in the Hotel Statler's glittering hall with over three hundred supporters, and the food had been sumptuous: succulent roast beef with mashed turnips and green beans, and a rich chocolate cream pie to finish. And plenty of coffee, strong and dark the way Ingeborg liked it. A meal like that made it easier to be back in the car on this frosty night, the breath steaming out of their mouths, instead of curled up in bed.

"That's not all," said Mabel smugly. Then she said, in a loud whisper, "They solved our petition problem."

Ingeborg's eyes opened wide. A wave of relief washed over her, and she twisted in her seat to gaze back at Mabel. "How?" she demanded.

"They've already collected four thousand signatures from suffragists across Michigan—they'll present them tonight," said Mabel, with quiet satisfaction. "When we add them to those you've collected on the trip we'll have plenty." She nodded with satisfaction. "Headquarters has this under control."

Ingeborg sighed with relief and faced front. "Good," she said. Then she frowned and looked back at Mabel. "Is that why the newspaper here says we have one million signatures?"

Sara groaned. "For God's sake! We have nowhere near that number."

Mabel's brow furrowed. "I missed that," she admitted. "What paper was it?"

"*The Detroit Free Press*," said Ingeborg. "It said the names from Michigan bring it to one million."

"I'll look into it," said Mabel. "We can blame it on careless reporting."

"Tell headquarters to stick with the half million," said Sara. "We may have narrowly escaped one disaster—let's not create another."

As they drew up to the county building, the hundreds of people assembled parted at their approach, laughing and cheering, and Maria pulled Emilie to the curb. Ingeborg peered up at the building and saw beautiful red lights burning from great stone urns arranged on the steps. Together they climbed up to meet the mayor's representative and the welcoming party waiting for them at the top.

An icy wind lifted their skirts and tugged at their scarves, and Ingeborg felt the warmth draining from her body. Just when she got warm again, they went back into the cold, she thought, shivering. And it was going to get worse. She could smell winter on the wind. She imagined them arriving in Washington as frozen blocks of ice, like the ones they chipped out of the lakes in the winter and stored in sawdust to be used in iceboxes in the summer. It might be easier to travel that way than constantly freezing and thawing and freezing again. They could just go to sleep, encased in their blocks of ice, displayed on the back of a flatbed truck for people to point and stare at, and then get thawed out in time to meet the president. She was picturing dripping on the White House carpet, fishing the last of the ice out of her pockets, when she realized that Mrs. Jennie Law Hardy had introduced Sara, who was now praising the skill and dedication of the Swedes. Ingeborg and Maria smiled and waved. The crowd applauded loudly.

Sara was in good form tonight, Ingeborg thought, watching her. She'd heard variations of the speech so many times that she'd almost stopped listening, but tonight the words flowed out of her, passionate and strong. "As we drove through the country and spoke in city after city we've felt the growing conviction and determination of the women. It has fueled our passage, our desperate 'gasoline flight' to win political freedom for the twenty million women who now lack it." The crowd erupted in cheers. Sara paused and then raised her hand for silence. "Women in the West have foresworn their political parties; they have just one plank now, women's political rights." She took a deep breath, and raised her voice still louder, saying "Women have become united, East and West, North and South, in this one cause, and they give each other absolute loyalty and support!" The crowd roared its approval.

Ingeborg hoped that would prove to be true but was skeptical. Hadn't they already witnessed the many fractures among women, voters or not? Antis. NAWSA supporters. Negroes. And don't forget the *ladies,* she thought scornfully.... And what "absolute loyalty and support" would they find when they reached Washington?

She watched now as the bishop stood forward to give the final blessing. He spoke approvingly of the work the Congressional Union was doing and, with a slight nod and the briefest of smiles at Sara, said only that she was one of those who were breaking the paths for a larger freedom in the world. Sara smiled back at him.

* * *

Sunday was a rest day. Sara spent the morning writing letters and the afternoon with her mother. Ingeborg and Maria slept gloriously late. As they entered the lobby in search of breakfast, a young woman rose from her seat behind a tall palm and approached them. "Excuse me,

Miss Kindberg? Miss—Kindstedt?" She pronounced their names with the hard "k" sound, like a hammer, as Americans often did, instead of the gentler shhhh sound that Swedes used.

Ingeborg stopped and peered at her. She was younger than Sara and had a confident bounce to her step, one Ingeborg doubted she'd ever had herself. Her dress clung to her slender frame, and it was cut scandalously short, barely to her knees. She wore her glossy chestnut hair just below her ears in a bob that emphasized her creamy neck, and a flower nestled between the swelling of her breasts. Ingeborg scowled politely and said, "Not now," and swung toward the hotel's front entrance, Maria in tow.

Undeterred, the young woman hurried to open the door for them and said, "I can recommend Mrs. Bea's diner—good food, cheap, and plenty of it. I'll walk with you."

Ingeborg stopped and faced her, jaw thrust out. "What do you want?" she asked, cranky now, annoyed that they had to fob off a stranger before their first sip of coffee.

"Ingeborg, don't be rude," Maria murmured.

The young woman seemed not the least deterred. She flashed an amused smile and held out her hand to Ingeborg. "Helen Bouchard," she said. "I need to talk with you."

"No talk before coffee," said Ingeborg, "It's a rule I have."

"And one to live by," said Helen, with a laugh. "I'll buy you coffee if we can talk afterward."

Mrs. Bea's was as good as Helen had said. They sat in a corner booth in the back, whose worn seats welcomed them like old friends. Empty tables were strewn with napkins and crumb-covered plates. The rush was over, and the remaining customers glanced at them but minded their own business. Once she'd sipped her coffee and was halfway through a plate of eggs and sausage, Ingeborg's mood improved and she eyed Helen curiously.

"What do you want?" she asked, in a friendlier tone this time.

Helen glanced around to see if anyone was listening, then leaned forward and, looking from Ingeborg to Maria, said, "I need a ride to Cleveland."

Ingeborg gave a short laugh. "We're not a car service," she said. "And we already have passengers." For once it might come in handy to pretend Frances was with them.

"You have one passenger," Helen corrected her. "Sara Bard Field is the only envoy." She sat back and smiled broadly at them. "I heard the other one is ill."

"Well, sometimes we have others," muttered Ingeborg, irritated by Helen's insistence. "Why should we take you?"

Helen leaned back in her chair and crossed one long leg over the other, lighting a cigarette. She inhaled deeply and blew the smoke off to the side before saying, "I need to get out of town for a while, and I have a sister in Cleveland who'll take me in. But I don't have the fare."

"Can your sister wire you the money?" Maria asked.

"She doesn't have it either," Helen said flatly. "I'll be all right once I get there."

"Why the hurry?" asked Ingeborg, mopping up egg yolk with the last of her toast before popping it in her mouth.

The young woman looked around the room again, and said in a hushed voice, "The vice squad is after me."

Ingeborg and Maria exchanged a glance. "What do you mean?" Maria asked.

Helen shrugged, and the corners of her wide mouth turned up in a smile, but Ingeborg saw that her eyes were worried. "The vice squad," she repeated. "You know, the moral police?"

Maria frowned. "Go on."

"I work in a shop," Helen explained, "Making hats. Six days a week, twelve hours a day." She shrugged again. "A girl likes to have a little fun, and what's it to anyone if I let a man take me dancing, or to a picture show?"

Ingeborg raised an eyebrow. "And…?"

Helen flushed. "What if I let him put an arm around me, kiss me? It's no one's business but my own!"

"Are you a prostitute?" asked Ingeborg.

"Ingeborg!" protested Maria, glaring at her.

Helen shook her head firmly and said, "No!"

Ingeborg rolled her eyes at Maria. "I'm not saying she is—but isn't that what they think?" she asked, turning back to Helen.

"They say I could be infected," Helen said, her eyes on her empty coffee cup as she tilted it back and forth, sliding the last drops around the bottom. She raised her eyes and looked at them. "With venereal disease. They say I must be tested—but I know I'm not sick." Her dark eyes flashed. "I'm afraid they'll lock me up. They took a friend of mine for three months. She'd never been with a man, no more than I have, but they said she had, and the medicine made her so sick. She had beautiful silky blond hair, and it fell out in tufts. She still isn't well."

"What if you refuse?" asked Maria.

"I told them no, but they say I must—that if I don't, the police will come and take me to the women's reformatory. But I've done nothing wrong!"

Ingeborg turned to Maria. "This happens?" she asked.

Maria picked up her empty cup and waved it at the waitress. "There was talk in Providence before we left, and for sure there were moral police at the Exposition—the girls in the suffrage booth mentioned it." The waitress approached and refilled the cups.

Ingeborg, smiled her thanks at the waitress, but waited until she'd stepped away to ask Maria, "Is that legal?"

"I don't know about the laws," said Maria, sipping her coffee. "But they always blame women for sex diseases." She looked over at Helen. "They take the men, too?" she asked.

"Of course not," Helen said, her cheeks flushing warm with indignation. "They only lock up the women—men go to clinics." She leaned closer. "They see all these single girls working in shops and factories with no family to mind them and they're worried what we'll get up to." The corners of her mouth lifted into a sly smile. "I'm not saying they're wrong, but it isn't fair to just lock up the girls."

Ingeborg sighed. Helen was right. Just like Eve and the apple—always the woman's fault. It was worrying. Every step toward independence brought a double measure of suspicion from those who wanted to keep women bound to men. If the police and the national guard could be called out to squash strikes like the one Rolf had been in, couldn't they come after women, too?

She raised her eyebrows at Maria, who nodded slightly. They should help the girl. Ingeborg had one last question. "What if we just give you train fare?"

"They're watching the trains," said Helen, simply. She leaned forward, pleading. "Look, you don't have to take me all the way to Cleveland, but at least get me out of Detroit. I don't think they'll risk coming for me if I'm with you."

Ingeborg gave in. "All right," she said. "We leave tomorrow morning. Just after dawn. Wait until we're in the car and then slip in next to Sara. We'll hide you until we're out of the city."

"Thank you!" Helen beamed, reaching for her hand. "Thank you!"

CHAPTER FOURTEEN

NOVEMBER 16-17, 1915

Ingeborg and Maria watched as the men loaded Emilie onto a long barge. Ice pellets blew sideways across the shipping yard, almost obscuring their view. They waited until she was safely loaded before turning away. Ingeborg felt strangely bereft at being parted from the little car, now as battered and dented as she felt herself. As many times as she'd cursed the long stretches of road, the breakdowns and tire changes, they hadn't been parted since they left San Francisco. She felt that Emilie was calling for them, straining at the binding straps, and as they walked away Ingeborg looked over her shoulder a few times before the barge was swallowed by the driving snow.

Early the previous morning they'd headed south out of Detroit, hugging the shores of Lake Erie under low clouds engorged with snow. The landscape was a uniform dirty brown, drained of other color by the threatening sky. The wind sweeping hard off the lake was raw and damp, and by the time they got to Cleveland the first flakes were swirling down.

They'd dropped Helen Bouchard in Cleveland not far from her sister's house.

"I appreciate the lift," she said as she climbed out of the car. "I hope you make it to Washington."

"We'll make it all right," Ingeborg told her. "You stay out of trouble." Helen had laughed and said she would, and the travelers sped on their way.

The storm allowed them to blame the low turnout on the weather rather than on Harriet Upton, who had urged her followers to boycott their meetings. Snow fell thickly over the handful of people shivering in front of them at their open-air meeting in Cleveland's Public Square, and they'd hustled through the program to release everyone from their misery. Later, they'd met with two congressmen who assured them they'd support the federal amendment when it came up in the House.

Their meeting with Cleveland's mayor, Newton Baker, was less successful. Baker was a pinch-faced man with smug self-certainty leaking from every pore. "I support your cause," he'd declared, in his squeaky voice, "but I couldn't possibly sign your petition. I find the word *demand* offensive, you see. I prefer womanly sweetness. I have never demanded anything from my government. Suffrage will come when it comes, which will be soon enough. There's no need to demand it. Have patience!"

As melting snow dripped from their hat brims, and their toes remained frozen from standing in the bitter wind in Public Square, the women glared at him as one. The mayor looked not one whit uncomfortable. He simply stood there with a smirk on his face, as if to say, *Ha! Now I've got you.*

Ingeborg was ready to claw his glasses off his face and stamp them under her boot. She blurted out, "We're sick of men pretending to think we're angels and treating us like idiots. We find that offensive."

Sara gave an icy chuckle. "Women have made little progress by asking politely—we believe a change of tactics is necessary," she told him. "How long must we wait for liberty?" Baker had shrugged and said that wasn't his concern, and the meeting broke up soon after.

It was more than 180 miles to Buffalo, their next stop, and the snow showed no sign of letting up. Mabel wanted them to forge ahead. "Think how glorious it will be when you arrive coated with snow, and tell of braving the storm to bring the message of suffrage hope to the women of the East," she'd said the next morning, over a breakfast of coffee and sweet rolls. "People will know then that nothing can stop us."

Ingeborg had regarded her sourly. "What if you drive the car and we take the train?"

"Too far, Mabel," agreed Maria. "Too risky. Cold would be hard enough but with this snow, too." She shook her head, scowling. "A barge can take it."

"You've managed everything else so far—remember that pass into Cheyenne? It's flat here and the roads are better. You can do this," Mabel had insisted.

Sara had been drooping over her coffee, her eyes closed, but at Mabel's words she opened them and straightened. "Oh, for God's sweet sake, Mabel," she said, wearily. "Have mercy. We can't possibly arrive on time in this storm. Put the damn car on a barge and be done with it."

* * *

It had been a luxury in some ways to take the train to Buffalo, watching the snow swirl past the train windows, but it was still uncomfortable traveling. The bench seats were hard, and they had to brace themselves against the swaying motion of the cars. Coal dust clung to every surface, and there was a strong odor of coal in the air. They'd passed the trip in silence, for the most part, Sara with her eyes closed and Mabel writing endless letters.

The snow had eased by the time they arrived in Buffalo, and they'd reunited with Emilie without difficulty. After a brief meeting in bitter cold, attended by only a few stalwart supporters, they'd retired to their hotel rooms.

Now they were speeding along toward Geneva, just outside Rochester, where they were to spend the night. There was no wind, so despite the cold they ran with Emilie's top down. The snow hadn't reached here, and the road was clear and in decent repair, so Maria sped along at a good clip. She crouched bear-like over the steering wheel with the thick fur hat Ingeborg had insisted she buy in Chicago pulled down to her eyebrows.

Ingeborg watched the scenery speed past, farmhouses nestled under the trees with woodsmoke curling from their chimneys, surrounded by fields wrested from the forest. She felt a sudden intense longing to pull Emilie into a dooryard and enter a snug farm kitchen, sit down next to the fire, pull off her boots, and just sit for a while. Again she felt a strong tug toward moving back to Sweden, a country she'd once been so desperate to leave. It surprised her to think seriously of returning for good. But she was homesick.

Through the trees a pond glinted in the cold sun, and she suddenly straightened up and peered out the side of the car. Skaters. Gliding along on the smooth surface, bent forward with the effort, scarves streaming behind them.

"Look, Maria, skaters!" she pointed out, excitedly. "Stop the car!"

"What?" squawked Maria, startled from her own thoughts. "Stop? What's wrong?"

"Nothing. Pull over by that wide place there," Ingeborg said. "Please, I want to see the skaters. Just for a minute."

Grumbling, Maria braked and steered Emilie over to a wide, level area at the side of the road. A thin layer of ice had formed on the puddles, and Ingeborg's boots crunched through them as she walked stiffly to the edge of the pond. The sun slanted through the trees, bathing the skaters in a honeyed glow as they sped by in long, whooshing strokes.

Maria joined her at the edge of the pond and peered out at the skaters. "What is this?" she asked Ingeborg.

Ingeborg laughed, a joyous sound in the frozen landscape. "Skating!" she said. "Did you never do it, in Sweden?"

"No. Too poor," said Maria, flatly.

"My uncle was a blacksmith—he made skates we strapped to our boots. I loved it." She inspected the ice at their feet. "Let's walk out!"

"Ingeborg! You're crazy. You'll fall through the ice," Maria told her, backing away.

But Ingeborg grabbed her arm. "Come, Maria. Slide your feet. Small steps. I'll hold you." She urged Maria forward, slipping an arm around her waist, and they took a few cautious steps away from the frozen mud at the edge of the pond. The ice was clear as glass, and they could see small rocks and tufts of weeds poking up from the sandy bottom. A minnow darted by.

Ingeborg laughed again, the years peeling back until she was a child skating into the wind, battling ahead until it was time to turn around and get blown back the way she'd come. How she'd loved that feeling!

Maria tried to hang back, but Ingeborg urged her forward. Suddenly the ice boomed and cracks shot out from beneath their feet, spreading in all directions.

"Ahh!" shrieked Maria, turning around and trying to scuttle back to shore.

Ingeborg held her fast. "Stop, Maria, you'll make us fall!" she ordered, laughing again. "Look, the ice is holding."

Maria eyed the ice beneath her feet dubiously. The cracks had branched across the surface, dividing it into sections. "For how long?" she asked.

Ingeborg pointed in front of her. "The ice is thick enough." She looked back out at the skaters. "Look at them! Oh, I wish I had skates, I'd go out right now and to hell with suffrage." She looked around. "Where's Sara?"

"Waiting in the car," said Maria. "We should go."

"Just a minute more, Maria," pleaded Ingeborg, eyes fixed on the skaters crisscrossing the pond surface, some arm in arm, others playing chase, darting and spinning. What was it her uncle used to say about sharp blades on smooth ice? "Friction—frictionless motion," she murmured.

"What?" said Maria.

"Frictionless motion," repeated Ingeborg, louder. "That's what my uncle used to say. When the lakes were very smooth the blades almost floated."

"Huh," said Maria, absently, eyeing the cracks at their feet. Then she snorted. "Better than motionless friction—sometimes this suffrage business is like that. All this work to go nowhere fast."

Ingeborg shouted with laughter and squeezed her arm hard around Maria's waist. "You're right." The two of them stood there, giggling.

They broke off as the ice released once more, a deep, guttural sound that echoed across the lake like thunder. Maria squealed again. Ingeborg let go of her and leaned over, tracing the cracks with her gloved fingers. The once smooth ice surface had divided into jagged sections. She looked up at Maria and pointed to the swatches of ice between the cracks. "Feminists and ultra-feminists, state or national action."

"Temperance and labor," Maria chimed in.

"Whites and Negroes," said Ingeborg, ruefully. She traced her eyes glumly around the pond surface. So many cracks.

They were quiet for a moment and then Maria chuckled and stamped her feet. Ingeborg looked at her.

"But look!" she said. "The ice holds. Never mind the cracks. Maybe suffrage will, too."

Ingeborg considered this gravely. "Maybe it will."

"Let's go," said Maria, and with a slow pirouette, she led the way off the pond.

* * *

Dusk was settling as they raced out of Rochester, having stopped there briefly before pushing on to Geneva. Overnight it seemed they were back in spring; the air was warm and thick with a low mist that swirled and shifted in the dim glow of the headlamps. They passed through a small hamlet with a garage spilling its contents out on the road, and then swerved around two shadowy figures who leapt to the side to avoid the rushing car.

Ingeborg had been trying to work out what day it was—she sometimes lost track as they raced from one town to the next. All that mattered was that they made the next meeting on time, day by interminable day. She squinted, considering. It was November, she was sure of that. And Mabel's itinerary had them in Cleveland on the fifteenth, so it must be the seventeenth. Almost two months since they'd left San Francisco. It was all a jumble in her mind.

As the trees flashed past in a solid wall, she lapsed into a half-drowsing fantasy of cupping her hands around a mug of hot, steaming coffee, a glistening slice of apple pie on a plate in front of her. Her nose twitched at the heavenly scent, and she imagined feeding herself bites of pie with her right hand, her left delivering sips of coffee.

Without warning Emilie's right front tire slammed into a deep hole and there was a deafening bang. Her nose pitched down and her rear end lifted briefly, pivoting around her right front tire and throwing her passengers forward and then to the side before coming to rest. They sat stunned and bruised. Someone sobbed, "Ahh, ahh!" and it was some moments before Ingeborg realized the sound was coming from her.

Blood trickled down her forehead and a stabbing pain sliced through her right shoulder. Carefully, she turned and looked at Maria, who was sitting behind the wheel holding her ribs, equally stunned. Then she turned and peered into the back seat.

Sara was gone.

"Sara!" croaked Ingeborg, frantic. She tried to think, but her head felt full of a thick, dark slurry. When had they last stopped? Had they left her somewhere? She twisted back to her right and saw Sara lying in a crumpled heap in the ditch, still as death. Ingeborg groped for the door handle and let herself out. She dropped to her knees by Sara, putting her hand on her shoulder and giving it a little shake. Had they managed to kill the envoy after all? She'd threatened to, but she'd never meant it. Desperate, she leaned low and pleaded, "Sara. Sara, wake up!" To her immense relief, Sara began to stir. Water was trickling through the ditch and Ingeborg saw that if they didn't move her quickly she'd be soaking wet.

"Is she dead?" Maria called, her voice thin and weak in the gathering gloom.

"No, but she's hurt." Ingeborg struggled to her feet and rummaged through the back of the car until she found and lit the lamp. Maria sagged against the car, crying, shaking with the shock of it. "I killed her," she moaned. "I killed Sara."

Ingeborg's own knees trembled, and the pain in her shoulder made her cry out as she heaved at the heavy buffalo skin, dragging it out of the back seat and arranging it roughly on the side of the road next to Sara. "Shut up!" Ingeborg snapped at her. "Come help me. There's water in the ditch—we have to get her out."

Maria limped over and stood by Sara's feet, still sobbing and cradling her ribs. With some difficulty she got down on her knees and put her hands under Sara's legs.

Ingeborg stood at Sara's head and got her hands under her shoulders. "Pull her legs," she told Maria.

As Ingeborg lifted Sara's shoulders, Maria strained and managed to drag her legs a few inches, but a searing pain from her ribs made her cry out. "Ahh, it hurts!" she wailed. Sara moaned, too.

"Once more. Look, her legs are almost out. Then you can rest."

Two figures loomed out of the darkness then and stood looking down at them, breathing hard. In the flickering light of the headlamps they seemed tall and menacing, and for a moment Ingeborg shrank back. They were far from a town and in unfamiliar territory; if the strangers meant harm there was nothing the three of them, bruised and battered as they were, could do about it.

Quickly she shook off her fear and asked, "Can you help us move her from the ditch?"

Without answering the taller figure moved around to Sara's side, picked her up and deposited her gently onto the buffalo skin. The smaller one crouched down and deftly flipped the skin over her body, cocooning her. Ingeborg sat back on her heels and breathed a sigh of relief.

Sara stirred again and her eyes opened, slowly focusing on her attendants.

"What happened?" she asked, her voice thin and weak.

"We hit a pothole," Ingeborg told her. "You were thrown out."

"Shit," said Sara. She tried to sit up.

"Stay still, Sara," said Maria, placing a hand on her shoulder. "Rest."

"I can't lie here all night," Sara complained, her voice stronger now. "Aren't we supposed to be somewhere?" She peered upward, for the first time taking in the strangers' faces. "Who are they?"

Ingeborg looked up at them. In the dim light she could just make out they were a man and a woman, clad in long overcoats with heavy bundles strapped to their backs. Brimmed hats were tugged down over their ears. She struggled to her feet. "I don't know," she said.

"You passed us," said the woman. "Near ran us over. We heard the crash and ran to help."

"Thank you," Ingeborg remembered to say. She squinted, trying to recall seeing them on the road. She was trembling all over and she ached from head to foot, her body a big throbbing bruise. She put her hand to her head and felt gingerly around a large, painful swelling with a small gash about at her hairline. It was sore but the bleeding seemed to have stopped. She thought she'd be all right; both Maria and Sara needed a doctor, though. She looked over at the car and swore. Emilie lay canted over at an angle with her front wheel in a deep pothole.

Despair washed over Ingeborg and she stood there, swaying. She had no idea how far they were from Geneva, or how they would possibly find someone to repair the car.

She turned her gaze to the couple and realized they were conferring quietly. Then, without a word, the man dropped his bundle and trotted off into the darkness, back the way they'd come.

"Your car's broken," said the woman. "He'll get help."

Ingeborg nodded. "Thank you," she said again, and stood there shivering, suddenly very cold and indescribably weary. Her head wound pulsated with pain, and her shoulder was stiffening.

The woman slung off her pack and moved around in the darkness collecting scraps of wood. Somehow, despite the dampness, she got a small fire going off to the side of the road near where Sara lay limp in the buffalo skin. Ingeborg helped Maria to her feet and they stood holding their hands out to the fire, grateful for the warmth and the way the light pushed back the growing darkness. Maria peered at the woman and asked her name.

"You can call me Phoebe," she said. She seemed to be a woman of few words. Ingeborg couldn't guess her age; not young, given the lines on her weathered face, but she moved with strength and purpose. They'd have been lost without her.

Ingeborg introduced herself and the others and asked, "Where are you going this time of night?"

"Coming back from the trading post," Phoebe said simply. "We live over there." She pointed up the road and into the woods.

"Thank God you came along," said Maria. She turned to lean over Sara, touching her arm, murmuring something Ingeborg couldn't hear. Then she stood and rummaged around in the back of the car for the water pouch and brought it back to Sara, who managed to prop herself up on one elbow enough to take a few sips. When she was finished Maria wobbled over and let herself carefully down to sit with her back against Emilie's fender. As if in sympathy, Emilie let go a puff of steam and settled a bit deeper into the hole.

Ingeborg stirred. "How long?" she asked. "I mean before he brings back help?"

Phoebe shrugged. "Not too long. If Enrico's home."

"Enrico?" Ingeborg asked.

"Owns the garage in the hamlet," Phoebe pointed back down the road and Ingeborg nodded, remembering. "What was your hurry?"

Ingeborg explained their mission. Phoebe shrugged again and looked away, and they stood there quietly for a bit, warming themselves at the little fire, leaning away or shifting places when the smoke drifted into their eyes.

Ingeborg eyed Phoebe, curious. The other woman spoke with a quiet confidence and an accent that Ingeborg couldn't quite place. Eastern Europe, perhaps? "Where are you from?" she asked.

Phoebe snorted. "Here." She glanced at Ingeborg.

"I mean where's your family from?" Ingeborg asked.

"Here." Phoebe paused, and when Ingeborg looked confused she said, "I'm Seneca—Indian."

"Oh," said Ingeborg. "I didn't expect to meet an Indian here—" She broke off, grimacing. No Negroes, no Indians on this trip, she reminded herself. She sighed. "I guess you know we weren't coming to talk to you about suffrage."

"No. White people don't let us vote in your elections—we're not citizens," said Phoebe. Ingeborg opened her mouth to speak, but Phoebe cut her off. "But we have our own government, the Haudenosaunee Confederacy. It's better—our women have more rights than you do."

Ingeborg blinked, surprised. "What do you mean?" she asked.

"We already vote," said Phoebe, with a small grin. "We're born into clans headed by a clan mother. Haudenosaunee women have many more powers and rights than you white women."

"Not really?" said Ingeborg, astonished. "How long has it been like that?"

Phoebe shrugged. "Since our people can remember, I guess."

"But how can that be?" Ingeborg screwed up her face and shook her head slightly as she tried to absorb Phoebe's words. She stared at Phoebe.

"It just is," Phoebe said flatly. "It's what we believe. Women must be respected by the men. If a man hurts his wife she can put him out of her house—for good, if that's what she wants."

Ingeborg's jaw dropped. It was like a fairy tale. Here they were, nearly killing themselves racing across the country just for the right to vote, and Phoebe's people already had it figured out. "Why don't we know about this?" she demanded. "Why didn't you tell us!"

"Hah!" Phoebe's laugh was a short, derisive bark. "You think we didn't? Your men didn't want to share power with women, I guess. But we never could figure why you women went along with it." She turned and stooped to add more sticks to the fire. It blazed up. "My grandmother was friendly with Matilda Gage—Matilda saw it right away."

"Matilda Gage?" Ingeborg asked. "Who's she?"

"She helped with some big meeting white women had—for equal rights. A long time ago, this was. Over in Seneca Falls, I think—my grandmother lived out that way." Phoebe cracked a branch across her knee and added the pieces carefully to the fire. The flames flickered higher, casting light on Phoebe's outstretched hands but deepening the shadow on her face. "Grandmother told me Matilda used to visit her, ask questions about the Seneca. Said Matilda wanted the whites to be like the Haudenosaunee. Like women having a say in the government. But that was a long time ago—and not much changed, from what I see."

"I can't believe it," muttered Ingeborg, again. She was stunned by what Phoebe said, and in her present state had trouble making sense of it. She walked over to Sara and crouched down next to her, knees protesting, putting a hand down to the ground to steady herself. "Sara, are you awake?"

Sara was curled up on her side but she stirred and opened her eyes. "Sort of." Her face was chalk white and she was limp as a rag, but her voice was clear.

"Phoebe says she has more rights than we do, with her people, the Seneca Indians. Did you know about that?"

"No," said Sara, and shut her eyes again.

Ingeborg went back to the fire and stood by it, frowning. She felt as if, like Emilie, she had come up hard against a new truth that turned her life upside down. As a girl in Sweden, and all these years in Providence, it was the same. Men made the laws and ran the businesses, and that was just the way it had always been. The idea of women being equal seemed as distant as the stars, sometimes, given how hard they were working just for the vote. And here the "savages," as white people still referred to them—when they thought of them at all—had it right all along.

CHAPTER FIFTEEN

NOVEMBER 19-21, 1915

Two days later Ingeborg shuffled into the crowded lobby of their hotel in Albany, struggling under the weight of her suitcase, a bag of petitions, and water flasks. Her right side still ached from the crash, and her head tilted slightly to one side due to her stiff neck. She paused, looked around, and spotted the hotel desk off to her left with a long line of guests queued up in front of it. With a sigh, she swung toward it. Suddenly, she jerked back and gaped at a woman crossing the lobby toward the elevator. Was that Frances Joliffe?

She stopped and dropped her bags as Sara and Maria came up behind her. "Look," Ingeborg pointed. "Frances!" They waved and called out to her as the elevator doors opened wide and she prepared to walk inside. Hearing her name, she paused and looked over at them, frowning, as if at some riffraff, and Ingeborg could see she didn't recognize them.

"Looks like you won the bet," Ingeborg muttered to Maria.

Just then Frances broke into a big smile and she waved, crossing the lobby to them in long strides, her stylish frock dancing around the tops of her calves. Ingeborg had forgotten how attractive she was, tall and slender, with eyebrows that arched over dark, expressive eyes, and skin so pale it was almost translucent. Her shiny brown hair was cut into a modish cap, tucked behind her ears. Ingeborg glanced quickly at her companions and almost laughed at the contrast—cheeks reddened from the wind and cold, slathered with road dust, shapeless in layers of coats and scarves and stooped and wobbly like the old women this trip had turned them into. No wonder Frances had frowned at them. She probably wondered why this swank hotel let beggars trawl through the lobby and hail guests by name. From the corner of her eye Ingeborg noticed a man sitting in a chair nearby with a newspaper spread open in front of him. He was watching this exchange with interest, but she forgot him as Frances came up.

Frances smoothed over her failure to recognize them, smiling and drawing each of them close for a peck on the cheek. "Heavens, look at you! What a journey you've been through! I couldn't imagine who was calling out to me—we didn't expect you for another hour or two."

"We flew," said Sara, looking pleased that Frances had finally shown up but also jealous that she looked so fresh and beautiful. "Thanks to Maria. When did you arrive?"

"Oh, two days ago," said Frances, smiling. "I wanted to be rested for the meeting with the governor. Train travel is so tiring, you know."

They stood there silently, gazing at her. Ingeborg gave a short bark of laughter. "We wouldn't know," she said, pointedly. She had just bent over to pick up her bags when the man she'd noticed earlier approached them, his newspaper now folded under his arm.

"Excuse me, ladies" he said. "I saw you arrive. I've been waiting for you, in fact."

They regarded him warily. Sara was the first to break the silence. "How nice," she said, her voice suggesting she felt the opposite. "And you are?"

"The name's William Harmon," the man said, extending his hand. "I'm a reporter with the *Albany Evening Journal*. You're the suffrage envoys, are you not? I wondered if we could have a word."

Sara shook his hand, summoning a smile to hide her unease, and didn't introduce herself or the others. "Yes, that's right," she said. "But we've only just arrived, as you see, and we're rather travel-weary and need to freshen up. Can we arrange a later time?"

Harmon ignored her and looked around at their faces. Ingeborg could see he was appraising the difference in their appearances. "I see," he said. "Now let me guess, which one of you is Sara Bard Field?" He looked at Frances, who raised her chin and gave him a cool stare.

"I am," said Sara, impatiently.

Harmon nodded at Sara and his lips twitched in a thin smile that didn't touch his eyes. "Ah, of course. Then which one of you is Maria Kindberg, the driver of your motorcar?"

Maria gave him a brief nod and said, "That's me."

He looked over at Ingeborg. "Then you must be Miss Kindstedt, the mechanician?"

Ingeborg nodded yes. She could see he was playing with them. He must know who they were, he'd have seen the press photos Mabel sent. And now he'd caught them reuniting with Frances as if they hadn't seen her in months, which in fact they hadn't. She felt her toes curl. Would the whole farce be revealed now?

Harmon turned and studied Frances. "Then you must be Frances Joliffe," he said. "Permit me to ask, I had understood you were one of the envoys, but I overheard you say just now you'd arrived by train two days ago. And, if I might add, you look a bit more—rested—than your companions."

Frances lifted her chin and stared down her nose at him, arching her brows. "That's correct, Mr. Harmon," she said smoothly. "I returned home because of illness in my family."

"Just when was it that you left the trip?" asked Harmon, pleasantly. He pulled a small notepad out of his pocket and leafed through it to an open page then raised his eyes to her, his pencil poised expectantly.

Frances opened her mouth to speak and then closed it, sliding her eyes over to Sara in mute appeal. How much did she know? Ingeborg wondered. Had Mabel told her the CU was pretending she was with them all along?

Sara hesitated. "Oh, I don't know," she said, and forced a light laugh. "You know how it is when you travel. We've come so far, so fast, all the days have blurred together until I can't put a time or a place to anything."

"I see," said Harmon, nodding. "I just wondered, because the notice we received at the paper said the four of you had made the trip and you've admitted that isn't the case. So I wonder, how do we know the whole thing isn't a giant sham?" He cocked his head and looked at each of them in turn, smiling pleasantly, but his sharp eyes missing nothing.

Ingeborg thought about Sara taking the train in Iowa, when she'd been so sick, and shipping Emilie up by barge to Buffalo from Cleveland to avoid the snow and bitter cold. But those were short distances and hardly counted. There were so many more miles they *had* been in the car, just the three of them, bad roads, good roads, snow, sleet and rain. She blurted out, "Look at us. We've driven more than four thousand hard miles from San Francisco to get here. My backside knows we did every one of those miles." Harmon nodded. "You wouldn't believe what we've been through."

Harmon bowed slightly and smiled. "Miss Kindstedt, I would never tell a woman she looked anything but lovely, but you do appear to have been, shall we say, intimate with the weather. I'm merely wondering when Miss Joliffe left you. And if the trip was as hard as you claim, it wouldn't be surprising if the rest of you also took time off along the way. Our readers will want to know."

"Mr. Harmon, we're suffragists," said Sara, her eyes flashing. "We have to be tough, or we wouldn't have gotten as far as we have. I can assure you that the rigors of travel have never stood in the way of our cause. The three of us have been together since San Francisco." Her eyes flicked to Frances and then back to the reporter. "Miss Joliffe, I now recall, left us in Sacramento."

"I see," drawled Harmon. "And you have evidence of this?"

"You're the reporter," snapped Ingeborg, her growing anger chasing the fatigue from her limbs. She'd always doubted the wisdom of the CU pretending that Frances was with them, and it looked as if she'd been proven right. Now the press would use it against them, say none of them made the trip, after everything they'd been through. She was damned if she'd come this far for nothing. "Go find it."

Sara shot her a warning look. "The newspapers have covered the trip in every city we visited," she said swiftly to Harmon. "You can obtain press clippings from all of them, I imagine. Mabel Vernon is here somewhere, and she has the itinerary, you can get it from her."

Harmon inclined his head. "I'll do that, thank you" he said. "And can you show me the petition? It must be enormous by this time—you say it's three miles long?"

With a flip of her hand, Sara said, "I couldn't tell you how long it is, but we left San Francisco with a half-million names on it, and we've added thousands more since then."

"Impressive," said Harmon, looking around at their baggage. "But where is it?"

"It grew far too large for us to travel with," Sara said, smiling sweetly at him. "We sent it ahead by train to CU headquarters in Washington."

* * *

That night the travelers gathered for supper in a corner of the hotel's main dining area. They all tucked into their food hungrily, plates of roast chicken and mashed potatoes, with plenty of salty gravy. All but Frances, who picked at her food and sipped a glass of wine.

"Did that reporter—Harmon—find you?" Sara asked Mabel. "He made me nervous."

Mabel patted her mouth with her napkin. "Yes, I spoke to him. I showed him some press clippings, and that seemed to satisfy him." She looked around at them, concerned. "Your wire said you'd had an accident. What happened?"

"Hit a pothole and broke an axle," said Ingeborg. "Sara was thrown from the car."

"Good God!" said Frances, horrified. "It's a wonder you weren't killed."

Sara shrugged. "We're all a bit banged up. We think Maria cracked a rib," she looked over at Maria with a sympathetic smile. Maria fingered the bandage beneath her breasts and nodded.

"That's awful!" exclaimed Mabel. She looked worried. "Did you see a doctor?"

"There wasn't time," said Sara.

"No time?" Frances repeated, faintly. She looked profoundly puzzled. "But you might have been badly hurt."

Ingeborg shrugged, proud now at how tough they'd been. It had seemed perfectly sensible at the time. "We could walk and talk. Why spend the money? I drove the rest of the way to Geneva so Maria could rest."

"How on earth did you get the axle repaired so quickly?" Mabel asked, more concerned about the car and not a bit troubled by their refusal to see a doctor. "I thought you'd be delayed at least a day."

"That was a small miracle," laughed Sara. "There was only one telephone in that hamlet, but I was able to reach the Willys-Overland company and they sent the part by train from Buffalo. A mechanic installed it for us and we were on our way later that evening. We got to Geneva early the next morning."

Frances remained shocked. "I just can't imagine what you've been through. Is it worth it, to risk so much?"

They looked at her in silence. Ingeborg frowned, turning the question over in her mind. It came to her that many things you didn't think you could manage became possible when the other option was starvation—people with no money learned that lesson young. It made life simpler, somehow. They just learned how to keep going. But Frances had never had to. It was no surprise that she'd left the trip so early.

Maria cleared her throat. "I wouldn't want to repeat it," she said. They all laughed. "But we've done a lot of good, I think."

Mabel smoothed her hair back behind her ear. "I'm here to tell you, ladies, that this is the hardest thing I've ever done. I know you've suffered in the car but it's not been a picnic for me, either. I've been shaken about on those wooden train seats 'til my teeth rattled. Baked and frozen, by turns. Once some cinders flew in an open window and burned holes in my dress. Try finding matching fabric in some backwater town."

They regarded her with sympathy. "I took trains when I worked those suffrage campaigns in Nevada and Oregon," said Sara, wincing at the memory. "It's a hard way to travel."

"And then there's fending off drunks and lechers—" Mabel wrinkled her nose in disgust. "I make a point of befriending other women so I can sit with them. I'm less bothered that way."

"I made the right choice to step out when I did," said Frances, with a delicate shudder. "You're all made of sterner stuff than I am. I feel a bit of an imposter, I confess. But I want to help now that I'm here. What's the plan?"

Mabel pushed her plate away and laid out the schedule. The next day they'd drive to Hartford, then from there to Boston and to Providence. From Providence they'd head to New York City.

"Anything special planned in New York?" asked Sara.

"We'll have a strong showing there," Mabel replied. "Mrs. Belmont is helping us, of course. A procession of one hundred motorcars will escort you into the city, and we'll all end up at Sherry's for tea. The acting mayor—McAneny, his name is—will sign the petition."

"What will NAWSA do?" asked Ingeborg.

"I don't expect much help, but they won't work against us, either," said Mabel. "The rumor is they're busy planning their next state referendum—this one for presidential suffrage only."

There was a chorus of groans from around the table. "Why would they settle for just voting for president?" asked Frances. "And why bother, when we're so close to getting the amendment through?"

"Don't ask me," said Mabel. "I couldn't believe it either." She frowned and took a sip of her tea. "They must think it will be easier to get since full suffrage lost here so badly two weeks ago. But perhaps wisdom will prevail. I hear they're planning to work on the federal amendment, too, so perhaps we'll get some help from them. But we're not waiting—as we have in all the other states, we'll use the publicity from your arrival to help form a New York branch of the CU—they don't have one yet."

Sara stared at Mabel, her eyebrows lifted. "Does NAWSA know this?" asked Sara. "I doubt Carrie Catt will be pleased."

Mabel shrugged. "Alice says she and Mrs. Catt had an agreement— we'd stay out of New York until after the referendum. It's over, it was defeated, and here we are." She looked around the table with a smile. "Besides, New York has other suffrage groups—the Women's Political Union, for one."

"Is that the one Elizabeth Stanton's daughter runs?" asked Sara. "I've forgotten her name."

"That's right," said Mabel. "Harriot Stanton Blatch. She's welcomed us, and there's talk her group will join forces with the CU." She shifted and smiled. "Here's something fun—one of her organizers is planning a séance. They want to contact Harriot's mother to see what she says about the prospects of getting the amendment through in the next session."

Ingeborg rolled her eyes and looked over at Maria, whose ears had perked up at this discussion. She placed great store in contacting the dead, but Ingeborg thought it was just another way to separate people from their money.

"A séance?" asked Maria, eagerly. "When? Can we go?"

"I don't know the details," said Mabel, smiling at her. "But yes, I think I can get you an invitation."

"And Thanksgiving?" Ingeborg broke in, changing the subject.

"Yes, we should talk about that," said Mabel. "We can't expect people to come out on Thanksgiving, so you'll have the day off." She looked over at Maria and Ingeborg. "That means you can stay in Providence for the holiday, if you like. We'll take the train back to New York City. But we'll need you back in the city by noon on Friday—that's when we'll have the big parade."

Ingeborg and Maria shared a glance. Maria beamed, but Ingeborg's belly had done a little flip at the mention of Providence. She had some unfinished business there. She frowned and fidgeted with her napkin, thinking about how to bring it up.

Mabel looked at her, now, curious. "Is something wrong, Ingeborg?"

Ingeborg hesitated, and then said, "We should talk about Providence...." She plunged into a description of last summer's riots, her scuffle with the policeman, and Maria hiding her in the Dexter asylum until they left for the Exposition. The three younger women listened to her account, wide-eyed, as the warmth leaked slowly from the room. "So, you see," she said, awkwardly, "Perhaps in Providence the publicity should just be for Sara and Frances. No mention of me or Maria."

Sara sat back in her chair, looking at Ingeborg with horror. "You almost killed a policeman, and then you were in an insane asylum? What else haven't you told us? Has this happened before?"

Ingeborg shook her head vigorously, "Almost killed? That's too much! Those head wounds, they bleed a lot."

"And I hid her in the asylum from the police, to let things settle down," Maria cut in, with an anxious look at Ingeborg.

Ingeborg cocked her head at the three younger women. Their faces were a mixture of astonishment, fear, and revulsion, like when a cat starts noisily chewing the head off a mouse on the parlor floor. She hadn't made them see how the whole thing was, how the workers had been driven to their limits so they'd had to strike, and then that last day when the police had attacked *them*, not the other way around.

She sighed, and leaned forward, her forearms on the table. "Look, I'm telling you, those police came at us, and that boy would have been killed. They beat his mother too. There was no time to think. But I don't—"

Sara broke in. "You threatened to kill me."

Mabel and Frances gasped, looking from Sara to Ingeborg.

Ingeborg heard Maria mutter, "No, no," and felt her face flush. "Oh, for God's sake, Sara! It was a bad time." She looked at Mabel. "When we didn't get to Topeka for the rally." She looked back at Sara, fighting a rising anger that choked her breath in her chest. "You went on and on, complaining. We were doing the best we could and you made it worse. You made me so angry, and I shouted to make you stop. Anyone might have said the same." She tried for a joking tone. "But you're still here, right? I never laid a hand on you."

Sara's eyes flitted past hers, then she lifted her shoulders and let them drop. "Perhaps I should have been more worried than I was," she murmured, and gave Mabel a wide-eyed stare, her eyebrows raised in a look that said, *You see what I've had to put up with? Riding with a madwoman?*

"She never meant to," Maria jumped in, her voice soothing. "She has a temper and says what she shouldn't—haven't you, sometimes? But she doesn't mean it."

Mabel said, "Of course not" and Frances murmured, "We all say things we oughtn't to," but Ingeborg could see the bond they'd shared was now, like the poor dead mouse on the parlor floor, mangled and headless.

Ingeborg was disgusted. Why did she still bother with them? After all the miles, they were further apart than when they started, strangers then but lifted by the send-off from the Women Voters' Convention and their blood filled with passion for their cause, the brutal hardship and tedium of the trip still ahead of them. She lifted her hands in a gesture that was both supplication and dismissal. "Believe what you like," she said with a shrug. "But remember we saved you at the Exposition. You wanted a hundred cars to make this trip—you couldn't find even one! What we've been through—I tell you, we deserve better." She turned to Maria. "Maybe we just take Emilie home to Providence and forget about this." She glanced back at the others and said bitterly, "Let the *envoys* find their own way to Washington."

Mabel was quick to soothe her ruffled feelings. "Of course we recognize all that you and Maria have done for us. We couldn't have managed without you. And this trip has been tremendous for suffrage." She looked over at Frances and Sara for agreement, eyebrows lifted. Silence hung in the air. "Isn't that right?" Mabel prompted them.

Sara struggled to compose her face and managed a grumpy smile. "That's so."

Frances cleared her throat, hesitated, and said, "Quitting is rather a delicate subject for me...." Her face was grave but her eyes twinkled, and then she grinned. They all laughed, and the tension in the room eased. She reached her hand across to Ingeborg and clasped her arm. "You've done so much already, and we still need you. I've only just come back. Please stay with us."

* * *

Ingeborg sighed and turned over on her side, easing her sore shoulder. She'd woken from a deep sleep when a noisy wagon had clattered by under her window and now her mind was like a baby in the night, wide awake and happy for the company when the sleepy mother comes to shush it. Her eyes opened, and she looked out at the hotel room. In the dim light of the streetlamps, she could just make out the shape of the armoire, and the straight-backed chair in the corner next to the washstand. She closed her eyes again.

They were in Boston, she remembered. She let her mind drift over the last couple of days, which had needed more delicate political maneuvering than she had patience for. The other suffrage group was strong in Massachusetts—two of its leaders lived there, Maude Wood Park and Katherine McCormick. NAWSA's leaders considered the CU an affront to womanhood, and they spent nearly as much time badmouthing Alice Paul as promoting suffrage. Mabel had worried they'd speak out against the envoys or use their influence to keep politicians from seeing them.

But NAWSA was still smarting from the losses in the four states that had just held suffrage referendums, when only about a third of the men could bring themselves to support it. They'd spent a great deal of money—and worked their organizers half to death—and were utterly discouraged by their poor showing. The word was they were taking a hard look at the federal amendment. It was starting to look more appealing, so they couldn't talk it down, but they also refused to fall in line behind the CU and openly support the envoys. Mabel had handled those negotiations in her usual diplomatic fashion, and she'd pulled off quite a coup.

In the end almost two hundred women had trooped up the steps into the capitol's rotunda to meet with Governor Walsh. He'd backed the state suffrage referendum and was clearly jittery about going against the voters when it had been defeated so soundly. "I believe in suffrage," he told them. His deep-sunk eyes darted here and there, and then fixed so hard on a point in the back of the room that Ingeborg turned to peer at who had come in behind them. The space was empty. "But I believe it should happen through state action. The voters here have spoken, and it seems a good majority of them don't want woman suffrage. You know men will generally vote as their wives tell them to," he assured them.

Ingeborg snorted softly in disgust, remembering. She'd glanced over at Elizabeth Glendower Evans, the local CU leader who had introduced the envoys. She wore a magnificent, broad-brimmed felt hat crowned with ostrich feathers, like a musketeer. Her bold brown eyes shot sparks, and she looked ready to skewer the governor with her walking stick. "Governor Walsh," she said crisply, "there are so many things wrong with that statement, starting with it simply isn't true. If it were, women would have voted long ago."

But Walsh had ignored her. "If the men defeated the recent referendum it can only be that their wives didn't want it, either." He produced a nervous chuckle and fingered his chin. "It appears to me that you have more work to do."

"What if women didn't marry?" Ingeborg asked him. "Or their husbands died?

"Surely they can find some man to influence," Walsh said with a shrug.

"Governor Walsh," said Sara, crisply. "Oregon voters defeated suffrage five times when I lived there but the governor still pushed for it. We've come all the way from San Francisco and you're just the second governor to refuse our petition, which now has almost a million signatures. Why, only yesterday Governor Holcombe of Connecticut signed it and told us that if the four million women voters of the West would stand behind the amendment, we'd have it through in no time."

Ingeborg saw Maria looking at her and raised an eyebrow. Back up to a million signatures?

"You have a long career in front of you, Governor," said Elizabeth. "Think about whether you care to be on the wrong side of history— the women of Massachusetts won't forget where you stood on this question."

Walsh frowned and put his head to one side, considering, and Ingeborg thought they had him. Then he said, decisively, "I can't sign your petition, but I'll write a letter commending suffrage, and you can use that as you wish."

That was that. They'd sailed off to meet Mayor Curley, but he never appeared, so they'd had to content themselves with standing in a circle outside his office and singing suffrage songs. Then it was on to the obligatory luncheon, with about seventy-five of Boston's braver suffragists in attendance. Ingeborg yawned. Another state behind them.

Beside her, Maria stirred and stretched, opening her eyes to the light now spilling over the windowsill. "Mmmmhh." She said drowsily. "What time is it?"

Ingeborg smiled at her. "Morn, morn. About seven, I think. We should get up. Providence today!"

Maria tugged the covers up to her chin and settled back into her pillow, closing her eyes. "That's not far. We can sleep a bit longer."

Ingeborg hitched over closer to Maria and wrapped an arm around her waist, inhaling her warm mix of musk and scented powder. She planted a soft kiss on her cheek. "Sleepyhead. Wake up."

"Why such a hurry?" Maria murmured. "Aren't you worried they'll arrest you?"

Ingeborg pulled away and sat up, swinging her legs over the side of the bed. "We live there. I have to go back sometime." She reached for her stockings and started to pull them on. "Mabel said she told headquarters to send only Sara and Frances's names to the papers. No photo. No one's interested in us anyway; we're just the help."

Maria sighed as she rose from the bed and walked over to the washbasin. "I wish we were going back to Providence for good," she grumbled. "I could sleep for a week. What will we do while Sara and Frances are in the meetings?"

Ingeborg shoved her feet into her boots and sat back down on the bed, brushing her hair out with short, quick strokes and pinning it up so it would fit under her hat. "Let's go home," she suggested. "You can visit with Minnie."

Maria glanced at her suspiciously. "And what will you do?"

Ingeborg's face was blandly innocent. "Visit friends," she said.

"What friends?" Maria demanded.

"Tommy Delano and Paulo Bianchi. SallyAnn if she's around," said Ingeborg, returning Maria's stare coolly.

Maria groaned. "Ingeborg! What do you want with the IWW now?"

Ingeborg shook her head. "You know they killed Joe Hill a few days ago. I just want to stop by the hall, see how they're doing."

Maria finished buttoning her blouse and pulled on her skirt. Then she pushed her feet into her boots and sat down on the bed, waiting for Ingeborg to tie them for her. Maria's ribs were slow to heal, and leaning over made her gasp with pain. Ingeborg stooped down and grabbed the left foot, setting it on her knee to begin tying it, then paused and turned her face up to look at Maria. "You always think I'm going to cause trouble," she said, her voice teasing. "Don't you trust me?"

Maria gave her a little nudge with her foot. "Not one little bit. You're always pushing, pushing, never content with the way things are. Then you get upset and you don't think and do things like break a policeman's head." Boot tied, Ingeborg set that foot down and grabbed the other. Maria leaned back on her hands. "He deserved it. But most people wouldn't do that."

"An injury to one is an injury to all," said Ingeborg, "That's what the Wobblies say. I was just—"

But Maria cut her off, stamping her right foot onto the floor. Her mouth was tight and her voice came harshly. She leaned forward and thrust her face into Ingeborg's. "I know what they say, but you listen to me, Ingeborg Kindstedt." Maria's voice came out in a hiss. "I won't go through it with you again. You go from cause to cause like a bee after flowers. Suffrage, labor, the race question. And I pay the price for it. I'm not like you—this trip has worn me out. You do what you like, but if you go to jail you're on your own this time."

"Maria—" Ingeborg protested.

Maria cut her off. "I mean it!" she said, glaring at Ingeborg.

"All right, Maria," Ingeborg said, solemn now. "Nothing will happen. Don't worry."

CHAPTER SIXTEEN

NOVEMBER 22, 1915

Ingeborg looked about eagerly as the small farms on the outskirts of Providence gave way to houses with gray, weathered clapboards, tenements with wash hanging from the windows, and a sprinkling of small grocers, butchers, bakers, and the occasional diner. Smoke from coal fires hung in the air, and the factory smokestacks rising in the distance belched out black smoke.

The road was thrumming with activity, delivery men offloading trucks and wagons, women with shopping baskets on their arms. Children raced in and out of the traffic and squatted in the dirt playing marbles. A backyard rooster crowed.

"What an adorable town," said Frances, from the back seat.

Ingeborg flushed a little. Looking at it through Frances's eyes she could see that this section of the city was small and poor; some of the buildings sagged and the packed dirt streets were edged with refuse. The pungent odor of horse manure rose from the road, laced with the occasional whiff of an overfull outhouse.

"It reminds me of places I've seen in Europe," Frances added, "So bright and lively. Very different from where I live."

Ingeborg glanced over at Maria, who shrugged and gave her a small smile. Frances was merely being polite about Providence—it could hardly compare to her home in San Francisco—but she didn't really care. It might lack the sunny beauty of California, the towering mountains of Salt Lake City or Denver, and the muscle of Chicago, but it was home. She felt a sudden rush of affection for it.

Maria pulled up and waited for a driver to back his delivery truck up to a coal bin. "It's not fancy. But it made a place for us."

Ingeborg agreed. "It's been good."

They'd decided, in deference to Ingeborg's situation, to drive into the city with Emilie's top folded down but without the We Demand banner and other suffrage signs and flags that would draw attention to them. After dropping Sara and Frances off at City Hall where the mass meeting would be held, Maria and Ingeborg would head to their home and stay there through Thanksgiving. The envoys would take the train back to New York City that evening.

After safely delivering their charges to City Hall, Maria maneuvered through the gathering crowd and swung Emilie onto Westminster Street, looking eagerly about until they arrived at their home in the West End at the base of Federal Hill. It was a bright cold day, very still. Brown leaves still clung to the few trees, and coal smoke rose from the chimneys.

Maria pulled up in front of 557 Westminster Street, a two-story old building with a furniture business in the first-floor storefront. It seemed to Ingeborg they'd been gone for years and she was mildly surprised to see that nothing had changed on their block. The Colonial Theatre, next door, was showing *Should a Wife Forgive?* starring Lillian Lorraine. Probably not, thought Ingeborg, but wondered if it would still be showing when they returned to Providence from Washington.

Maria owned the building and sublet rooms to other tenants. One of these was her own nephew, Richard, who'd emigrated from Sweden about five years before and lived there with his wife, Minnie, and their new baby. This arrangement was in part how she'd managed to save enough money for the trip West and to buy Emilie. She was careful with money, often going without new clothes or other small luxuries Ingeborg told her many times that she could afford.

Minnie was a fresh-faced farm girl who had grown up outside of Providence and had come to the city to work at a woolen mill. Richard had met her at a dance, and before long they'd married and she'd moved in. Maria's frugal habits had been a source of some conflict with Minnie, who liked nice things and often pressured Richard to buy her luxuries Maria thought she could live without. A new dress when the old one could be mended or made over. New shoes when the old ones still had plenty of wear in them. "You should save that money," she scolded. "You'll want your own place one day." But Minnie was a good cook and pitched in with housework, so both Ingeborg and Maria had grown fond of the girl.

Richard was at work but Minnie met them at the door and seemed genuinely pleased to see them. "Welcome home!" she said, holding the door open wide. She held the baby, Juliana, on her hip. Juliana had been born in June, and when they left she'd still been an infant, content to eat and sleep with a tendency to colic in the evenings. Now, at five months, Juliana was a plump and beguiling baby, with blue eyes like Richard's, her mother's bow-shaped mouth, and a mop of toffee-colored curls. She chortled and waved at the travelers, who exclaimed over her.

"Look how big she is!" said Maria. "Will she let me hold her?"

"Let me help you with your coats," protested Minnie, laughing, and beamed with pride as Maria cooed over the baby.

"Oh, you sweet thing!" said Maria in Swedish, planting a moist kiss on Juliana's cheek. "Aren't you beautiful?" She looked up at Minnie and switched back to English. "Oh, Minnie, she's precious." Maria had taken a keen interest in Juliana, the closest thing to a grandchild she'd ever have, and as they'd gotten closer to the East, she'd started talking about the baby and how she'd have changed while they were gone.

Ingeborg had been less excited—babies never interested her much. Since leaving the Salvation Army orphanage in Sweden so long ago, Ingeborg had been around children very little. She'd been largely indifferent to Minnie's pregnancy and paid scant attention to Juliana once she'd arrived. She'd been so consumed by the strike last summer she'd hardly thought of anything else. But the rush of love and delight she felt on seeing Juliana surprised her, and when it was her turn she reached out her arms happily to hold the child, holding her so awkwardly it made Maria and Minnie giggle.

Juliana was good-natured about the commotion and began fussing only when it was time to be fed, busily nursing but stopping at intervals to turn her head and peer owlishly at the strangers. Later, she napped peacefully in her cradle in their kitchen as Minnie served them coffee and slices of cardamom cake she'd made that morning, allowing them to get caught up on events of the last few months.

Minnie had never left Rhode Island, and their stories left her open-mouthed. "My word, you two," she said, laughing. "I had no idea when you left that you were setting off on such an adventure."

"Nor did we," said Maria, drily.

"It's a wonder you're still alive," said Minnie, as she sliced off more cake and added it to their plates. "Wait until Richard hears. But you say you're not back for good?"

Ingeborg shook her head. "We'll be here for Thanksgiving," she said, and then sketched out the rest of their itinerary "But we go back to New York City the next day for meetings, and make our way down to Washington from there. Congress opens on December sixth— there's a big meeting on the steps of the Capitol and we must be there for that."

"And we meet with President Wilson later that day. Imagine that!" said Maria, beaming.

"President Wilson himself?" exclaimed Minnie, visibly shocked that anyone she knew would call on the president in the White House. "Isn't that something!"

Ingeborg peeked at her watch. The afternoon was slipping by, and she still wanted to stop by the IWW hall. But she was also anxious to know if anyone had come looking for her after they'd left. They'd decided against telling Richard and Minnie about Ingeborg's fight with the policemen, figuring the less they knew the better in case they were questioned. To explain Ingeborg's absence while she was at the asylum Maria had simply told them she'd gone to help a cousin in New York City who'd taken ill. It was a common enough story, and with a new baby, Minnie and Richard hadn't cared to know the details.

Ingeborg rose to her feet and carried her plate and coffee cup to the sink. "I have to go check over the motorcar," she said, vaguely. "I'll be back in a little while." She kept her voice casual. "Before I go, did anyone come looking for me after we left?"

Minnie's face scrunched up as she tried to remember. "Let me see, it's all a blur with Juliana and all…were you expecting anyone in particular?"

"No," said Ingeborg, relief washing through her. The policeman who'd said he knew her must have been lying. "I just wond—"

"Wait!" said Minnie. "My goodness, how could I have forgotten? I think you'd been gone about a week when a policeman knocked at the door. I remember because I'd been nursing Juliana when he knocked, and I was a bit flustered—she was howling because she wasn't finished and I could hardly hear him for the racket." She giggled a bit, remembering. "I think Juliana put him off, he didn't stay long."

"A policeman? I wonder why?" asked Ingeborg. She feigned surprise but her stomach did a little flip.

"He said he had some questions, I forget what about, exactly, but he seemed annoyed not to find you." Juliana stirred and let out a squawk, so Minnie stuck out her foot to nudge the cradle to rocking. "I told him I wasn't sure when you'd be back."

Ingeborg's eyes met Maria's. Maria looked alarmed and gave her head a little shake, mutely asking her to not to go, but Ingeborg ignored her.

"That's strange," said Ingeborg calmly. "Did he come again?"

"No," Minnie said, glancing at her curiously. "What was it about, do you know?"

Ingeborg shrugged into her coat and buttoned it. "No idea," she said, as she stuck on her hat. "I'll be back." And she headed down the stairs.

* * *

Ingeborg smiled happily as she entered the IWW meeting hall, a low-slung brick structure that had once been a warehouse. It felt good to be back—it was like her second home. The Wobblies had paneled the space with bits of wood scavenged from dumps and lifted from jobsites; what could have been a visual disaster was saved by the creative way the wood had been pieced together, forming a tapestry of workers and symbols that was pleasing to the eye. Labor slogans hung from the walls—a new one she recognized from Joe Hill was "Don't Mourn, Organize!" with a little shrine to Joe below it, along with the old familiar ones: "Direct action gets the goods," "The boss needs you, you don't need him," and "Bosses beware—when we're screwed, we multiply!"

She looked around. The place was mostly empty. A few hoboes sat with their bedrolls in the corner, in between jobs or on their way to some other city. The IWW hall doubled as a flophouse at night. It offered little else but a safe place to sleep out of the cold, but it was free.

Paulo Bianchi and SallyAnn O'Connor were sitting at a table in the corner, poring over some documents. They looked up as Ingeborg approached and SallyAnn gave a little cry of pleasure.

"You're back!" she said, hustling over to give Ingeborg a welcoming hug. Paulo followed, smiling and shaking her hand.

"It's good to see you," said Ingeborg, and meant it. She gazed at them, feeling again as if she'd been gone for years, not months. She recalled that SallyAnn's daughter had been quite ill in the summer and asked after her.

"She's better," said SallyAnn. "We thought we might lose her, but somehow she pulled through. I watch her baby and help some with the cooking, but she'll soon be back on her feet."

"Good," said Ingeborg, and looked over at Paulo, who lived with his wife and five children in a three-room flat. "How's your family?"

He shrugged and gave a tired smile. "We're getting by—mostly. Niccolo's apprenticing at the tailor on Broadway. He likes it. The others are doing good in school—trying to keep them there."

Ingeborg nodded. Paulo didn't make much as an organizer, and more than once Maria and Ingeborg had helped with their rent. His wife, Ilaria, took in sewing, and the girls helped when they were done with their schoolwork. Like most immigrant families, Paulo and Ilaria knew schooling was the ticket to a better life for their children, but to make ends meet sometimes they had to send them to work. "Tell Ilaria I said hello—I'll come by when we're back for good."

"What do you mean?" asked Sally. "You're leaving again?"

"We have business in Washington still. But we're back for Thanksgiving and I wanted to see you."

"Where did you disappear to?" asked SallyAnn. She was a large, matronly woman with a mop of blond hair spilling down her back. "We've been so worried—you look like you've been through hell. Sit yourself down, I just made coffee." She pulled out a chair for Ingeborg and quickly brought over a tray with a coffeepot and three chipped mugs.

Ingeborg felt a pang of guilt at having left without saying good-bye. "After the strike we caught a boat for San Francisco." She was gratified to see their eyes widen as she sketched out their drive for the CU. She left out the part about hiding in the Dexter Asylum.

Paulo was a wiry little man with thick eyebrows that rose comically above his deep brown eyes. He tended to flap his hands around when he got excited, and Ingeborg's eye was caught, as always, by the two fingers missing on the right one, from a mill accident. His hands rose up out of his lap now. "My God!" he chuckled. "They lucked out when you and Maria showed up. There's no one tougher than you two."

SallyAnn's broad face was wreathed in smiles, and she reached her hand forward to give Ingeborg's forearm a gentle squeeze. "To think of you meeting all those important people. President Wilson, you say? It's a wonderful thing you're doing," she said warmly.

Ingeborg's face flushed and she squirmed with pleasure under her friends' praise.

SallyAnn continued. "You do look used up, though. How is Maria?"

"She's fine," Ingeborg said. "Tired, like me. Ready for this to be over."

Paolo looked around at the hoboes in the corner, then sat forward and lowered his voice. "It was good you got out of town when you did," he said quietly. "Them cops came around looking for you, said they wanted to talk about a thrashing you gave one of them."

Ingeborg's heart beat a little faster, but she feigned nonchalance. "I'd like to talk with them about the thrashing they gave the strikers!"

"They came back one other time, as far as I know," said Sally. "About a week later. They seemed mad they couldn't find you, but we couldn't help them. Not that we would've. But we had no idea where you were."

She looked at Ingeborg over the rim of her coffee cup. "When you didn't come back, we were worried."

"I'm sorry I left like that," said Ingeborg, feeling chagrined. She'd been so absorbed, first by her own misery and then by their adventures, that she hadn't thought what it had been like for her friends after she'd left. "But it was all so crazy and Maria was convinced I'd be arrested." She stopped and considered. "Are they still after me, do you think?"

Paolo and Sally looked at each other, and then back at Ingeborg.

"Who knows?" said Paolo, with a shrug. He lifted his hat and scratched his scalp for a moment, considering; then he set it back down over his tight curls. "But no. I don't think so."

Ingeborg took a big swallow of her coffee, trying to suppress a leap of hope. "Why not?" she asked. She looked over at SallyAnn and was surprised to see a wave of sadness wash over her friend's face. "What is it?" Ingeborg asked. "What happened after I left?"

Paolo shrugged again. "They won," he said simply. His voice grew bitter. "Flour prices went down, for about a week. Now they're higher than when we went out on strike. They blacklisted a bunch of workers—it's been real hard for them. Some had to move to find work. And the bosses are back to speeding up the line and cutting pay. Same old thing."

"Paolo's right," agreed SallyAnn. She smoothed her hand down her sleeve and picked at a hanging thread, then looked up at Ingeborg. "Folks've lost the will to fight. I doubt they'll be after you now— why bother?"

Ingeborg looked sadly at her friends. She saw now how their faces were worn and tired, their shoulders a little slumped. Their spirits seemed as thin as the coffee they served her. She shook her head. "I thought the strike would change things. It seemed like we could win."

"These are hard times," said Paolo, "and they ain't getting better." He motioned with his head over at the little shrine. "I guess you heard about Joe. The sonsabitches killed him."

"I know," said Ingeborg. "It's awful. But I saw him! In Salt Lake City. I went to the prison, and I saw him."

"Ingeborg, you didn't!" said SallyAnn, plainly awed by the thought.

"How was he?" asked Paolo, eagerly. "How was old Joe?"

Ingeborg paused, thinking of what to say. In her mind she saw him in his prison uniform, thin and sick at heart, wondering if he'd done any good. But then she remembered how he sat tall again when she asked him for a message for President Wilson, how some of the old spirit flashed in his eyes. She rubbed her neck and fingered some stray hairs, tucking them back under her hat. "He said prison wasn't so bad, he got three meals a day and had time to think and write. He'd had worse, he said." Paolo and SallyAnn looked at each other and grinned. "He was tired, though," she admitted. "He was ready for it to be over. But he gave me a message for President Wilson—said I should ask him what's radical about wanting a fair shake for people who work themselves to death to make the bosses rich?"

"That's Joe for you," Paolo said, sitting up and slapping his hand on the table. "Union to the end!"

Ingeborg felt a rush of warmth and added, "When I told him about our suffrage trip, he said we should go to Washington and give 'em hell!"

"Give 'em hell," Paolo repeated, smiling broadly. "You hear that, SallyAnn?"

"That's our Joe." SallyAnn beamed. "I like to think of him strong like that, on our side right up to the end. Takes a little of the sting out of losing him."

Ingeborg felt a pang of guilt for dressing up her meeting with Joe in finer cloth than it deserved, perhaps, but what could she do? Her friends looked beaten down, and if she could pass on a little of his spirit to help them with the struggle, why not? And he really had said those things. That's how he should be remembered.

She rose to her feet. "Time to go," she said. "Maria will be looking for me. We'll be back for good in a couple of weeks."

CHAPTER SEVENTEEN

NOVEMBER 27, 1915

Ingeborg looked around the small drawing room with interest. It was located in a tidy brick building a few blocks from the headquarters of the Women's Political Union in Manhattan. There were about a dozen women altogether, most unknown to her, crowded onto chairs set around the room. In one corner was a small round table with a dusky purple cloth draped over it; in its center was a flickering candle under a glass chimney. Madame Rosen sat behind the table facing the rest of the room, her eyes closed and hands loosely clasped. She'd wrapped a brightly flowered shawl around her shoulders and wore a jeweled gold headscarf over her hair. Gold bangles covered her bare forearms. She hummed, a nasal drone that rose and fell without repeating and grew gradually louder. The onlookers spoke sparingly and in hushed voices, with one eye on the medium. The gas lights on the wall were turned down, and the walls melted away in the low light, opening the door into the next world.

Maria sat bolt upright beside Ingeborg, her eyes wide as saucers. She was certain it was possible to talk to the dead and claimed to have seen this many times. As a midwife, she worked in that flickering borderland where life met death. Women in the agony of labor often called on a dead mother or grandmother for relief when wracked with labor pains. A baby's first breath might be her mother's last, or the baby would die while the mother lived. Maria argued if the spirits were ever going to be present, surely they would be hovering around a mother giving birth, ready to escort a new spirit into the afterlife.

Ingeborg was skeptical. She thought that people who were hungry, ill, grief-stricken, or homesick were easy prey for tricksters pretending to connect them to loved ones they missed desperately. People believed anything when their lives were nothing but misery. And she'd read how mediums fooled people by rapping with their toes or throwing their voices.

But ever since Mabel had mentioned the séance, Maria was determined that they should come, and Ingeborg felt she owed her partner this given everything she had been through on this trip. Maybe it was true, as people claimed, that spirits could peer into the future. They needed all the help they could get, and if Mrs. Stanton could tell them how to get the amendment passed, who was Ingeborg to argue?

Besides, anything was better than another night driving New York City's freezing streets to preach suffrage to anyone they could find. It was warm in the drawing room, and she removed her outer wrap, feeling her toes and fingers tingling back to life. She looked across the room at Harriot Stanton Blatch, Elizabeth Cady Stanton's daughter. Harriot was a formidable suffrage leader in her own right, and just that day she had pledged to merge her group with the Congressional Union. It was the talk of the hour, and everyone was excited about it. Harriot brought a tough fighting spirit and a knowledge of strategy that could only have come from being mentored by her mother and Susan B. Anthony.

Harriot's silver hair curled around her face, and she had a look of calm intelligence, though to Ingeborg's eye she also looked a little queasy to be in this setting. Ingeborg felt a rush of sympathy for her. What if it was all a hoax? Frances Joliffe sat beside Harriot, speaking quietly to her. Sara was off trying to sell Erskine's poem to a publisher, and Mabel had gone to Trenton to prepare for the meeting there.

While she waited for the séance to start, Ingeborg thought back over the last couple of days.

Was it just yesterday morning they'd returned to New York? Every fiber of Ingeborg's body had protested at climbing into Emilie once again. It felt as if their little home, after welcoming them back, had wrapped its arms around them, straining to prevent their departure. As they headed out a damp wind swept in off the harbor, and it was bitter cold, so they were shivering even before they got to the outskirts of Providence. But they were due in the city at noon, with almost two hundred miles in front of them, so even with the better roads in the East that meant an early start and a long drive. Maria was glum, and Ingeborg could think of nothing to raise her spirits, so a heavy silence blanketed the car.

Fortunately, the snow held off, and the sun even peeked out in the afternoon, glinting off the procession of almost one hundred automobiles—all draped in purple, white, and gold—as they drove slowly down Fifth Avenue, waving to those on the sidewalk and tooting their horns. Ingeborg's ill humor lifted. The attention they received was so positive it was hard to believe New York had just defeated suffrage so soundly.

New York was tricky terrain for the CU. The National was very strong here. While they'd lost the recent suffrage referendum by almost two hundred thousand votes, in the end over a half-million men did support it, the best showing they'd ever had. "We'll win this next time!" Ingeborg had heard many local suffragists declare. In October, Carrie Catt had assembled a parade of suffrage supporters five miles long to march down Fifth Avenue, nearly shutting down the city in a show of strength people were still talking about. Ingeborg smiled as she recalled that in his remarks, acting Mayor McAleny had confused the NAWSA parade with the envoys' cross-country trip. That would annoy Catt, no doubt, who was ever vigilant at drawing thick black lines between the two suffrage groups.

Still, Alva Belmont was leading the charge for the CU, and she was also a force to be reckoned with, Ingeborg conceded, even if she didn't much like her. When introduced to them out in San Francisco, Mrs. Belmont had eyed them deliberately from head to foot, taking in their worn travel outfits, graying hair, and plain, workaday hats. She'd almost visibly recoiled when she heard their thick Swedish accents, and it was a short time later that Alice Paul had declared that Sara and Frances had to do all the public speaking. Ingeborg had always suspected Mrs. Belmont was behind it.

The CU organizers all said Mrs. Belmont had a vicious temper and a tendency to seize control of planning events, riding rough-shod over those unfortunates assigned to work with her. She terrified them. Only Alice Paul was able to manage her, they said, but since Mrs. Belmont held the purse strings, even Alice hesitated to intervene except when absolutely necessary.

As she shook Mrs. Belmont's hand at Sherry's, where they gathered after the parade, Ingeborg felt suddenly shy and cursed herself for it. Maria stood beside her, absolutely mute, which didn't help. Ingeborg scolded herself. Who cared if her clothes were plain and dusty? Who had driven all the way across the country, something few people had done? Could Alva Belmont change a tire or fix a car? Hold your head up! she scolded herself. So she threw back her shoulders and gave her a sweet gap-toothed smile. "How nice to see you again, Mrs. Belmont," she said.

Mrs. Belmont was immaculate in a tailored wool suit and a hat whose towering plumes almost tickled the restaurant's famous chandeliers. She had chestnut-colored hair that had to have been professionally colored, as Ingeborg judged her to be even older than Maria. She looked back at them, her eyes flat and expressionless. "We so appreciate what you've done for us," she said. "I understand you've been subjected to absolutely appalling conditions. And I'm afraid it shows." She took out a lace handkerchief and dabbed her nose delicately.

Ingeborg stiffened and only just managed to avoid sniffing her armpit. Was their odor that strong? They washed regularly, but their clothes had less attention, especially their travel-stained outer coats.

Then Mrs. Belmont smiled, revealing the charm for which she was equally famous. "But wear it as a badge of honor because you've accomplished something that few have even attempted, and many—if not most—would have failed trying. Congratulations, ladies! The CU is in your debt!"

Ingeborg had reeled from the braided insult and praise. "It has been very hard," she'd acknowledged, leaning forward to whisper conspiratorially, "especially for us older women, as you would know."

She moved back, noting with satisfaction how the silky plumes on Mrs. Belmont's hat jerked and a wary look came into her eye. Ingeborg gazed back at her, innocently. "But we're glad to do it for suffrage." Then she and Maria had moved away as Mrs. Belmont turned to greet someone else. Maria pinched her arm and hissed, "Behave!"

At the séance, Ingeborg's attention was brought back to the present as Madame Rosen abruptly stopped humming and took a few deep breaths. Her eyes remained closed.

"Death is but a doorway between rooms," Madame Rosen said dreamily. "Those in the afterlife, if they so choose, can lend a hand to us, who still live in the earthly present." She opened her eyes and looked around the room briefly, then shut them again.

"Tonight we summon the spirit of Elizabeth Cady Stanton," she said, her voice now clear and low. "Her daughter—is she with us?"

"I am," said Harriot. She looked excited at the prospect of speaking with her beloved mother, but also nervous, as if worried her mother might criticize the frock she was wearing, the sort of thing Ingeborg's mother might have done even after a long separation. How personal could spirits get? Ingeborg wondered. If they existed.

Madame Rosen nodded, her eyes still closed. "Your presence will draw her. She will speak through me, but to you alone." With that, she threw back her head and cried "Elizabeth Cady Stanton, we call on you as a woman of power to attend us in this room tonight and give us your counsel!"

There was utter silence and Madame Rosen stiffened for several seconds. Maria found Ingeborg's hand and clutched it, trembling with excitement. Then the medium relaxed, her face changed expression, and she began speaking in a voice very different from the one she had used previously. It was eerie, and despite herself Ingeborg felt her scalp prickle.

"I am come to visit my daughter and her friends. What is it you wish from me?" said the voice.

Was that Elizabeth? Ingeborg looked over at Harriot, whose hands rose to her mouth in shock. When she spoke, her voice shook and it was thick with tears.

"Mother!" Harriot cried. "Is it you?"

"Yes, my darling."

"I've missed you so," Harriot choked.

"As I have you," replied Elizabeth lovingly. "I am so very proud of what you have accomplished. But we must hurry. One never knows how long these connections may last—how may I help you?"

Harriot blew her nose with her handkerchief and wiped her eyes. "Yes, Mother," she said, pulling herself together. "As you know, we remain engaged in the suffrage fight that you and Aunt Susan started. And we've made progress but we still have far to go."

"I like this renewed focus on the federal amendment," said Elizabeth, approvingly. "Susan would, too."

There were a few chuckles around the room. Ingeborg realized she'd been holding her breath and let it out slowly, feeling the tension leave her body.

"I'm quite taken with Alice Paul. And this stunt the CU has undertaken, the automobile trip with the petitions, that's brilliant! It reminds me of what Susan and I used to do, though we received much less attention, of course."

Ingeborg's jaw dropped foolishly as she heard this. She looked over at Maria, who gave her a smug nod and a little dig with her elbow as if to say, What did I tell you?

"Oh," Harriot said. "I'm glad you approve, Mother. We think so too. In fact, the envoys are here with us now."

"Congratulations, ladies. Well done! Now Harriot, how may I help you?"

"Can you tell us what to expect when the envoys reach Washington? How will President Wilson receive them? Will Congress advance our bill in the next session?"

Elizabeth, said, "Hmmmm." There was a pause, and then she said, "No."

"No?" Harriot demanded, taken aback. "The petitions will make no difference at all?" The group stirred and murmurs drifted around the room.

"I didn't say they'd make no difference—but you won't get the bill through in the upcoming session. You'll have to campaign against

Wilson and the Democrats in 1916. Make them feel vulnerable politically."

"I understand," said Harriot. "We're preparing to do that but hoped it wouldn't be necessary."

"There's something else, though," said Elizabeth. "America will be pulled into this war in Europe—we see new souls from the war every day. I'm surprised it's not more crowded here," she mused, almost as an aside. "But never mind that," she continued, her voice strengthening, "You must resist calls to suspend your suffrage campaign and work on the war to prove you are deserving of the vote. Heed me now! Remember what happened after the Civil War—Negro men got the vote, and women are *still* waiting." She huffed in irritation. "Susan and I worked our entire lives for the vote and died knowing it was still not won. Have you any idea how frustrating that was?"

Harriot gave a small smile. "I know, Mother. That's why I'm here. That's why we're all here," she said, looking around the room. There were nods of confirmation from the women, all round-eyed and solemn in the presence of this suffrage icon. Maria sat bolt upright, eyes locked on the medium, scarcely breathing, straining to hear every word. Ingeborg squeezed her hand.

Elizabeth continued, "Tell those men that every bit of flesh and blood used as cannon fodder on the battlefields was created by women, so we demand a seat in the councils of war to decide when—and whether—to call for that sacrifice. You have no need to prove your loyalty once again—they just want to distract you with war work. Above all, never trust their promises about suffrage after the war. God knows who else there is to enfranchise except the women—but they will surely try to find someone else instead. Maybe children, at least the boys."

"We thank you for that advice, Mother," said Harriot, her eyes shining with pride and unshed tears. "Is there anything else you can tell us?"

"Don't worry about antagonizing the men," instructed Elizabeth, firmly. "Of course they'll whine about it, they always do. Just keep making suffrage a national campaign issue."

"What about NAWSA?" asked Harriot. "Is there any chance they'll come over to our side? It seems to us we could win suffrage sooner if we worked together, but they're dead set against us."

Elizabeth clucked her tongue. "Once I believed persuasion could take the place of force, but that underestimates our adversaries and the depth of change required to win rights for women. Remember when we published the *Woman's Bible*? What an uproar! We saw it as a prybar to free women from the stifling claptrap of Christianity that confined them to domestic servitude. Oh, how they howled and threatened us with fire and brimstone! And yet, in the end, many came around to our way of thinking. My advice is to ignore them and go about your business!"

"Yes, Mother," said Harriot, beaming.

"Is there anything else?" Ingeborg thought Elizabeth's voice was beginning to fade. She leaned forward, unwilling for the session to end.

Harriot reached out and gripped the medium's hand, desperate to continue the connection. "Mother, please stay with us!"

"I am trying, but—" Her voice was definitely softer, more distant.

"Wait—when will we win the vote? How long will it take?" Harriot implored her.

"As long as it takes, my dear daughter. You know that. Not as long as it has already been, though. I think it will be soon. You will live to see it happen, though Susan and I did not. Remember, truth is ever the only safe ground to stand upon." With that, Madame Rosen gave a gasp and slumped forward over the table, unconscious.

For a moment silence gripped the room, and then everyone started talking at once. Madame Rosen's assistant appeared beside her and applied a moistened handcloth to her cheeks and forehead, then rubbed her back soothingly and called her name in a soft voice. Presently the medium stirred and woke, and was led, still groggy, from the room.

Maria gazed at Ingeborg, eyes shining in triumph. "What did I tell you? Spirits exist and they can speak to us!"

Released from the spell of the medium's voice, Ingeborg felt her skepticism return. She would need to think about this. She shook her head doubtfully. "She did seem real, Maria, but I just don't know."

"What are you saying?" exclaimed Maria. "You heard for yourself." She leaned forward insistently. "The spirit knew about our trip. She praised us!"

Ingeborg shifted uncomfortably. "I heard that too, Maria, but Madame Rosen could have read about it in the newspapers. I've heard most spiritualists are suffragists; perhaps she took an interest."

"You think too much sometimes, Ingeborg," said Maria, standing up and drawing on her coat. "Sometimes you have to trust what you see, what you hear. Her own daughter thought it was her." She gestured over toward Harriot who sat wiping away tears, comforted by her friends.

That was the part Ingeborg found most unsettling. If Harriot were faking, she belonged on the stage—her act had been utterly convincing. But why would she do that? Frowning slightly, Ingeborg pulled on her own coat, buttoned it up, and found her gloves. She looked over at Maria. "If she was real, and I'm not saying she was, I hope she was telling us the truth. Harriot's older than us, so if she'll live to see women get the vote then maybe we will, too."

CHAPTER EIGHTEEN

DECEMBER 6, 1915

Ingeborg sat rigid in Emilie's passenger seat, Maria crouched over the wheel beside her like an enormous badger, coat buttons straining over several shawls, a thick beaver fur hat pulled low over her ears. Her wide mouth was set in a straight line, and she'd had little to say all morning. Ingeborg couldn't tell whether she was excited or sad or anxious—she just seemed set to endure whatever came next. For herself, Ingeborg's heart was banging in her chest, and there was no time to think about why. Today must go perfectly, and that meant they had to start right away if they were to reach Stanton Square at noon. It was there they'd meet the parade that would escort them to the US Capitol. After ten weeks of hard travel, they were finally in Washington, DC. Soon their trip would be over.

It was a damp, chilly day that had forced them to keep the top up as they spun down the wide roads from Baltimore, where they had spent the night. As they entered the Washington city limits they'd stopped to decorate the car one last time with the Great Demand banner slung across the rear, and a purple and white On to Congress! banner across the front. All five of them—Mabel had joined them for this leg—slipped the CU's tricolor sashes over their shoulders, Ingeborg's and Maria's straining to fit around their broad shoulders and bulky garments.

Ingeborg turned around to look at the three women in the back seat and smiled slightly. "Ready?"

Frances's nose was red, and bright spots of pink bloomed on her cheeks under her large, dark eyes. She nodded. Mabel gave a last pat to her hair pins and smiled, her eyes intense in a face that had grown far too thin and sagged with exhaustion. Sara gave Ingeborg a crooked smile, her tanned face tired but resolute. "Let's go," she said.

Maria switched on Emilie and pulled away from the roadside, the suffrage pennants on the side windows snapping and fluttering in the breeze. Ingeborg kept her eyes pinned to the road ahead of them, ignoring the houses, shops, and people they passed. She had the directions in her hand and called them out to Maria. Left here. Right there. Watch out for that wagon—those horses could bolt. Today, nothing must go wrong. Today, the suffragists were taking over the city, at least the section around the Capitol and the White House.

The petition would meet them at the park. Mabel had assured them that the CU had sorted it out, but Ingeborg remained uneasy that their ploy would be revealed as a sham—that they had nowhere close to the signatures they claimed to have. That was still secret information to which few people were privy. Mabel said the CU had never learned what happened to all the signatures they'd collected in San Francisco, but through some miracle they had enough to create an impressive scroll. She hoped it would be enough to satisfy the curious.

At length they swung around a corner onto Maryland Avenue and saw Stanton Square ahead of them, thronged with horses, marchers, automobiles, and curious onlookers. Maria tooted the horn and a great cheer went up as the waiting women surged forward to meet them, bringing the car to a momentary halt. The marchers pressed in, calling out a welcome and patting Emilie's flank, and Emilie wheezed happily in return. Ingeborg's face split into a broad grin and her body tingled—and for once it wasn't a heat storm. For a moment she felt she'd happily stay right there in the midst of the raucous, adoring crowd. How she loved these women! This moment made the hard traveling worthwhile, like the send-off from San Francisco but all the sweeter now because their trials were behind them.

She reached over and grabbed Maria's hand, holding it tight as a wave of emotion swept through her, crumpling her face and making her mouth wobble. Glancing sideways she saw that Maria was similarly moved, tears trickling down her weathered cheeks. But she was smiling, her eyes sparkling, and she nodded a little at Ingeborg as if to say, We made it. Isn't this sweet?

Looking up, Ingeborg saw two mounted policeman forcing their way through the excited marchers and pushing them back away from the car. From a bench at the edge of the park a young woman with a megaphone called the marchers into formation. Drumbeats from a military band rolled across the square and bounced off the nearby houses, filling the air with sound and silencing the chatter. Mrs. John Jay White had been tasked with serving as the grand marshal of the parade, and she sat astride her horse now, resplendent in a plumed tricorn and a tricolor CU sash across her chest. Silver-haired and regal, she urged her horse forward to the front of the parade, followed by the holders of the Great Demand banner. The first mounted escorts edged their horses in behind and the band struck up the tune of "La Marseillaise" as she raised her arm high in the air, pointed forward toward the Capitol, and led off.

One after another, the groups of women and girls slotted into their assigned places in the line of march: women carrying tricolor banners; girls in liberty caps; over three dozen marshals wearing flowing white capes trimmed with the purple, white, and gold colors of the CU; and groups of women representing doctors, lawyers, the WCTU, social workers, homemakers, the states that were free and those that had yet to win the franchise.

They'd been told that to maintain order there would be close to two hundred police officers along the route. The District police were determined to avoid a repeat of what had happened back in 1913 when men had mobbed the streets and forced the suffragists to a standstill.

Ingeborg cried out and pointed when she saw the petition scroll. Two women held it between them on a spool and it was unfurled one hundred feet behind them, held up by twenty petition holders, ten to a side. Alarm squeezed Ingeborg's heart; the press had been told the petition was four miles long. She didn't know how big that might look rolled up, but she guessed it would be much larger and heavier than what the women were carrying today. She shot Mabel a worried look and Mabel just shrugged. What could they do about it now? They'd have to play it out and hope for the best.

"There's the Women's Liberty Bell!" Sara called out, and Ingeborg craned her head around to look. Pennsylvania suffragists had manufactured a replica of the famous Philadelphia bell for use in their recent statewide referendum. The original bell was engraved with the words "Proclaim Liberty Throughout All the Land Unto All the Inhabitants Thereof," but in the suffragists' version the clapper was muted—fastened to the side—to symbolize women's lack of political freedom. The CU had brought it all the way out to San Francisco for the Exposition, and it was always a hit when it appeared. It felt like seeing an old friend.

Dozens of automobiles driven by women followed the bell, and a mounted escort brought up the rear. In the midst of all this someone waved Maria forward to ease Emilie into place. Well-wishers lined up along the few blocks of Maryland Avenue between the park and the Capitol, clapping and adding their voices to the din. Ingeborg gazed about, answering their smiles with her own. She forgot her exhaustion and drank in the outpouring of love and triumph.

Soon the ornate white dome of the Capitol loomed up above the marchers and the band switched to "Dixie." As they inched onto the grounds, those in front swung off to the left and right, leaving the envoys to motor up and park alone, with Emilie's nose pointed toward the steps. For a moment they sat looking up at the Capitol. This moment they'd been racing toward all these weeks began now, at the foot of the steps. Would they be successful in persuading the Democrats? Or would their journey have been in vain, as Darrow had warned them back in Chicago?

She noted with satisfaction that the steps were packed tightly with congressmen, suffragists, and dignitaries, with some men—and a few women—standing out on the wings of the terrace, at the base of the soaring columns. A broad corridor remained open in the center of the steps. Alva Belmont and Anne Martin waited for them at the bottom, along with a third woman Ingeborg hadn't seen before. She'd heard they'd be joined by Cora Smith King, the treasurer of the National Council of Women Voters, so that must be her.

"Here we go," muttered Sara. Her voice was tight with tension although her face betrayed no emotion. All of the other meetings they'd held across the country had been dress rehearsals—this stage was where their performances really mattered.

Ingeborg and Maria remained seated as Sara opened her door and stepped out of the car; Frances did the same on her side, followed by Mabel. Ingeborg felt herself trembling. Several days ago Mabel had told the Swedes to wait in the car during the ceremony.

"But we've always stood there with Sara," Ingeborg had said to her, angrily. "Even if you never let us speak, we've always been up there."

Mabel could barely look them in the eye. "There just won't be room for all of us at the top of the steps," she'd explained, lamely. "That's what's been decided, and there's nothing I can do about it." She'd turned away, but Ingeborg was damned if she'd sit there like the hired help, and the night before she'd convinced a very nervous Maria to join her in a forbidden push to stand with the envoys at the ceremony.

"What can they do?" Ingeborg had asked Maria. "Do you think they'll stop the ceremony and scream at us to get back in the car? In front of all those congressmen?"

Maria frowned. "I just don't want anyone to be angry, Ingeborg. We've come all this way. Let's end on a good note."

"No, Maria," Ingeborg had insisted. "They owe us this. We've been on every platform since we left San Francisco. We deserve to be there." She'd refused to back down, and Maria had finally agreed to follow her lead.

Ingeborg stood up and prepared to leave the car, waiting until Mabel, Sara, and Frances had reached the party waiting for them at the bottom of the steps. Then she and Maria quickly jumped out and smoothly attached themselves to the end of the procession, and it wasn't until they'd reached the top of the steps that anyone realized they were there. As Mrs. Belmont caught sight of their insubordination her eyes widened briefly and a look of pure rage swept over her face. She sent them a venomous stare. Ingeborg flinched inwardly, hoping she blocked Maria's view of Mrs. Belmont, because it would surely have sent her scuttling back down to Emilie.

But they were committed now, and she saw with relief that while Mabel looked worried, Sara and Frances were trying to suppress smiles. When they reached the top, Ingeborg turned and backed into the women already in place to create a space for her and Maria, ignoring the angry mutterings that buzzed like angry bees at her back. Maria, still wearing her thick beaver-fur hat, had her eyes half-shut against an errant sunbeam that broke through the clouds and washed over them. Ingeborg stared flatly at the CU leaders, daring them to order her back to the car. An uneasy silence reigned as they shifted and eyed each other, unsure of how to respond to this incursion. The unruly clouds blotted out the sun once again.

Cora King broke the silence, presenting them to Congressman Frank Mondell and Senator George Sutherland as the men who would introduce the amendment into their respective chambers later that day. Frank Mondell was all smiles and greeted them like old friends.

"Wonderful to see you again," he said warmly. "Congratulations on bringing this momentous journey to a successful conclusion. It cannot fail to move it closer to passage in Congress."

Senator Sutherland was more reserved, but equally gracious as he welcomed them to the Capitol. Then they all turned to watch the white-clad marshals solemnly carry the petition up the gray granite steps to the terrace. A damp, raw wind buffeted the paper the women clutched in their hands. The clouds parted, and again a sunbeam shot out to illuminate the procession in splendid benediction.

As the marshals advanced, the pages came into focus, glued together tightly, end to end. Ingeborg could see that they were spotted with dust, and some were wrinkled from rain, souvenirs of where they were collected and their eastward journey. She couldn't make out the individual signatures, but it moved her to imagine the person behind each one, a man or a woman who thought it high time the simple act of voting should be guaranteed by the nation's Constitution. It occurred to her that the pages of all the many petitions, gathered over decades from white women and colored, from Eastern or Western states, by Susan B. Anthony and countless others, would stretch for hundreds of miles, not the four, or eight, or whatever the CU claimed this one to be, and every page would have carried the hopes and dreams of both the signers and the collectors.

What a wretched waste of time it all had been, she thought, suddenly angry. Surely the generations of women who had worked so hard to reach this moment could have set their hands to some better purpose. How many more petitions would be required to end this one battle? There were so many battles left to fight, after all, so much unfinished business before women were truly equal with men.

But what if this were the last suffrage petition ever submitted? She thought back to the seance with Elizabeth Cady Stanton and her prediction that the Democrats wouldn't act in this session, that they'd force the CU to campaign against them in the 1916 elections. Her gaze swept the assembled members of Congress—how many were here today? Eighty or a hundred, she guessed. Her heart lifted at the show of support though she knew there were still far too few—they would need a two-thirds majority in both houses to pass the amendment. Still, perhaps once there had been only one congressman brave enough to stand with the women. Slowly they had found one supporter after another and, as Stanton had said, the fight would have to go on—"as long as it takes." Ingeborg shivered, remembering how Stanton had then said quietly, "You know that," the simple statements less a command than a covenant uniting the suffragists of the past with those who would see it through to the end.

Just then the two lead marshals reached the top step and stopped. The petition unspooled one hundred feet down to the bottom steps between the two lines of marshals, each clutching her piece of it and looking up at them expectantly.

Frances Joliffe spoke first, her words lifted by the wind. "We represent the women voters of the West, met in convention last September at the Exposition in San Francisco. They sent us here to the halls of power in Washington, DC, on a sacred mission, not to beseech, not to request, but to *demand* that Congress pass the Susan B. Anthony Amendment!"

The crowd stamped and clapped, roaring approval, even the congressmen joining in. Ingeborg looked around with satisfaction while Frances finished her remarks, and Sara stepped forward.

"Voting rights for women is an issue of paramount importance before the people of this country," she said. "As we took this 'gasoline flight' east we found, in small hamlets and in our great cities, an outpouring of support for women's enfranchisement. This support comes from men as well as from women—and we do thank our enlightened men for that." Claps and cheers met this statement as well.

Now Sara raised her voice, and her words snapped out a warning. "But one of the enduring features of this trip is the uniting of women to achieve a common goal—women's political freedom throughout these United States, so that a woman may vote no matter where she lives. Four million women in the West now possess the right to vote. They have pledged to put women's enfranchisement above party affiliation—they will recognize no party until women win the right to vote through national action." More applause met this statement. "So, yes, gentlemen," Sara concluded, "We are playing politics as never before. We will be watching the actions Congress takes in this coming session, and hope you will aid us in our long quest for political equality."

She made no specific threat as to the CU's plans, Ingeborg saw, but perhaps she didn't need to. Every man there knew of the CU's attempt in 1914 to persuade Western women to vote against the Democrats, and they were now on notice that the CU was prepared—better prepared, as a result of this trip—to do so again in 1916. And this time they would campaign directly against President Wilson as well.

Senator Sutherland and Representative Mondell both made clear in their remarks that the envoys' message was not lost on them and that it "would receive the most serious attention of Congress."

Representative Mondell noted that today would be the fifth time he had introduced the measure. "We trust that the pressure of other matters of national importance will not be made an excuse for delaying or postponing action on woman suffrage," he said. "Under free government there can be no more important question than one involving half the people."

"Hurrah and vote for suffrage!" came a voice behind Ingeborg, and the call rippled through the crowd.

With that, the envoys formally presented each man with copies of the resolutions the Woman Voters Convention had passed in September, and the meeting broke up.

Ingeborg avoided Mrs. Belmont's gaze and descended the steps back to Emilie, who looked travel-stained and weary alongside the gleaming automobiles parked nearby. Ingeborg felt a rush of affection for the plucky little car, and ran her hand over her fender as she walked around the hood to the passenger side.

She and Maria settled themselves back into the car and waited while the parade reassembled around them. Ingeborg looked over at Maria. "That went all right," she said.

Maria smiled back. "Not bad," she agreed. Suddenly her smile disappeared and she looked frightened at something behind Ingeborg's head. Ingeborg swiveled around and saw Mrs. Belmont storming up to the car, her face white and furious.

Ingeborg barely had enough time to collect herself before Mrs. Belmont was there beside her. She felt the disadvantage of looking upward at the angry woman from her seat in the car, and briefly considered forcing open the door into Mrs. Belmont's knees so she could stand and face her. A familiar prickle started in her lower back and spread up her spine, pushing a wave of heat before it. Despite the cold she felt droplets of sweat trickling down her chest, and she felt a sudden urge to remove her hat. Though moments before she'd felt happy and excited, now irritation surged through her until she felt ready to snap. Willing herself to stay calm, she locked eyes with Mrs. Belmont and said, "Yes?"

Mrs. Belmont rapped on Ingeborg's door with her gloved hand and hissed "What do you think you were doing with that little stunt?"

"Claiming our rightful place, the same as you, Mrs. Belmont. Isn't that what we're all trying to do?"

"You were told to stay in the car!" said Mrs. Belmont, thrusting her face closer to Ingeborg's.

Furious, Ingeborg's chin came up and she stared coldly at Mrs. Belmont. "Some women are more equal than others, is that it?" From the corner of her eye Ingeborg saw Sara and Mabel hurrying over, Frances a few steps behind.

"You should know your place! From now on you follow orders," Mrs. Belmont said, her voice full of menace.

Know your place! Ingeborg wondered briefly if it were possible to explode from anger, because she felt ready to. She shrugged off Maria's warning hand on her arm and rose up to her feet—standing in the car she now had a height advantage over Mrs. Belmont and looked down at her with blazing eyes, hands on her hips.

"We're the envoys!" she shot back. "We belonged up there." Behind Mrs. Belmont a little crowd was gathering.

Mrs. Belmont backed up a pace as if worried Ingeborg might take a swing at her. She gestured to Sara and Frances as they came up. "You are merely the drivers—these two are the envoys. You do as you're told."

The insult and injustice almost took Ingeborg's breath away. "Just the drivers!" she fired back. "We bought the car and paid our own way! You were happy enough for us to do that."

Mabel said with authority, "Please, ladies." Ingeborg flicked a glance at her and saw she was a bit pale, but determined to put a stop to this. Sara was beside her, wheezing slightly, a hand on her heart. "Let's not have this discussion now," Mabel said firmly, looking from one furious face to the other. She gestured to the marchers who were trickling back to their places. "We can't hold up the parade—we have an appointment with President Wilson."

Sara had complained to Maria and Ingeborg of Mrs. Belmont's snobbery and high-handedness. But she'd also confided that Mrs. Belmont needed a new personal secretary and had offered Sara the job. Sara was torn because she desperately needed the money, but the thought of trailing around after Mrs. Belmont made her queasy. It would also keep her in the East, far away from her children—and Erskine. Now, she put a hand on Ingeborg's arm and tipped her chin up at the CU's benefactress. "These two are not just drivers, they're the best damn drivers ever! They saved my life more than once, and if we had more women like them, this campaign would be over tomorrow. I don't care what we call them. They're with us."

Stunned, Ingeborg looked down at Sara. She must have decided against the job—standing up to Alva Belmont in public seemed a sure way to have the offer withdrawn. But Mrs. Belmont evidently saw this was a battle she wouldn't win—at least not at that moment—so she simply muttered, "We'll see about that." She then wheeled around and stalked back to her car.

A taut silence reigned as Sara, Frances, and Mabel settled themselves in the back. Ingeborg lowered herself onto her seat and sat staring straight ahead. Her heat storm had passed. Now she felt gripped by an icy fury and had to remind herself to breathe.

The wind gusted sharply, throwing a handful of sand against the car, and Ingeborg reached up mechanically to tug her hat more firmly on her head. She squinted up at the Capitol, the steps emptying rapidly as the congressmen hurried inside and the women resumed their places for the march to the White House. The ornate dome gleamed dully against the racing clouds, and she thought bitterly about this American democracy everyone was so proud of. Government of the people, for the people…but which people?

An image came to her of Ida Wells Barnett stepping out of the crowd two years before to join the Illinois delegation in the CU's great march. What had been said to Ida, afterward? Had she been scolded like this? "There's room in your car for someone who looks like me," Ida had told them when she and Maria visited her in Chicago. Well, Ingeborg thought, I have it better than the Negroes, but still.…

Mrs. Belmont's venom made her shiver. Once, America had been the place where people could make a life for themselves with hard work and a little luck, safe from whatever oppression they had escaped in their own country. But now it felt as if the country were turning against them, and she wondered how secure their future might be. The joy and triumph of the morning felt shattered.

A part of her wanted to order the three women in the backseat out of the car and tell Maria to drive away, to leave all this ugliness behind them. Return to their cozy rooms on Westminster Street and to hell with Mrs. Belmont and the CU. But she set her jaw and looked out the windshield. She wouldn't give Mrs. Belmont the satisfaction.

The band started up again and the marchers fell into place until, with a flourish of her staff, Mrs. White led them off. Maria switched Emilie on and steered her into their spot in the procession.

With a heavy sigh, Mabel broke the silence. "I'm sorry for what Mrs. Belmont said. She means well, and she knows how much you've done for us. I'm sure she didn't mean to hurt you."

Sara gave a brittle laugh. "Oh, Mabel, of course she did! She meant to put them in their place. It was wrong to say they should stay in the car, and we should have stood against her."

Mabel grimaced. "You're right," she said, in a low voice. "But the CU needs her money—and her influence. We wouldn't have gotten this far without it."

"That doesn't give her license to run roughshod over everyone," Sara retorted. She gripped the front seat with both hands and leaned forward. "I meant what I said to Mrs. Belmont," she said, looking from Maria to Ingeborg. "It never could have happened without you two. You just kept going. There were days I sat there and marveled." She sat back.

Mabel was quick to agree. "Of course. I've said that all along."

Ingeborg felt the icy grip on her limbs thaw a little. It helped to have Sara come to their defense now, but why hadn't she had spoken up before? She met Maria's worried glance and gave her a short nod. She was still angry, but she wouldn't explode. Not yet. She half turned in her seat and looked at the three women in the back. "Thank you for what you said just now. But if you want help from working people—immigrants like us—you must treat us better," she said stiffly. "We won't wait in the shadows to be pulled out when it suits you, like puppets."

Maria spoke suddenly, raising her voice to be heard over Emilie's rattling engine. "Apologies are easy," she said. "Standing up to injustice is harder. Do the right thing the first time so you don't have to apologize later."

Shocked, Ingeborg looked over at Maria, who appeared as relaxed as if she were out for a Sunday drive. Her partner so rarely spoke up on these matters—but people listened when she did.

"You're right, Maria," said Frances.

Ingeborg's eyebrows shot up. The high-class Frances agreeing with Maria? Ingeborg smiled. When Frances had left the trip so suddenly, she'd become the symbol of how privileged people dallied in suffrage but weren't really serious about it. They'd speculated about her pampered life as they rattled over bad roads and wagered when or even if she'd come back. But she'd held her own these last few weeks, always respectful of what the other three had done. In her speeches she always told of working women's need for the vote rather than focusing on women like herself. She treated Maria and Ingeborg as equals and never complained. Ingeborg had been surprised to find herself warming to Frances and wondered if it might have been better to have her along the whole way. Perhaps she would have softened their quarrels. Or perhaps they'd have had to coddle her the way they did Sara, especially during the hard days. She shrugged. Here they were now, it was almost over. They continued on in silence.

The crowd was thinner along this section of the route, but the people they passed waved and cheered them on all the same. The wind came in fierce gusts that threatened to yank the banners out of the marchers' hands, and they were sometimes pushed off balance as they fought to hold onto them. The horses pranced and skittered, shying at bits of newspaper that blew past them as their riders struggled to keep them from trampling those on foot.

The parade swung right onto 15th Street with the massive US Treasury Building looming in front of them, and then left by Lafayette Square and into the parking area in front of the White House. Ingeborg felt a bit shivery inside at the prospect of meeting President Wilson. Never in a thousand years would her family in Sweden believe this.

It took some time to gain entrance to the East Room of the White House, as three hundred CU supporters crowded in there with them. Ingeborg had known this would happen, and she saw the sense of having numbers to back them up, but she secretly wished that only the five of them would be meeting with him.

Her eyes flicked to the door as an aide announced President Wilson's arrival through a set of double doors that were swung wide to allow him entry. Ingeborg watched him closely and thought he flinched when he saw the size of the crowd of women, but he recovered quickly and stretched his lips in a thin smile that barely hid his protruding teeth. He introduced the thickly mustachioed man accompanying him as his military aide, Colonel William Harts. Why have a military aide with him? Ingeborg wondered. Is that a nod to the campaign the CU had mounted against the Democrats? Or for protection?

Anne Martin was a CU Executive Committee member from Nevada and a veteran of other deputations to Wilson. She stepped forward to introduce the envoys, making sure to include Maria and Ingeborg. To Ingeborg it seemed that he was especially impressed to learn that they were the driver and the mechanician.

"Is that so?" her said, looking at them intently. "Quite an accomplishment." Ingeborg grinned her best gap-toothed smile at him and saw his lips twitch. She suddenly felt emboldened to deliver the message Joe Hill had given her for the president. She had only half-meant it when she'd asked Joe for a message to Wilson back in Sugar House Prison. For weeks she hadn't been sure she would deliver it—or how she could do it—with access to the president tightly controlled. Then, too, the CU was claiming millions of women were setting aside all other interests and cared only about voting rights for women; not labor or anything else. Maria would surely have been scandalized to hear she was even thinking of such a thing. And yet, ever since she'd seen her IWW friends in Providence she'd remembered Joe's words, and the way his blue eyes had blazed with intensity as he'd given his message for the president.

Abruptly, Ingeborg leaned in and said quietly. "I have a message to you from Joe Hill."

Wilson looked at her in surprise.

Ingeborg looked intently at him, and said rapidly. "I saw him right before he was executed. He said to tell you the strikers want to work but bosses don't pay them enough to take care of their families. He asked what's radical about wanting a fair shake for people who work themselves to death to make the bosses rich? He said give women the vote and they can help clean things up." Ingeborg needed to finish— she could see from the corners of her eyes that people were looking alarmed, and were about to swoop in and push her back. She put out a placating hand to them and said hurriedly, "And to tell you thanks for trying to get him out of prison." She fell back and stood quietly watching the president, feeling Maria glaring at her.

Wilson maintained his polite smile and murmured, "Thank you" to her, but behind his glasses his eyes were startled and his brow furrowed.

Anne Martin stepped in hastily and brought them back to the focus of their visit. "We met a year ago," she reminded President Wilson. "You congratulated me on the success of the Nevada suffrage campaign. Since that time we have been greatly cheered by you becoming more favorable to woman suffrage, even voting for it in New Jersey last month."

Wilson inclined his head in acknowledgement.

"We here today represent not just woman *suffragists*, but woman *voters*, Mr. President," Anne continued, looking him in the eye and giving those words extra emphasis. She paused while he absorbed that bit of information, and then added, "You have told previous deputations that you could not speak *for* your party; we ask you therefore to speak *to* your party and impress on your members in Congress the importance of passing the suffrage amendment."

Frances Joliffe then added "Mr. President, I am a Democrat who campaigned hard for you in 1912. I raised money and spoke at rallies all over the state, because I believed in the high ideals of the Democratic Party. I did the same in 1914 to help preserve a Democratic majority in Congress. My home is in California, where women have won the right to vote, but this right would be denied to me should I move to this city—or to New Jersey."

Ingeborg shifted from one foot to the other, feeling warmth steal back into her limbs under her heavy wraps. All she had ever heard about Frances was that she was a socialite who could help with fundraising. It was news to her that Frances had applied those skills to the Democratic Party, and it explained why the CU had insisted on including her. She looked at Frances with new respect.

"We are asking for nothing radical or revolutionary," Frances went on. "We women of America simply want the vote. And there is a great fund of gratitude—and votes—awaiting the party that will hear us." She stopped and looked at him meaningfully.

Wilson nodded his understanding, but made no comment. His smile looked pasted on, Ingeborg thought, and she wondered if he were actually listening to their words. He had that slightly glazed look men got when they wanted women to think they were listening but were someplace else entirely in their minds; thinking about lunch, perhaps, or a knotty business problem.

"As a loyal Democrat, I was happy to travel throughout California to work for you, and I have never asked for anything from the Democratic administration. Now I plead not for myself, but for the nine million working women whose average wage does not exceed six dollars a week and for all the other women who need the strength the vote will give. Finally, I ask for your help in the name of the three generations of women who have fought for the Susan B. Anthony Amendment."

Applause for this sprang up spontaneously from the three hundred suffragists crammed into the East Room.

Frances waited for them to subside, her gaze never leaving Wilson's face, and then finished up. "Mr. President, there are a great many things to do in this nation, and we want to help you with them. But you must help us first—help us to a new freedom and a larger liberty."

With that, Frances stepped back, and Sara came forward. She spoke at length about the trip, the reasons for it, and the hardships they'd endured as they drove across the country, braving the pass into Cheyenne in the blizzard, the many long miles in blazing sun, wind, and rain, getting stuck in the Kansas mud, and flat tires and mechanical problems. Again he looked over at Maria and Ingeborg with evident respect, as did Colonel Harts. Ingeborg nodded back as if to say, Yes, we did this impossible thing, and we're coming for you next. Be worried.

Sara then handed him a copy of the resolutions that had been passed at the San Francisco Woman Voters Convention. "I'm afraid they're a bit battered, having come a long way, but that in no way diminishes their importance." She quoted them to him from memory.

Finishing up, she said, "Mr. President, we overcame these hardships because we had at our backs the wishes of the four million women voters of the West. But, you see, the demand for suffrage comes from throughout our great country. Last month one million men voted for it in the East. We have seen that, like all great men, you have changed your mind on other matters, such as war preparedness, and we believe this show of support must alter your mind on the subject of suffrage."

With that, she asked him to view the petition, which Mrs. Hopkins and Miss Hurlburt were still holding, fully furled. Sara grasped the end of it and pulled it out to a length of about twenty feet, telling Wilson that while the bulk of the signatures had been collected in San Francisco many politicians and other supporters had also signed it as they passed through their states. Wilson made a show of examining the signatures while Ingeborg held her breath, hoping Wilson wouldn't ask any probing questions about how many they actually had. He came close. "And I was told this is eighteen thousand feet long?" he asked, at one point.

"Of course, we weren't able to bring them all today, as that would be too heavy to carry," explained Sara, brightly.

"Naturally," said Wilson, as he helped the women roll it back up. Then he turned to address the envoys, his voice carrying throughout the room.

"I did not come here anticipating the necessity of making an address. I hope it is true," and here he smiled at Sara, "that I am capable of changing my mind, and indeed I hope to be a learner throughout my life. Nothing could be more impressive than the presentation of such a request in such numbers and backed by such influences as undoubtedly stand behind you."

Ingeborg breathed a sigh of relief and looked over at Mabel, who raised an eyebrow and nodded back. If they could get the petitions past the president—get through today—then it would all be behind them, and the press would move onto something else. No pesky reporter would demand to see the entire petition, or to count all the signatures. She returned her attention to President Wilson, who was explaining why he couldn't—to his infinite regret—include any mention of suffrage in his address to Congress the following day. The women frowned at him as one.

"All I can say is that I hope I shall always have an open mind, and I shall certainly take the greatest pleasure in conferring in the most serious way with my colleagues at the other end of the city regarding what is the right thing to do in this great matter," he babbled on. "I do not like to speak for others until I consult others and see what I am justified in saying." The group of women eyed him balefully, but he saw his exit and plunged on to the end. "This visit of yours will remain in my mind not only as a delightful compliment, but also as a very impressive thing which undoubtedly will make it necessary for all of us to consider very carefully what is right for us to do." With that, he thanked them all for coming, gave them a little wave, and strode quickly from the room, the colonel marching along behind him.

There was a brief silence, and then the tension left the room, and it seemed everyone began speaking at once. "Did you hear that?" said one. "Won't refer to suffrage in his speech tomorrow," grumbled another, "He could have done better," declared a third voice as they all turned and jostled toward the door. Slowly, the women flowed out of the White House and sorted themselves into their automobiles, pulling out of the parking area one by one.

The travelers returned to Emilie and sat there for a moment in silence. "Where to now?" asked Maria.

They paused, considering. Where indeed? It came to Ingeborg that the trip was over. They had just met with Congress and the president, the unwavering goal that had consumed them night and day for almost three months, and to which they had almost literally given their lives. They'd done it. She thought she ought to feel relieved, even joyful at being released from the tyranny of the trip, but instead she felt unsettled, directionless, unable to think for herself what she ought to do next. She watched a flock of pigeons peck aimlessly at the frozen mud, then bolt for the sky as someone walked past them, only to return to the spot they'd just left. All she wanted was to sit and rest with a cup of strong coffee. Maybe a slice of cake.

She said slowly, "For weeks I've been looking forward to this day and now—I hardly know what to do." She looked over at Maria, who smiled but also gave her a warning glance that said, Don't even think about volunteering for something else....

"Let's go to our hotel," said Sara. "I want to rest a bit, and I must send a note to Erskine."

"Drop me off at headquarters," said Mabel. "I'm staying there."

Maria slipped the car in gear as Mabel directed her to what the suffragists dubbed "The Little White House" on Lafayette Square, just across Pennsylvania Avenue from the actual White House.

Meanwhile, Sara grumbled. "When it comes to tariffs, he's out there in front, leading the charge, but he's not about to do the same for suffrage." She lowered her voice, mimicking his clipped words expertly: "'I do not like to speak for others until I consult others.'" She resumed her own voice, crying out impatiently, "Well, sweet Jesus, there are at least a hundred men at the other end of Pennsylvania eager to be consulted. Talk to them, Mr. President!"

Her voice and tone so perfectly mimicked Wilson's that Ingeborg laughed, a deep, liquid chuckle that burbled up her throat and out her mouth before she could stop it. She couldn't remember when she had last laughed, and that struck her as funny, too, so she laughed harder and was soon undone, helpless and sputtering. It was so unlike her that the others joined in, and as Maria pulled up and parked in front of headquarters they were all in stitches, laughing until their sides ached, giddy and delighted and relieved and thoroughly spent. Maria clutched the steering wheel, red-faced, with tears streaming down her cheeks, and Ingeborg could hear howls from the back seat. They must have been heard from three streets away, but Ingeborg simply didn't care, and the curious faces peeking through the windows at them from headquarters sent her into fresh whoops.

At length they subsided, and Mabel began pulling herself together, looking for her bag and groping for the door handle. As she clambered out, she stood looking at them and said simply, "Oh, you lovely ladies. Thanks for that, I needed it. Once you've freshened up come back here; remember there's a reception this evening."

They smiled and said good-bye, and Maria steered Emilie back into the wide streets on the way to their hotel.

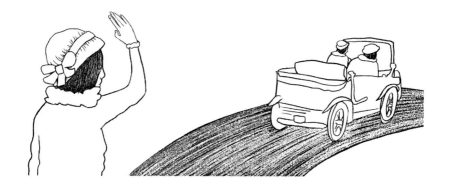

CHAPTER NINETEEN

DECEMBER 6-12, 1915

The rest the envoys needed so desperately at this point continued to elude them. Their arrival had led off the CU's first annual convention, so their days were filled with meetings and there was a reception of some sort every evening. It seemed everyone recognized the weary travelers and their battered car, greeting them warmly and asking after their health, wanting to hear more details of their trip.

Ingeborg had been wary at first, fully expecting the spotlight would pass over them to shine on someone else, but to her surprise and delight the praise seemed heartfelt, and it continued throughout the week. She'd steeped herself in the convention sessions, always sitting near the front and taking copious notes on how to boost her little suffrage organization in Providence. Over the week she became friendly with a number of CU members who shared her passion for labor organizing and race relations, and she huddled with them to plot strategy every chance she could. Gradually, the admiration and kind words she heard from nearly all the CU members soothed her flayed feelings until she was inclined to forget how much of the trip she'd been angry and bitter, and yes, jealous of the attention Sara and Frances had received.

The most loyal and influential volunteers were invited to the convention's closing reception at CU's headquarters. President Wilson's daughter, Jessie Sayre, was the special guest and was full of praise when she met Ingeborg and Maria. "I know of few women who could have undertaken such a strenuous trip—and achieved the great success that you did," she told them graciously. "The CU is in your debt. I know my father was quite taken with your story—he repeated it to us at dinner that evening."

What! The president had mentioned them at the presidential dinner table? Ingeborg was thrilled. She wanted to ask more about what he'd said, but asked instead, "Did we convince him to support the amendment this session?"

Mrs. Sayre had shaken her head and raised a hand in exasperation. "If only you knew how often I speak to him about it," she said. "But we must keep up the pressure—and the publicity. More stunts like yours will help."

Later that evening Ingeborg had been stunned when the CU had presented beautiful silver watches to Maria and herself as a gift for their service, accompanied by a very pretty speech about the importance of their contribution. As she turned to face them first Frances, then Mabel and Sara, and then the whole crowd of women rose to their feet and gave them a thundering ovation. It was little enough for all they'd done, she told herself, but for all that she'd felt humbled to be honored in this way. Her throat choked up alarmingly, and tears welled in her eyes. This was unfortunate because, as the applause died down, someone called "Speech!" and it caught hold until the walls rang with the demand that the Swedes say a few words.

Ingeborg looked out over the crowd and struggled to contain her emotions. She was struck by the irony that now—when she was finally given the chance to speak—she found herself unable to do so. Helplessly, she looked over at Maria, who raised her eyebrows and gestured with her chin as if to say, Well, go ahead!

The women began settling back into their seats as Ingeborg took a deep breath and thought of how to begin. "Thank you for your gift and your tribute. Although our trip was at times very difficult, we were glad to be of service. It was the trip of a lifetime...."

Maria leaned over to Ingeborg and said, in a stage whisper, "Perhaps many lifetimes." The audience laughed.

Ingeborg agreed, smiling. "By now you know some of the stories of our trip—crossing a pass in the snow, stuck in the mud, a broken axle, and cracked ribs. And these things happened, just as it happened that we met many politicians and collected their signatures on the great petition we brought with us from San Francisco." She paused and looked out over the smiling faces tilted up at them, every one of them white and most young enough to be her daughters. They were smart and worked so hard—suffrage headquarters was always bustling. Some knew so much about the inner workings of Congress that Ingeborg was a bit in awe of them. But she was determined to bring up the subject they had avoided all week.

She raised her voice and continued. "I hope one day you will drive from coast to coast as we did—though I wish better roads for you." There were some chuckles from the audience and she warmed to her theme. "America is much bigger than Sweden, where we come from. And so many different parts—deserts, mountains, high plains. Great lakes and rivers. And the ocean! In Providence the sun rises over the sea. Watching the sun set over the Pacific was strange for us."

Ingeborg could see some side glances as people wondered where her remarks were headed. She hadn't even mentioned the word suffrage, for heaven's sake. She could feel Maria's eyes on her as well. Nervous, Ingeborg plunged on. "Those different parts make our country strong. Some produce crops, some lumber or coal. Things we all need. In the same way, the different people in our country make us strong—farmers and miners, factory workers and shop girls. Together, we do more than we can alone.

"We met so many people on this trip. Some looked like all of us in this room. Others had darker skins. Some were born here. Others were born someplace else but came to America—as we did—to find better lives.

"Some want votes for women to make things better—for themselves or their families. I believe in that. Others say it's about fairness and justice. I believe that too. Everyone says our trip has done much to wake this country to the justice of women voting. But"—and here

Ingeborg looked around the room—"how we can talk about justice when we know the South will keep Negro women from voting, just as they have the Negro men?" Her question hung in the air.

"In Dayton, Ohio, Negroes and whites belong to the same suffrage association—they just have one. Think of that! They say they're stronger together. When we get back to Providence, we'll do the same. Why do we let ourselves be divided? Ask yourself! Winning this suffrage needs the strength from all of us. But they need our help, too. Fairness and justice for all. Isn't that what we say we want?"

Ingeborg stopped and gazed out over the audience. Smiles were fading, people looked down at their hands, and some of the women wore disgusted frowns. She sensed that she'd said as much as she could; they had stopped listening. Polite applause broke out as she turned abruptly and with Maria walked stiffly back to her seat. The color rose to her cheeks and it felt as if tight bands squeezed her chest, but she held her head high as the last speeches went on with no reference to what she had said. The meeting broke up soon afterward.

Ingeborg went to find the washroom and spotted Alice Paul sitting in her office, a pile of mail in front of her. Ingeborg stopped and looked in at her, marveling to see her already back at work. Miss Paul turned her head and met her gaze.

"Come in and have a seat." She waited while Ingeborg came into the room and perched on a rickety spindle chair next to Miss Paul's battered desk. "You will continue working with us, I hope," Miss Paul said, stating it more as fact than a question. "If the Democrats support the amendment in this session...." Her voice trailed off.

"Will they?" Ingeborg asked her.

Miss Paul shrugged. "If they don't, we will campaign for their defeat in the suffrage states during the 1916 elections. There is no other choice. And we will have far more impact than we did last year—in large part because of your trip."

Ingeborg nodded.

"But we may have to increase the pressure still further," Miss Paul went on. "In that event we will be in great need of strong women with no husbands or children to keep them home. Women willing to push themselves to the limit, as you and Maria have done the last few months."

Despite herself Ingeborg blushed a little at this praise. Why did this much younger woman always make her feel like a tongue-tied schoolgirl? She managed to smile and thank Miss Paul, but added, "I think maybe Maria will not be willing to help. Not at headquarters," she added hastily. "She will work on suffrage but only in Providence. She wants to be home. But I'll help however I can."

Miss Paul sat back in her chair and eyed Ingeborg steadily. "I see," she said. "We always need organizers, especially those willing to travel. Perhaps you could simply stay here and continue your work?"

Ingeborg's eyebrows shot up and she looked intently at Miss Paul, feeling a tingle of excitement in her chest. "Do you have a job for me?"

"Of sorts. We can't pay you, but we can offer room and board."

Ingeborg regarded Miss Paul steadily. "I have to be paid."

"I thought perhaps Maria might support you?" asked Miss Paul.

Ingeborg flushed. More than once over the years she and Maria had argued over this. Maria always wanted her to earn more, but Ingeborg kept giving her heart to causes that had no money. Just a few days ago Maria had made it abundantly clear that she expected Ingeborg to get a job—one that paid—when they returned to Providence. The trip had been more expensive than they'd planned, and she wanted to build their savings back up. Maria would go back to midwifing.

Now Ingeborg looked at Miss Paul, raised her shoulders, and let them drop. "I'm sorry, no," was all she said.

Miss Paul nodded and then cleared her throat. "Ingeborg, I spoke of limits a moment ago. There are some limits I fear may be too difficult to overcome—at least all at once." She nodded toward the hall where the speeches had just ended. "I refer, of course, to your remarks. I may agree with you privately but we simply cannot afford to dilute our efforts by embracing other causes. We can scarcely muster the funds we need to conduct the suffrage campaign as it is."

Ingeborg cocked an eyebrow at her. "What about justice?"

Miss Paul held her gaze. "There's justice, and there's politics. Don't confuse them. Working with the Negro suffragists, it might be years before we win the franchise—if ever." Miss Paul picked up a paper knife and slit open an envelope. "Without them, our path is much clearer." She looked up at Ingeborg and shrugged. "You understand this, do you not?"

"Perhaps," Ingeborg began, "But—"

Miss Paul smiled briefly and said, "Stay in touch, Ingeborg. As I said, we always need organizers." Then she pulled the letter out of the envelope and unfolded it on her desk, preparing to read.

Ingeborg pushed herself to her feet and, with a muttered good-bye, went and found the washroom. She looked at herself in the mirror and saw a gaunt face, her graying hair pulled back under her hat. She looked years older than she had just last summer—deep grooves carved along the sides of her nose down to the corners of her mouth. A network of fine lines blossomed under her browned skin. She felt suddenly overcome with exhaustion and put her hand down on the sink to steady herself. This flitting about on suffrage work is a young person's game, she said to the face in the mirror. Go home and rest.

* * *

Their parting with Sara was strained. They said their good-byes in the hotel lobby, eager to be shed of one another after traveling in a pressure cooker for so long. Ingeborg had so often been resentful or furious over something Sara had done, and she'd comforted herself with the thought that they'd leave her behind for good when the trip was over. Now, though, Ingeborg felt a tinge of nostalgia for those crazy days, and something that was almost regret. Would they ever see Sara again? Would they ever learn if she recovered from the trip, ended up with Erskine, or got back to writing poetry? She was nonplussed by these feelings, and when she opened her mouth to speak could think of nothing to say.

In contrast, Sara was businesslike and ready to wrap things up. She immediately bestowed on them the buffalo skin Erskine had bought for her in San Francisco.

"I expect to be in the East for some time," Sara had said. "I can't lug it around with me on the trains—that would be ridiculous. Take it. It belongs to you and to Emilie. I know Erskine would approve."

Maria beamed at her, delighted. "It will remind us of you."

Ingeborg added, "And of being lost in the desert at night."

Sara laughed. "And all those other times we damn near died." She shook her head and looked at them, her brow furrowed. "It seems like a crazy dream. Every morning I wake up in terror thinking I have to get back in the car and hurtle over bad roads for a hundred miles to give a speech, and then I remember—it's over, I can go back to sleep. How did we do it?"

"The same as we manage everything else," said Ingeborg, finding her voice at last. "We're women, and we're tough." She fiddled with her scarf and gazed at Sara, suddenly embarrassed by how often she'd been angry with her.

Maria jumped in to cover the awkward moment, saying, "When do you go back home?"

"I'm not sure," said Sara. "Alice wants me to stay, and there's still that job with Mrs. Belmont." She shrugged. "And I still need money. So my work is here for now, I guess."

Ingeborg peered at Sara, shocked. Just when she thought she knew her all the way through, Sara could still surprise her. "You signed up for more? Be careful—those two will be the death of you."

Sara grimaced. "I'm well aware! But I'm better suited to this work than a factory, and this will pay me better, anyway."

"What does Erskine say?" Maria asked, curious.

"He has his own decisions to make," Sara replied. Her voice hardened a little, and she looked away. "He knows I love him. He says he loves me. But he's still in Portland with his first wife." She looked back at Maria, her face equal parts courage and woe, and said simply, "I don't want to live apart from him, but this trip has taught me I can. I'm better off here."

Maria smiled and nodded at her, and then said quietly, "That's good, Sara. I hope it works out."

After a final hug Sara had turned and trailed off to her room.

* * *

The following morning Maria and Ingeborg drove north out of the capital toward Providence. A bitter, damp wind drove the cold into the car and the threatening clouds pressed down on the roof. Ingeborg shivered and peered up through the windshield as a few snowflakes whirled past them. "I hope that's all the snow we get," she said.

Maria made no reply. She was hunched over the steering wheel, mute and obstinate, her lips pressed into a thin line. They had quarreled over whether to leave that morning, after Ingeborg pointed to signs of a storm. Maria had refused to hear it. "Honestly, Ingeborg, sometimes I think you don't want to go back to Providence," she'd said crossly, folding the last of her gear into her travel bag. "Just stay here and work for the CU if that's what you want. I'm leaving today."

But Ingeborg would not let her go alone, and so here they were in the car again, just the two of them. The way it was supposed to have been all along. She smiled to think of how they'd naively imagined "driving the petitions to Washington" simply meant a few extra boxes in the back seat they'd deliver to CU suffrage headquarters on their way home. That the petitions would be an amusing side story they would later tell about their trip, instead of becoming its sole purpose. Emilie felt curiously light and unburdened with just the two of them, and she fairly leapt along the road. Yet Ingeborg still felt Sara's presence in the back seat very keenly, and wondered how long she'd remain their invisible traveling companion. She drew the buffalo skin up to her chin and got a faint scent of Sara's perfume.

Mabel had appeared just as they finished stowing the last of their bags in Emilie, preparing to depart. "I'm so glad I caught you!" she called as she came hurrying up, her lean face touched pink by the cold. "I'd meant to say good-bye last night, but when I looked around, you'd disappeared. Don't think I'd let you slip away so easily."

"Quick, Maria, start driving!" Ingeborg exclaimed, in mock horror. "Mabel has another job for us." She grinned at Mabel, though Maria stood by half-glowering, uncertain if it was really a joke.

"Must you go? I hate to say good-bye," said Mabel, smiling warmly at them.

Maria managed a smile despite her ill humor. Her face was drawn with exhaustion, and she was edgy and tense in a way that was unusual for her. "In Sweden we say, 'Away is good but home is best,'" she said. "I miss my home."

Mabel nodded. "I understand," she said. "You two have given all we asked of you and more. We have no right to ask for more sacrifice."

"No," agreed Maria vaguely, and reached over to grip the handle of Emilie's door, preparing to climb in behind the wheel.

"We have no right," repeated Mabel, "And yet, we know now how extraordinary you are so I feel sure we'll see each other again. I can think of dozens of ways you could be useful."

Maria's smile looked frozen on, as though she truly believed that, just at the very moment they were going to escape the CU's clutches, Mabel was going to reel them back in. She sent Ingeborg a warning glare.

Ingeborg chose to ignore Maria's signals and looked at Mabel, eyebrows raised. "Such as?" she asked.

Mabel's bright eyes opened wide and she ticked ideas off her fingers. "Of course it depends on Congress, but there's organizing against the Democrats in the 1916 elections, if we have to. We can always use help at headquarters. Street speaking." She looked at Maria and smiled. "And we could always use a mighty car and two fearless drivers."

Maria stamped her foot. "Perhaps later, when we're rested," she said. Her voice was high and tight, her jaw set, and her eyes welled with tears.

Ingeborg, seeing how upset she was, relented and went to hug Mabel. "We must go. Be sure to rest yourself. Don't let Miss Paul order you around."

Mabel hugged her back. "I'll be fine. Don't worry about me." She walked over to embrace Maria, whose face was now damp with tears.

Maria clung to her for a moment and her body convulsed in sobs before she collected herself. "I'm sorry," she said, wiping the tears from her face. "I'm just so tired…I can't do this anymore."

Mabel gave her another squeeze and said, "Go!" She stood there waving until the little car was lost in the distance.

* * *

Now, speeding through the wintry morning, Ingeborg thought back to that night at the Exposition when they had watched the fireworks exploding over the San Francisco Bay, and she had yearned to be part of some great forward movement of humanity. She still believed that had led to a prolonged dash across the country for the CU. She slid a glance over to Maria, driving with her fur hat jammed down onto her head to her eyebrows, pointedly ignoring Ingeborg, still cross from their earlier quarrel. Ingeborg felt a pang of regret for the trip that might have been, and then straightened in her seat as an idea popped into her head. Perhaps she could talk Maria into another trip, just the two of them and Emilie, no suffrage business whatever.

She felt a rush of affection for her partner and reached over to place her hand on Maria's knee, giving it a gentle squeeze. Maria looked over at her and Ingeborg smiled. "We're going home," she said. Maria smiled back.

They settled into their seats as the snow thickened, edging the trees and covering the road ahead with a thin white blanket that boiled out beneath Emilie's tires, hiding the road behind them.

From left to right, Sara Bard Field, Maria Kindberg, Ingeborg Kindstedt.
National Woman's Party Records, Manuscript Division, Library of Congress.

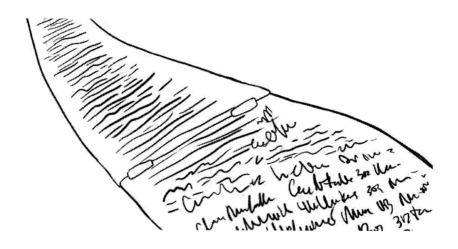

AFTERWORD

This book is based on a true story. Ingeborg Kindstedt and Maria Kindberg were middle-aged, Swedish immigrants who really did travel by ship to the Panama–Pacific International Exposition intending to buy a car and drive it back to their home in Providence, sightseeing on the way. Exactly how and why they came to volunteer to drive the petitions to Washington, DC, is unclear, but I believe the way I portrayed it is close to the truth.

I retraced the route of the original trip in the fall of 2015, almost exactly a hundred years later, intending to write a nonfiction book about it. On my trip I interviewed women's rights and other activists, and met with a number of League of Women Voters branches, trying to understand what difference having had the vote meant for women in the preceding hundred years. I blogged about it at www.suffrag-eroadtrip.blogspot.com.

This journey—literal and figurative—brought me hard up against the history of racism in the suffrage movement and the US as a whole. Clearly, it mattered from whose perspective the story was told. Native Americans weren't enfranchised by the Nineteenth Amendment—the federal government didn't even recognize them as citizens until 1924, and in some states voting rights came much later. The Voting Rights Act of 1964 was required in order to ensure Blacks could vote. And that was just voting rights; as with women, there were many other inequalities that we are still working to address.

The more I thought about it, the more determined I was to tell the story from the perspective of Ingeborg and Maria, whose experience of early twentieth-century America would have been quite different from the more affluent white suffrage leaders who, until recently, have been almost the sole face of the American suffrage movement. Most of what is known about the original trip comes from Sara Bard Field's letters to her lover, newspaper accounts, articles in *The Suffragist*, the National Woman's Party archives, and oral histories of Sara, Mabel Vernon, and Alice Paul conducted in the 1960s by Amelia Fry. Virtually all of this was from the majority white, affluent point of view. But despite extensive research (including a trip to Sweden), I could find very little additional information about Ingeborg and Maria.

"The Swedes," as Sara and Mabel refer to them, appeared to have left no personal record of the trip, at least that I was able to find. Since Sara and Frances were designated the "suffrage envoys," Maria and Ingeborg were not allowed to speak from the stage on their trip, though they were occasionally interviewed by more curious reporters. More often they were simply omitted from newspaper accounts entirely—Frances was more frequently mentioned than they were, even though she had abandoned them in Sacramento. Descriptions of the trip included in more recently published suffrage histories also sometimes fail to even mention them.

So I decided to write the book as historical fiction, blending what I could find out about their trip with what might have occurred given the time at which they did it. Readers are understandably curious about what did—and did not—happen, so here's an attempt to separate the two.

Maria Ingeborg Kindstedt was born in Glava near Karlstad in the county of Värmland on May 8, 1865. She emigrated to America from Karlstad in August 1890. In 1933 she returned to Sweden and Karlstad, where she died on August 5, 1950.

Ingeborg joined the Salvation Army in Karlstad in 1888 and was admitted to their officers' school in Stockholm in August of that year. She did move to Stockholm but soon left and returned to Karlstad and her family. There are two letters from her to a Major Hellgren in Stockholm; in the last letter she says that her father has bought her a ticket to America.

She emigrated in 1890 and became a naturalized citizen in 1898. She was never married. She had a number of different small businesses—including serving as the matron of the Swedish Young Women's Home. She later advertised herself as an investigator with an "intelligence" business—providing references for Swedish household help. Exactly when and where she met Maria is unknown, but in 1895 they were both listed at 311 Blackstone. By 1911 they had moved to 557 Westminster Street—Ingeborg is listed as a "lecturer" who boards there; Maria as the primary owner or tenant. Ingeborg was described by Sara and Mabel as the more difficult of the two, while everyone loved Maria, who was motherly and sweet.

Maria Albertina Kindberg was born in Ryd, near the town Skövde, in the county of Skaraborg, on October 7, 1860. She did not have the name Kindberg then, as her mother was not married, but by 1880 this was her last name. She emigrated to America from Sventorp in May 1888 and became a naturalized citizen in 1909. She was a midwife by profession, and told Sara that she had delivered over two thousand babies. She traveled back to Sweden in 1912 but never returned there for good; she died in Providence by suicide in 1921. According to the census she was able to speak, read and write English. There is no record that she ever married.

In the book, they travel the same route they did in 1915. My account of their send-off from the Panama–Pacific was based heavily on newspaper accounts from the time, though in fact they did not leave San Francisco until over ten days later. The man they hired to drive them did get them lost in the desert east of Reno, they were the only car to make it over the pass from Laramie to Cheyenne that snowy day, and they did get stuck in a mudhole in Kansas. I had to invent some details and dialogue around those incidents but they are reasonably faithful to Sara's description of them. Also true were Sara's hope that she would be pregnant with Erskine's baby, the Episcopal Bishop in Detroit having second thoughts about Sara due to rumors about her lover, and Sara getting thrown from the car when they broke an axle in a pothole in western New York. Most of the suffragists and political leaders they meet in the book were people they actually met at the time, and I relied heavily on reports of the actual settings and arrangements made for each stop, including the meetings with Congress and President Wilson. At times I quoted or paraphrased speeches that were made. Mabel Vernon did serve as their advance agent in the way I described.

They did purchase an Overland Six as described, though I made up that they christened her Emilie after Sweden's first suffragist.

The mass meeting in Topeka, Kansas was the only one they missed entirely due to getting lost and their car problems. We don't know if Ingeborg threatened to kill Sara as they raced to that particular meeting, but Sara insisted in her oral interview that she had done so at some point; she couldn't recall exactly where they were. She also claimed, after the trip, that she'd learned Ingeborg had been in some sort of mental institution prior to having left for San Francisco.

I played up Ingeborg's resentment at not being treated as an envoy, but, in her oral history, Sara does mention her belief that this was at least partially the source of the animosity Ingeborg appeared to have toward her. In contrast, Maria was described as warm and motherly, though I played that up as well. I did find articles about the trip in several different Swedish-language newspapers, and they focus on Ingeborg and Maria, sometimes not even mentioning Sara or Frances. I don't know if Ingeborg was responsible for them.

Here's what did not happen. Joe Hill was being held in Sugar House Prison for the crime I described when they came through Salt Lake City but Ingeborg did not meet with him. He was executed in November 1915. There is also no record of them having met as a group with Frank Walsh, or with Ida. B. Wells Barnett, or Clarence Darrow (though the bit about Sara's sister Mary being Darrow's mistress for many years is true—as is Darrow turning against suffrage, though that happened a bit later). The chance meeting with Phoebe also did not happen, though the history of the Haudenosaunee is accurate.

The strike I describe in Providence happened a bit earlier in the year than I said it did, and there is no record of Ingeborg having been involved in it, but I wanted to have a reason that she might have been hospitalized prior to their departure (though we don't know if it was in the Dexter Asylum). It was not uncommon for troublesome women to be committed to mental institutions by their husbands or the authorities, not because they were mentally ill, but because they wouldn't obey. I chose to have Ingeborg hide out at the Dexter Asylum to avoid being arrested for assaulting the policeman, as opposed to having a mental illness as Sara claimed.

Ingeborg actually did emigrate with her brother Rolf, but she did not meet up with him in Denver. I invented his back story about losing his wife and child and chose to place him in locations and at events that could have been true. Sadly, the Ludlow massacre did take place as described, though of course I have no idea if Rolf was there. The government did call out the National Guard to fire on protesting miners and force them back to work. In ways that are frighteningly similar to events happening today, there was significant anti-immigrant sentiment across the United States, and anti-union sentiment as well.

I don't believe there were many counter-protests from antis on their trip, but the sentiments uttered by Mrs. Talbot and Reverend Brandenburg were expressed by antis in Ohio at the time. The incident with the gun did not take place.

Another completely fictional account is the meeting with the medium. The early spiritualists were often suffragists, and there was great interest at that time in communicating with the dead. I thought it would be fun to bring in Elizabeth Cady Stanton's voice in that way.

Finally, the centennial of woman suffrage in 2020 brought a lot of criticism that the suffragists were racist. Like many people learning about suffrage history for the first time, I didn't want to believe that my heroes, these amazing women, were racist. I now understand that, while that's not inaccurate, it also unfairly tags them as being somehow more racist than the country as a whole. The record shows that the entire country was racist, and to some degree the suffragists had to respond to that reality, regardless of how they might have felt themselves. Ingeborg grappling with this issue is my attempt to have that discussion, though I'm sure I haven't done it justice and many may fairly object that she didn't do more to stand with Black suffragists. But that's not what happened, and for the purposes of this book I thought it more important to reflect that reality than to invent a different storyline that cast the suffrage movement in a more favorable light. It's intriguing to think how things might have changed if whites had been more willing to speak out, but that's another book.

Many whites believe that since many early suffragists were abolitionists, how could they be racist? I confess I used to reassure myself that way, too. But the reality is, you could believe that slavery was wrong and still be racist, in the sense that you didn't want a Black family to move in next door, your daughter to marry a Black man, or to have a Black person as a boss. That's what I mean when I say the entire country was racist. After the Civil War, everywhere in America Blacks were legally excluded from employment, paid less for equal work, excluded from many colleges and universities, and were prevented from living where they wished no matter how educated or affluent they were, and that's just a short list of the wrongs they suffered.

At some level I can understand why the suffragists chose to focus exclusively on the vote. As with any other social movement, women and their male allies came to suffrage from a variety of different interests; temperance, peace work, the labor movement, protecting families, women's equality, to name a few. They united under the banner of suffrage with the hope that the vote would lend power to women's voices in whatever areas they chose to work once suffrage was won. So it wasn't suffrage *only*, but suffrage *first*. They had been working on suffrage for over three generations already, and while in 1915 they were closer to getting the federal amendment through Congress than they had ever been, they had no assurance they would be successful. And then they would need to persuade thirty-six states to ratify. Ultimately, ratification came down to one legislator's vote in one southern state, Tennessee. It was that close.

For me, I think the real sin was their failure to stand with their Black brothers and sisters after suffrage was won. That sin remains with us as a country today.

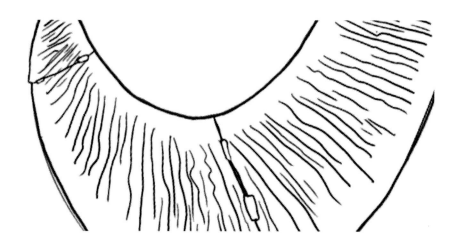

ACKNOWLEDEMENTS

When I embarked on this project, I had only a vague idea of retracing the suffragists' route by myself, more or less anonymously, and doing as much research as I could along the way to learn about their trip. I intended to write a nonfiction book.

What ended up happening was so much better! As my planning evolved, I named my project "We Demand: Women, Suffrage, and a Century of Change." I decided to interview women's rights activists and speak with Leagues of Women Voters as I made my way across the country, trying to understand what difference having had the vote meant over the preceding century. This made the experience a much richer one for me and gives me many more people to thank. While their stories didn't make it into this novel, I gained critical insights into history that ultimately changed how I thought about the original trip and what I would write.

First, the Huntington Library in San Marino, CA, houses the papers of Charles Erskine Scott Wood, Sara's lover, where I was able to find her letters to him from the trip. The staff there were generous with their time as well. I was also able to access issues of *The Suffragist* from the Bancroft Library at UC Berkeley, which gave me invaluable background on the planning and progress of the original trip.

I am indebted to the staff of the (then) Sewall–Belmont House & Museum (now the Belmont–Paul Women's Equality National Monument) in Washington, DC, particularly Jennifer Krafchick. Jennifer and her staff provided priceless historic photos of the trip and retweeted my blog as I came across the country.

The Library of Congress houses the collection of the National Woman's Party papers, and I used the microfilm versions residing in their partner libraries to understand the planning behind the trip, whom they met with, and the reception they got.

Before leaving San Francisco in September 2015, I stayed for several days with my husband's cousin Marian Doub, her father, Terry Doub, and her partner, Bob Thawley, who gave me a warm welcome. They are dedicated activists, with a proud history of actions and arrests, making them the perfect launchpad for my trip. It was Marian who pointed out the importance of asking who benefited from the Nineteenth Amendment, which ultimately transformed the way I thought about the project.

Prior to the start of my trip, Robert ("Bob") P. J. Cooney, author of *Winning the Vote: The Triumph of the American Woman Suffrage Movement*, graciously invited me to his home in Half Moon Bay. In addition to providing much needed encouragement, Bob introduced me to a friend of his, Erskine's great-granddaughter Sara Wood Smith. Sara introduced me to Sara Caldwell, Sara Bard Field's granddaughter, and it was my pleasure to visit with her in Oakland before I left San Francisco.

Sara also brought in her sisters Cynthia Matthews and Laura Smith, and their cousin Eliza Livingston. Together they helped organize a reception we held in the Cannon House Office Building in Washington, DC, to celebrate the culmination of my trip. I could not have managed the reception without them; Cynthia even served as master of ceremonies. The descendants also gave me important insights into Sara's complicated history with their family, which helped steer me in the direction of writing the book from the Swedes' perspective.

Maine US Representative Chellie Pingree reserved the room at the Cannon House Office Building in which we held the reception, and I am grateful to her and her staff for arranging that. Maine Senator Susan Collins also met with me when I arrived in DC.

My friends Andrea DeLeon, Bev Roy, Janis Visser, and Carole DeTroy flew down from Boston to attend the final reception, as did my husband, Rick Leavitt, and my daughter Emma. I will be forever grateful to them for their loving support and friendship. My sister Vicki Gass also housed Rick, Emma, and me for several days while we were in DC. Her life and work also influenced my thinking about this book and the direction it took.

As I made my way across the country I met with a number of people who deepened my understanding about women's rights history, and who did—and did not—benefit from the Nineteenth Amendment. I can't possibly thank them all, but what follows is a partial list (note, their titles and affiliations are from 2015 and may have changed): LisaRuth Elliott of Shaping San Francisco; Sue Englander of Bolerium Books, and author of *Class Conflict and Class Coalition in the California Woman Suffrage Movement, 1907–1912: The San Francisco Wage Earners' Suffrage League*; Paula Lee, co-President of the Sacramento League of Women Voters; Lyn Bremer and the Nevada Women's History Project; Jenn Donnelly, co-President of the Utah League of Women Voters; Emmylou Manwell, Visitor Services, Utah State Capital; Kate Kelly, Planned Parenthood Association of Utah; Nonie Profitt; Michele Irwin; Colleen Denny, Gender and Women's Studies, University of Wyoming; Jamie Smith, student, University of Wyoming; Dennis Perrin and Ladonna Fulmer; Emporia (Kansas) League of Women Voters; Sylvia Stevenson, KC chapter of the National Congress of Black Women; Robert Barrientos, Latinos of Tomorrow in KCMO; Sherry Miller and the Lincoln (Nebraska) League of Women Voters; Kären M. Mason, Iowa Women's Archives; Maria Socorro Pesqueira, President & CEO of Mujeres Latinas en Acción (MLA); Kaethe Morris Hoffer, Executive Director of the Chicago Alliance Against Sexual Exploitation (CAASE); Anne Ladky, Executive Director of Women Employed (WE); Patrick McLaughlin; Cynthia Canty, Michigan Public Radio; Susan Hesselgesse, Executive

Director, Greater Dayton LWV; Ann Fabiszak Payne, President, Toledo LWV; Derek Moore, Curator of Transportation History, Crawford Auto Aviation Collection; Judy Merzbach, Lucy Watson, Jim Scully, and the Hawken Middle School; Sheri L. Scavone, Executive Director, Western New York Women's Foundation; Deborah L. Hughes, Executive Director, National Susan B. Anthony House & Museum; Marilyn Dunn, Schlesinger Library at the Radcliffe Institute for Advanced Study; former Tufts University students Lisa Setrakian, Ann Louangxay, Krista Speroni, Paige Bollen, and Emma Leavitt; Vickie Choitz and Ted Poppitz; Dona Munker; Lucy Beard, Executive Director, Alice Paul Institute; Gwenn and Brett Elliott and the LWV of Delaware; Congressman Sam Farr and Congresswoman Anna Eshoo, both from California.

I also want to thank my advance readers, beginning with my friend, the distinguished writer Michelle Cacho-Negrete, author of *Stealing: Life in America: A Collection of Essays* (as well as many other published pieces). I spent several years on this book project floundering, questioning my direction, and above all doubting my ability to produce a novel after a lifetime of nonfiction and business writing. I finally reached the point where I knew I had to share it with someone, so I summoned the courage to ask Michelle, who graciously agreed to read my manuscript. When I was near collapse, just shy of the finish line, it was Michelle who picked me up and carried me across. I am so grateful to her for her encouragement, and for her wise suggestions on ways to improve the book.

Bob Cooney also provided extensive edits and saved me from committing several egregious factual errors. Marsha Weinstein, Russ DeSimone, Jennifer Pickard, Tiffany Wayne, Eileen Eagan, Ellen Alderman, Sara Wood Smith, Christine DeTroy, Phil Ohman, Meta Ohman, Nancy Murdock, Lorraine Glowczak, my husband Rick, and my son Silas Leavitt all read early drafts and provided much needed encouragement and suggestions. It is unquestionably a better book as a result and any errors are mine alone.

Maine Authors Publishing provided much needed editing and design assistance, and it has been a pleasure to work with them again (they published my first book as well).

Many thanks to my daughter Emma Leavitt (Solei Arts) who, at the last minute, willingly agreed to create the chapter illustrations and help design the cover. She has been my biggest champion and it was a real delight to work with her on this project.

Finally, my husband, Rick Leavitt, provided significant logistical and financial support, starting with accompanying me on the 2015 trip. I hadn't originally planned on this; I assumed he'd be unable to take time off from work. But he found a way to work in coffee shops, hotel rooms, and even in the car, and his presence made the trip easier in so many ways. As I struggled through the writing process, Rick would ask periodically "How's that book coming?" and I'd hang my head and make excuses, but he never conveyed doubt or impatience, either of which might have been fatal. I'm so fortunate to have him in my life.

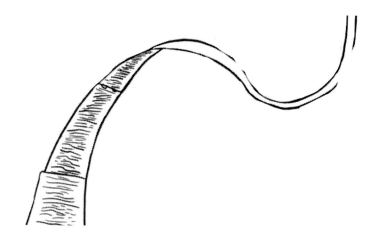

RECOMMENDED READING

ARTICLES

Brook, Michael. "Radical Literature in Swedish America: A Narrative Survey." Swedish Pioneer Historical Society, 1969.

Fry, Amelia R. "Along the Suffrage Trail: From West to East for Freedom Now!" *The American West*, January 1969, 16-25.

Fry, Amelia R. "Sara Bard Field: Poet and Suffragist." Suffragists Oral History Project, University of California, 1979.

Fry, Amelia R. "Speaker for Suffrage and Petitioner for Peace: Mabel Vernon." Suffragists Oral History Project, University of California, 1976.

Ancel, Judy. "Frank P. Walsh – Labor's Tribune." Expanded from a talk given October 17 and 24, 1992. The Institute for Labor Studies. https://pendergastkc.org/works-cited/frank-p-walsh-labors-tribune, viewed February 8, 2017.

BOOKS

Ackley, Laura A. *San Francisco's Jewel City: The Panama-Pacific International Exposition of 1915*. Berkeley, CA: Heyday, 2015.

Adler, William M. *The Man Who Never Died: The Life, Times, and Legacy of Joe Hill, American Labor Icon*. New York: Bloomsbury USA, 2011.

Bengston, Henry, trans. Westerberg, Kermit B., Edited by Brook, Michael. *Memoirs of the Scandinavian-American Labor Movement*. Carbondale, IL: Southern Illinois University Press, 1999.

Bruno, Lee. *Panorama: Tales from San Francisco's Pan-Pacific International Exposition*. San Francisco: Cameron & Company, 2014.

Downing, Sybil. *The Vote*. Albuquerque: University of New Mexico Press, 2006.

Doyle, Sir Arthur Conan. *The Wanderings of a Spiritualist*. London, Hodder and Stoughton, Project Gutenberg, E-Book #39718, 2012.

Eason, Andrew Mark. *Women in God's Army: Gender and Equality in the Early Salvation Army*. Montreal: Canadian Corporation for Studies in Religion, 2003.

Gustafson, Melanie; Miller, Kristie; and Perry, Elisabeth Israels, ed. *We Have Come to Stay: American Women and Political Parties, 1880–1960*. Albuquerque: University of New Mexico Press, 1999.

Hamburger, Robert. *Two Rooms: The Life of Charles Erskine Scott Wood*. Lincoln, NE: The University of Nebraska Press, 1998.

Harzig, Christiane; Mageean, Deirdre; Matovic, Margareta; Knothe, Maria Anna; Blaschke, Monika. *Peasant Maids, City Women: From the European Countryside to Urban America*. Ithaca, NY: Cornell University Press, 1997.

Helquist, Michael. *Marie Equi: Radical Politics and Outlaw Passions*. Corvallis, OR: Oregon State University Press, 2015.

Hoffert, Sylvia D. *Alva Vanderbilt Belmont: Unlikely Champion of Women's Rights*. Bloomington, IN: Indiana University Press, 2012.

Kersten, Andrew E. *Clarence Darrow: American Iconoclast*. New York: Hill and Wang, 2011.

Leavitt, Judith Walker. *Brought to Bed: Childbearing in America, 1750-1950*. New York: Oxford University Press, 1986.

Lintelman, Joy K. *I Go to America: Swedish American Women and the Life of Mina Anderson*. St. Paul, MN: Minnesota Historical Society Press, 2009.

Ljungmark, Lars; Westerberg, Kermit B., trans. *Swedish Exodus*. Carbondale, IL: Southern Illinois University Press, 1979.

Marshall, Susan E. *Splintered Sisterhood: Gender and Class in the Campaign against Woman Suffrage*. Madison, WI: The University of Wisconsin Press, 1997.

Moberg, Vilhelm. *The Emigrants: The Emigrant Novels Book 1*. St. Paul, MN: Minnesota Historical Society Press, 2009.

Ptacin, Mira. *The In-Betweens: The Spiritualists, Mediums, and Legends of Camp Etna*. New York: Liveright, 2019.

Renshaw, Patrick. *The Wobblies: The Story of the IWW and Syndicalism in the United States*. Chicago: Ivan R. Dee, 1967.

Southard, Belinda A. Stillion. *Militant Citizenship: Rhetorical Strategies of the National Woman's Party, 1913-1920*. College Station, TX: Texas A & M University Press, 2011.

Tax, Meredith. *The Rising of the Women: Feminist Solidarity and Class Conflict, 1880–1917*. New York: Monthly Review Press, 1980.

Tetrault, Lisa. *The Myth of Seneca Falls: Memory and the Women's Suffrage Movement, 1848–1898*. Chapel Hill, NC: University of North Carolina Press, 2017.

Wagner, Sally Roesch. *Sisters in Spirit: Iroquois Influence on Early Feminists: Haudenosaunee (Iroquois) Influence on Early American Feminists*. Summertown, TN: Native Voices Books, 2010.

Zahniser, J.D.; Fry, Amelia R. *Alice Paul: Claiming Power*. New York: Oxford University Press, 2014.

COLLECTIONS

National Woman's Party, et al. *National Woman's Party records.* Manuscript/Mixed Material. Retrieved from the Library of Congress, <lccn.loc.gov/mm82034355>.

C. E. S. Wood papers, 1829–1980 (bulk 1870–1940), Huntington Library, San Marino, CA.

ABOUT THE AUTHOR

Anne B. Gass is the author of *Voting Down the Rose: Florence Brooks Whitehouse and Maine's Fight for Woman Suffrage,* published in 2014. Anne is Whitehouse's great-granddaughter, and she speaks regularly on Florence and women's rights history at libraries, museums, colleges, high schools, and other venues.

Anne has continued her great-grandmother's activist tradition. She is the founder and principal of ABG Consulting LLC, a small business supporting nonprofits, local and state governments, and foundations in their efforts to help people in need build stable, productive lives. She serves on the Steering Committee of the Maine Suffrage Centennial Collaborative and as the Maine Coordinator for the National Votes for Women Trail, a project of the National Collaborative for Women's History Sites. She also serves on Maine's Permanent Commission on the Status of Women and is Vice President of the Gray Town Council.

When not writing or volunteering, Anne can be found hiking, wild ice skating, traveling, or backcountry skiing with her husband, Rick.